I looked down at the paper, still touching the tip of my shoe.
I reached for it, flipping the page over to look.

A girl lay back on a bench, roughly sketched in scrawls of ink.

A sick feeling started to twist in my stomach, like motion sickness.

And then the sketched girl turned her head,
and her inky eyes glared straight into mine.

Also available from Amanda Sun
and
Harlequin TEEN

The Paper Gods series:
(in reading order)

SHADOW (ebook prequel novella)
INK

AMANDA SUN

Recycling programs for this product may not exist in your area.

ISBN-13: 978-0-373-21071-8

INK

This edition published by arrangement with Harlequin Books S.A.

For questions and comments about the quality of this book, please contact us at CustomerService@Harlequin.com.

Printed in U.S.A.

For Emily

1

I made it halfway across the courtyard before I realized I was still wearing my school slippers. No lie. I had to turn around and slink all the way back to the *genkan,* the stifled laughs from my classmates trailing me as I mustered what slippered dignity I could.

God, way to scream *foreigner.* You'd think after a couple of weeks I'd have the routine down, but no. I'd gone into that mode again, the one where I forgot everything for a minute and walked dazed through the sounds of the Japanese being spoken around me, not fully comprehending that it wasn't English, that I was on the other side of the world, that Mom was…

"Katie!"

I looked up to see Yuki running toward me, breaking from a group of girls who stopped chatting, staring at us. Their stares weren't unfriendly—they just weren't exactly subtle. I guess that's expected when you're the only *Amerika-jin* in the school.

Yuki grabbed my arms with her slender fingers. "You do *not* want to go in there," she said in English, motioning at the school entrance behind us.

"Um, I kind of have to," I answered in broken Japanese. *Forget English,* Diane had said. It's the easiest way to get fluent faster. It's easier to forget everything, I guess. *Forget I ever had any other kind of life.*

Yuki shook her head, so I pointed at my slippered feet. "You still shouldn't," she said, this time in Japanese. I liked that about Yuki—she knew I was trying. She didn't insist on English like some of the other kids. "There's an ugly breakup going on in the *genkan.* Really, really awkward."

"What am I supposed to do, wait?" I said. "I'll just be in and out, ten seconds." I held out my fingers for emphasis.

"Trust me," she said, "you don't want to get in the middle of this."

I peeked around her shoulder, but I couldn't see anything through the glass. I tapped the toe of my slipper on the ground; it felt so flimsy.

"Some big shot?" I said in English, and Yuki cocked her head to the side. "You know, a *daiji na hito* or something?" If Yuki was worried, it was probably gossip-worthy.

She leaned in conspiratorially. "Yuu Tomohiro," she whispered. In Japan, everyone went by their last names first. "He's fighting with Myu."

"Who?"

Yuki's friends giggled behind us. Had they been eavesdropping the whole time?

"Myu, his girlfriend," she said.

"No, I know Myu. The other one," I said.

"Yuu Tomohiro?" Yuki said, her arms waving wildly as if that would jog a memory I didn't have. "Top of the kendo team? They let him get away with almost anything. You don't want to draw his attention, trust me. He has this cold stare. I dunno...he seems dangerous."

"So, what, he's going to stare me down?"

Yuki rolled her eyes. "You don't get it. He's unpredictable. You don't want to make enemies with a third year in your first two weeks, do you?"

I bit my lip, trying to peer through the glass door again. I didn't need more attention, that's for sure. I just wanted to blend in, get my homework done and drift through school until Nan and Gramps could take me in. But I also didn't want to stand in the courtyard in a pair of slippers, stuck for who knows how long. Anyway, it's not like they could make my life a living hell if I left Japan, and it would all be sorted out soon, right? This wasn't where Mom intended me to end up. I knew that.

"I'm going in," I said.

"You're crazy," Yuki said, but her eyes shone with excitement.

"They don't scare me."

Yuki raised her fists up to her chin. *"Faito,"* she said. *Fight.* In her most encouraging, you-can-do-it voice.

I grinned a little, then stepped toward the door. Even from outside I could hear the muffled yelling. When it died down for a minute, I took my chance.

Just in and out. I'm in slippers, for god's sake. They're not even going to hear me.

I pulled open the door and let it close quietly behind me before I stepped onto the raised wooden floor. My heartbeat pounded in my ears. The yelling was still muffled, and I realized the couple were on the other side of the sliding door into the school. Perfect—no way they'd see me now.

I snuck between the rows and rows of shoe cubbies looking for mine. It wasn't hard to find—it was the only one with a pair of leather shoes sticking out approximately a mile, surrounded by the neatly tucked-away slippers in everyone else's boxes. We all wore slippers in the school to keep it clean, but they weren't your typical cozy bedroom slippers. They were more like papery white flats. Japan had slippers for everything—school, house, toilet room, you name it.

I reached for my shoes as Myu's high and whiny voice echoed from the hallway behind the sliding door. Rolling my eyes, I pulled off the first slipper and then the other, clunking my shoes onto the floor and sliding my feet in.

And then the door slid open with a crash.

I crouched down, jolted by the footsteps stomping toward me. I did *not* want in on this performance.

"Matte!" Myu shouted, followed by a flurry of shuffling footsteps. "Wait!"

I glanced at the door to the courtyard—too far to make it without being seen. And just by trying to plan my escape route, I'd waited too long. If she saw me now, the way I was pressed against the wall all spylike, she'd think I was eavesdropping, and I didn't need rumors circulating about me. I was already a *gaijin,* an outsider—I didn't need to be a weirdo, too.

"Oi," said a second, annoyed voice. It was deep and rich—must be Yuu Tomohiro, dangerous kendo star. He didn't sound that dangerous. In fact, he sounded pretty disinterested. Cold, like Yuki had said.

Myu rapidly churned out Japanese words I didn't know. I caught a particle here and a past tense there, but let's face it—I'd only been in the country for a little more than a month and studying for five. I'd crammed all the Japanese I could, but I realized the minute I was on the plane that it had all been useless if I wanted to have a real conversation. At least

I could name just about all the fruits and vegetables in the grocery store.

Great plan there. Real useful. Things had improved since I arrived, but still, talking to Yuki or taking notes in class was not the same as following the high-pitched babbling of a major social breakup like this one. That was hard enough in English. I could really only make out the most important detail, which was that she was seriously pissed. You didn't need much vocab to tell.

I peeked around the wall of cubbies, hugging the wooden frame so I wouldn't be seen. Yuu Tomohiro had stopped in his tracks, his back to me and his head tilted back, staring up at her. Myu's long legs made her school uniform look scandalously short, her kneesocks slumped in coils around her ankles. She clutched a black book at the top of the steps, her nails painted neatly in pinks and glittery silver.

"What is this? What is it?" she said over and over, waving the book in Yuu's face.

Um...I thought. *A notebook?*

Yuu Tomohiro shrugged and climbed the steps back up to the sliding door. He reached for the notebook, but Myu whisked it behind her. He sighed as he leaned back against the opened door, his slipper pressing against the wooden frame.

"Well?" Myu said.

"What's it look like?" he said. "A notebook."

I rolled my eyes, even though my answer had been pretty much the same.

"Baka ja nai no?" Myu shrieked at him.

He was taller than her, but not when he slouched like that against the wall. And the more she fumed at him, the farther he seemed to slouch into the door. He shoved his hands deep into the pockets of his navy blue school blazer and tilted his head down, like he couldn't stand to even look at her or something. His copper hair, too bright to be natural, flipped in every direction like he hadn't taken the time to brush it, and he'd grown his bangs long—the way he was staring at the floor made the tips of them brush against his eyelashes.

I felt the heat rise up my neck. Yuki had not warned me he was so, well, pretty. Okay, gorgeous. I almost expected sparkles and rainbows to burst out of the walls anime-style, except his lips were turned in a smirk, and the way he crumpled against the wall exuded a smug superiority.

It was obvious Myu got the message. She looked absolutely *livid.*

"You think I'm stupid?" she said again. "Or are you?"

"Does it matter?"

What the heck had I walked into?

I couldn't tear my eyes away. Myu's face was puffy and pink, and every now and then her words got all choked up in her throat. She threw a string of questions into the air and they hung there with no reply. She became more frantic, the silence more tense.

What the hell did he do?

Cheat on her, maybe. That was the obvious answer or she wouldn't be so pissed. And he had no reply for it, because really, what could he say?

Yuu Tomohiro shook his head, the copper strands dancing around, and his head suddenly twisted to the cubbies beside me.

I shrunk flat against the wall, squeezing my eyes shut and praying he didn't see me. Myu had stopped ranting and a thick silence fell over the *genkan.*

"Is someone there?" she said.

Oh, crap—he *had* seen me. It was all over. I'd forever be

the *gaijin* who has no life and eavesdrops on bad breakups to sate my emo side.

"No one," he said, but it sounded off.

I couldn't bear it and I peeked around the cubby wall. Yuu was looking away. So he hadn't seen me after all. Thank god—I could go back to just being the Slipper Slinker.

Myu's eyes puffed up and overflowed, the tears streaming down her cheeks. "So it's really true," she said. "She's pregnant."

Oh my god. What is *this? Who* are *these people?*

"Sou mitai," Tomohiro smirked, which was way too casual a yes. A response like that was downright cruel. Even *I* knew that.

Myu's glittery fingernails tightened around the book. She raised it high above her shoulders, the loose papers inside it slipping until it was a mess of corners.

Then she hurled the book at the floor.

The notebook exploded with pages as it trailed down, the papers catching in the air and filling the room like rain. They twirled and twisted as they came down, white edges framing thick lines of black ink and charcoal. They fluttered down to the floor like cherry petals.

One of the drawings fell in front of me, tapping gently against the end of my shoe as it came to a rest.

"What the hell?" Yuu shouted, picking up the book from the floor.

"What did it all mean, then?" she whispered. "What was I to you?"

Yuu straightened to his full height and tilted his chin back until his gleaming dark eyes gazed straight into hers. He took two swaggering steps toward her, bending forward until their lips almost met. Myu's eyes widened.

He stood silently for a moment. Then he looked to the

side, and I saw a pained look in his eyes. He breathed heavily, his cheeks pink, his eyes glossy. So he did have feelings after all, the beast. He started to reach for her chin with his fingers. And then his hand suddenly dropped into his pocket and he laughed.

"Betsu ni," he said in a velvet voice. *Nothing special.*

You're lying, I thought. *Why are you lying?*

But Myu looked like she'd been punched in the gut. And even with the cultural barriers that stood in my way, it was clear to me that he'd just discounted all her suffering, her feelings—the whole relationship. He looked like he didn't give a shit, and that's pretty much what he'd said.

Myu's face turned a deep crimson, and her black hair clung to the sides of her snot-streaked face. Her hands squeezed into fists at her sides. Her gaze of hope turned cold and listless, like a mirror of Yuu's face.

And then Myu lifted her hand and slugged him right in the jaw. She hit him so hard his face twisted to the left.

He lifted his hand to rub his cheek, and as he raised his eyes, they locked with mine.

Shit.

His gaze burned into me and I couldn't move. Heat flooded my cheeks, and shame tingled down my neck.

I couldn't look away. I stared at him with my mouth open.

But he didn't call me out. He lifted his head, flicked his gaze back to Myu and pretended I didn't exist. I let out a shaky breath.

"Saitei," she spat, and I heard footsteps. After a moment, the door to the hallway slid shut.

I let out a breath.

Well, that was today's dose of awkward.

I looked down at the paper, still touching the tip of my shoe. I reached for it, flipping the page over to look.

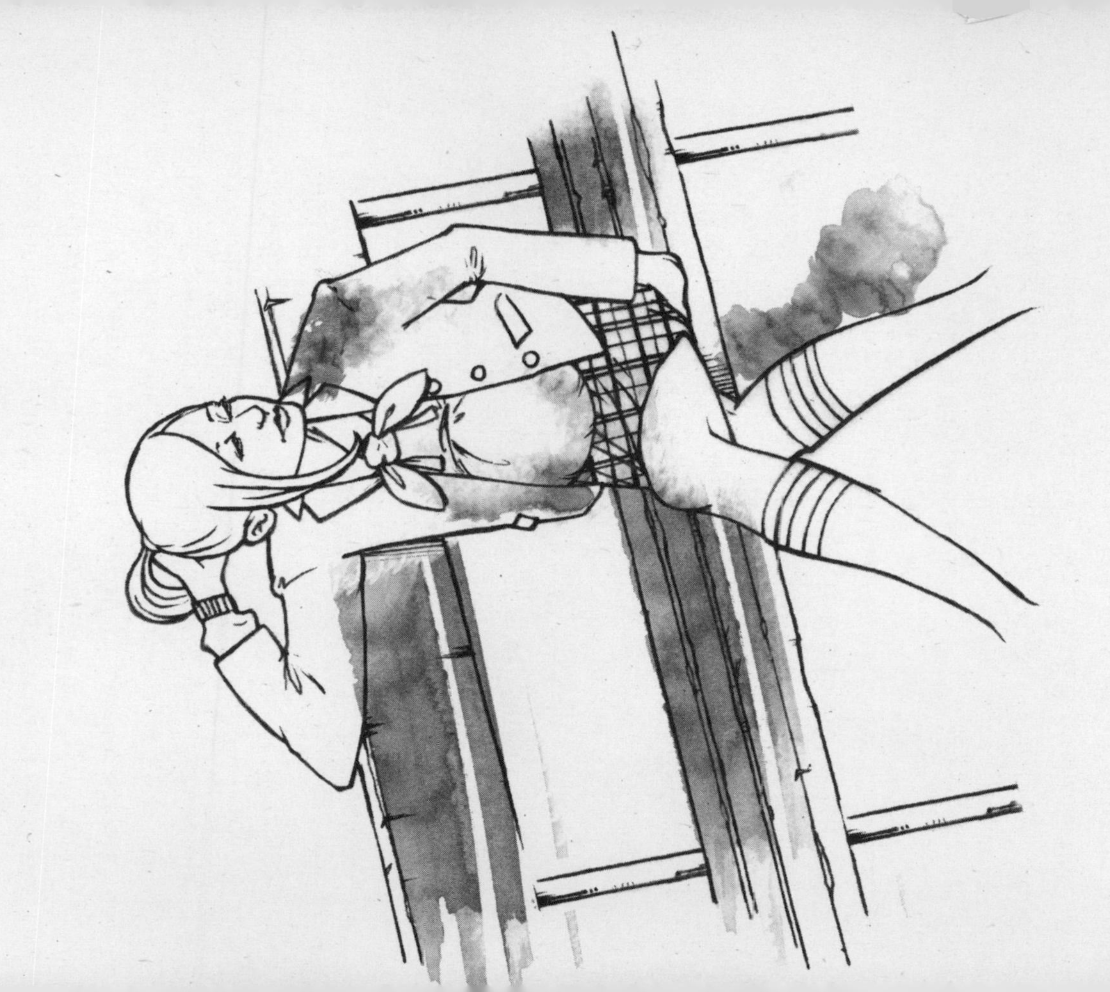

A girl lay back on a bench, roughly sketched in scrawls of ink as she looked out over the moat of Sunpu Park. She wore a school uniform, a tartan skirt clinging to her crossed legs. Little tufts of grass and flowers tangled with the bench legs, which had to be creative license—it was still too cold for blooms.

The girl was beautiful, in her crudely outlined way, with a lick of hair stuck to the back of her neck, her elbow resting against the top of the bench and her hand behind her head. She looked out at the moat of Sunpu Park, the sunlight sparkling off the dark water.

A pregnant bump of stomach curved under her blouse.

The other girl.

A queasy feeling started to twist in my stomach, like motion sickness.

And then the sketched girl on the bench turned her head, and her inky eyes glared straight into mine.

A chill shuddered through me.

Oh my god. She's looking at me.

A hand snatched the paper out of mine. I looked up, my mind reeling, straight into the face of Yuu Tomohiro.

He slammed the page facedown on top of the pile of drawings he'd collected. He stood too close, so that he hovered over me.

"Did you draw that?" I whispered in English. He didn't answer, staring hard at me. His cheek burned red and puffy where Myu had hit him.

I stared back. "Did you draw it?"

He smirked. *"Kankenai darou!"*

I looked at him blankly, and he sneered.

"Don't you speak Japanese?" he said. I felt my cheeks flush with shame. He looked like he'd settled some sort of battle in his mind, and he turned, walking slowly away.

"She moved," I blurted out.

He stumbled, just a little, but kept walking.

But I saw him stumble. And I saw the drawing look at me.

Didn't I? My stomach churned. That was impossible, wasn't it?

He went up the stairs, clutching the papers to his chest.

"She moved!" I said again, hesitant.

"I don't speak English," he said and slammed the door. It slid into the wall so hard it bounced back a little. I saw his shadow against the frosted glass of the door as he walked away.

Something oozed through the bottom of the sliding door, sluggish like dark blood. *Did Myu hit him that hard?*

The liquid dripped down the stairs, and after a moment of panic, I realized it was ink, not blood. From the drawings she'd thrown, maybe, or a cartridge of ink he'd kept inside the notebook.

I stood for a minute watching it drip, thinking of the burning eyes of the girl staring at me, the same flame in Yuu's eyes.

Had Myu seen it, too? Would anyone believe me? I wasn't even sure what the heck I'd seen.

It couldn't be real. I was too tired, overwhelmed in a country where I struggled to even communicate. That was the only answer.

I hurried toward the front door and out into the fresh spring air. Yuki and her friends had already vanished. I checked my watch—must be for a club practice. Fine. I was too jittery to talk about what I'd seen anyway. I ran across the courtyard, sans slippers this time, through the gate of Suntaba School and toward the weaving pathways of Sunpu Park.

When my mother died, it didn't occur to me I would end up on the other side of the world. I figured they would put me in foster care or ship me up to my grandparents in Deep

River, Canada. I prayed they would send me up there from New York, to that small town on the river I had spent almost every summer of my childhood. But it turned out that Mom's will hadn't been updated since Gramps's bout of cancer five years ago, when she'd felt it was too much of a burden to send me there. And Gramps still wasn't doing well now that the cancer had come back, so for now I would live with Mom's sister, Diane, instead, in Shizuoka.

So much sickness surrounded me. I could barely deal with losing my mom, and then everything familiar slipped away. No life in Deep River with Nan and Gramps. No life in America or Canada at all. I'd stayed with a friend of Mom's for a while, but it was only temporary, my life stuck in a place where I couldn't move forward or back. I was being shipped away from everything I knew, the leftover baggage of fading lives. Mom never liked leaving American soil, and here I was, only seven months without her, already going places she wouldn't have followed.

And seeing things, hallucinating that drawings were moving. God, I'd be sent to a therapist for sure.

I told Yuki about the fight the next day during lunch, although I left out the part about the moving drawing. I still wasn't sure what I'd seen, and I wasn't about to scare off the only friend I had. But I couldn't get it out of my mind, those sketched eyes glaring into mine. *I wouldn't imagine that, right?* But the more I thought about it, the more dreamlike it felt.

Yuki turned in her seat to eat her *bentou* on my desk. I wasn't used to the food yet, so Diane had packed my *bentou* box from side to side with squished peanut-butter sandwiches. Yuki gripped her pink chopsticks with delicate fingers and scooped another bite of eggplant into her mouth.

"You're kidding," she said, covering her mouth with her

hand as she said it. “I still can’t believe you went in there.” She’d pinned her hair back neatly and her fingernails were nicely painted, reminding me of Myu’s delicate pink-and-silver nails. I wondered if they’d chipped when she hit him.

“You didn’t even wait for me to come out,” I said.

“Sorry!” she said, pressing her fingers together in apology. “I had to get to cram school. Believe me, I was dying inside not knowing what happened.”

“I’m sure.” Yuki did like her share of drama.

She lifted her *keitai* phone in the air. “Here, send me your number. Then I can call you next time I abandon you in the middle of the biggest breakup of all time.”

I turned a little pink. “Um. I don’t have one?”

She stared at me a minute before shoving the cell phone back into her bag, then pointed at me. “Get one. *Maa,* I never realized Yuu Tomohiro was so mean.”

“Are you kidding? You told me he was cold!”

“I know, but I didn’t know he was cheat-on-your-girlfriend-and-get-someone-pregnant cold. That’s a different level.” I rolled my eyes, but secretly I tried to break down the number of words she’d just used. I loved that she had faith in my Japanese, but it was a little misplaced. We switched back and forth between languages as we talked.

Across the room, Yuki’s friend Tanaka burst through the doorway, grabbing his chair and dragging it loudly to our desks.

“Yo!” he said, which sounded less lame in Japanese than English. He tossed his head to the side with a friendly grin.

“Tan-kun.” Yuki smiled, using the typical suffix for a guy friend. I looked down into the mess of peanut butter lining the walls of my *bentou.* Tanaka Ichirou was always too loud, and he always sat too close. I needed space to think about what I’d seen yesterday.

"Did you hear about Myu?" he said, and our eyes widened.

"How do you know?" said Yuki.

"My sister's in her homeroom," he said. "Myu and Tomo-kun split up. She's crying over her lunch right now, and Tomo didn't even show up for class." Tanaka leaned in closer and whispered in a rough tone, "I heard he got another girl pregnant."

I felt sick. I dropped my peanut-butter sandwich into my *bentou* and closed the lid.

That curve of stomach under the sketched blouse…

"He did!" Yuki squealed. It was all just drama to them. But I couldn't stop thinking about the way her head turned, the way she looked right at me.

"It's just a rumor," said Tanaka.

"It's not," Yuki said. "Katie spied on the breakup!"

"Yuki!"

"Oh, come on, everyone will know soon anyway." She sipped her bottle of iced tea.

Tanaka frowned. "Weird, though. Tomo-kun might be the tough loner type, but he's not cruel."

I thought about the way he'd snatched the paper out of my hands. The sneer on his face, and the curve of his lips as he spat out his words. *Don't you speak Japanese?* He seemed like the cruel type to me. Except that moment…that moment where he'd almost dropped everything and kissed Myu. His hand reaching for her chin, the softness in his eyes for just a second before it changed.

"How would you know?" I burst out. Tanaka looked up at me with surprised eyes. "Well, you called him by his first name, right?" I added. "Not even as a senior *senpai,* so you must know him pretty well."

"Maa…" Tanaka scratched the back of his head. "We were in Calligraphy Club in elementary school—you know, tra-

ditional paintings of Japanese characters. Before he dropped out, I mean. Which sucked, because he had a real talent. We haven't really talked much since then, but we used to be close. He got into a lot of fights, but he was a good guy."

"Right," I said. "Cheating on girls and making fun of foreigners' Japanese. What a winner."

Yuki's face went pale, her mouth dropping open.

"He *saw* you?" She put a hand over her mouth. "And Myu? Did she?"

I shook my head. "Just Yuu."

"And? Was he angry?"

"Yeah, but so what? It's not like I meant to spy on them."

"Okay, we need to do damage control and see how bad your social situation is. Ask him about it after school, Tan-kun," Yuki said.

I panicked. "No, don't."

"Why?"

"He'll know I told."

"He won't know," Yuki said. "Tanaka's sister told him about the breakup, remember? We'll just slip the conversation in and see how he reacts to you."

"I don't want to know, okay? Drop it please?"

Yuki sighed. "Fine. For now."

The bell rang. We tucked our *bentous* into our bags and pulled out some paper.

Yuu Tomohiro. His eyes kept haunting me. I could barely concentrate on Suzuki-sensei's chalkboard math, which was hard enough considering the language gap. Diane had been so set on sending me to a Japanese school instead of an international one. She was convinced I'd catch on quickly, that I'd come out integrated and bilingual and competitive for university programs. And since she knew how much I wanted to move back with Nan and Gramps, she wanted to hit me over the head with as much experience as possible.

"Give it four or five months," she said, "and you'll speak like a pro."

Obviously she didn't realize I was lacking in language skills.

When the final bell rang, I was relieved to find out I didn't have cleaning duty. I had a Japanese cram school to go to, so I decided to cut through Sunpu Park and get on the east-bound train. I waved to Yuki, and Tanaka flashed a peace sign at me as he rolled up his sleeves and started lifting chairs onto the desks. *Pretty sure that counts as two friends,* I thought, and in spite of everything, a trickle of relief ran through me. I headed toward the *genkan* to return my slippers—I wasn't going to make that mistake again—and headed out into the courtyard.

School began in late March at Suntaba, and the spring air was fresh but cool. Green buds had crept onto each of the spindly branches of the trees, waiting for slightly warmer weather to bloom. Diane said everyone in Japan checked their cell phones daily to find out when the cherry blossoms would bloom so they could sit under them and get drunk. Well, okay, that wasn't exactly what she said, but Yuki said a lot of the salarymen turned as pink as the flowers.

I was nearly at the gate when I saw him. He slouched against the stone entranceway, hands shoved deep in his pockets. The sun glared off the neat row of gold buttons down his blazer and splayed through his hair, gleaming on the copper streaks.

Yuu Tomohiro.

My footsteps slowed as dread leached down my spine. There was no other way off school grounds; I'd have to pass him. The back of his hand curved over his shoulder, his book bag pressed against his back. He stared straight at me, as if he was waiting for me.

He wasn't…was he?

Maybe he wanted me to keep my mouth shut about what had happened. But he hadn't understood what I was saying, right? He didn't speak English.

His face was turned down in a sour frown, but his eyes shone as he stared at me, like he was trying to figure me out. A bluish bruise was set in his cheek, and the skin looked a little swollen. I looked down first and then straight at him, but I couldn't stare at him long. Nothing could settle the pit I felt in my stomach, like I was going to be sick.

If he did make that drawing move… No, that was impossible. I'd been tired, that's all.

I stood there ten feet from the gate, unable to move, squeezing the handles of my bag as tightly as I could. My navy skirt felt short and ugly against my bleached-out legs. I was out of place at this school and I knew it.

Move! Just walk past and ignore him! Do something! my brain screamed at me, but I couldn't move.

I let out a shaky breath and took a step forward.

He uncoiled from his slouch like a snake, rising to his full height. I wondered why he always slouched when he could look like *that,* but the thought sent prickles up my neck. He was a jerk anyway, even if I hadn't seen the drawing move. He'd cheated on Myu, got someone else pregnant and still had the nerve to laugh at it. Except that he looked like he'd been lying that he didn't care about her. And Tanaka had said he was a good guy deep down.

Must be *really* deep down.

His shoes clicked against the cement as he stepped toward me, and despite all my common sense, I couldn't stop shaking. His eyes burned as he stared me down. He was only two feet from me, and now only a foot. I'm sorry, was I the only one at the school who worried he was psycho?

His eyes flicked to the ground suddenly, his bangs slipping forward and fanning over his face as he walked straight past me, so close that his shoulder grazed mine. So close that I could smell spices and hair gel, that I could feel the warmth radiating from his skin. The heat sent a shudder through me and I stopped walking, listening to the *click, click* of him walking farther away.

He's screwing with me, I thought. Trying to intimidate me or something. Shame flooded through me as I realized I'd let him get away with it. He'd reeled me in, and despite everything I knew, despite drawings staring at me and pregnant girlfriends and humiliating language barriers, I'd still let my heart twist at his gorgeous eyes.

When did I become so shallow? I scrunched my hands deeper into the leather of my book bag, until the zipper dug into my knuckles.

"Ano!" I said to get his attention, squeezing my eyes shut as I said it. The clicking of his shoes stopped. Around us the noisy chatter of other students buzzed in my brain, fading into background noise like ringing in my ears. All I could focus on was the silence that had replaced his footsteps, the sound I imagined of his breathing.

Now what? I wanted to ask why he'd been staring at me, why everything felt off when he was there. And about the drawing, the memory sitting unsettled in my gut. But how could I ask him that? He'd think I was nuts. The limits of my Japanese shoved against me, which only proved his point and pissed me off more. What was I thinking to confront him? And what exactly could I say that wouldn't make me look like an idiot?

A moment passed, and I heard a single laugh under his breath. Then the click, click, click of him walking away toward the eastern wall. The clicking suddenly sped up, and I turned to look. He ran at the wall, leaping up the stone face and grabbing the branches of the *momiji* tree above, slipping over the wall and out of sight.

I'd let him do it again, let him tip me off balance for the second time in five minutes. I shuddered with anger as I stared at the branch, still swaying, dusting the wall with maple leaves.

The branch.

I didn't spend my summers hiking in the woods for nothing.

My shoes pounded against the cement as I raced toward the wall. Students backed out of my way just in time, breaking apart their little groups out of curiosity about what I was about to do next. Slippers were about to take a backseat.

I threw my hands around the tree trunk and pressed my feet against the slippery bark. My book bag clattered to the ground as I reached for the branches, hoisting myself up. Leaves and twigs tangled in my hair, but I climbed higher and higher, until I cleared the wall and the street on the other side came into view.

I scanned the sidewalks for the Suntaba uniform—there, behind the line of salarymen. He was combing a hand through his copper hair, his blazer draped over his arm.

"Yuu Tomohiro!" I shouted at the top of my lungs. He jerked to a stop, but didn't turn around. I stared at the curve of his shoulder blades under the white dress shirt as he breathed in and out slowly.

Then he turned, looking up in slow motion when he didn't see me on the street.

"That's right, Tarzan, look up!" I screamed in English. "You're not the only one around here who can make an exit!" My lungs burned with adrenaline as I watched him stare at me.

I couldn't help it. The grin spread across my face, knowing I'd beaten him at his own game.

He waited a minute, completely still, and I wondered if he hadn't understood a word I'd said. Not that it mattered. He'd still get the point. I was the winner.

"What do you have to say now?" I shouted.

Still nothing.

And then he slowly raised his arm, his finger pointed.

"I can see up your skirt," he said.

Oh god.

I'd totally forgotten I was wearing my short uniform skirt.

Crap, crap, crap!

I twisted to look down at the ring of students gathered around the tree trunk. They were starting to giggle, and if they hadn't been looking up my skirt before, they definitely were now.

A couple of squealing girls reached into their bags. *They better not be bringing out cell phones to immortalize my humiliation.*

I let go of the branches with one hand to press my skirt tight against my legs. I turned back to look at Yuu. He was smiling, beaming even, like this was some sort of amusing moment we were sharing. Like it was just the two of us. And worse, the smile made my stomach twist. Then he beat his fists against his chest a couple times Tarzan-style and turned, walking out of sight.

My fingers tightened around the branch. Why did he act like two different people? A giggle from below and my anger surged up again.

All right, Mr. Creepy Sketch Guy. You want war?
You're on.

The maze of Sunpu Park calmed me down a little. It always did, with the twisting hedges and the murky moats in deep channels. An old castle towered over the eastern side of the park, but I didn't see much of it on my way home. I headed south over a long concrete bridge above the water teeming with koi, and then twisted past the underground walkways to Shin-shizuoka Station.

I scanned my pass, and the little metal doors slammed into the sides of the barriers to let me through. I walked slowly to the platforms, my eyes squinting at the signs of scrolling kanji. The train was coming in three minutes, so I sat on one of the light blue benches and rested my bag on my lap.

I noticed a twig caught in the wool of my skirt, and I pulled it from the fabric.

"Why did I do that?" I groaned, slumping my chin on my bag. As if fitting in wasn't hard enough, I had to go and climb a tree to yell at a boy and flash my underwear to half the school population.

Maybe I should be sick tomorrow.

A group of girls suddenly rushed in front of me, laughing as they punched out texts on their cell phones. One of them tripped over my foot, and her friends caught her by the shoulders as she stumbled.

"Sorry!" I burst out, tucking my feet as far as I could under the bench.

The girl looked at me for a minute, and then the three of them shuffled away, mumbling loudly to each other. Their green-and-blue-tartan skirts showed me they were from a different high school, so why should I care if they were being snobby? I wanted to stick my tongue out but stopped short. It was too much—I didn't fit in at school, and I couldn't even blend in at the train station. How the heck was I supposed to survive here anyway? Without Mom, without anything familiar. The tears started to blur in my eyes.

I heard a muffled greeting as a boy called to the girls. They didn't answer him. Typical. *Rude bunch of—*

He said hello to them again. They still didn't answer. What was their problem?

"Domo," he tried again, and this time I looked up.

His dark eyes caught mine immediately. He had black hair that flopped around his ears, with two thick blond highlights tucked behind them. His bangs trailed diagonally across his forehead, so they almost covered his left eye. A silver earring glinted in his left ear as he nodded at me.

Wait. He's talking to me.

"Hi?" I managed. It came out like a question.

He smiled. He wore the same uniform colors as the girls—a white dress shirt and navy blazer, a green-and-blue tie and navy pants—and he leaned against the pillar near the bench. His body was turned away from the clique, and they seemed a little pissed that he was talking to me. From the smile on his face, I wondered if that was the point.

"You go to Suntaba?" he said, pointing at my uniform.

"Yeah," I said.

"You must speak Japanese well, then."

I smirked. "I wouldn't say that."

He laughed and walked toward me. "Can I sit?" he said.

"Um, it's a free station."

"What?"

"Nothing." Okay, so when did hot guys from other schools start trying to pick me up on train platforms?

He leaned in a little, so I leaned back.

"Don't let them get to you," he mumbled. "They're just airheads anyway."

"Them?" I said, looking over at the girls. They pretended they weren't staring, which only made it more obvious.

"Yeah," he said.

"It's fine," I said. "I've been through worse."

He laughed again. "Rough day?"

"You have no idea."

"Jun!" one of the girls squealed at him—an ex he was trying to make jealous, maybe? He leaned in closer and winked like we were coconspirators. And then a little chime flooded the station, and the train roared past, the brakes squealing as it slowed.

I grabbed my bag from my lap and we lined up by the giant white arrows on the floor. The cars opened up and we filed in. I grabbed the metal rail by the door so I could make a quick getaway at Yuniko Station. It's not like I didn't appreciate attention from Jun the *ikemen*—and was he ever gorgeous—but I just needed some space to myself to think.

The doors closed behind us and the train lurched forward. But in the crowds outside the window, I saw a tall figure in the Suntaba uniform. With copper hair and a puffy bruise on his cheek.

I stepped back as the train jolted, nearly knocking me over. It pulled slowly out of the station, barely moving along the platform.

"You okay?" Jun said behind me.

Impossible. Why would Yuu Tomohiro be here when I'd watched him walk the opposite direction? He looked different when no one was watching, like his features had softened. He waited in line for a Roman bus, emerald-green with an old motor that made the vehicle bump around as it idled. When it was his turn to get on, he actually stepped to the side with a smile and helped a gray-haired lady behind him up the steps.

Was I hallucinating again? *That did* not *just happen.*

Then I lost his face in the crowd, and the train reached the end of the platform, speeding up as it snaked across the bustling city.

"I'm fine," I said when I found my voice again. "Just saw a guy from my school over there." I waved my hand vaguely at the window, but the sight of the bus was long gone.

"Tomodachi?" Jun said. "Maybe *koibito?*"

I choked. "What? No! We are *not* friends. Not even close."

Jun smiled. "You just looked flustered, that's all." He tucked a blond highlight behind his ear, rubbing his earring between his fingers.

"Because I'm tired," I said a little too sharply. "It's nothing."

"Ah," he said, giving the earring a tug. "The rough day you mentioned."

"Right."

"Sorry," he said, dropping his hand into his blazer pocket. In the corner of the train car, the group of girls was still whispering about us. Jun stood beside me, silent as he stared out the window. I felt a little guilty shutting down the conversation, but I couldn't help it. My thoughts were a tangled mess.

I watched the buildings blur outside the window as the train sped past.

What was I thinking, climbing a tree and yelling at Yuu like that? So much for a fancy exit—I'd just dug a deeper social hole to curl up and die in. And I couldn't stop thinking about the smile on his face, as if we were in on the same joke. He'd looked harmless enough helping that woman onto the bus.

But that's not how he'd looked staring at me from the gate.

2

"Okaeri," Diane said in a singsong voice when I opened the door.

"I'm not saying it," I said, kicking the toes of my shoes against the raised floor until they slipped off my feet.

"Oh, come on," Diane whined, appearing around the corner. She'd draped her navy-and-pink-flowered apron over her teaching clothes, and the smell of curry rice wafted from the kitchen. "If you want to learn Japanese, you have to use it all the time."

"Not interested," I said. "I've been speaking it all day. I need some English right now." I strode past her and collapsed onto the tiny purple couch in the living room. It was ugly, but definitely comfortable.

"So how was school?"

"Fine." *Other than the part where half the school looked up my skirt.*

I picked up the remote and started flipping through variety shows. Bright kanji sprawled across the screen in neon pinks and greens, quoting outrageous things guests said. Not like I could get the joke, of course.

"It's curry rice again. I got held up with the Drama Club

meeting." Diane stepped into the kitchen and lifted the lid of the pot, the spicy fragrance wafting around the room as she stirred. I flipped the channel, looking for something English to watch, some reminder of the fact that I was still on the same planet.

"And how was cram school?" The rice cooker beeped and Diane shuffled over to turn it off. I leaned back so my head faced the kitchen upside down.

"It was crammy," I said.

"Could you at least set the table?" She sighed, and then I felt guilty.

"Sorry," I mumbled. I flipped the TV off and tossed the remote onto the couch, setting plates on either side of the flimsy table.

I hadn't known Diane much before Mom's funeral, but she'd never struck me as the motherly type. She'd spent most of the service shoving hors d'oeuvres at everybody with a fake smile, like she was a balloon ready to pop. She'd insisted on my calling her just Diane. I think "Aunt" emphasized the fact that her sister was gone, and made her feel like we were some sort of dysfunctional family, trying to keep going after the fact. Which, of course, we were.

She'd picked me up at the airport with the same over-excitement, waving wildly at me to make us even more of a spectacle. "Katie!" she'd screeched, like this was some kind of fun vacation, like we weren't terrified of each other.

The bullet-train ride made my ears pop and sting, and once we got to Shizuoka, I stood out even more. There were a lot of *gaijin* in Tokyo, but in Shizuoka I rarely saw anyone foreign.

Diane lifted the lid of the rice cooker, and steam swirled out, fogging up her glasses. She reached for my plate and paddled the rice on, and then dumped a ladle of curry on the side.

"Great," I said.

"You mean '*itadakimasu.*'"

"Whatever."

"So any new friends yet, or are they still being shy?" Diane sat down and mixed the curry and rice together with her chopsticks. I pushed my rice into a sticky mound and dug my fork into a carrot.

Well, let's see. Cute guy on the train from another school, and annoying senior who has it out for me at my school. But friends? "Tanaka, I guess. He's Yuki's friend." Big mistake. Diane clasped her hands together and her eyes shone.

"That's great!" she said.

"It doesn't matter," I said. "I figure it won't take too long to settle the whole will dispute. I'll be in Deep River before we know it." Diane frowned, which looked almost clownish in her thick plum lipstick.

"Come on, it's not that bad here with me, is it?"

"Why would it be bad in a country where I can't even read where the bathroom is?" Speaking was one thing; even writing phonetic hiragana and katakana had come without too much study. But learning two thousand kanji to read signs and newspapers was a slow, grueling process.

"I told you, it'll take time. But you're doing great. And you know Gramps still isn't in the best of health. It's too much of a strain on them right now, at least until we know the cancer is in remission for sure."

"I know," I sighed, pushing my potatoes around in the thick curry.

"So tell me about Tanaka."

I shrugged. "He's into calligraphy painting. Tall, skinny, pretty loud when he comes into a room."

"Is he cute?"

"Gross, Diane." I slammed my fork down in disgust.

"Okay, okay," she conceded. "I just wanted you to know that we can talk boys, if you need to."

"Noted."

"Do you want some tea?"

I shook my head. "I've just got some kanji sheets to write out and some math homework. Then I'm going to bed."

"No problem. Do your best. *Ganbare,* as they say." Diane's cheerful tone had returned. I rose to take my plate to the sink.

"Like I give a shit what they say."

"Hey, watch it. You know your mom wouldn't be impressed with that kind of talk."

I paused, thinking of Mom. She was always a prude, which is why I was stunned to find out she'd dated someone unpredictable like Dad. Maybe he'd set her on the straight and narrow after he ran out on her. Kind of like Yuu Tomohiro was doing to Myu now.

"Sorry," I mumbled. "I just had a crazy day."

"I just… I hope you'll be a little happier here with me," Diane said gently. It was about the most serious voice I'd ever heard from her, and I suddenly felt like a jerk. She'd always been the piece that didn't fit, Mom said, the one searching for herself on the other side of the world. Kind of the way I felt now. And even then she'd opened up her tiny world here for me when I'd needed her the most.

"You're right," I said. "I'll try." Diane smiled, and I wondered if she realized we were both lost now, adrift together but somehow alone.

The moment over, I headed to my room to suffer writer's cramp copying pages and pages of kanji.

I was sure Yuu Tomohiro would be waiting the next morning, leaning against the Suntaba plaque on the gate. I'd flipped through my dictionary after cram school, perfecting what I was going to say to him. When he wasn't there, I wondered whether I felt more relieved or disappointed.

I slid into my seat behind Yuki, putting my book bag on the ground and reaching in for my textbooks.

"Ohayo," Yuki said, twisting in her chair.

"Morning," I said. "You didn't see Yuu come in, did you?" Okay, so I was just a little anxious to know. I was ready to take him on and get some answers.

Yuki shrugged. "Probably early morning *kiri-kaeshi,*" she said.

"Early morning what?"

"You know, for Kendo Club."

"Morning!" Tanaka sang as he burst into the class, striding toward his seat.

"Okay," I said, "he's got way too much energy for the morning." I lifted my hand in a feeble wave. Tanaka nodded at us and broke into a huge grin. The conversation with Diane surfaced like bad heartburn, and I turned to look at my desk, desperately ignoring the fact that Tanaka was a little cute. Jeez, thanks, Diane. I did not need to be looking at one of my only friends like that. What if I lost both friends over a dumb crush? Life was complicated enough right now. I shoved the feeling down and concentrated on the cover of my textbook.

Advanced Mathematics. Fascinating.

"Did you decide which clubs to join?" Yuki said.

"You should at least join English Club," said Tanaka, inviting himself into the conversation. Yeah, English Club wouldn't make me stick out. But Tanaka looked so sincere and I really only had the two friends....

"Okay, okay."

"Yatta!" Tanaka said, throwing his fist high in the air.

"No fair!" whined Yuki. "You have to join at least one club with me. *Sado? Kado?"*

"Kado?"

"Flowers."

"I have allergies."

"Then Tea Ceremony. You get to have cakes and learn the roots of Japanese culture…?" Yuki sounded like a brochure, but I was starting to crack under the pressure. Anyway, it wasn't like I wasn't interested in Japanese culture—just homesick, disoriented. Orphaned.

"Okay," I relented. "Sado it is."

Suzuki-sensei stepped into the room. We stood, bowed our good-mornings and opened our books.

I scribbled notes from the board but pretty soon got bored and started doodling. And as I sketched flowers and snails down the margins, the eyes of the inky girl from Tomohiro's drawing flooded my thoughts. I didn't think I was coming apart at the seams—why would I be seeing things?

The look on Tomohiro's face when he'd grabbed the drawing out of my hands still bothered me. Half anger, half worry. What was he trying to hide? He'd got some girl pregnant and humiliated me in front of the school. But I was pretty sure he'd also lied to Myu about how he really felt. And the smile he'd given me when I was up in the tree—like we were on the same team, like we were friends…

I felt itchy suddenly, my head throbbing the way it had when I'd stared at his sketch. I kept picturing the inky girl looking at me, the way her hair curled around her shoulders. I could hear the birds singing in the park, the water in the moat sloshing along. I could feel the breeze on my skin.

The corner of my notebook flipped up, lifted by a cool

spring wind. Wait, that couldn't be—we were indoors, and the windows were shut. Then the whole side of the book started to ripple.

The flowers I'd doodled started to bend in the breeze. One of the petals fell to the little bit of ground I'd sketched. A snail tucked himself into his shell.

Is this happening? Is this real?

The pen was hot in my hand and I gripped it tighter, watching the pages of my notebook flutter in the wind, watching the snails leave glittering trails across the page…

Watching as they turned and came toward me, mouths full of sharp, jagged teeth I didn't know snails had, teeth that I hadn't drawn….

The pen shattered beneath my fingers, drowning the doodles in ink. Shards of plastic flew across the room and scattered on desks and floors. Students shouted in surprise, jumping back from their desks to their feet. Suzuki-sensei whirled around from the board.

"What happened?" he snapped.

Tanaka and Yuki stared at my hand, covered in ink.

"Katie?" Yuki whispered.

"I—I'm sorry," I said, my throat dry.

And then I saw Yuu Tomohiro standing in the hallway, his startled eyes watching me, his fingers wrapped around the door frame. He looked almost afraid. Had he seen it, too? Or maybe—maybe he'd caused it.

"Go clean up," Suzuki-sensei said, and I forced my head to nod. My chair squeaked as I pushed it back to stand up, the whole class staring at me. Ink dripped off the side of my notebook and onto the floor.

"Sorry," I choked again and ran into the hallway.

When I got there, Tomohiro was gone.

I ran to the washroom and scrubbed my hands, splashing water on my face.

I stared at myself in the mirror. I looked thin and frightened, barely there.

The ink spiraled down the drain. I carved lines through it with my fingertips.

There was no way this was a hallucination. The whole class had seen the pen explode. And the drawings definitely moved. I could still smell the murky moat water; the breeze had left tangles in my hair.

And Tomohiro had been there when it happened, just like before.

I splayed my inky fingers under the rush of clean water.

He was doing something to the drawings. I just didn't know what.

"Ready to go?" said Yuki.

We stepped out of the *genkan* door and into the courtyard, Yuki and Tanaka laughing about something Suzuki had said—I'd missed that joke, too. The sunlight was streaming down, and a gentle, warm breeze blew through the branches of the *momiji* and *sakura* trees.

I took a deep breath and looked up at the gate to the school.

He wasn't there.

Relief flooded through me. At least I could put off my planned confrontation for now. I just needed time not to think, time to forget everything that had happened.

Except I couldn't. It was all I saw every time I closed my eyes.

I wanted my life with Mom back. I wanted to be normal and not see drawings move.

I started to giggle along with Yuki, pretending I understood the joke, pretending I wasn't shaking inside. But Tanaka suddenly shot out his arm.

"Oh!" He pointed. "It's Tomo-kun!"

You've got to be kidding.

I looked up, and there he was, leaning against the stone wall and chatting with a friend. The other guy had bleached his hair so white it looked like he was wearing a mop on his head.

"Introduce us!" Yuki squealed. "We can get the whole story about Myu!"

"Please don't," I whispered, but Tanaka was already running across the courtyard. Yuki grabbed my arm.

"Come on!" she said, squeezing my elbow and rushing us forward.

"*Oi,* Tomo-kun!" Tanaka shouted.

Yuu Tomohiro looked up slowly, his eyes dark and cold. His friend sagged back against a tree trunk, watching us approach with mild amusement.

"It's me, Tanaka, from Calligraphy," said Tanaka, panting as he stopped beside them. He placed his hands on his knees and then gave Yuu a thumbs-up.

Yuu's face was blank at first, but then remembrance flickered into his eyes.

"Oh," he said. "Tanaka Ichirou."

"This is Watabe Yuki and Katie Greene," Tanaka said. He didn't reverse my name because *gaijin* never put their last names first. Yet another way I stood out. Yuki bowed, but I couldn't bring myself to do it. I squeezed my hands into fists and tried to do the same with my fear—I tried to squeeze it into anger.

Tomohiro didn't bother to introduce his friend or say hello to us. He leaned his head forward slightly so his bangs fell into his eyes, then exchanged a side glance with Bleached Hair. I got the message—they wanted us gone.

But Tanaka didn't clue in. He laughed, nervous, grasping for things to say.

"It's been a long time, huh?" he said.

Tomohiro nodded, his bangs bobbing curtly. "You got taller, Ichirou."

"Well, I had to fend for myself after you left." Tanaka grinned before turning to us. "Tomo-kun used to get into fights over everything."

Tomohiro smirked. "That hasn't changed," he said, staring directly at me.

So he was picking a fight with me. But over what? He was the one doing creepy stuff, not me. He ran a hand through his hair and looked over at Bleached Hair, who rolled his eyes.

Yuki spoke up. "Sorry about you and Myu."

Tomo's eyes snapped back to mine. I bet he was wondering how much I'd told. Was he worried I'd spilled about the drawing, too?

"Maa," he said with a dramatic sigh, pressing his slender fingertips to his forehead. "Some people don't know when to keep their mouths shut."

Fire spread through me. "I didn't say anything," I blurted.

"My sister told me," Tanaka said quickly. "Keiko's in Myu's homeroom."

"It doesn't matter," Tomohiro said, rubbing the back of his neck. "You don't have to cover for her. The whole school knows anyway."

But it did matter. I didn't want to give him the satisfaction of being right when he wasn't.

"He's not covering," I said. "I have better things to do than gossip about you."

"So you have a new girlfriend now?" Yuki piped up again. She was determined to drag the gossip out at any cost.

Tomohiro tilted his head. "Why? Are you confessing?"

That's what they called it here when you admitted you liked someone. Yuki turned bright pink.

"It's—it's not like that," she said, waving her hand back and forth.

"Oh, her, then?" he said, motioning at me.

My heart almost stopped. "Excuse me?"

"It's a joke," Bleached Hair said. "Calm yourself."

"Um," Tanaka said, looking from Tomohiro to me and back with wide eyes. "Um, so are—are you going to join the *Shoudo* Club this year?"

A dark look crossed Tomohiro's eyes. "I don't do calligraphy anymore," he said quietly.

"Tan-kun told us you were really talented," Yuki bubbled, but Tomohiro took a step toward her, glaring at her from behind his bangs.

"I don't paint anymore," he said, and I wondered why he had to get so uptight about it. "It doesn't interest me."

"Oh, that's too bad," Tanaka said, laughing politely to smooth things out. "With me in the club, they need all the help they can get." Tomohiro let out a small laugh, which only egged Tanaka on. "God help us if they put my drawings on display!"

"You did always draw the lines too thickly." Tomohiro grinned. The storm in his eyes looked as if it had passed. I could see a faint image in my mind of what he must have been like in elementary school, when he and Tanaka had been friends.

"Sou ne…" Tanaka trailed off, staring into the distance,

deep in thought. He tapped his fingers against his chin. "How do I fix it?"

Tomohiro gripped his fingers together, as if he were holding a paintbrush. "If you hold it like this," he said, "with the right support here, and move like this..." His arm moved gently through the air, making light brushstrokes, and even I, who had no background in calligraphy—heck, even my school notes were illegible—could tell there was something more going on here.

"Try to load less paint on the tip of the brush," Tomohiro said. "And move like this."

Tanaka smiled and crossed his arms as he watched. "You're really good, you know? A natural."

Tomohiro's arm stopped suddenly like a dance cut short. It hung there in the air, rigidly, until he dropped it down to the side and shoved his hand into his blazer pocket.

"I told you," he said sharply, "it doesn't interest me anymore."

Tanaka's face fell while Bleached Hair leaned back into the tree, grinning. *What the hell?* I thought. Tanaka and Tomohiro used to be friends, and now he treated him like this?

"You don't have to be a jerk about it," I snapped. "Tanaka's just trying to be nice to you."

"Katie," Yuki whispered, urgently squeezing my arm.

Tomohiro sneered. "You're always sticking your nose in, aren't you?"

"So are you. You're everywhere I turn. What, are you a stalker, too, or something?"

"If I was, I wouldn't stalk you."

"Oh, I'm not your type, huh? You don't like *gaijin?*"

"I don't like annoying girls who think they know everything."

"Unless they have a skirt to look up, right?"

Tomohiro grinned, and my nerves flipped over. It was that same secret-alliance look. I almost expected him to wink like Jun had at the train station. I took a deep breath.

"So if you hate art so much, how come you had a sketchbook full?"

The grin vanished.

"And how come they move?"

"Move?" Bleached Hair said.

"That's right," I fumed. "I know you're doing something."

I looked at Tomohiro, and did he ever look pissed!

Good. I'll finally get some answers.

"Oh, are you working on another of those animations, Tomo?" Tanaka said.

Tomohiro smiled.

No.

"He used to do these really neat ones on the edges of his notebooks."

No! Don't give him an escape hatch!

"Right, Ichirou. Animation."

"On one page?" I sneered.

"On lots of pages," he said. "That's why I had so many drawings. It's a project for my cram school. I didn't want to draw, but I have to if I want full credit."

Yuki nodded knowingly.

The answers were slipping through my fingers like sand.

"But I saw you in the hallway," I said, "when my pen— I know you're trying to freak me out with all your ink stuff."

Tomohiro stepped toward me, his eyes studying mine. He was a little taller than me, and his bangs feathered around his eyes like the hairs of a painter's fan brush. My stomach twisted and I focused hard on hating him.

“Why would I want to freak you out?” he said in a smooth voice.

“I don’t know,” I said. I could hear my pulse in my ears. Tomohiro smiled, his eyes gleaming from behind his bangs. So he could look normal after all, I thought. Okay, more than normal. *Damn it! Focus!*

“Greene-san,” he said in accented English, giving me just about the politest suffix he could, “I assure you, I don’t have the time or the intention to scare you. I’m third year, yes? I have two cram schools to go to and I have university entrance exams to take. If you don’t want to see me, then don’t look for me at the school gate every morning.”

English. He was speaking English. Not only that, but calling me by my last name like I wasn’t some outsider, as if I belonged. I felt off balance, like he’d rolled a single marble to my side of a plank and the sudden change of weight might cause me to topple over. He’d turned this into a game, and he was winning.

Bleached Hair grinned. “I didn’t know you spoke English so well, Yuuto.”

“You understood me that day, in the *genkan,*” I whispered. I felt nauseous and wished he would stop looking at me and turn away. “You told me you didn’t speak English.”

He smirked, but his face was pale. “And you told me you didn’t speak Japanese,” he said. “So we’re even.”

“I don’t—” Wait, was he complimenting my Japanese?

“Look, we’re already late for kendo practice.” He turned to his friend and snapped, *“Ikuzo.” Let’s go,* trying to sound like a tough guy. He took off toward the *genkan,* followed by Bleached Hair.

There was more to it all—I knew it. How could he hate something that had made him come alive? I saw the way his arm arced through the air, the graceful way he moved, the look in his eyes and the softness of his voice as he sketched the kanji with his fingers. And he hadn't denied the ink moving. He hadn't said no.

My head flooded with questions, too many to handle. I wanted him to leave me alone—didn't I? I never wanted to see him again—right? I just wanted things the way they were before. My whole world was shaken up. I didn't want to see things that weren't there. I didn't want to lose whatever it was I had left without Mom. And every step he took away from me was a step away from normal. I needed answers and I needed them now.

I panicked and grabbed his left wrist with my hand. He turned, his eyes wide with surprise.

His skin felt warm beneath the shirt cuff, and time felt like it stopped.

"Katie," Yuki whispered. Tanaka's mouth was half open, half shut. I guess you didn't just grab someone in Japan. I was making a spectacle of myself again—but it was too late. I clung to the softness of his skin, unsure what to do next or what I had been thinking.

"Oi," Bleached Hair said, annoyed. The whole courtyard was staring at me. Again. Tomohiro looked at me, face flushing pink, his eyes wide and gleaming. He even looked a little frightened. I opened my fingers and let his wrist slip away.

"I—"

"Stay away from me," Tomohiro said, but his voice wavered, and his cheeks blazed red as he turned and took off. I looked down at my hands.

Stay away from me.

Isn't that my line?

And then I saw the pads of my fingers, covered in dark ink.

I screamed and wiped them on my jeans. But when I lifted them to look, the ink was gone. There was nothing on my jeans, either.

"Katie." Yuki, looking worried, grabbed my arm and steered me away from the scene I was making. "Let's go, okay?"

I followed, my mind racing.

I hated myself for the heat that flushed through me when I thought of the warmth of his wrist against my fingers. I tried to crumple up the feeling and toss it away like I had with Tanaka, but when I thought I'd crushed it, it dripped back into my thoughts like black, sluggish ink.

I walked silently through Sunpu Park, Yuki with a sympathetic arm around me.

"Don't worry," she said. "It's not like everyone saw. I mean… um."

"You okay?" Tanaka said.

"I don't know," I said. "I didn't like how he was talking to you. He said he's your friend, and then he goes all crazy when you ask him about calligraphy. I just feel like he's hiding something. Sometimes he looks so pissed, and other times he looks worried or like I'm in on some kind of secret. I don't get it—I want to know what's going on."

"Katie," Yuki said, squeezing my arm. "That's just how Yuu is. I've been talking to the second years, and he's just touchy like that."

"Right," said Tanaka. "He likes his space. My sister told me he's always disappearing somewhere—a loner or something, right? I know he's cold, but don't take it personally."

Disappearing somewhere? *So he* is *up to something.*

Yuki flipped her phone open to check the time. "Listen,

I have to go. They'll kick me out of cram school if I'm late again. Later, okay?"

We waved as she took off ahead of us.

"Tanaka," I said quietly as we walked.

"Hmm?" he said, tilting his head to the side.

"Why did Yuu quit Calligraphy Club?"

"*Eh?* Oh," Tanaka said, looking a little embarrassed. Maybe I'd hit a sore spot. "He was getting into a lot of fights, and sensei warned him he'd have to quit the club if it continued."

"So he got kicked out."

Tanaka shook his head. "He was doing all right for a while. We had a big show coming up, our winter exhibit. Tomo-kun was working so hard on his painting. He chose the kanji for sword, and it was supposed to be our feature piece. Anyway, he practiced so many times and then went to paint the one for the display."

"And?"

"Somehow he cut himself on it. Some sharp nail in the back of the frame or something. It was a deep cut, and he bled across the canvas. After all his hard work, his painting was ruined."

I struggled to imagine it, Yuu Tomohiro throwing himself into creating a work of art. It didn't mesh with his tough image, that was for sure.

"So, what, he just quit?"

"When I came into the arts room the next day, his canvas was ripped in two in the garbage. I still remember the sound of the ink dripping into the trash can."

I stopped walking. "Ink dripping…"

Tanaka nodded. "He must have used a lot of pigment. It was really thick. I remember how weird it looked, kind of an oily sheen with dust or something. He never came back to Calligraphy Club. And shortly after he switched schools."

"Switched schools? Isn't that a little drastic?"

Tanaka laughed. "Different reason," he said.

Ink dripping in ways it shouldn't, with sparkling clouds of dust. So Tanaka had seen weird stuff, too. "Kanji only have so many strokes. If he's so talented, why didn't he start over?"

"I thought so, too. But after that, the fights started getting worse. When I asked what was going on, he said his dad made him quit. Of course, he wouldn't want to admit it if he just gave up. Probably the ruined painting was the last straw for him."

"Why would his dad make him quit?" I said, incredulous. Tanaka grinned and his whole face lit up. He looked handsome, but not in a way, I noticed, that distracted me.

"Well, I didn't really hang out with Tomo-kun outside of school," he said, "but I wouldn't be surprised if his father was pushing him to study harder and spend less time on the arts, even the traditional ones. My mom is always pushing my sister and me to study harder."

"Hmm." I wondered what sort of home Tomohiro went to at night, where he slipped off his shoes, whether he had curry waiting for him, too. "So why did he switch schools?"

"You like him."

My heart stopped. "What?"

"Trust me, I can tell. But you should probably keep your distance. Tomo switched schools because he was almost expelled. There was a really bad fight with his best friend, Koji."

"The white-haired guy?"

"No, no, I don't know him. I haven't seen Koji since…well, since it happened. It was bad. There was a lot of pressure to expel Tomo. So he withdrew and went to a different school."

"How bad is bad?"

"Enough to put Koji in the hospital. But don't freak out or anything, okay? I mean, no one's really sure what happened, and knowing Koji, he probably started it."

I felt a chill as fear replaced the memory of Tomohiro's skin against my fingers.

"Anyway, this is as far as I go," Tanaka said, and I slipped out of my thoughts.

"Oh, of course. Thanks," I said.

"Don't fall for him, Katie. Choose someone less complicated. Like me, okay?"

I stared at him until he clapped me on the arm.

"I'm joking." He laughed. *"Jaa ne,"* he said, waving.

"Jaa," I said, but my mind was far away. I wandered the maze of pathways and moats of thc park. Sunpu Castle loomed above the tree branches, entangled like crosshatching around its base. The arching castle bridge gleamed in the crisp sunlight, and the moat below bubbled in its murky, thick movements.

The castle had seen generations rise and fall, had even burned down and been rebuilt. I bet from the roof you could almost see the whole park, paths and moats and bridges crossing, the buds on the trees almost ready to burst.

Maybe living in Shizuoka with Diane wasn't that bad. Once it was time, cherry petals would fall gently into the cloudy water, swirling on its surface and painting the park pink and white for spring. Dancing across the sluggish waterways, dripping slowly down their channels, almost oozing like ink…

Shit.

Why did all my thoughts have to turn to him? He wanted to mess with my head and he'd managed to do it. I decided to kick him out. Thank god it was the weekend, where I could go home and not have to see him for two whole days.

The castle vanished behind me as I twisted down the pathways. I ended up walking way too far—all the paths looked the same. Students from different schools always cut through the park on their way home from after-school clubs, so when I saw the couple standing by the wooden bridge out of the park, it wasn't unusual. At least, not at first.

The girl wore a deep crimson blazer and a red-and-blue-tartan skirt. Definitely a uniform from another high school, but I wasn't sure which one. She was sobbing, quick, hiccupy breaths stifled by the back of her hand. She looked familiar, but I couldn't place her.

The boy with her was from my school, dressed in our dark navy blue. His copper-dyed hair gleamed in the sunlight.

Give me a break. Not here, too. Didn't he say he had kendo practice, or was that just another cover so he could disappear, like Keiko said?

The girl with him wasn't Myu—that's for sure—and her stomach curled outward under her skirt in a way that it shouldn't.

I covered my mouth when I realized why.

A moment later Tomohiro embraced her, pulling her and her blooming stomach toward him.

The girl's teary eyes flicked toward me as her head pressed into his shoulder.

The same burning eyes that had stared at me from the paper.

I turned and ran, spraying the gravel stones as I raced toward Shizuoka Station. I didn't slow until I was across the bridge, down the tunnels and through the doors of the station.

She's real. It's her.

I felt like the station was spinning. And even though most of me was freaking out that the girl from the drawing was real, the shallow part of me was flipping out because Tomohiro was hugging another girl. A pregnant girl.

I stumbled through the crowds, desperate to be anonymous. I just needed a break from all this, just for a few minutes. Just so my heart could stop pounding.

I tried to lose myself, but as much as I wanted to be alone in the great mass of travelers, my blond hair assured I could never really blend in.

3

"Okaeri!"

"Are you going to do that every time?"

"Until you play along."

I sighed.

"Tadaima," I muttered in a flat tone. "I'm home. Happy?"

Diane's mouth curved into a slanted frown. "Not really."

I kicked my shoes against the raised foyer until they dropped off my feet, and headed toward the couch.

"Hey, rough day?" Diane said, looking worried.

"No," I mumbled. "Just tired."

"You're home late," she said. "Did you join a club at school?"

"I went to a café with Yuki," I said. It was probably for the best not to mention the encounter with Tomohiro. Or, you know, that my drawings were coming at me with pointy teeth.

"That's great! See, you're making friends!"

I shrugged.

"And I got dragged into the English Club at school."

"Ah," said Diane. "Yes, that generally happens to *gaijin*. Did you join anything else?"

"Tea Ceremony, with Yuki."

"Glad to see you finally taking an interest in the local culture."

I rolled my eyes. "You know it's not that. It's not like I'm not interested in Japan."

"I know. It's homesickness." And what she didn't say. *It's Mom.* And that's a home I can't go back to.

"So how was your day?" I asked. She looked shocked and way too happy that I'd asked.

"Busy," she said. "The other English teacher is getting married soon, so I'm having to sit in on an extra period until we hire a temp. I don't have any prep time now."

"You need a temp because she's getting married?"

"She's going to quit to be a housewife," Diane said. "A lot of women do in Japan. Not as much anymore, but Yamada is really traditional. So no prep period for me."

"Taihen da ne," I drawled, stretching my legs out on the couch. Diane beamed at me.

"Yes, it is tough," she said. "And I can see that cram school is really paying off."

"Give me four or five more months." I smiled.

I helped Diane ladle out plates of spaghetti and we ate our dinner in exhausted silence. In the middle of dinner, Diane's friends phoned to go out for drinks, and she hastily clipped on dangling gold earrings as I assured her for the fifth time that I would be just fine by myself.

"I *am* sixteen, you know."

Diane gave me a once-over and arched her eyebrow. "I know."

"I'm fine," I said, pushing her out the doorway. "Have fun."

"You have my *keitai* number if you need me," she stuttered.

"Go!" I said.

"Ittekimasu."

"Yes, yes," I said, but she stood there with her frowny face until I gave in and muttered the response. *"Itterasshai." Go and come back safely.*

I wished I could go anywhere without having to think about Tomohiro. And now I was in an empty apartment, flooded only with silence and the image of him hugging his crying, pregnant girlfriend.

I flicked on the desk light in my bedroom and lifted the lid of my laptop. As the colors swirled to life and the computer hummed, I thought about Tanaka and Tomohiro in calligraphy class, about the ripped canvas dripping into the trash can.

Wouldn't the ink have dried overnight? How much did he load onto the brush? And what the hell did he do to his friend Koji?

I had an email from Nan, an update on the custody situation. What it really boiled down to was Gramps's health, and it wasn't great. But he was on his second-to-last round of chemo, and then they'd check to see if he was back in remission. *Please let him be.* I didn't want to lose anyone else.

I tapped out a reply, then closed the lid on the laptop and collapsed onto my bed. In the dim glow of my desk lamp, I stared at the ceiling. Thin lines of light spread across the wall from the back of the metal shade. I tried to picture the kanji for *sword,* but had no idea. I sat up and grabbed my dictionary from the desk; Diane had an electronic one, but I still couldn't read the kanji easily enough to use it. *Sword* didn't look that complicated to write, at least not for Tomohiro. It took all of ten strokes: 剣.

I closed the dictionary and lay back, trying to picture Tomohiro standing in the arts room, holding a delicate painter's brush between his fingers. Curving his arm in the smooth strokes he had sketched with in the school courtyard.

He slouched a lot, but Tomohiro didn't strike me as clumsy. He moved with precision, and I didn't think he'd cut his hand on a mounted canvas.

Maybe there'd been a loose nail or staple, like Tanaka said. But if he was painting, why would he touch the back of the canvas?

I imagined the stark spray of red across the kanji, black as night. The ripped canvas, ink and blood dripping into the trash, sluggish like the ink that had dripped down the steps of the Suntaba *genkan*.

And if his dad really didn't approve of his time "wasted" on the arts, then I could imagine what he had to say about Tomohiro's pregnant girlfriend.

If he knew, which he probably didn't.

Not that any of it really mattered. Or it shouldn't. I had my own life to worry about. I didn't need moving drawings with sharp teeth and exploding pens. I didn't need to cross paths with a guy who beat up his best friend and switched schools because of it. I'd just have to tell him to get lost so I wouldn't have to stare at his gaudy highlight job anymore.

I closed my eyes to the spray of light in my room, and my thoughts spiraled into sleep.

The week blurred past between cram school and *Sado* Club, learning how to twist a teacup three times in my hand to admire the sketched cherry blossoms and leaves encircling the lacquered *chawan*. Hand-copying stroke after stroke, page after page of kanji. Schoolwork was getting easier, Japanese more natural, and I started to wonder if Diane was right. Maybe I'd really underestimated my language skill.

"Guess what?" Diane gushed at breakfast. I looked up from my pancakes and honey.

"What could possibly have you so giddy?" I asked.

"Cherry blossoms," she said. "They've spotted the first ones in Kyoto and Osaka, and someone found a whole tree in bloom in Kamakura."

"So Shizuoka will be next?"

"I wouldn't be surprised if you see a few on your way to school."

Sure enough, the odd tree in Sunpu unfolded in sprays of pink and white, dotting the bare park with color. Most of the trees still lay dormant as buds, but my eyes hunted for *sakura* trees as I snaked through to Suntaba.

When I slid open the door to our classroom, the whole class was going on about the trees. Was it really such a big deal?

"Katie-chan!" Yuki called out, and the friendly suffix she'd used wasn't lost on me. She waved me over to where she sat huddled with her friends, who smiled shyly.

"Morning," I said.

"The *sakura* are blooming. We're going to go on the school picnic on Friday!"

"Picnic?" I said. "Nice!" Missing school to be outdoors was like skipping without getting into trouble. Everyone had trouble sitting through class, restless with thoughts of the upcoming picnic. We peered out the windows at the floating cherry petals, watching them spiral down from the trees until the final bell rang.

Tea Ceremony Club started after Yuki and I finished wiping down the blackboards and emptying the garbage cans. The teacher droned on about how to spin the whisk in our hands, the murky green in our cups frothing into a thick, bitter tea. She brought homemade sweets to go with the tea, pink *nerikiri* flower cakes and *manju* filled with red-bean paste. At first the texture of red bean had bothered me, but after almost two months in Japan, I guess I was adjusting.

Diane woke the next morning at five-thirty so she could cook *karaage, onigiri, nasubi* and stewed eggs for my picnic *bentou.*

"You can't take peanut-butter sandwiches for flower viewing," she said, and for once I agreed with her. "Only thing is, I don't know how to make *dango,*" she added, embarrassed.

"Oh, *dango,* yeah," I said.

"Tell me you know what *dango* are."

I shrugged.

"Yuki will probably bring some. Eat them."

I only found out after, when I peeked inside the delicate pink handkerchief she'd tied around my lunch, that she'd switched my box for the more expensive one she had, a traditional black-and-red *bentou* with two layers—lots of food to share.

It clicked then, in my memory—Diane hiding under platters of hors d'oeuvres at Mom's funeral. *This is how she copes,* I thought. *This is how she tries to be family.*

I wrapped my arms around the *bentou* as I continued toward the park. There's a saying in Japan, and it has to do with cherry-blossom viewing—*hana yori dango. Dumplings over flowers.* It basically means that someone should value needs over wants, substance over appearance. As in, make sure you have food and shelter before you burn money on something extravagant. And, you know, choose genuine friends who will be there for you over pretty, shallow ones. Don't get carried away by beauty if it leaves you empty.

But it was hard to believe in dumplings over flowers when I reached the southern moat and stepped onto the arch of the

Sunpu bridge. The beauty took my breath away, and for a minute I believed I could live off the flowers alone.

The entire park was bathed in pink, thousands of petals floating on the breeze as if it were raining *sakura.* The papery petals caught in my hair, on my uniform and on the leather of my book bag. Cherry blossoms littered the gravel paths, the bright green grass and the sluggish moats that pulled the petals from the park.

I walked slowly toward the castle, watching the petals falling. It was like an alien rain, something I had never experienced before. The crowds in the park were huge, salarymen, families and friends all gathered on tarps at the base of the cherry trees. They shared food as they laughed, beer cans and tea bottles lining the edges of the blankets. I closed my eyes, walking slowly, feeling the petals as they grazed my skin and floated downward. For the first time, I felt truly happy in Shizuoka, carrying my special *bentou* in a forest of pink under the clear sky.

I rounded the corner to shouts and howling laughter. Three guys—younger than me, probably thirteen or so—and one girl, who dabbed at her eyes with her *seifuku* sleeve. One of the boys chugged away at a can of something or other I couldn't read, and another held the girl's book bag up in the air, laughing.

"Give it back!" she begged, but the boys snorted and passed the can back and forth, tossing the book bag out of her reach to each other.

I stood there frozen. No way could I take on three punks, even if they were younger than me, but I had to do something.

I stepped forward, taking a deep breath.

A voice echoed through the park.

"*Oi!* Leave her alone."

The boys looked up as a student from Suntaba stepped forward, petals clinging to the buttons of his open blazer. My mind churned—Tomohiro. The boys swore at him, and I secretly hoped he'd back off. They looked like seriously bad news.

But he swore back, apparently with a worse word, because one of the guys threw his can down and started rolling up his sleeves. They dropped the book bag, forgotten, and the girl raced over to pick it up. She darted away, running past me so fast that the breeze rushed against my face. The three came at him, shouting. Tomohiro lifted his hands slowly, and panic shot through me.

There's no way he can handle three of them, even if he does get into a lot of fights.

The boy with the rolled-up sleeves swung at Tomohiro, but he ducked and pulled the guy's arm so hard that I thought it might rip from the socket. The second guy lunged and clipped Tomohiro's face, but Tomohiro swung his leg around and kicked the guy at the back of his knees. He stumbled forward and Tomohiro punched him in the back, shoving him into the third guy.

Rolled Sleeves was up again, and he kicked hard. With three of them, there was no way Tomohiro could avoid all the blows. The blood trickled down his face.

And just when his bruise from Myu was fading.

Then Tomohiro took hold of one of the wiry boys and threw him through the air. The boy's awkward body arced, suspended for a minute among the falling petals, and then thudded hard against the sharp gravel. In a minute he was up again, running across the park followed by the second guy.

Tomohiro grabbed Rolled Sleeves' collar and walked him

backward, shoving him against the fence that overlooked the deep, cold moat. Tomohiro muttered something and Rolled Sleeves flinched. Tomohiro dropped him, wiping at the blood dripping from his nose.

But as Tomohiro walked away, the boy stood up slowly and pulled out a switchblade.

Oh my god.

My legs started moving before I could think. "Watch out!" I screamed, running at Tomohiro. He looked up in surprise and then saw the boy behind him. He caught the boy's arm as it swung down, squeezing his wrist hard until he dropped the blade. I grabbed it from the ground and threw it into the river, where it was sucked into the water with a sploosh.

"Teme!" the boy shrieked at me.

"You need some manners!" Tomohiro shouted and punched the boy so hard I could hear the crack of his nose as it snapped.

Rolled Sleeves felt around his nose as the blood soaked his chin. He stumbled to his feet and took off, swearing at Tomohiro. Tomohiro swore back and the boy sped up.

The blood trickled down Tomohiro's face as he heaved in every breath.

"Are you—are you okay?" I said.

Tomohiro nodded, his shoulders moving up and down as he panted. "You?" he said.

"I'm fine."

He wiped at his nose with the back of his arm, and as he dropped it down again, I saw a gash across the skin.

"He cut you." I panicked.

"What?"

"On your wrist!"

He looked down, then quickly pushed the cuff of his sleeve down.

"Just an old injury. It's nothing," he said.

It didn't look like nothing.

"Thanks," he said finally. "For the warning."

"Um, no problem," I said.

He paused. "But just for your own safety, maybe you shouldn't run toward boys with knives. You know, in the future." The corner of his mouth lifted as he tried to keep the grin off his face.

I found myself grinning back. "I'm sorry, are you insulting me after I saved your butt?"

He laughed, and the warmth of the sound spread through me.

"I'm just saying you should avoid running toward sharp objects and dangerous guys."

"Like you," I said. It just popped out—I didn't mean it to.

The grin faded, and he was serious again. "Yeah," he said quietly. "Like me." He kicked the toe of his shoe into the gravel. "*Che!* What the hell am I doing?" He turned, his shoulders lifting with a breath, and then he ran.

"Wait," I said. "I just wanted to—"

The gravel sprayed across the grass, tiny drops of blood clinging to the stones. Except, some of the drops didn't look like blood. They oozed like…like black ink.

The shower of pink petals rained down.

I stepped forward, one foot, then the other, numb to the beauty of the park. I bent down and lifted one of the stones. The droplet of ink spilled onto the side of my finger before dripping back to the ground.

He'd been warm, laughing, the weight of something lifted. And then he'd stopped. *What the hell am I doing?* he'd said. *What are you doing, Yuu?* He was keeping something secret, something about the ink. He wanted me to stay away. But he'd forgotten.

And it was nice.

The castle rose as I neared the picnic site, and I saw the classes spread out under the branches laden with hundreds of pink-and-white blooms. I spotted the Class 1-D tarp, and Yuki waved wildly at me.

"Hey, slowpoke, what took you so long?" she said.

"Yuu Tomohiro," I said. "Where's 3-C?"

"They're not coming until this afternoon," she said. "They have class."

I said nothing. It was still early enough that he could have been on his way to school through the park. With no book bag. Maybe. Or maybe he was headed somewhere else.

More drops of ink where they shouldn't be. And all I could think about was his face lighting up with that laugh.

We ate our lunch amid the excited chatter of first-year senior high students. Yuki's friends sat with us and shyly exchanged a few pink, white and green *dango* sticks with me for some of Diane's *karaage*. The *dango* looked like pastel traffic lights and tasted overwhelmingly sweet.

After the picnic, I helped fold up the tarp and carry it back to the school with Tanaka. We resumed our afternoon classes, but no one's heart was really in it, even the teachers'.

I had cleaning duty—the bathrooms—and I wrinkled up my nose when I heard it. I headed toward the ones by the gym, armed with my brush, my apron, my hair tie and my gloves. Not the most fun task, but I scrubbed away anyway. Making students clean the school toilets would never fly in my school back home, but here it was just expected. When everything was clean, I washed my hands in the sink and opened the bathroom door.

Shouts erupted from the gym, a chorus of tired voices yelling in unison and the clatter of wood hitting wood. I walked toward the sound, carrying my toilet brush with me, and pulled the gym door open a fraction.

About forty students were decked out in black armor, masks of screen mesh covering their faces. They wore long black skirts down to their ankles and stepped barefoot across the gym in pairs. Each student held a long bamboo stick with both hands, and at the shout of the teacher, they clashed them against each other. The noise echoed to the rafters of the gym and rang in my ears.

One of the teachers, chemistry, I think, saw me peeking and hurried over.

"I see you're interested in kendo," he said in English. He had a broad smile and a towel scrunched around his neck. The veins almost popped out from his head, and thick-rimmed glasses hunched over his nose.

"Kendo," I said. So this was what Tomohiro and Bleached Hair were always running off to. "Japanese fencing, right?"

"Yes," the teacher said. "We're practicing for the ward competition coming up."

I'd wanted to take karate in New York but always chickened out at the last minute. I couldn't bring myself to willingly sign up for something that involved sparring.

The students moved in unison, like ghostly visions of samurai dancing. They swung their bamboo swords in the air, each movement timed to the other teacher's strained voice. The students lined up along the edge of the gym, called forward in pairs to challenge each other.

"You want to try?" the chemistry teacher asked.

My eyes popped. "Me?"

He nodded.

"No. No, I mean, I..." I trailed off. It's pretty rude to flat-out refuse something in Japanese, so I decided to find a more subtle way out. "I'm already in a few different clubs, so…" The chemistry teacher looked crestfallen.

"Sou ka…" he mused. Then he shook his head. "Well, never mind. Come in and watch for a bit, *ne?*" I couldn't think of a way to refuse, so I shuffled into the gym, slumping down against the wall where the students waited for their turn to duel.

"Okay, next pair!" the other teacher shouted. The chemistry teacher nodded at me with a smile and started across the floor. Throaty shouts echoed through the gym as the pair came at each other. They pressed their swords against each other's, circling at arm's length. With lightning speed, one approached and smacked his sword on the other's helmet.

"Point!" the chemistry teacher yelled. I stared wide-eyed. It had happened so fast it was almost a blur. The skirts of the fencers swayed as they moved back and forth, coming at each other and drawing back.

Another pair was called forward, and another. I watched in amazement until I'd lost track of time.

"See you next week!" the teacher called, and I stared down at my watch. Really?

The students untied their helmets and wiped the sweat off their foreheads with their arms. There were a few girls, but mostly guys. I scanned the group as they walked toward the change rooms.

And then Bleached Hair strode past me, followed by Tomohiro.

So. This was why he could take care of that fight. Next to this, the fight with three thirteen-year-old morons was probably nothing to him.

"What did you think?" came an English voice beside me.

I looked over, startled, into the glowing face of the chemistry teacher.

"Oh," I stuttered. "It was, um, great." The other teacher had walked over now, another senior-level sensei that I didn't know.

"This is the foreign student at Suntaba," said the chemistry teacher. *Thanks, real subtle.* The man arched his eyebrows.

"You going to join our club?" he asked. I began to protest, unsure how to word it. I looked over at Bleached Hair and Tomohiro rubbing their faces with towels and chugging water bottles. Tomohiro had a white-and-navy sports bag strapped over his shoulder and he grinned as he chatted with his friend. He glanced over, and I couldn't tell if he was smirking or actually smiling.

"Well? What do you think?" said the teacher. "Give it a try?"

I stared at Tomohiro. I wanted to figure out why he'd ditched calligraphy for kendo and what that glimpse of him in the park had meant. And anyway, the way he stared at me felt like a challenge. Like I had to prove that I could do it, too.

"Sure," I said, glancing at Tomohiro. "I want to try." The teachers smiled, sputtering about how wonderful it was, while the grin slipped from Tomohiro's face. He looked away, turning toward the end of the empty gym.

"I joined the Kendo Club at school," I said to Diane over dinner. She went bug-eyed and just about dropped the shrimp straddled between her chopsticks.

"You what?"

"I joined the Kendo Club."

"I thought you hated contact sports."

I shoved in a forkful of salad. "I do."

"*Kendo* does not translate to 'ballet,' Katie."

I rolled my eyes. "I know. I sat in on a practice today. And anyway? Ballet isn't easy, either, thanks very much."

"It's dangerous. You could get hurt," Diane said, but I shrugged.

"You could get hurt crossing the street."

"Katie, I'm serious. Are you really sure you want to do kendo? Did the teacher talk you into it?"

"No, I want to do it." I poured my cup of green tea over my rice and mashed it in.

Diane sighed. "I don't know about this. What would your mom say if I let you try it? And don't pour your tea in your rice, Katie. You'll ruin it."

"Tanaka said it tastes better this way," I said. "And don't worry. Mom would say, 'Good for you, Katie! Japan needs more girls taking kendo!'"

I could almost hear her voice when I said it. Mom had always been like that, making sure I knew girls could take on anything. If Mom couldn't be here to say it, then I would say it for her. I swallowed the sadness back, biting my lip. I could keep her alive, just a little bit. I wouldn't have to let go. Not entirely.

Before the tears could start, I rose to my feet and started clearing up my empty dishes. Diane stared down at her pile of shrimp tails and I knew I'd won when her shoulders sagged. I knew she was thinking about Mom, too, about what she would want for me.

"All right," she said eventually. "It's okay with me, but take it slowly and be careful. If you get hurt, I'm pulling you out."

"Diane, come on," I said. "What's a contact sport without contact?" Okay, so I was egging her on, but I couldn't help it. A sport where I was expected, even encouraged, to smack Tomohiro. What could be better? I placed my dishes in the sink with a clank and raced to my room before she could say anything.

I sank into the quilt of my bed, the comfort of a Friday night where I didn't have to slave away at homework. Diane shouted that our favorite drama was on, but by then I was half-asleep, dreaming of the clatter of bamboo swords.

Oh god. What had I signed up for?

4

On Monday, I slipped out the front door of Suntaba just as Tomohiro pedaled away on his white bike.

Where's he sneaking off to all the time anyway?

I watched with frustration as he cycled out of sight. If he was trying to keep me at a distance, it couldn't be good. I knew better than to spy on a boy who put his best friend in the hospital. I did. But I couldn't get him out of my mind. And it's not like I wanted my drawings to come at me again with pointy teeth, ever. Maybe I needed to preempt the next weird ink encounter.

"Diane," I said, when she finally got in from a late night of drinking beer and slurping noodles with her coworkers—a required social thing.

"Hmm?" she said, slipping off her high heels and rubbing her feet. Her face looked worn and tired.

"Can I get a bike?"

"You want a bike?"

"It is a long way to school," I said. "Most of the kids bike anyway. Tanaka does." Diane arched her eyebrows, like she'd understood something.

"Oh," she said, "you want to go biking with Tanaka."

"Ew. Please don't start that again."

"All right, all right," she said, but she looked unconvinced and suspicious. "You can take my bike on Wednesday, and I'll see about getting you your own if you decide you like biking so much."

"What about you?"

"Wednesdays I have a prep period first. They finally hired another English teacher, so it's not a problem. And you may find you prefer walking, in which case I can get my bike back."

There was no way I preferred walking. That Wednesday I hoisted Diane's thin white bike from our balcony and shoved it into the elevator with me. I almost knocked out our neighbor with the wheel when I got to the lobby, but once I was on the streets, it was a breeze to maneuver through the traffic. The tires spewed up gravel in the park, so I had to slow down to avoid spraying passersby. With the slow speed, I almost collapsed on my side, but once I'd found the right rhythm, it was perfect to cycle under the shower of pink petals, which would be hopelessly tangled in my hair by the time I reached Suntaba.

The breeze whipped my hair behind me and closed my ears to the noise of *hanami*-goers in the park. All I could hear was air, birds, the odd traffic signal beeping across the moats from the city, all buzzing together in a blurred combination. I pumped the pedals hard as I crossed the northern bridge, falling back into the city on the other side and through the gate of our school.

Class passed by slowly, and I kept staring out the windows, where I could see the pink snow of *sakura* from the tree in the courtyard. Yuki said the blossoms only lasted a couple weeks. Pretty soon I would wake up and discover the branches all bare.

Tanaka offered to help Yuki with the bathrooms because I'd mopped the floors for him the day before, so I managed to leave school earlier than usual, just in time to see Tomohiro straddling his bike.

I fumbled with my lock as he sped out of sight. Although I guess I didn't have to hurry that much—I knew he'd end up at the station because he'd turned left first, which meant he was trying to throw everyone off his trail.

Always with the tricks. What was so important no one else could see?

I pulled the rusty lock off and scrunched it into my book bag, slipping the leather straps over the handlebars and yanking the tire out of the rack. I sped through the gate, nearly knocking out two second-year boys, and headed south.

I stopped for a breather at Shizuoka Station. I had a few minutes at least before he'd finish his wild-goose-chase route, and when he showed up, I'd be ready.

"Guzen da!"

I may have jumped clear out of my skin. I whipped around, but it wasn't Tomohiro. For one thing, this guy had floppy black hair and blond highlights tucked behind his pierced ear.

"Jun!"

"You remembered." He smiled. "Are you waiting for someone?"

"Oh, no, no," I stammered. I could feel my face turning red. It was a million kinds of obvious that I was.

Jun grinned. "A guy, maybe? The one you saw on the train?"

Was I that transparent?

"What are you talking about?" I stuttered.

"Sorry," he said. "None of my business, right? You just have that same flustered look again." He reached for the heavy bag on his shoulder and pulled on the strap. "I'm on my way to practice, but I saw you and thought I'd say hi."

"Practice?"

"Just a sport I'm into," he said.

"Oh," I said, trying to peer around him without looking like I was peering around him.

He leaned in a little, and whispered, "Who are we spying on?"

"Okay, fine, it is the guy from the other day," I said. "Jeez, what are you, some kind of detective or something?"

"I watch a lot of police dramas." He grinned. He lifted his left palm and pretended to take notes on it, his fingers poised around an imaginary pencil. "So is he giving you trouble or somcthing?"

"He's not— Well, I mean. Kind of?"

Jun frowned. "Kind of?"

"He's just up to something, that's all." I thought of the inky eyes staring at me—they still made my heart flip over when I thought of them. "He draws these sketches that creep me out. It's almost like they're alive or something."

"Creepy sketches? That's definitely criminal activity," he said, madly tracing kanji onto his palm.

My cheeks blazed red. "Forget it. It's stupid," I said, and he dropped his hands to his sides as he shook his head.

"It's not stupid if he's bothering you," he said.

"He's not bothering me. I mean, he is, but—" The words tangled as much as my thoughts. What exactly was he doing? "Sometimes it's like he's picking on me. And then other times, he looks like he's scared of me, or like I'm in on some kind of secret."

"Ah," said Jun. "Now that, I understand."

"So?"

"He likes you."

I snorted. "You're way off base, *keiji-san*. He even has a girlfriend."

"I guess I'm losing my touch." He laughed. "That just seemed like the obvious answer."

Then he stared at me intensely and started to lean in.

"What are you doing?" I said, my pulse racing. How was this happening? His eyes were soft and dazed, like he was looking at me while half-asleep. The blond highlight tucked behind his ear escaped and fanned over his cheek, the longest strands brushing the corner of his lips. He reached his hand out toward my hair. I flinched and tried to back up, but I was on my bike and huddled against a wall. There wasn't anywhere to go.

I felt the soft brush of his fingers through my hair, and then he leaned back.

"Cherry blossom," he said, the pink petal pressed between his fingers. He let it flutter to the ground as we watched, and then he looked up at me. "So beautiful," he whispered.

My heart might possibly have stopped for a second.

And then Tomohiro whizzed past with his unmistakable hair slicked to the sides of his head. Jun must have seen the urgency on my face because he turned to watch him go by.

"Ah," he said, and I wondered if I imagined the hurt in his voice. "He's here, the boy who draws things. You're flustered again."

"I'm not flustered! I'm just—"

"I know, I know. But I'm late for practice, so I'll catch you later, okay?"

Yeah, right. He smiled as he walked away, limping a little under the weight of the sports bag. I watched him go, wondering if I imagined it. *So beautiful.* He meant the cherry petal—right?

No time to think about it. Tomohiro veered toward the walkways and I was on his tail, coasting down the hill and looping around pedestrians. This was my chance to finally figure it all out. What he was hiding, why he was pushing me away. Sure, there was the I'm-a-jerk component, but after the fight in the park, there was more than that. There had to be.

The city thinned as we moved forward, and then I really got nervous. Maybe he was onto me. Maybe he was messing with me again, because I didn't see anything out of the ordinary here. I half expected him to stop his bike and look back at me with a smug grin and a slow clap.

But then a tipsy Roman bus snorted along the street, and relief washed through me. He was just following the bus route.

A mass of trees in fresh bud spread in front of us like an emerald beacon amid the city streets, and I realized where we were headed.

Yuki had told me about it—Toro Iseki, an excavated archaeological site in the thick of Shizuoka City. A chain-link fence surrounded the area, and suspended from the barrier was a big orange sign with kanji I couldn't quite read—but there was a big picture of a bowing, apologetic workman with a hard hat, so I got the idea.

Tomohiro coasted along the side of the fence, his fingers strumming the chain links as he went. He leaped off his bike and pushed in on the side of the fence. It lifted from the rail and he ducked under, pulling his bike through the gap. When he disappeared into the trees, I pedaled up to the loose fence.

There was a thin trail on the other side—not very noticeable, but I had spent every summer in the forests of Deep River, and clear as day I saw the stomped-down grass and broken branches.

A slip of ripped paper fluttered in the grass, with little torn holes like it was pulled from a notebook. Something had been scribbled on it. And I bet it was Tomohiro's.

I peeked around me, my heart pounding. Even when friends egged me on, there were lines I never crossed. I couldn't believe I was even considering breaking into a restricted area.

I stared at the tuft of forest, the trees bursting upward. I knew Tomohiro was there, and I had to know what he was doing.

I took a deep breath. Hot adrenaline raced into my fingertips and down my tired legs.

I pushed the chain-link fence in and ducked under.

The tension prickled down my neck and shoulders, but nothing happened. The park was silent except for the chirps of strange birds grating against each other.

I bent over and lifted the scrap of paper, rubbing the grainy notebook page between my fingers. With a deep breath, I flipped it over. Scribbled, panicky lines had somehow woven together into the end of a dragon's tail, curved with shaded-in scales. Tufts of hair and ridges sprawled from the tail in sharp, ragged scrawls of ink.

I squinted as I stared at the paper. Something was off—the proportion maybe, but part of the tail looked funny. One spike looked too long, but then it looked fine again, and then another patch of scales seemed out of place. I scrunched up my face, trying to figure it out, as a gust of wind almost blew it out of my hand.

The tail flicked from one side of the paper to the other.

I dropped the scrap, my heart pounding.

I stood there, unsure what to do. Should I let Tomohiro know I was here and make him explain? I'd probably come off as a wacko. Not that spying on him from afar was any better, but it's not like I'd planned this out well. I just wanted to know what the hell he was up to. I shivered as I thought of the pregnant girl's eyes on me, the horrible moment that had started all this weirdness. I had to know the truth.

The forest wasn't as dense as it had seemed, and a few meters ahead the trees thinned into the clearing of Toro Iseki. My breath caught in my throat as I stepped forward.

Bathed in the pink of *sakura,* the white of late *ume* plum blossoms and the vibrant greens of fragrant spring leaves, walking into the silent ruins of Toro felt like walking into an ancient painting. The floating petals rained on the thatched rooftops of the old Yayoi houses and collected in the grasses around them.

Tomohiro sat beside one of the huts, his knees tucked up and a black notebook balanced on them like a canvas. His hand arced over the paper quickly, black spreading across the stark white page. Every now and then he had to stop to blow the cherry and plum petals off his work.

I hung beside the trees on the edge of the clearing, watching him.

Without lifting his head, he said into his drawing, "You might as well sit down instead of standing there gawking at me. It's annoying."

Heat coursed through my cheeks, and my ears burned with embarrassment.

When I didn't reply, Tomohiro stopped drawing. Still not looking up, he moved his hand to a spot on the ground beside him and patted it. "Sit."

I smirked. "What am I, a dog?"

He looked over and grinned, the breeze twisting his spiky hair in and out of his deep brown eyes. I almost melted on the spot.

"Wan, wan," he barked, the Japanese version of a dog's noise. I nearly jumped back at the sound of it, and his eyes gleamed with twisted delight. "I'm the animal around here, right?" he said with a smirk. "Don't sit if you don't want. I don't care." He turned back to the page.

I took a deep breath and stepped forward, walking slowly toward his back, curved over his drawing.

My eyes flicked nervously to the drawing, a sketch of a wagtail bird. The drawing was beautiful, but I was relieved to see it didn't move around.

Tomohiro shook his head.

"You just don't get the message, do you?" he said, his pen curving around the back of the wagtail. High in the trees I saw a wagtail in a cherry tree, singing while other birds darted through the branches.

"You told me to stay away from you," I said.

"And so you followed me to Toro Iseki." He looked up at me, but I gazed back suspiciously.

"I just think—"

"You think I'm up to something."

I nodded. He tilted his notebook toward me.

"I'm up to this," he said, tapping the page.

I said nothing, but the heat rose to my cheeks.

"You think Myu had the right idea, don't you?" he said. "You want to slap me, too?"

I stared at him. Why so much attitude? The way he'd saved that girl in the park, the moment we'd had after, even the softness of his face when he'd waited for the Roman bus—it didn't match up with this I-don't-give-a-shit act he was pulling now, the one he always put on at school.

"Well?" He stared at me expectantly, and I forced my mouth to move.

"I'm not going to hit you, but I think it was pretty shitty of you to cheat on her." He smirked and glanced into the trees, lifting his pen to shade the wagtail's beak. "Why did you lie to her?"

"Lie to her?"

"Yeah. Myu didn't mean nothing to you. I saw it in your eyes, how you really felt."

He paused in his drawing.

"That," he said, "is not your business."

A moment passed before either of us said anything. The tip of his pen made a loud scratchy noise as it scribbled back and forth across the paper.

"Okay, so how about something that is my business? Tell me why your drawings move, and how you made my pen explode."

"Animation, and a faulty pen."

"Like crap it was," I said.

"Watch if you don't believe me," he said, and I stared at his page. Completely normal. "You must be seeing things. You should probably get that checked out."

"Shut up," I said, but the comment worried me. I'd done an internet search of the symptoms of hallucinating, and apparently, grieving the loss of a loved one was a big one.

"So Watanabe-sensei and Nakamura-sensei say you've joined kendo," Tomohiro said after a minute.

"Yeah," I said. He grinned and leaned forward to brush the *ume* petals off his paper. His bangs slipped over his eyes and he tossed his head to the side.

"You're doing a thorough job of stalking me," he said.

"I'm not stalking you!" I snapped. "I couldn't care less what you're doing with your time."

"Which is why you followed me here."

"Like I said, I thought you were up to something."

"The arts."

I lowered my voice, embarrassed. "I see that."

He stopped drawing abruptly, and the wagtails peeped high-pitched warnings to each other. He scratched thick black strokes through his drawing, scribbling it out of existence. I watched with surprise.

"It wasn't that bad," I said. He didn't answer, but flipped to a fresh page. I could hear his breath, tired and labored like when he'd fought in the park. After a moment, he swallowed and his hand started moving across the paper, sketching what looked like a plum tree.

"Why did you quit calligraphy?" I asked, watching his hand pause a moment as he studied the foliage of the nearby *ume*.

"My dad," he said. "He thinks art is nonsense. He wants me to study medicine or go into banking like him."

"But you're really good at it," I said. "I mean really good." Tomohiro sketched in a few more ink leaves. "Maybe if your dad saw your work—"

"He's seen it," Tomohiro snapped darkly. The ink blotted from his pen and trickled down the tree. "Shit!" he added, scratching violently through the drawing.

I rolled my eyes. "You kiss your mother with that mouth?"

"My mother's dead," he said.

I stared at him, my hands shaking. I'd been standing until then, but my legs buckled under me and I sank down to my knees beside him. I opened and closed my mouth, but no sound. I'd never expected we were connected in this way.

"Mine, too," I managed.

He looked up from the page, his eyes searching my face, and I felt like he was seeing me for the first time, really me, how broken I was.

"Sorry," he said.

"What…what happened to yours?" I asked. His eyes were intense, and I felt exposed suddenly, like I'd told him too much. And maybe I had, but for a minute I'd felt like maybe he could understand me.

"It was an accident," he said. "I was ten." Not recent, then, like mine. Not like mine at all. His voice was all softness and velvet. "Yours?"

My eyes started to blur with tears. Having this in common knocked all the fight out of me. I could barely get out the words. "Heart attack, eight months ago. One minute she was fine and then…"

"No warning, then," Tomohiro said. "Like mine." Oh. I guess it was like his after all. Except his voice was steady as he spoke. Time healing all wounds and all that, like everyone kept telling me. He was where I'd be in seven years. Without the attitude, hopefully. He was where I'd be if I let myself forget my old life.

I watched him draw for a little while in silence, and even though he was just doodling with a pen, each drawing was so beautiful. But he was critical of his work. He'd start and stop drawings like he had a short attention span. He'd scribble things out, sometimes striking them out so hard the pen tore through the paper and blotted onto the next page of the notebook.

"They tell you you'll forget how it used to be," he said suddenly, and the sound of his voice startled me. "You'll get used to it, that it's better to move on. They don't realize you can't. You're not the same person anymore."

My eyes flooded again and I stared at his blurry form through them. This wasn't what I'd expected him to say. I mean, when he had half the school staring up my skirt, I was pretty sure he didn't even have a soul.

"Don't let them tell you you'll be fine," he said, looking at me urgently. His brown eyes caught the sunlight and I could see how deep they were before his bangs fell into them again. He tucked the bangs to the sides with his slender fingers; I couldn't help wondering what his fingertips felt like. "Be angry, Katie Greene. Don't forget how it was. Because there'll always be a hole in your heart. You don't have to fill it."

Satisfied with his pep talk, he gave me a small grin and then turned back to his drawing. The wind caught the cherry and plum petals and they spun in drifts before my eyes.

And I felt that I wasn't alone, that Tomohiro and I were suddenly linked. No one had told me I *wouldn't* feel better. No one had let me be empty and changed. I knew which side of him was real now, and it wasn't the part everyone else saw.

When he moved his hand across the drawing, the cuff of his white school shirt caught on the edge of the paper and rolled up his arm. He left his palm up as he studied the Toro houses, and that's when I saw the scars that slashed across his wrist, the ones I'd seen in Sunpu Park. The biggest one spanned from one side to the other, interlaced with the rest. They were smaller and not as deep, but they looked ragged, fresher and not anywhere as neatly healed.

Concern welled up in me. *Oh—he's a cutter.* Now that I looked, I could see the pattern of dark scars that trailed up his arm beneath the thin fabric of his shirt. But when he saw my expression, he looked down at his wrist and grinned, like he thought my assumption was funny.

"It's from the sword," he said.

"The what?"

"*Sword.* The kanji. In elementary Calligraphy Club? I'm sure Ichirou told you about it."

"Oh," I said. "That's a pretty bad scar."

"It was a deep cut. I had to go to the hospital for it." He switched to English and tried to explain, and I got the message that he'd needed stitches and lost a lot of blood. All I could think of was how he'd put his friend Koji in the hospital, too. At the moment, he didn't seem capable of it.

"Sorry," I said, but he smiled grimly.

"Art is a dangerous hobby," he said, and somehow I couldn't tell if he was joking.

"So how come you draw here?" I asked.

"It's safer here."

"You mean your dad doesn't know?"

"Something like that. Anyway, look around the clearing. People lived here almost two thousand years ago. There are birds, trees, silence. Ever try to be alone in a city like Shizuoka?" He ran his hand through his copper hair and shook it from side to side, flower petals tumbling onto his notebook. I thought of Jun reaching for the flower petal in my hair. *So beautiful.* I quickly pushed the memory aside with shame. I felt like I'd betrayed Tomohiro by thinking of it, which was dumb, but I felt it anyway.

"You know you're trespassing here," I said. Tomohiro broke into a broad grin.

"A place like this doesn't belong to anyone," he said. "They can't keep me out like they can't keep the birds in."

It was surreal among the ruins, and I could see why he risked coming in here. Besides, with his entitled attitude, the orange sign on the gate was probably a challenge, a dare, more than anything else.

He stopped sketching and a bead of sweat rolled down his face. He drew an ugly rigid line through his beautiful sketch of a Yayoi hut and slammed the cover of the notebook closed.

"Why'd you wreck it?" I asked as he shoved the notebook

deep into his book bag. When I thought about it, he'd crossed out every single drawing.

He shrugged it off, but his eyes were dark. "They're not good enough," he said. "Let's go."

Go? Together? I struggled to push down the panic that rose to my throat and reminded myself what a jerk he could be. And he was a taken jerk, on top of it. Cheater. Pregnant girlfriend. Koji in the hospital. It was a mantra I repeated in my mind, but somehow it wasn't working.

He strode ahead into the trees and I followed, reaching for my bike as he lifted his. When we were both through the chain-link fence, he let go and it clanged into place.

We leaped on our bikes, coasting across the street and up through the thickening maze of Shizuoka.

He led the way, but competitiveness overtook me and I pedaled past him, coasting in front and weaving around the traffic. He didn't challenge me but sat back and relaxed, following my lead and riding in my wake.

Maybe there was something to his friendship with Tanaka. He wasn't acting the same as before, different than the Tomohiro that Myu had slapped.

Not different than the one who'd tenderly embraced his crying girlfriend in the park, though. The memory flashed through my mind like a good slap to the head.

We stopped at Shizuoka Station.

"I go north from here, to Otamachi," he said.

"I live west," I said. "Near Suruga."

He nodded. "You hungry?"

I just stared at him. My hunger was definitely clawing at the sides of my stomach, but I wasn't about to admit it.

It was like he knew what I was thinking. He smiled, then burst into another of his grins, looking down and shaking his head as he laughed.

"You should see your face," he said between laughs. "Like I'd just asked you to jump off the top of Sunpu Castle!"

I flushed red.

"Come on," he said. "There's a good café in the station."

I grasped for words, reasons, that I could not go.

"Won't your girlfriend be upset?" I said.

He tilted his head to the side. "Girlfriend?"

"The pregnant one? Or do you have more than one?"

He stared at me blankly and then burst out laughing.

"So that made it into the rumor?" he managed to say. He looked pretty pleased with himself. My face would have turned redder if I'd had any humiliation left in me.

When he saw how pissed I was, he stopped laughing. "Oh, right. You heard Myu say it. I don't have a girlfriend. Especially a pregnant one."

"But I saw you. In the park," I said and regretted the words the minute they came out. His eyes went wide.

"You really have been spying, *ne?*" he said. "Shiori's not my girlfriend. She's more like a sister, and I promised her mom I'd look out for her. Students are giving her a rough time because she's keeping the baby."

I didn't know what to say to that.

"Now, come on. I'm hungry."

I protested, but he just walked his bike toward the station, waving his arm in the air like he wasn't going to hear it.

I stood there for a moment, squeezing the handlebars of my bike. I could just take off for home and ignore him. But when he turned around to see if I was following, I hurried forward, like I didn't control my own legs anymore.

I ordered a melon soda and he got a platter of *tonkatsu* curry.

"You sure you don't want something to eat?" he said, breaking his wooden chopsticks apart. I held up my hand.

"I'm fine," I said. He narrowed his eyes at me.

"I know what it is," he said. "You're scared I'm going to try and pay for you."

The heat prickled up my neck. "It's not that at all," I stuttered.

"No problem," he said, "because I'm not going to."

"What?"

He raised an eyebrow and shone a cocky grin at me.

"I'm pretty broke at the moment. So order yourself something and I won't protest, promise."

"Fine," I mumbled. I called the waitress over and ordered a bowl of *gyudon.* Tomohiro picked at his meal until mine came, and by then his curry was cold. But even though I insisted he go ahead and eat, he just prodded it.

When my bowl of teriyaki beef and rice arrived, Tomohiro just about leaped out of his seat.

"Itadakimasu!" he shouted, clasping his hands together and wolfing down the pork cutlet.

He took a gulp of his water to wash it down. "I'm starving," he said, but the sound of the childish words he chose made me snort. *"Peko peko"* coming from the mouth of someone like Tomohiro.

"So are you convinced now that I'm not up to anything?" he asked, his chopsticks suspended in the air between bites.

"Not even close," I said. "But why did you do that to me, the day after I saw you with Myu?" I said. He raised his eyebrows and looked sincerely puzzled.

"Do what?"

"Oh, please, like you don't remember. You waited for me at the gate, and then you walked past me all dangerous-like." *And too close,* I added to myself. The smell of his vanilla hair gel, the heat of his shoulder grazing mine. And then, you know, he proceeded to look up my skirt, but did we really need to remember that part?

I wondered if it was the wrong thing to say. It must have been, because Tomohiro's grin faded, replaced by a look of concern. His eyes focused on some distant object that wasn't there. I wanted to choke back the words, but it was too late. The silence pressed against me, the tension pushing against the back of my neck and down my spine.

"Anyway, it doesn't matter," I said weakly, but it didn't help. Tomohiro picked at his curry.

"I wanted you to stay away from me," he said, but the voice didn't sound like his. It was too cold and distant, like his voice at school.

"Why?"

"Ichirou told you, right? I'm always getting into fights. So you'd only have trouble if you made friends with me." Was that really the reason? I couldn't believe anything he said in that tone anymore.

I scoffed. "Why should you care whether I get into trouble?"

"Why do you have to see everything as a challenge?" Tomohiro snapped. "Fine, okay? Maybe I shouldn't have stared you down at the gate, but you're the one who spied on me all the way to Toro."

"You gave me reason to."

"I never intended to be so interesting to you." He slammed his chopsticks down and I felt too sick to eat any more of my rice. "I told you to stay away, didn't I?"

"Ha," I snorted. "Like you're not going around making my writing utensils combust. Like you didn't cheat on Myu like the lowest scum of the earth!" He grinned darkly, like he enjoyed all the fuss about him.

"You still believe that, after I explained?" he said, and that's when the shame washed over me, when I realized the mistake.

"You were lying," I said. "There never was another girl, was there? And you lied when you told Myu she didn't matter. Why would you want to break up with her if there was no one else and you still cared about her? And how am I supposed to know when you're telling the truth about anything?"

The waitress came by and Tomohiro put down his money while I counted out my yen.

"Whatever," he said. "Take it how you want, but what I did was a warning to stay away." He rose to his feet and lifted his book bag off the chair. He stared into the distance for a minute and I could barely look at him, utterly humiliated that I'd agreed to go for dinner with him like this.

He took a deep breath and sighed. "But that was before," he said.

"Before?"

He shook his head. "You didn't take the warning, so I guess it's void." He tilted his head back and grinned, and his bangs slid out of his eyes and to the tips of his ears. "Follow me to Toro again. It's nice to have company when I draw."

And just as suddenly he was gone from the café, the bell on the door ringing and me feeling off balance like my head was spinning.

It took me a few more minutes to realize he'd paid the entire bill.

5

By the time I left the café, the cherry petals were spinning through the darkness, lit only by the lampposts lining the streets. The blossoms appeared briefly in the sky, fluttering down, and then winked out of the light's beams and disappeared.

The first time I told Nan I was going to live in a mansion, she'd flipped with excitement. But Japanese mansions are just newer buildings divided into tiny apartments—no caviar or butlers included.

I entered the automatic doors of our mansion, the bright golden lights of the lobby a stark contrast to the city streets outside. I hoisted the bike into the elevator, and when I fumbled with the lock on our door, Diane's footsteps thundered to the other side and she yanked it open.

"Katie," she said, pulling me inside. "I was worried out of my mind! I almost called the police, you know. I thought you'd been in an accident."

"I do know how to ride a bike," I said.

"Why didn't you call? Do you know what time it is?"

"Sorry," I said. "I didn't know it got so late."

Diane sighed and rubbed her forehead. She stopped suddenly and felt around with her fingertips.

"I think you're officially giving me wrinkles," she said and walked toward the bathroom mirror.

"You're just being dramatic," I said as she poked and prodded the skin.

"So where on earth did you go? Even with cleaning duty, it wouldn't make you this late."

"Um." The moment in Toro Iseki felt precious suddenly, and I was unwilling to share it. "Just out. With a friend."

"Yuki? Doesn't she have Sewing Club on Wednesdays?"

Shit.

"A different friend." I could feel my cheeks blazing.

"Katie, is something going on that you don't want to tell me?"

The hairs on the back of my neck started to rise. I did not want a conversation like that.

"Like what, host clubs filled with beer and pretty boys? Pachinko? Drugs? Nothing like that, Diane. You know I'm not into any shit."

"I know, I'm just scared that someone will influence you. And watch it, by the way."

"Sorry."

"Just tell me the truth, Katie. Where did you go?"

I stood there, frozen. Telling her I broke into Toro was not a good idea. Telling her drawings were looking at me was not a good idea. Telling her I went for dinner with a senior boy who put his friend in the hospital was not a good idea, even if it was just as friends, or rivals, or whatever exactly we were. I broke under the pressure.

"I went for a bike ride and dinner with Tanaka," I said. Diane's expression changed in an almost comically slow way.

It was like she finally got it, and I felt a little guilty that she was so off the mark.

"Katie, why didn't you just tell me? I would've understood."

I was trapped in my own lies, and I wished I could just hightail it out of there.

"It's kind of stuff I want to keep to myself, you know?" I said. My arms and neck felt itchy.

"Well, but if you want to talk... I want you to be smart about things, Katie. I'm not as...traditional as your mom, and I'm not going to assume that you'll be fine without any advice."

"Ew." It popped out; I couldn't help it. "Diane, it was just dinner and a bike ride. It wasn't sex." Diane's face turned bright red and I wondered who this conversation was really the most awkward for.

"I know, but these things have a way of speeding up," she stuttered.

"Okay, more than I want to know or think. Please spare me."

"Fine, but we also need to put some sort of system in place. I can't be wondering where you are all the time." Great. So now she was going to limit my freedom. Bring on the lockdown.

"Please don't tell me you're inflicting Japanese-style curfews," I said. Yuki had told me horror stories about hers.

Diane smirked. "I'd like to put enough trust in you that you don't need a curfew," she said. "I know your mom always hated those. It's not how much time you're out there. It's what you're spending that time on and who you're spending that time with."

"So the deal is...?"

"The deal is we'll get you a *keitai,* and I want you to let me know when you go places and where you are."

I couldn't really see a downside to that, so I just shrugged. "Sounds fine," I said.

"Good. I just worry, Katie, you know? I'm just not used to this whole being a—" She stopped just short of saying it. *A mom.*

"I know," I said, my throat dry.

"Your mom's counting on me."

I saw the sadness then in her eyes, the way her brows knit together the way Mom's always did. The same creases on her face, the small bridge of her nose, the thin lips that curved into a worried frown. She was like her somehow, an older vision of the same spirit.

I felt the hot tears well up in my eyes and I blinked them back.

"You're doing great," I said, squeezing her arm. I breathed slowly as I passed her, walking toward my bedroom and sliding the door shut.

I turned off the light and lay on my bed. I let my breath escape, and then I let the tears come, the ones I'd been holding in since Toro Iseki. I could be angry if I wanted. I could be changed. I could be myself.

What would Mom have said about him? I felt like the real Tomohiro was tangled in this other personality that wasn't his. How could he be gentle, understanding, beautiful like that, and still treat Myu with such cruelty? I was sure now that the cold badass at school wasn't who he really was. But why all the lies? What was he hiding?

I grabbed another tissue, trying to cry quietly. I didn't want Diane to hear, even though I bet she knew and was giving me space. She was doing her best. I knew it. But this just wasn't home, and she'd never be my mom.

There would always be a void. And my shoulders shook with relief that I didn't have to fill it.

Friday morning the clouds gathered over Shizuoka, and by the time I reached the school, the rain had drenched the city in the way that only a spring rain can.

I could barely focus on the equations Suzuki-sensei scribbled onto the board in last class. When the bell chimed and students began gathering up their books, I got to my feet and packed up my book bag, then stuffed it into my desk. I wiped off the blackboards and mopped the classroom floor while Tanaka lifted the chairs and flipped them upside down onto the desks, pushing the units against the walls.

By the time we'd scrubbed the classroom spotless, sweat was dripping down my forehead.

"We're going for *okonomiyaki,*" Yuki said. "Can you come?"

I shook my head. "I have kendo," I said.

Yuki nearly dropped her mop. "Kendo?"

"*Naaa,* Katie-chan." Tanaka sighed.

"What?" But I knew what.

"Tan-kun, is she—?"

"It's true," he said, shaking his head.

"Guys, can you not talk about me like I'm not here?"

"You like Yuu Tomohiro." Yuki sighed.

"That's not true," I lied. I mean, I didn't want it to be true, but…

"Katie, if you like him, then go for it," Tanaka said.

"What?"

"What?" Yuki echoed.

"That's not what you said last time."

"Last time?" Yuki said.

Tanaka grinned. "You're not going to listen to us anyway, right? And I know he's become a little lost—"

"A little!" Yuki said, but Tanaka glared at her.

"—but I've known Tomo-kun a long time. He's nice. He didn't even make us call him *senpai,* even though he's older. He treated us equally. Just be careful, that's all. He's mixed up in stuff."

"I know," I said, and Yuki and Tanaka exchanged a glance.

"You don't know," Yuki said.

"What's that supposed to mean?"

"It doesn't matter," Tanaka said. "If you want this, go for it with your whole heart, okay?"

"When did you become so inspirational?" I laughed, leaning my mop against the wall, and Tanaka shrugged.

"I read a lot of manga," he admitted with a goofy grin.

"Life doesn't work like that!" Yuki sighed, smacking Tanaka on the arm.

Tanaka laughed and shook his fist in the air. *"Faito, ne?"* Like Yuki had said to me when I went into the *genkan* to get my shoes. Fight. I nodded at him and went into the hallway, and the minute I was out, Yuki started whispering harshly at him.

"It doesn't matter," he kept telling her. *What doesn't matter? The girlfriend? The fights he gets into?*

I wove through the hallways and entered the gym, where the Kendo Club members—*kendouka*—circled the floor with cloths, cleaning up the gym before practice. Other students buckled armor around themselves, slipping out of the change rooms in their gray *hakama* skirts and fitting the *dou* plates on their chests. I scanned the group for Tomohiro and Bleached

Hair, but no luck. They were probably still in the change room putting on their *hakama*.

Watanabe-sensei looked way too pleased that I'd actually shown up, and sent some of the senior girls to help me put on the armor.

When we slipped out of the change room, the class was already forming into lines, so I hurried into place. Nakamura-sensei shouted out something and all the students knelt, placing their bamboo *shinai* swords on their left sides.

Crap. I didn't have one.

A shadow draped over my head, blotting out the gym lights that beamed down on us from the ceiling. I looked up, straight into the face of Yuu Tomohiro, and the sudden closeness of him shuddered through me like a shock. He was in my space again, his face way too close to mine. He knelt and the bright lights beamed over his shoulders. He placed a *shinai* at my side, lining the hilt up carefully with my knees.

"Thanks," I whispered, while Watanabe-sensei shouted and all the other students bowed, hands down on the floor.

Tomohiro nodded and strode slowly to a break in the line where I saw Bleached Hair waiting for him. He eyed me suspiciously, looking from me to Tomohiro, and then he stared with outright hatred. I looked away, my pulse buzzing in my ears.

We did twenty-five push-ups to warm up, and as I stared at my little square of varnished gym floor, I couldn't stop thinking about Bleached Hair's glare. He'd stared at me like I'd destroyed something, invaded where I shouldn't have. And maybe that was the truth, because I didn't belong in the world of someone like Yuu Tomohiro, and he didn't belong in mine.

After the exercises, the students fell into a drill, and Watanabe-sensei helped me hold my *shinai* properly while he taught me the basic stances.

There was a lot of yelling involved in kendo. Sometimes the *kiai* shrieks broke through my concentration and I looked up to watch two students advancing on each other in more and more complex drills. They slipped the *men* helmets into place, the metal bars caging their faces in shadow, and swung at each other, the crack of the *shinai* rattling through my thoughts.

I practiced with the junior *kendouka,* learning to control the *shinai* with my right hand but power my hits from the left. It took more concentration than I had expected, and after fifteen minutes my shoulder throbbed. It was a relief when Watanabe-sensei ordered us to take a break and observe the senior students, and we knelt in a line, *shinai* placed neatly by our sides, to watch.

Tomohiro rose to his feet, and Bleached Hair was called on to spar with him. Tomohiro swung his *men* in his hand as he approached the lines of *kendouka.* He hoisted the mask over his face, jostling it until it fell snug on his shoulders. The straps flared out and bounced as he walked into place, bowing to Bleached Hair, who slipped behind his own mask. They looked like two mysterious samurai now as they crouched down, their *hakama* skirts draped across the floor.

As they lifted, they drew their *shinai,* and a *kiai* erupted from Tomohiro, a terrifying sound in the silence of the gym. The wildness of it drove fear into my heart, as if I didn't really know him at all—and maybe I didn't. The kindness of bringing the *shinai* to my side and lining it up carefully was lost with the ferocious shriek as he moved forward and cracked his *shinai* against Bleached Hair's, as he swung again and again.

Maybe Yuki and Tanaka were right. Maybe Tomohiro was more dangerous than I realized.

Bleached Hair growled back, and the sound of them fighting was like wild animals. No lie. They struck over and over, keeping each other at sword's length. Bleached Hair slammed his foot down as he swung at Tomohiro's *dou*—a hit, a point. Some of the older students murmured to each other, studying their form. All I could do was watch, the shouts echoing in my ears. Tomohiro whacked Bleached Hair on the right side of the *men* near his neck, their *shinai* looking as if they would splinter as they cracked together.

As they fought, I noticed a splash of color on Bleached Hair's arm. At first it moved like a blur, but from his *kote* glove to the sleeve of the *keigoki,* I was certain I'd seen the broad outlines of a tattoo.

I watched the rest of the match with my mind occupied. Tattoos weren't as big a deal in New York—rebellious, maybe, and sometimes beautiful. But in Japan, tattoos were linked to gangsters and the Yakuza. I stared at Bleached Hair in a new way. *Impossible,* I thought. *He's only in high school like us.* But the more I tried to convince myself, the more the suspicions loomed over me. Was this what Yuki and Tanaka had meant when they said Tomohiro was mixed up in things?

The match finished and Nakamura-sensei dismissed us. Tomohiro and Bleached Hair swung their masks off, sweat dripping down their faces. Bleached Hair jabbed Tomohiro in the arm and they laughed, walking past like they didn't even see me. I stared at them as they disappeared into the change room. Did Tomohiro really keep such dangerous company? Is that why he'd wanted me to stay away?

And if they were both in the Yakuza, then I'd already delved too deep into that dangerous world.

But it was just a tattoo. It didn't have to mean that. And

why would Bleached Hair be so careless to get one where it would be seen?

Did Tomohiro have one, too?

The senior girls helped me unbuckle my armor. The rain outside was so heavy it pounded against the roof of the gym, echoing with the sour sound of aluminum.

When I came out of the change room, Tomohiro and Bleached Hair had already left, and there was nothing for me to do but head home.

I walked slowly to the *genkan,* dreading the drenching ride home. I'd brought Diane's bike again today, in some feeble hope that Tomohiro might head for Toro Iseki again.

When I slid open the door to the torrent of rain, Tomohiro's bike wasn't in the racks with the abandoned ones, slick with rain.

I couldn't leave the bike at school; Diane needed it for Monday. Taking a breath and lifting my book bag over my head, I stepped out into the coolness of the spring rain, soaking in the thick raindrops that pelted from the gray sky.

I reached the bike, but it took me a moment to realize it was mine.

Someone had hooked a clear plastic umbrella to the handlebars.

The rain slicked down the sides as I lowered my book bag.

I stood there a long time, staring at the umbrella in the rain.

On Wednesday I went to school with the umbrella under my arm. The rain lasted all weekend and knocked what was left of the cherry petals out of the trees into soggy piles all over the city. The beauty of *hanami* now lay as a shriveled ugliness on the ground. The trees still towered above in bright late-spring greens, and the heavy rains sprouted lots of new flower stalks from the dank earth. I sneezed the whole way to school. It smelled of spring—or would've, if my nose wasn't plugged from allergies—even if there were no petals to catch in my hair, no shower of blossoms on my walk to and from Suntaba.

When I saw Tomohiro's bike in the racks, I hooked the umbrella over the handlebars. Then I hurried into the *genkan,* slid on my school slippers and raced down the hallway to homeroom.

At the end of the day, he was waiting for me at the bike racks, straddling his seat with his foot on the pedal. He checked his watch as I approached and narrowed his eyes.

"You're late," he said.

We never talked about the umbrella.

Tomohiro headed out first, twisting north out of the Suntaba gate to throw everyone off. "I don't need any more stalkers," he said. "One's enough." I rolled my eyes, until he added, "At least she's a cute one." He grinned and set off.

Oh, jeez. I was definitely in trouble.

We met up near Shizuoka Station and twisted past the underground walkways. We took turns leading the way through the crowds, but Tomohiro was much more at ease with the task. He cut razor-sharp lines through the traffic, so following him was terrifying and thrilling at the same time.

We laid our bikes down in the curtain of forest and sat down by a Yayoi-period hut. Tomohiro had said the houses were almost two thousand years old, and I stared at them, terrified to touch them in case they crumbled to dust or something. The rain had let up the day before, but the grass was still a little soggy. Tomohiro didn't seem to care. He leaned back into the hut and let the tall grasses soak into the back of his school blazer.

I spread my blazer on the ground and sat down in the

middle of it. That should help keep me at least a little dry from the dewy grass. I took out the book I'd brought with me and some strawberry-cream sandwiches I'd saved from lunch, my favorite of the ones Diane made. I hesitated, then passed one to him.

He eyed it suspiciously.

"What?"

"Is it poisoned?"

"Hey, you're the creepy one, not me," I said.

He grinned and took a bite, crumbs dropping onto his sketch of a horse.

"You're good at the anatomy," I said.

"The proportions are all off," he said. "I've never seen a real horse."

I stopped eating.

"Never?"

"There aren't many horses in Shizuoka, Greene."

"Well, haven't you traveled around Japan or outside the country?"

"My father took us on a business trip once to Paris, in the days when he was happier."

"Paris?"

"Mais bien sûr, mademoiselle." The French rolled off his tongue, and every nerve in my body tingled. This was a bad idea, spending more time with him. I should be at home, trying to forget him, falling for Tanaka, or maybe Jun. Tomohiro didn't notice that I was silently falling apart beside him; he was lost in the memory. "I disappeared and he and my mom panicked. They looked everywhere for me, even called the police. I was about six, I think."

"So where were you?" It was hard to conjure up an image

of a six-year-old Tomohiro, lost and crying somewhere for his mommy.

Tomohiro smirked. "I was drawing pictures in my sketchbook inside the Louvre."

Of course he was.

"You really love art, don't you?"

"I can't explain it," he said, curving around the tail of the horse with his pen. "It's not really a love of art. I have to draw. It's…a compulsion."

"Isn't that the same thing?"

"Sou da na…" he mused.

"Yuu?"

"Hmm?" He drew gentle strokes to build the horse a wild mane, and it looked so lifelike I could almost smell the dank locks, feel them tangled between my fingers.

"Your friend from Kendo Club, the one with the…" I wasn't sure of the term in Japanese, so I switched to English. "You know, with the bleached hair…"

"Bleached?" he repeated in English. I wasn't sure how to translate.

"Lighter than blond hair," I said. "Almost white."

Tomohiro scoffed. "Sato?" he said. "Ishikawa Satoshi?"

So he had a name.

"Does he draw, too?"

Tomohiro laughed, and the sound rang in my ears.

"Zenzen," he said. "He can barely draw a straight line."

"I was curious," I said, biting my lip and taking a breath, "because I thought it looked like he had a tattoo."

Tomohiro dropped his pen. It rolled across the page and fell with a gentle thud into the long, dewy grass. A moment later he wrapped his fingers around the black cover of his notebook and closed it. The drawing of the horse flashed out of sight, but I swore he'd drawn the head curving down, not over the shoulder like it was now.

"What are you saying?"

"I'm not saying anything," I said. "It just looked like he had a tattoo."

He breathed slowly, hunched over his notebook.

"Yes," he said. "He has a tattoo."

The truth screamed out inside my head. *It's all true. Why else would he act like this?*

"Ishikawa…is he—"

"Does it really concern you?" he said in a sharp voice. I felt the shame burning up my neck, but it only made me angry. I hadn't said anything wrong.

"He's your best friend," I said. "It kind of concerns me if he's into dangerous stuff."

"I told you to stay away, didn't I?" he snapped.

"Would you cool it already?" I said, but the expression was lost in the translation and he looked puzzled. His eyes clouded over, and his head hung lower and lower until he rested his chin on his notebook. Then I saw the dark ooze dripping out from between the pages.

"Yuu!" I said. "Are you bleeding?"

Tomohiro shot up, stared at his hand and then the dripping liquid. His hand was fine, but he grabbed the pen, opened up the notebook a sliver and scribbled over the horse drawing.

"The ink blots sometimes," he said. "It's from the pen."

I stared with wide eyes at the bloodlike liquid, how it shimmered as it pooled on the grass. "What the hell kind of ink are you using?"

"Look," Tomohiro said. His tone was even now, and he looked up at me. I was suddenly aware that I was sitting too close to him, but I couldn't back up without looking like I was recoiling. "Sato is mixed up in some things that are no good. He gets me into a lot of fights, but I'm not into that stuff, okay?"

The unasked question hung in the silence of Toro Iseki. I could barely form the words, but Tomohiro's eyes told me I didn't need to.

"Yuu," I said, my throat thick and dry.

"Yes," he said, but he didn't raise his voice like a question. He knew what I was going to say, and he was ready to answer.

"Is Ishikawa in the Yakuza?"

Tomohiro stared straight at me, and I could already see the answer.

"Yuu, you have to stop hanging out with him."

"We've been best friends since elementary school," he said. "He was the only one who was my friend after…"

"After what?" I whispered.

"After I—switched schools." Koji. After Koji. *What the hell happened, Yuu?* "I can't abandon him. Anyway, I can take care of myself. And he's not that involved. He hasn't taken a sake oath or anything. He just does…odd tasks."

Fear coursed through me slowly, nerves prickling with the information I didn't want to know.

"When you were warning me to stay away…I had no idea."

Tomohiro snorted and his eyes fell to the cover of his notebook.

"You *have* no idea," he said.

A surge of panic cut through the pins and needles prickling down my spine.

"What do you mean?"

"It's nothing," he said. "You won't have to worry about it."

"You're scaring me," I said. He looked up and smiled warmly, like that would melt the fear in my heart.

"Daijoubu," he said. *It's okay.* "I won't let anything happen to you. Just like—" He stopped.

"Like what?"

"Nothing," he said. "I'll watch out for you."

"I don't need your protection," I said. "I just don't want ties to the Yakuza."

"Greene, I'm not in the Yakuza. I've made my intentions clear to them. You don't have to worry. Sato doesn't bring it up and I don't ask."

Tomohiro opened up his book bag and pulled out two cans of sweet milk tea. He pressed the cold drink into my hands and we said nothing, listening to the wagtails sing, their tails bobbing up and down like they were sketching, too. Tomohiro opened up his notebook to a fresh page and started drawing.

Ishikawa was his only friend after the fight with Koji. After he cut himself on the calligraphy project. I felt like I was standing too close to a painting, like I couldn't see the whole picture or put the fragments together. None of it made sense on its own. I couldn't piece him together.

"Yuu?"

"Hmm?"

"I've got to know. About the drawings. And don't tell me they're animated. My own doodles came at me with pointy teeth."

"I didn't do that," he said.

"So you're saying I'm doing it?"

"I'm not. I'm saying *I* didn't do that."

"Which means you did some of it, just not that."

Silence.

Bingo.

"I'm going to figure it out," I said.

"I'm sure you are."

"Yuu—I'm serious." I reached for his arm so he would look at me, but stopped. The cold way he'd told me to stay away from him the last time I touched him—I pulled my hand back. "Why did you transfer schools?"

"You ask too many questions, Greene." His pen traced the edge of the horse's leg.

"Katie."

"What?"

"My name is Katie."

Tomohiro's hand froze, and his cheeks started to turn a deep crimson. I'd been in Japan long enough to know what I was saying. A first-name basis was a step up the relationship ladder. "I'm a *gaijin,* remember?" I added quickly. "I'm not used to being called my last name. Don't you usually call *gaijin* by their first name anyway?"

He paused a moment, and I realized I shouldn't have said it. I was moving too fast—just because I felt something for him didn't mean he felt something for me, right? But then his hand began to move again, drawing the lines slowly as if he feared they would jump off in directions he couldn't control.

"All right, Katie," he said, and for the first time I relished the sound of my name on his lips. So rich, so lovely, so safe. He didn't sound dangerous, not here. I leaned back on the grass, watching the clouds float over the ancient city, wondering what tangled mess I'd gotten myself into.

"So you're not going to tell me what happened?"

"Nope."

"Why?"

"Because it doesn't matter."

"It matters to me."

"Then because it's not your business."

"You always say that." I rolled my eyes.

"Because it's true," he said. And then he closed the book and lay down beside me in the soggy grass. Every breath became shallow as I focused on the fact that he was right beside me. His knee pressed against mine by accident and I pulled away. A moment later I sat up.

"A-re?" he said in surprise. Then he sat up with a wolfish grin on his face. "Are you scared of me, Katie?" He rolled onto his knees and pressed his hands into the grass, leaning forward so his face almost reached mine. I could feel his warm breath on my skin. My stomach grew wings and battered around my insides. He wasn't going to… I mean, he wouldn't try to kiss me, would he?

I didn't want him to.

I wanted him to.

God he was beautiful. Dangerous things usually are. What the heck was I playing around with?

"Who's Koji?" I blurted out. Tomohiro froze, his eyes gleaming from behind his bright copper bangs. And then he pressed backward with the palms of his hands and stood up.

"Fuck," he said, walking a few steps away.

I got to my feet, my legs shaking. Tomohiro ran his hand through his hair.

"Who told you about him? Ichirou?" His voice was like stone.

"Yeah," I said. "Tanaka did."

A long pause.

"Koji was my best friend," Tomohiro said. "I didn't mean to… God, there was so much blood."

"How could you do that to your best friend?" I asked quietly. Tomohiro spun around, a wild look on his face. He was frightening again, like he'd been at kendo.

"It's not like that!" he shouted. "It's not what everybody thinks." He fell to his knees, folding his head into his hands. "They don't know what happened," he said quietly.

"Then tell me," I whispered. "I'll listen."

He didn't say anything. Then, "I can't."

"Why?"

"I can't, okay?" he snapped. "We were messing around, and he got hurt."

"But Tanaka said—"

"Tanaka knows shit!"

"If it was an accident, why didn't Koji say so?"

"He did, but they didn't believe him. No one would."

I took a breath. "Okay, so it was an accident. I believe you. Chill out, okay?"

Tomohiro looked over at me, then pressed his palm against his forehead. "I'm gonna kill Ichirou for telling you."

I smirked. "I would've found out from someone else eventually."

"Ha." Tomohiro laughed, and then he grinned. "I wouldn't expect less from you. I just wish you wouldn't think about all that too much. You know, my past and stuff. Can't you just forget it?"

"What do you mean?" I said. That glossing over the past meant there was some bad stuff there.

"I mean can't I just like a girl without it getting so complicated?" He raked another hand through his hair, shaking his head a few times, but all I could hear was my own heartbeat in my ears. Then he turned to look at me, his brown eyes deep and unafraid. The breeze was chilly against my dew-soaked back, but all I felt was warmth. I wanted to ask what he'd said, to hear it again, but the words lodged in my throat.

"You mean Myu?" was what escaped. Tomohiro didn't even grin. He just moved forward, looking intense.

"What I mean is..." he said. *"Ore sa."* His voice was made of honey. *"Kimi no koto ga..." About you,* it meant. *I, you know, I...*

And his *keitai* phone went off, and we both jumped away from each other. He flipped it open, cursing under his breath. He stared at the name, his finger hovering over the button.

"I... Sorry, I have to..."

"It's okay," I said, and he pushed the button. I felt like I was floating. This couldn't be real. My mind repeated over and over what he'd said. *Can't I just like a girl? About you, I, you know...*

He clicked the phone closed, his bangs sweeping over his eyes. "I have to go," he said.

"Your dad?"

"No, it's nothing," he said. "I just have to go."

"Some girl?" I joked, only I wasn't joking.

"Maji de," he said. "Are you the jealous type?" He flashed a mean grin.

"Shut up. I don't care."

"It's Sato," he said. "He's in a situation."

"Oh." And it hit me yet again that I had fallen for the wrong guy. A dangerous guy, going to help his gangster friend.

"I'll— Listen, give me your *keitai* number." And he held up his phone and flipped it open. "Please?"

I reached for mine, pretty sure this wasn't what Diane had in mind when she got it for me. I pushed a few buttons and the infrared sent my number over to his phone with a beep. Another beep, and I had his.

"Yosh," he said, clicking it shut and shoving it into his

pocket. "I'll see you tomorrow?" I nodded, and he nodded, and then I nodded again. "Okay, *jaa,*" he said, and then he headed toward our bikes. He only got about five steps before he tripped, but he kept going, cursing under his breath. Well, at least we were both feeling awkward. I'd thought he only had one mode, and it was suave.

I ducked under the fence and grabbed my bike, walking alongside it as I watched Tomohiro cycle out of sight. If he was so dangerous, why did I feel like I might float away?

Too late to step away now. I wanted to see what was going on.

I hopped on my bike and followed him.

6

Tomohiro coasted south for a while, until the streets became narrow and crowded, and he walked alongside his bike. I followed him at a distance, finding it easier to hide in the crowds. My phone went off, and since it was so new, it took me a minute to realize it was mine. I pressed it to my ear.

"Moshi mosh?" I said.

"Katie!" Tanaka's voice rang out.

"Tanaka?"

"And Yuki. She's done with Sewing Club, and we want to hang out. So…coffee?"

"Oh. Um."

"I told you" came Yuki's slightly muffled voice. "She's busy flirting with Yuu Tomohiro."

"I'm not—Tanaka, put Yuki on the phone."

"And let you yell at each other? No way. Have fun, Katie-chan. We'll talk later."

"I'll call you!" shouted Yuki from the background. "I want all the details!" So did I. The more Tomohiro didn't want me to delve into his past, the more I needed to.

"Wait!" I said, and for a minute I was worried Tanaka had hung up.

"Hmm?" he said. I veered my bike around the thinning crowd, trying not to lose sight of Tomohiro.

"Koji," I said quietly. "What happened to him, Tanaka?"

"I don't think you should ask him about it."

"Fine, but just tell me. Please."

"His dad was going to file assault charges. I think he got paid off or something."

"Tomohiro said it was an accident," I said, watching the copper spikes bob a few yards ahead of me.

Tanaka let out a long sigh. "I always thought that, too. I want to think it, because that's not who Tomo-kun is. But… that's impossible."

"Why?"

"Katie." I could tell Tanaka had cupped his hand around the phone, his voice quiet and serious. "Three long slices to the eye with a blade. Multiple stab wounds on his arms. He almost lost his eye. There's no way all that was an accident."

"Holy shit." I felt like I was going to be sick.

"Except," Tanaka said, "there was a lot of talk that it was an animal, you know, not a knife that—"

There was the muffled sound of Yuki grabbing the phone. "Katie, I didn't know that before. Tanaka, are you stupid? Telling her to go for a guy like that? Get out of there, Katie. Don't speak to him again. Please."

I was crumbling to pieces. Parts of me were blowing away on the wind.

The one person who understood me, and he goes at his best friend with a knife. No, I still believed Tomohiro. It was an accident, somehow, wasn't what it looked like. But if it was an animal, why not just say so?

Multiple stab wounds…

"Katie?" Tanaka said. "I'm not sure it's true. Koji always said it didn't happen like that. Katie—"

I closed the phone and put it in my pocket. There wasn't enough of a crowd around to blend in, to forget what I'd heard. I didn't want to follow Tomohiro anymore. It didn't matter what Koji had said. How could Tomohiro explain away those kinds of wounds as accidental? *I can't,* he'd said. More puzzle pieces adding up to nothing.

I wasn't paying attention to where I was going, and in front of me Tomohiro had met up with Ishikawa. I stopped abruptly. Another few minutes and I would've crashed into them.

I stared at Tomohiro as he greeted Ishikawa, as they smacked hands and Ishikawa pointed at a guy with a knit hat pulled over his head, as Tomohiro grabbed hold of the guy's shirt collar and shoved him back a foot while Ishikawa laughed. The guy approached and Tomohiro leaned his face in close to the other guy, forcing him to walk back a few steps before shoving him again. Ishikawa reached out his palm, coaxing the hat guy to either fight back or give them something, I couldn't tell.

And then I saw the backs of Tomohiro's fists, drenched in black ink, dripping onto the ground.

Only, the others didn't seem to notice it, and when he pushed the knit hat guy again, none of it came off on his shirt. It dripped, thick as blood. I blinked and it was gone.

Was that how his hands had looked when he attacked Koji?

I backed up quickly, the warmth of Tomohiro's words to me turning cold and slick like sweat. I was seeing things again. It couldn't be true. I'd told him I believed him that it was an accident. He'd seemed so genuine, filled with regret, but it wasn't the kind of event I could ignore. How dangerous was Tomohiro? It was starting to give me a headache.

I turned and walked away, but it was a bad neighborhood, and the roads were too crowded to bike.

"Hello," said a creepy voice in English, and it was like a warning shot going off into the air. I was too terrified to look. A tough-looking guy, grubby and smelling of thick smoke, started walking alongside me. He was in bad need of a haircut, and bright tattoos circled his beefy arms. "Hello, pretty girl. You American?"

I walked faster, but he kept pace with me. For a minute I considered going back to Tomohiro. Which was safer, going forward or going back? I didn't know.

"You lost?" the guy said in English.

Like I would ever tell him in a million years. "I'm fine," I said, my voice shaky.

And suddenly someone wrapped his arm around me and pulled me into his warmth, away from the guy. My body went rigid, ready to kick away whoever this new threat was. And then I saw a flash of blond tucked behind his ear.

"She's not lost," Jun said. And then to me, "Sorry I made you wait. Shall we go?"

I nodded numbly, pushing the bike forward, letting my body lean into Jun as he pulled me closer.

The angular guy grunted and fell back, and for a few minutes it was the sound of my heartbeat in my ears, the warmth of Jun and the slightly sweet smell of his hair gel.

"You okay?" he said quietly, and my eyes filled with grateful tears. "What are you doing down here anyway?"

"I could ask you the same," I said, wiping my eyes with the back of my hand. In a fluid movement, Jun whisked my bike to the other side so he could push it and I could freely dab at my eyes.

"There's a great pasta place near here," he said. "I used to live in Ishida and I crave the manicotti sometimes. Lucky for you."

"Thank you," I said. We seemed far enough away, but Jun didn't drop his arm from my shoulder. He had a black wristband around his wrist, and then his muscular arm disappeared into the sleeve of his school blazer. When he saw me staring, he smiled, pulling his arm away.

"Glad I could help. Shizuoka's a pretty safe city, but it's still better to stick to main routes, okay?" I just nodded. Between following Tomohiro and being on the phone with Tanaka and Yuki, I hadn't paid any attention to the maze I'd stumbled through.

"We keep running into each other." He smiled. "Are you an exchange student? Or have you moved here?"

"Moved here," I said. "I'm living with my aunt. She's an English teacher."

"Ah." He smiled again. "Maybe you can teach me sometime. My English isn't that great. But your Japanese is really good. I'm envious." He talked easily, like we were old friends.

I could see Shizuoka Station now, rising in the distance. Thank god, too, because the sun had disappeared from the sky and darkness was setting in.

"You know where you are now?" Jun grinned.

"Thank you," I said again, and he nodded. Then the smile slipped from his face and he looked all serious. He dipped his head down and his bangs tumbled from behind his ear, swaying in a blond wave in front of his eye. The fading sunlight glinted off his earring.

"I was thinking maybe you'd like to have coffee with me?"

I'm sorry, what? He looked up, his dark eyes somehow cold. I guess I'd expected him to look a little more nervous asking a question like that, but I couldn't read how he was feeling.

"Um," I said. "I really appreciate it, I do, but…it's getting late and if I'm not home soon…"

"I understand," Jun said. "You don't want your aunt to worry. I can walk you the rest of the way if you like."

I shook my head. "I'm okay from here," I said.

He nodded.

"Maybe another time?"

"Sure." He smiled. He turned to walk away, hands shoved in his pockets, then looked over his shoulder at me. "Is that boy still drawing things?"

"Oh," I said. "No, it's not that, I—" But it was that. And he knew it.

"I hope he draws for you," he said, and then he was gone.

When I got home, Diane was just serving up dinner. I pushed it around the plate, forcing myself to eat and make pleasant conversation until I could escape to my room. I stared at the ceiling, trying to picture Koji's injuries.

"There's no way," I said to myself. Tomohiro had been really worked up about the accident. He seemed as shaken as I was about it.

I flipped open my computer and did an internet search of Yuu Tomohiro and Koji together. When that didn't work, I added in Shizuoka. It came up, finally, a single old article about the incident. Of course, it was also written using hundreds of kanji I was still learning. It might as well have been in hieroglyphic.

I sighed, running the article through a translation site. Hopefully I'd get the gist of it.

I read the garbled translation. Interview snippets with Koji—"He's my best friend. He'd never hurt me. It was an accident."—and comments about dropping the case. The payoff Tanaka mentioned, I guess. No pictures of Koji, but I didn't really want to see anyway. And then a description of the wounds—punctures and claw marks, like an animal did it.

And then, in the final paragraph, Koji insisting they broke into a construction site, that the guard dog attacked him. Police insisting dogs couldn't inflict those kinds of bladelike slices on his eye.

I reread the paragraph. But claw and bite marks would make similar kinds of wounds, wouldn't they? So…not a dog, but something else?

Tanaka didn't know what had happened, but he'd thought it might be an animal, too.

Attacking a friend with a blade? That wasn't my Tomohiro. I felt it in my heart. He wouldn't do that, but he would sneak into a construction site and take the fall so they didn't get into more trouble. And once it came to light about the animal, maybe Koji's dad would've doubted what happened and dropped the case.

Satisfied, I lay down on my bed. And then I realized what I'd said.

My Tomohiro.

7

Tomohiro and I barely spoke at kendo, but that suited me just fine. I wanted to keep my distance from Ishikawa, and from the way he glared at me, he felt the same. He and Tomohiro had a few faint bruises on their faces, and I didn't really want to think about how they'd got them. We went on through club practices like we didn't know each other at all, and we kept our trips to Toro Iseki secret. Tomohiro feared his dad would learn he was drawing, despite him forbidding it—which I thought was crazy, but I chalked it up to a strict, unhappy workaholic—and I was scared of trespassing charges.

"What if they deport me?" I ranted, but Tomohiro smirked.

"Isn't that what you want anyway?"

Just like in our kendo matches, where we only felt briefly safe with our *shinai* thrust between us, keeping each other at arm's distance was the only way to trust each other. That way, no one would lunge, and either of us could retreat.

We lived in parallel worlds, somehow held together by the axis of each other.

The vibrant greens of spring dulled and the chirps of the wagtails drowned under the whirr of summer cicadas.

Two weeks before the big Aoi Ward tournament, Tomohiro didn't show up in the courtyard after school. He texted me that night that his uncle had died and he was going with his father to Chiba for the funeral.

I felt his absence more strongly than I'd expected. I felt off balance when he wasn't there, and while Eto-sensei droned on about world history, I thought about Tomohiro, how he had changed somehow. Maybe he hadn't changed at all, just opened like a bud on the rough branch of the *sakura* tree, suddenly blooming and floating on the breeze; free, wheeling wherever he might land, dragged only by the current.

His kendo movements were unpredictable like that. No one could keep up with him except Ishikawa, and the two were the hope for the tournament. But no matter how Tomohiro unwrapped his strategies to me, I couldn't match him in the gym, when all the eyes were watching and we were both shrieking our *kiais* at each other. The kendo teachers were always pairing us with *kendouka* we had no chance of beating. For the experience, they said. If we only fought at our own level, we'd never be challenged, never improve. But it was frightening to fight with Tomohiro. When he shouted and brought the *shinai* toward me, all I could think about was Koji, even though I'd mostly figured out the truth. It still frightened me, what Tomohiro might be capable of.

And yet, against all common sense, I'd fallen for him. I'd told myself for a while it was to figure out what was going on, to get my life back. He understood about my mom. But I wasn't sure anymore what I wanted. I just knew I wanted to be near him.

Tomohiro was absent from practice for the funeral, but there was hardly time to think as Watanabe-sensei barked out the orders. One hundred push-ups for the junior members, twice as many for seniors. One thousand *men* strikes and countless laps of footwork around the gym. We would be up against some of the toughest schools in the ward, Nakamura-sensei said, in particular Katakou High. They had one of the best kendo clubs in the ward, and their secret weapon? National *kendouka* champion Takahashi.

"All our hope this year is placed in Ishikawa and Yuu," Watanabe said, "so give them your support."

So the juniors could "improve" for the tournament, and the seniors could practice beating us to a pulp, the sensei paired us with older *kendouka.*

"Not today." I sighed to myself. I didn't feel like getting my butt handed to me.

"Greene and Ishikawa!" Watanabe belted out, and the pins and needles rushed up my neck.

You're kidding.

Ishikawa flattened his mop of bleached hair under a tight headband and slipped on his *men.* My breath condensed on the mesh of the helmet's screen; the stiflingly hot armor had become almost unbearable.

It had to be a joke. He was a much higher level than me. Pairing me with Tomohiro was bad, but pairing me with Ishikawa was suicide. He wouldn't go easy on me the way Tomohiro did.

"Sensei?" I said to Watanabe, but he nodded at me.

"We want you to compete in the tournament," he said. "It would look great for our club to have more girls and more *gaijin* competing. So you need as many challenges as we can give you before you go out there. Take it lightly, Ishikawa, okay? Let her get warmed up first." Ishikawa gave a faint nod, but his eyes were piercing. He wasn't going to go easy on me. I knew that.

Ishikawa and I crouched to the floor, *shinai* at our sides.

We pulled them from their imaginary sheaths and pointed the tied bamboo slats at each other.

Ishikawa shrieked as he ran at me, and two thoughts snapped into my head: how different his movements and *kiai* were from Tomohiro's, and how his yell rattled even Tomohiro. He often said Ishikawa would be the better fighter if he didn't let the rage block his thinking, but the upcoming tournament had made him ferocious, so that panic grasped my mind as his *shinai* came at me. I tried to block, but within a minute his *shinai* slammed down on my wrist for a *migi-kote* point.

It was like I forgot all my training, like I was regressing. Watanabe barked combinations at me, but my mind was so murky I could barely hear him. I was drowning in my own fear, off balance. Through the metal screen, Ishikawa's dark eyes glared at me, a shock of white hair clinging to his forehead.

When the match finished, Ishikawa had managed four good hits, and I'd only had one pathetic swing to his *dou*. And missed.

Class wrapped up, and Ishikawa pulled off his *men* and walked toward me, towering over me the way Tomohiro had done before.

"You think you're so important to Yuuto," he sneered, his voice low and hushed. His hot breath was in my ear, and the sounds of students unfastening armor and pushing open the change room doors all blurred into the background. "But he'll lose interest in you, like he did in Myu. He always does."

"We're just friends," I said quietly, but Ishikawa snorted.

"Yuuto always liked girls who were weak," he said. "His interest in you will end, and then he'll cast you aside."

"Shut up," I said. My whole body shook and my ears

buzzed from the blood rushing through them. "What do you care anyway?"

"Because he's my best friend," Ishikawa said, combing a hand through his bleached hair. "And you're distracting him."

"From what?"

"His destiny," he said. "Anyway," he added, cupping his arm around his helmet, "he already has a girlfriend, so you're wasting your time."

My fingers squeezed so hard against my palms that I could feel my nails digging in. "Not that I care, but some best friend you are. He doesn't have a girlfriend."

Ishikawa looked blank for a moment and started to laugh. It was a wicked laugh, cold and scornful, and as much I wanted to tell him to go to hell, the sound of it made my whole body shudder.

Ishikawa leaned in right beside my ear. He smelled of kendo leather and sweat.

"What did Yuuto tell you?" he said quietly. "Did he tell you his pregnant girlfriend was only a cousin? A sister? A family friend?" He smirked and turned away, his gray *hakama* swaying as he walked.

The words pulsed in my head. I felt like I'd lost my sense of direction, like I'd just spiral down to the floor and collapse. I forced myself into the change room, unfastened all the *bogu* armor and pulled the *tenugui* headband from my sweaty hair.

My head was spinning, and I could think of nowhere to go to clear it but Toro Iseki. I didn't have Diane's bike, so I hurried for the local yellow-and-green bus that Tomohiro and I often took on rainy days. It cut the trip in half, which was a good thing because I felt like I might pass out on the way.

I tried to call Tomohiro's *keitai,* but it was off. I started a text, but the kanji kept grouping into the wrong ones and I was too embarrassed to send a message with only phonetic hiragana. *Damn auto spell!* Eventually I sent a message in English.

Call me when you're back from Chiba. —Katie

I hit Send, but when I pushed the button, I immediately regretted it. He would get the message at his uncle's funeral, and for what? So I could accuse him of lying to me?

No, it wasn't that. Tomohiro and I had become close, and Ishikawa was jealous. He was just trying to piss me off. I was sure of it. But I also knew it had worked, and I needed help to pull myself out of the spiral.

Renovations at Toro Iseki were almost complete by the summer. I ducked under the fence with no trouble and stepped into the belt of forest around the site. The pungent smell of humid summer forest flooded my nostrils and clogged up my nose. Damn allergies. I wove between the trees, trying to avoid the patches of wildflowers. Cicadas whirred all around me, and the wagtails leaped from branch to branch above, their tails bobbing like they'd had too much caffeine.

I leaned against a tree trunk, finally able to face what Ishikawa had said.

Tomohiro was drawn to me because I was weak. He really did have a pregnant girlfriend. I was keeping him from his destiny.

What destiny? We'd kept our meetings private, so he couldn't mean study time for entrance exams. Was I distracting him from kendo? But that wasn't his destiny.

Joining the Yakuza? Maybe.

The wagtails' songs turned erratic and I looked up, trying to figure out what had happened. They jumped around and chirped high-pitched warnings to each other. Were they that worried about me?

Then I saw the problem—an intruder among the birds. It was another wagtail, but his tail feathers stretched out longer than the others, his round eyes void and vacant like…like the sketched girl in the *genkan*. All the wagtails were white and black, but this one looked papery, like he would crinkle in the breeze. His feathers were jagged, messy scrawls, and when he beat his wings to move to another branch, little swirls of shimmering dust trailed his flight.

Oh my god. He's…he's a sketch.

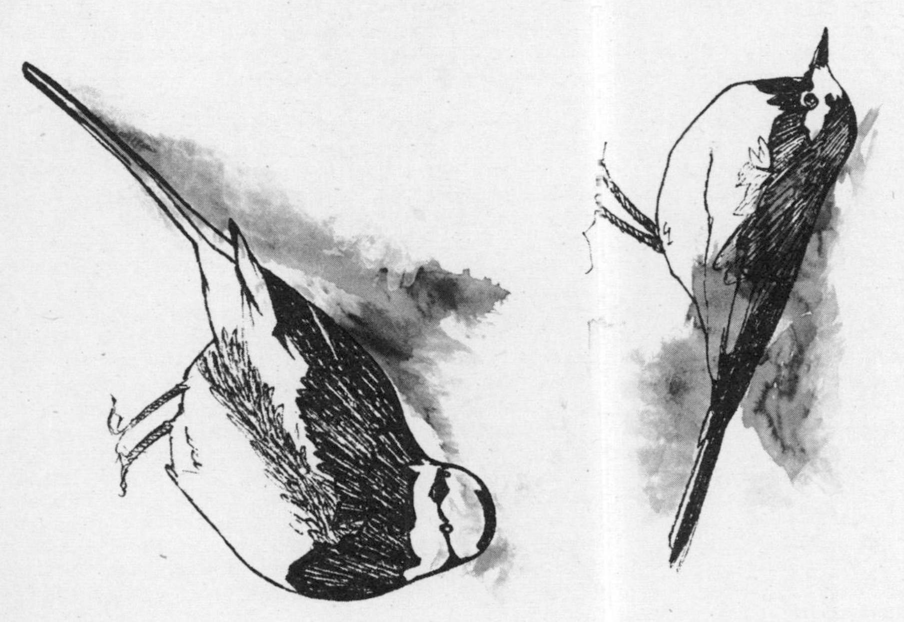

The wagtail hopped toward another bird and lunged. Red sprayed across the black-and-white victim, and the shock of color sent my head spinning.

He's attacking them. The way my drawings came after me.

In a flurry of feathers, the sketched wagtail lunged at the others, clawing at them, pecking at their eyes and throats.

I flailed my arms around to scare him away, then found a twig and threw it at the patch of birds. It clipped his wing and he took off into the air, chased by some of the puffier wagtails. He soared across the clearing of Toro Iseki, the trail of black dust following him. I took off after him.

Suddenly my *keitai* phone chimed with a text, and the sound scattered the whole flock of wagtails, their wings beating like a crashing waterfall. My heart pounded at the sudden electronic notes beeping through the chirps of the birds.

And just as suddenly, the sketched wagtail stopped in midair like he'd slammed into a glass wall. He plummeted to the ground, landing with a thud in the grass.

I stepped out of the trees and ran to where he fell. I scanned the long grasses, but I couldn't find his body anywhere. Black dust fell from the sky like snow, gathering on my shoulders like an oily sheen.

"Katie?" a voice said, and I knew it instantly.

Tomohiro.

I turned and saw him there, sitting with his sketchbook balanced on his knees.

"What are you doing?" he asked.

"The wagtail," I said. "It— What are you doing here? I thought you were in Chiba for the funeral."

Tomohiro motioned to the blazer he'd discarded beside him, a bracelet of wooden Buddhist prayer beads resting on top of it. He wore his red-and-navy-striped tie, part of the boys' school uniform, but he'd loosened the knot so it hung unkempt around his neck.

"The funeral was this morning," he said. "My dad had a business meeting, so we caught the afternoon train back. Are you okay?"

"Not really," I said. My head was pounding. Tomohiro's face wrinkled with concern and he patted the ground beside him.

"Sit down," he said.

"I have to find the bird," I said, scanning the ground.

"What bird?"

"Didn't you see it? It attacked the other birds," I said. I crouched down and bent the grasses out of the way with my hand.

"You mean like rabies? I didn't see anything."

"Maybe. But it looked weird. There was something wrong with its feathers. And it just dropped all of a sudden out of the sky, like it smacked into something. It looked like it was… made of paper."

"Katie, sit down," Tomohiro said, and there was something in his voice that made my thoughts snap into place. I turned to him, all my suspicions colliding in my head.

"Yuu, why do you destroy your drawings?"

"What?"

"I swear to God I saw them move."

"We've been over this."

"And the dragon tail."

"The what?"

"I found a scrap from your notebook. It moved, too."

"Katie, what the hell?" Tomohiro snapped. "Do you know how crazy you sound?" He sounded ticked off, but somehow his face didn't line up. It didn't add up.

What was Tomohiro's destiny, and why did Ishikawa think I was in the way?

"Ishikawa said Shiori is your girlfriend," I said. Tomohiro narrowed his eyes.

"Satoshi is full of shit," he said darkly.

"Is he?"

"Katie! You seriously believe him over me? He's just messing with you. I told you Shiori is like a sister. She's a family friend." He looked down at his closed sketchbook, and his bangs fanned over his dark eyes.

"How do I know?" I said. "Tell me why my drawings moved, Yuu. Tell me why my pen blew up and why I saw ink on your hands that wasn't there. Tell me what really happened to Koji. You've always been keeping something from me. Ishikawa said you're drawn to me because I'm weak. What does he mean?"

"How are you weak, Katie?" Tomohiro looked up at me, his eyes shining. "You're far from home, in a country you don't fully understand, speaking a language you haven't fully mastered, and all of that leaves you isolated to deal with your mom's death." Tomohiro stepped toward me and placed his hands on my arms. His palms felt warm through the thin summer sleeves of my uniform. "Tell me how that's weak," he urged quietly.

"You wanted me to stay away from you," I said. "I thought it was because of the Yakuza. But there's more, isn't there?"

Tomohiro smiled. "There's nothing more—"

"Cut the crap," I shouted and shook his hands off. He stood staring at me and I felt the shame rise in me. But I had to know.

"Show me your sketchbook," I said.

"What?"

"I want to see your sketchbook," I said, pointing at the black cover. Tomohiro turned and stared at it. "Maybe Ishikawa was messing with me. I don't know. But I need to know what's going on. Please, Yuu."

"Katie. Just trust me, and don't ask this." Tomohiro's eyes were wide and gazed at mine with pleading. But I'd gone this far, and I couldn't go back.

"Yuu, you know I have to see it." He hesitated. "Please," I said.

He backed up slowly, each foot dragging through the grass, then bent over and picked up the sketchbook. He held it out to me with one hand, and I took it, even though his eyes looked so sad.

My hands shook as I pressed my fingers into the cover. I pulled it open slowly, flipping through the drawings I'd seen him sketch over the past several weeks. They all looked weird, in poses I didn't remember, each with the same thick lines scribbled through them, scraped right through the pictures, rendering them ugly and useless. The horse had his nostrils flared, his head over his shoulder—not the way he had been drawn.

I fanned the pages until I reached the blank ones, and turned backward until the last sketch came into view.

I stopped and looked at the drawing.

A wagtail, with a thick X across its neck. His eyes gleamed like vacant pools of ink, and his feathers jagged out in awkward directions.

I stared at the picture. Tomohiro said nothing.

I looked up at him slowly.

"You drew him," I said. "You *made* that wagtail."

He didn't make any excuses. He just looked at me with a heaviness in his eyes.

"How did you do this?" I said, my voice barely a whisper. "What's going on?"

His gaze was piercing and I wished he'd drop his eyes to the ground. Shivers of fear pulsed through my body, but I couldn't tear myself away from him. I'd had my suspicions, but they couldn't have prepared me for the truth. My heart pounded in my ears.

"What are you?" I said.

"Katie. Calm down."

"Calm down? Either your fucking drawings are coming to life or I'm losing my mind! How the hell am I supposed to calm down?"

"It's not you, okay? Sit down, and—and I'll answer your questions."

"Well, you better!" I shouted, but he looked about as threatening as a puppy. When I thought about it, he actually looked more frightened than me.

I stayed standing.

"Is this why you quit calligraphy?" I asked.

He gazed at me with gleaming eyes. "Yes."

"Is this why you destroy your drawings?"

Another pause. Then a nod.

"And the girl really looked at me, in the *genkan*. And you made my pen explode."

"Yes."

My mind went blank. Hot tears carved their way down my cheeks. I sobbed and didn't care how wretched I looked. The reality I'd believed in and the reality that existed were too different, and there was no way to reconcile them. It was like seeing a ghost or a miracle, or someone fly. Something impossible. My brain throbbed as I tried to rationalize it.

"Katie." Tomohiro's gentle voice cut through my sobs.

He reached out his hands for the sketchbook, or for me. I wasn't sure.

I took a shaky breath and moved toward him. I pressed the notebook into his hands, the metal spiral cold beneath my trembling fingers.

"You can't tell anyone," he said, and I snorted.

"That's your major concern here?"

"Please," he said again. "Especially Sato."

"Tell them what?" I said. "That your drawings come to life? They'd send me to the loony bin."

He shook his head. "Satoshi will believe you," he said quietly. "He's been trying to prove it for years and I've always denied it. If he knew the truth… He'll try and get the Yakuza to use me. Do you understand? It will put us both in serious trouble if anyone knows."

"But knows *what?*"

Tomohiro sighed, and his eyes brimmed with tears that he blinked back.

In a shaky whisper he said, "I'm a Kami."

"Kami?" My head cycled through its mini-dictionary of Japanese. *Kami* meant "paper," but something else sparked in my mind. *Kami* also meant "god."

"Shinto talks about the *kami,* right?" Tomohiro said. "There are thousands of them."

"Gods, you mean?"

"Gods," he said. "Or spirits. Beings that inhabit things in nature, like trees, or waterfalls or stuff. Shinto's all about a spark of life in everything."

"So you're some kind of spirit, is that it?"

"That's just Shinto tradition. But there's more than that. There's a reason *kami* means 'paper' *and* 'spirit,' Katie."

"Just spit it out, Yuu."

"Okay. The most famous *kami* is Amaterasu, the goddess of the sun. She's part of the creation story. But she's more than that." Tomohiro stared into the distance. "Amaterasu was real. Not a goddess maybe, but a real person with some kind of… power. And the real Kami are descendants of that power."

"You're kidding, right?"

He raised an eyebrow.

"Did you, or did you not, see the drawings move?"

"Point taken."

"There was a time when the Kami were well-known. We can…do something with our minds. I don't understand it. Anyway, all the myths come from bits of truth. The drawings, poems, folklore…it's all by Japanese trying to understand where the Kami came from."

"And you're one of these Kami," I said, but he didn't answer.

"Do you know what one of the conditions of surrender was at the end of World War Two?" he asked. "Emperor Hirohito had to publicly deny his divinity. Japanese always believed emperors were descended from Amaterasu. I guess Westerners thought it would be humiliating for Hirohito to denounce this claim."

"So it sort of knocked him down a rank?" I said.

Tomohiro leaned in. "Yeah, but it wasn't just a tradition of myth. The royal family really *are* Kami," he said. "When Hirohito denounced his power, it was a message to the Kami to scatter. Families with the ability went into hiding, and now those who know the truth keep quiet out of fear. There are dangerous people in Japan, you know."

"You said Ishikawa would make you work for the Yakuza," I said.

"I'm afraid of it," he said, and I saw the fear in his eyes, that he was freaked out by all of this, too.

"So these Kami, they can all draw things that become real?"

"I'm not sure. For me, it's something in my mind when I draw. I don't really know any other Kami."

"You've thought it all out," I said.

"My dad told me most of it. But I've tried to learn more since he won't tell me everything."

"Your dad knows about this?"

"It's why he's forbidden me from drawing," he said.

"Is he a Kami, too?"

Tomohiro shook his head. "He won't give me a clear answer, but I know my mom was. She'd have to be, to pass the power down to me." A sudden thought sparked through my head, and I was almost too afraid to say it.

"Yuu," I whispered, "your mom..."

"It had to do with her accident, yes."

My throat felt thick.

"That's why you can't tell anyone, Katie. We'd both be in danger."

"But why did my drawing move? Why did the pen explode?"

"The pen was me," he said. "I didn't know what else to do. If the drawings had reached you..." He didn't need to complete the thought. They might have been tiny, but mouths of razor-sharp teeth don't lie. "So I burst the pen and drowned them before they could get to you. I just told the ink to go every direction, and it was strong enough to break the plastic."

"But I'm not a Kami," I said. "Why would my drawings move?"

"It's all my fault," he said and crouched on the ground, his hands in his hair. "They were reacting to me being there. I didn't do it, but I couldn't stop it, either. I've tried so hard to keep it a secret, but somehow when you're around I can't control the ink as well. I've been trying to figure it out, believe me. But when I'm near you, I can't—it's like everything gets fuzzy."

"What do you mean, 'fuzzy'?"

He sighed. "The ink wants something from you. I don't know what it is, believe me. You're some kind of ink magnet or something. It's getting really hard to control my drawings, to—to control myself."

"Stop drawing, then," I choked. *After me? Why?*

Tomohiro twisted the tall grasses around his fingers. "I have to draw. But I don't use inkstones or *sumi* anymore. It's too dangerous. I couldn't even think straight, like it wasn't my own mind or something."

"The time you cut yourself," I said, and he frowned.

"I cut myself on the kanji," he said. "The last stroke of *sword* flicks to the left. When I drew the line across the page, the word cut into my wrist. I was lucky it didn't kill me."

"Shit," I said, crouching beside him. And then another thought occurred to me.

"Koji," I whispered. He looked at me with glassy eyes.

"I was just a stupid kid," he said, his voice barely audible. "I tried to hide it from him, but…he just wanted me to show him what I could do."

There was no break-in, no guard dog. I realized that now. The drawing, whatever it was, had ripped into Koji. And Koji had protected Tomohiro even then.

"I never told Sato about the ink. It would've been a death sentence for him to know. But I can control things better now.

You don't have to worry. I would never let it happen to you. But Koji—oh god, Katie. I still have nightmares about it."

I took his hand and flipped it palm up, pushed his shirt-sleeve back to expose the scars and cuts up his arm.

"Sometimes the drawings still scratch or bite me. This long one is from a dragon claw."

"Dragon?" I said. "Like the tail I saw? It moved even though the page was ripped."

"I don't really understand how it works," he said, gazing down at the scars. "Destroying the pictures doesn't destroy the creatures. It contains them somehow, stops them from coming off the page. But they still move around."

It was too much for me. My head filled with a fog of confusion. It ached to wade through this new, unwanted knowledge. I tried to focus on concrete things I knew were real. The wagtails chirped and the breeze blew, first the scents of thatched wood and flowers, then the smell of Tomohiro's hair gel and his skin. The smell of funeral incense clinging to his clothes. The fact that I was technically holding his hand. The heat of his skin where it touched mine.

The warmth rushed up my neck and into my cheeks. I dropped his hand, but I realized how close I was sitting to him, the way his loosened tie flapped in the wind. The little buttons undone at his throat. The soft tan skin of his collarbone.

"Yuu," I said.

"Don't be afraid of me," he said. "Please." He reached out for my hand with his. His fingers were softer than I'd thought, slender and gentle as they wrapped around mine.

My voice was barely a whisper. "I am afraid."

"I know. But I would never hurt you, Katie. I would never let it hurt you." He pulled me close to him, so that my face pressed against the fragrance of incense caught in his white shirt. The warmth of his neck and chin pressed against my hair, and I could feel his heartbeat pulsing against my shoulder. And the way his strong arms shook as they held me, I knew he was afraid, too. "I'll fight it."

I wanted to press myself closer to him, and at the same time I wanted to step away.

"Fight it?"

He leaned back and shook his head. "I'm marked, Katie. That's what the nightmares keep telling me, that there's only suffering ahead. You saw the wagtail attack the other birds, right? There's something darker than ink that seeps into the sketches. I don't know if it's the Kami bloodline or…or something in me. Maybe my true self is evil and it's fighting its way to the surface."

"You don't believe that!" I said, but fear gripped my spine.

"I don't know why it's trying to get you. But I won't let it."

The power itself was as scary as hell, but the idea that it was something awful, that Tomohiro was something worthy of lurking in the shadows…

And that, whether it was him or something else, it was after me, too…

"That's bullshit," I said.

The corners of his mouth lifted, but the smile was brief.

"I hope so," he said.

He pulled me close again and we stayed like that for a long time, the pages of the sketchbook flipping in the wind.

8

It was almost dark by the time I made it home. I considered sending a text to Diane from the bus, but she was out with her coworkers, so she wouldn't have noticed me missing anyway.

I flicked on the lights in the empty mansion, wishing for once that she was there with her corny welcome. Anything but this silence that flooded the house and left me alone with the fog in my head.

I trudged to the fridge, my feet as heavy as lead. I poured myself a glass of cold oolong tea and took the leftover curry to zap in the microwave. I sat at the kitchen table, the bowl of steaming curry in front of me. I said *itadakimasu* to nobody at all, and ate.

In my mind I kept seeing the scars on Tomohiro's wrist, the wagtail snapping backward in midair and dropping to the ground with a cloud of sparkling ink dust.

I shoveled more rice and chicken into my mouth, willing the spices to overpower my thoughts.

It didn't work.

The drawings moved. They looked at me.

Worse. They *saw* me.

And Tomohiro said they were after me, that he lost control

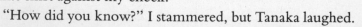

sometimes when he was around me. But I didn't have any special powers. Why did they want me? Because I knew about them?

Or because with me they could overtake Tomohiro, make him lose control—and then what?

And what if it *was* Tomohiro after me, subconsciously or not?

When my *keitai* chimed, I grabbed for it gratefully.

"Moshi mosh," I said, holding my forehead up with my hand and twirling my spoon into my rice.

"Katie-chan? You okay?" It was Tanaka. I straightened up like he could see me.

"Tan-kun," I said. "I'm okay. Just an intense kendo practice."

"I had a busy day, too," he said. "I just got out of cram school. We're going for karaoke. Come on!"

I hated the sound of my own singing, not because it was awful but because it sounded just like Mom's. I wished she could be here now, to brush my hair and hold me, to tell me everything would be okay.

"I can't really sing," I said. I heard some other voices on the end of the phone, the sounds of Tanaka walking the streets of Shizuoka.

"You can't say that every time!" he said. "You've been so busy with the kendo tournament coming up, we've hardly seen you. Yuki is coming, too."

"I don't know," I said, but I was close to caving. It was that or being alone with my thoughts.

"Look," Tanaka said, his voice changing. It sounded like he'd clamped his hand around the phone. "People are going to talk if you spend any more time with Tomo-kun."

Heat spread through my body; I could almost feel the crisp white shirt against my cheek.

"How did you know?" I stammered, but Tanaka laughed.

"It's obvious," he said. "So you need to take a break and come be with your friends before everyone else figures it out."

"Okay, okay. Jeez, I never pegged you for blackmail."

He laughed. "I'm not above it. See you in ten."

I met Tanaka and his cram-school friends halfway to Shizuoka Station, and once Yuki arrived, we went for karaoke in a winding wing of shops attached to the platforms. We ordered a round of melon sodas and cold iced teas, and Tanaka sang first, bursting out off-key but with lots of gusto. I thought Yuki would be shy around Tanaka's cram-school friends, but when her voice rang out, it was beautiful and clear. We performed a duet together, since I was too embarrassed to sing by myself.

The waiter brought the drinks in, and my heart froze when I saw him.

Ishikawa.

He stood there in his white apron, lowering the tray of drinks slowly onto our table.

"*Oi,* Tomo-kun's friend, right?" Tanaka waved. "He's from our school," he told his cram-school buddies. "Sorry, I don't know your name…."

"Ishikawa-senpai," Yuki supplied. "From the kendo team." Trust her to know everyone at school.

Ishikawa bowed swiftly, avoiding my gaze, and hurried back out the door, clicking our room shut.

The sight of him sent my thoughts racing again, back to the kendo match, the poison words that had soaked into me. What sort of things lurked in Tomohiro's dark destiny? Tanaka's boisterous voice blurred into background noise while my thoughts swelled in my head. I couldn't block them out.

"Katie?" Yuki said. I couldn't breathe.

"I just need a sec," I said and bolted past Tanaka into the hallway. In the bathroom I took out my *keitai* and dialed. I lifted it to my ear, listening to the tinny ring. It rang once, and I breathed. Again. It was only after a click and the recorded voice that I started to feel embarrassed, not even that I was running to him, but the reason why. Ishikawa hadn't even said anything, and I was already running to Tomohiro for help, when he had one hundred times the burden to carry that I did and more to lose from dropping it.

He'd carried this frightening knowledge with him since elementary school, and I couldn't even carry it through an evening.

I sighed and slipped my *keitai* into my purse, pushed the bathroom door open and headed down the hall to our karaoke room.

I crashed into Ishikawa in the hallway.

"Sorry!" I said out of instinct, before I saw his white-blond hair and his stark-white apron.

He smirked. "Yuuto know you're on a date with Tanaka?"

"Get a life," I said and tried to push past him. But then I saw the switchblade in his hand. He snicked it shut and shoved it into his pocket. "What the hell?" I said.

"You didn't see anything," he said, but I saw how his hand was shaking, just a little bit. He kept checking over his shoulder.

"Ishikawa—"

"Just get back in your karaoke room, okay?" He pushed my shoulder in the direction of the door.

"Watch it!" I said, startled.

He breathed out slowly through his teeth, the sigh sounding like *sssssss*. Then he said quietly, "I'm waiting for someone. So could you just get inside?" The edge of his tattoo was startling against the white of his uniform.

"You're going to attack someone?" I whispered.

Ishikawa stared at me, annoyed. "No, stupid. It's just, you know, in case."

"Yuu doesn't know, does he?" I said. "How far in you're getting."

He didn't answer me. After a moment he glanced down the empty hall again, his fingers curling into a loose fist.

"Ishikawa."

His eyes snapped to mine, and in them I saw the fear he was trying to hide. "Look, it's too late to worry about that now. It would be a lot easier if he'd admit what he was and help me."

I paled. "What do you mean?"

"Never mind," he said, but I already knew what he meant. Tomohiro was right—Ishikawa *was* suspicious he was a Kami. "Just get in there."

"Fine," I said, but my heart was pounding. I opened the door of our room to the sound of Tanaka's tone-deaf singing. I tried to shake off the icy reality that froze my thoughts solid. I couldn't let on to Ishikawa that I knew—ever. And yet I couldn't think about anything else, the wagtail falling in my thoughts over and over, filling me with cold dread.

"Maybe we should go," I told Tanaka.

"One more song," begged Yuki.

"Listen, Ishikawa is…" But no one was listening to me over the loud music. I opened the door a crack and peered down the hallway. Ishikawa had vanished.

The song finished up and after I pleaded with them, we finally packed up to go. I saw Ishikawa walking down the far end of the hallway, a tray of drinks balanced on his arm. I guess whatever meeting it was had gone well and without puncture wounds.

But what about the meetings that didn't?

On our way home, we passed a shrine in Mabuchi. The gate was locked, but floodlights illuminated the orange-and-green arch on the other side.

"Oh!" Tanaka said. "We should pray for the midterms coming up."

"It's closed," Yuki said, motioning at the gate.

"You going to let a gate stand in the way of good marks? Come on!" He started toward the stone wall.

"Count me out." Yuki giggled, holding her hand over her mouth.

"Katie, you coming?"

"I'm fine."

"You can pray for your kendo tournament."

"I'll stay here with Yuki," I said. I didn't mention that I would feel like a hypocrite breaking into a shrine to pray.

"Fine," Tanaka said. His friend lifted him over the wall and we stood on our toes to watch him over the top of the gate. He bobbed down the gravel path toward the shrine, where a rope thicker than his fist hung down from a giant rusty bell. Tanaka dug in his pockets for change, and the coins rattled as they spilled into the big wooden tithe box. He grabbed hold of the fat, braided rope and swung it vio lently from side to side, until the bell jingled and clanged. He clapped his hands twice and bowed his head, but then a light flicked on from an adjacent building and he raced for the gate, laughing and gasping as his friends pulled him back over. We took off, thundering down the streets to outrun the robed, groggy priest.

"You rang it too loudly!" Yuki shrieked between terrified giggles.

"That's so the *kami* will hear me!" Tanaka shouted back, and I wondered if anyone would want to get their attention if they knew the truth, what they were capable of. What had really happened to Koji.

What could happen to me.

I wasn't sure I could ever go back to Toro Iseki again, knowing Tomohiro's drawings really were alive and possibly wanted me dead, or at least maimed by pointy teeth.

On top of that, as dumb as it seemed in comparison, I was afraid of seeing him after he'd held me. Even if I'd felt the shift from rivalry to friendship, opening like *sakura* buds on the trees, it didn't make it any easier to face the blossom it had become. We felt the same before and the same after, but something had changed, so that when I thought about him my arms prickled with goose bumps.

I watched the senior kendo drills in the last practice before the ward tournament, Tomohiro and Ishikawa moving in unison through the practice katas. I wondered how they could claim to be best friends when there was so much darkness between them; I wondered if Tomohiro would be pissed at Ishikawa for the you're-weak speech he'd given me. He'd better be.

Saturday finally arrived, and despite my pestering not to, Diane came to watch the tournament. She probably thought it was what mothers did, but she looked too genuine to just be filling a role. Anyway, she made a better aunt than a mother.

Maybe the pieces were starting to fit after all.

I knelt in *seiza* with the other juniors, waiting for our turn to present katas. Okay, so maybe I wasn't the most elegant *kendouka* out there, but I was proud that I'd come from unknowing to knowing, and I performed every move carefully. I stepped with calculation, striking my *shinai* with loud cracks of bamboo. I stared down my opponent from behind the bars of my *men* and felt alive. I saw Diane's jaw drop in the stands, but it only made me scream harder.

In the corner of my eye, I saw the senior match unfolding across the host gym; the way the student moved, I knew it was Tomohiro. A red scarf dangled from the back of his *men,* but the referees moved their red-and-white flags so quickly that before I could see whether he'd made a hit, my eyes flickered back to my own opponent.

Seeing Tomohiro brought everything back, and my heart raced under the hard shell of the *dou* laced around my chest. The secret, so dangerous I could never share it with anyone, had left me with nightmares about the Yakuza kidnapping my mom—until I woke drenched in sweat and remembered she was already gone.

I couldn't stand it anymore—feeling helpless, useless, trapped in the bars of my *men* cage. Knowing the ink was after me, knowing that one wrong word could put the Yakuza on my tail. I shrieked at the top of my lungs and cracked the *shinai* down on my opponent.

"Point!" the referees shouted, and three white flags lifted from their sides. The match ended; I lost, but damn that point felt good. Now I knew why Tomohiro had taken refuge in kendo.

My set completed, I untied my helmet. Sweat trickled down my neck from under my headband, so I pulled that off as well and wiped at my face.

I heard a familiar *kiai* shout. Tomohiro.

I moved quietly along the lines of watching students. Watanabe saw me and motioned at an empty spot where I knelt to watch the match, my *shinai* lined up at my side.

The guy fighting Tomohiro, a white ribbon tied to his back, was about half a foot taller and his shoulders broader.

His footwork was tidy and fast, and he dodged attacks as if Tomohiro were stuck to the floor.

The guy's *kiai* rattled through my rib cage and turned my insides to jelly. I'd heard lots of different shouts in practice, and they came in all kinds; Ishikawa's was one of the worst, the way it shook around in my head. But this guy's was controlled, less ruthless than Ishikawa's. It was chilling, although it was hard to put my finger on exactly why. Maybe because it was so cold, so emotionally vacant, like this match wasn't even an effort for him. Like he would snap you in two without a second thought.

"Point!" the referee shouted. My eyes flicked over to see the white flags rise. I wondered if the humidity in the gym had finally gotten to Tomohiro. The only opponent who ever gave him trouble was Ishikawa. But Watanabe had warned us about the caliber of the Katakou School team, and I watched with dread as the match ended.

Tomohiro missed a final *tsuki* hit and lost the match.

He pulled the *men* from his shoulders, and Ishikawa handed him a bottle of water. He gulped it down, the sweat rolling down his neck, spikes of copper hair poking out of his headband.

There was a final match—Ishikawa against the guy Tomohiro couldn't beat. Tomohiro walked over and knelt beside me, resting his *shinai* on the floor with a clack.

"He's tough," he whispered, and I felt the heat of his breath on my ear. He said it just like that, as if nothing else had happened between us. I hated him for the way he could be so casual. I also hated him for making my insides melt just by sitting next to me.

"He's from Katakou, right?" I asked, pretending I didn't feel awkward.

He nodded. "Their star *kendouka.* He placed sixth in the nationals last year. Takahashi."

So this was the famous Takahashi. "Doesn't look that special."

Tomohiro snorted. "I think that's part of the act."

Ishikawa and Takahashi were circling each other now. They held each other at sword's length, *shinai* clacking against each other as they stepped round and round.

Ishikawa lunged. It was a move that had scored a point against me in practice, but Takahashi parried and struck for the *men.* Ishikawa slipped out of the way, retreating across the arena until they were apart again.

"Okay, so maybe he's good," I admitted.

Tomohiro sat forward, eyes narrowed. I knew he was looking at the way Takahashi moved, the mistakes Tomohiro had made that had led to his defeat.

But Takahashi seemed flawless as he parried Ishikawa's next hit, and the next, and the time ticked by without either having a single point.

Ishikawa stumbled, wavering from foot to foot.

"It's the heat," Tomohiro murmured. Takahashi noticed, too, and lunged, swinging from the right.

"Point!" shouted the referees, lifting three white flags.

"Shit." Tomohiro cupped his hands around his mouth. "Sato! *Ganbare!*"

Takahashi sprung forward. He leaned a little too far and Ishikawa smacked his *shinai* into the *dou.*

"Point!" Three red flags flashed upward.

"Yes!" Watanabe-sensei clapped from the sidelines.

Takahashi shifted to the left and then struck to the right, but Ishikawa blocked just in time. The loud crack echoed to the rafters.

Takahashi didn't let up. He lunged over and over, forcing Ishikawa into a corner. *Crack, crack, crack.* The jarring *kiais* and the pounding of feet on the floor.

Takahashi swung; Ishikawa sidestepped and brought his *shinai* down hard. This was his chance.

The sword exploded on impact, huge splinters of wood spraying across the floor. The leather binding the slats together unraveled as what was left of the *shinai* connected with Takahashi's head.

The shards clattered onto the floor, into a tiny pool of dark blood.

The match stopped instantly. A tournament medic ran forward to check the two were all right and to find the source of the blood.

Only it wasn't blood. I could see that, even if they couldn't.

Because it was like my pen all over again.

I glared at Tomohiro. He only shook his head like it wasn't his fault.

I started making a mental list of schools I could transfer to.

Ishikawa stooped to the tiny puddle and ran his fingers through. He looked over at Tomohiro. Takahashi followed his gaze and looked at us.

My heart almost burst from my chest. Could they tell I knew something? Did they know it was us? If they did, Ishikawa was going to have a *lot* of questions.

The medic finished her inspection—clean bill of health and no bleeding, surprise, surprise. The audience burst into applause. The referees deliberated for a tense moment and finally lifted their flags.

Red.

Watanabe gave Ishikawa hell for being lazy about taking care of his *shinai,* but behind the speech, his eyes were shining. Ishikawa was the winner and advanced to the prefecture finals. And so did Tomohiro, who scraped by thanks to his other matches.

Takahashi unbound his headband, and his jet-black hair flopped down around his face. His angled bangs almost covered one eye and trailed down to his ear, pierced with a shiny silver ring. He tucked two thick blond highlights behind his ears.

Oh my god.

It's Jun.

My face turned as red as the flags. I looked away in case Tomohiro got the wrong idea, but he was already walking over to congratulate Ishikawa.

All I could think about was the ink. Was this my life now, to be punctuated with drips of ink wherever I went? And had the ink spilled the truth to Ishikawa?

And Jun. Takahashi Jun shaking hands with Tomohiro and Ishikawa, the three of them chatting there, not realizing they were standing on the edge of a dangerous cliff. Maybe Tomohiro knew; maybe he'd gone to smooth things over.

He's here, the boy who draws things. Sketches that look alive, I'd told him. *You look flustered again.*

I felt like I'd fallen into a cold river. I'd told Jun about Tomohiro's drawings. He'd put it together and we'd be found out.

I watched them laugh as they chatted.

I was overreacting, I knew it. Why would Jun invent something impossible?

No one would believe what I knew. Even I barely believed it.

So why was I shaking?

9

A muffled chime rose from my book bag. I'd forgotten to put my *keitai* in manner mode, and Yuki raised her eyebrows at me.

"Good thing it's lunch," she said as I ruffled through the bag. "They have a way of never coming back after Suzuki-sensei confiscates them."

"Sorry," I said absentmindedly. I pulled the phone out and flipped it open to the text.

Talked to Ishikawa. He won't bother you again. Join me today. I'll wait for you there. —Yuu

"From Tomo-kun?" Tanaka chimed in. I snapped the *keitai* closed and slipped it back into my bag.

"Not your business," I said, and he grinned.

"You know, Katie," said Yuki quietly. Her eyes were round and sad, and I knew what she would say. I'd thought about it myself after the kendo match. "Please don't get involved with someone like him. What he did to his friend… And you saw what he did to Myu. Even Yuu's friends are bad news."

"He was always a good guy," said Tanaka thoughtfully.

"He got into a lot of trouble, but when it came down to the wire, he always did the right thing."

"Right," I said. "And you were right about Koji, Tanaka. It was an accident."

"Hai?" Tanaka's jaw hung open, and I realized what I'd said. It wasn't like I could tell him what had really happened—now what?

"Um. They broke into a construction site, and there was a guard dog." More lies, but closer to the truth than Tomohiro stabbing him.

"I knew it!" he shouted.

I took a deep breath and turned to Yuki. "And he didn't cheat on Myu, you know. The pregnant girl? She's a family friend, and he's only trying to help her." There was a pause while Tanaka and Yuki absorbed this.

"Well, even if that's true," Yuki said doubtfully, "you saw the way he broke up with her. It wasn't pretty." It was true; he'd been heartless to her, cold and ugly. I'd spent so much time remembering the way the drawing looked at me and not enough thinking about the dark look in Tomohiro's eyes as he broke up with Myu, the way he'd slouched against the door frame while she wept. I knew he'd been lying, but even then—that was cruel.

Maybe they were right. I had to admit it had been on my mind since the tournament—okay, so since I'd learned he was a Kami. Did I really need the nightmares he came with? But every time I decided to step away, my heart twisted.

"It's not like we're a serious couple or anything," I said. "He hasn't even confessed." But I knew how ridiculous I sounded. If his phone hadn't gone off that time, what would he have said? What would I have said?

"Not serious at all. He's just sending you texts for a date,"

Tanaka said. I picked up his packet of *furikake* seasoning and smacked him with it.

"Sonna wake nai jan!" I whined with a Japanese accent. *It's not like that.* But from the look of them, I'd already lost the argument. I took my black chopsticks and lifted the left-over croquettes from my *bentou* into my mouth. The taste of peanut-butter sandwiches had drifted away with my old life. I wondered who I was then, when I couldn't speak or read or eat, totally immobilized by the change in my world. Vines were entangling the hole in my heart, buds sprouting on the outskirts. There was still a void, a pocket of emptiness. But around it, my heart was blooming.

Tomohiro sat in his usual place beside the Yayoi house, his notebook resting on his pulled-up knees. That was the only thing that was the same. Clouds of shimmering dust encircled him, wisps of inky swirls that glinted in the sun-light. They curled in slow motion, spreading around him like waves of fireflies.

I gasped. He heard me and looked up, a grin plastered on his face, and I began to understand how much effort it had been to keep all this from me. This was why he'd al-ways stopped so abruptly in the middle of a sketch, why he'd scraped those desperate lines across the paper. It was to keep me safe from the truth, when all the time this was supposed to be *his* safe haven.

"Katie," he said, his hands still. The clouds faded and swirled into nothingness as his pen stopped.

"Does it always do that?" I asked, walking forward slowly and clutching the handles of my bag.

He laughed. "No. Don't you think the Calligraphy Club would've noticed?"

"That's where I come in, right? Where you lose control like the kendo match?"

"That," he said, "was not my fault."

"I've heard that before."

"*Oi.* I'm serious."

"Okay," I said. "So if it wasn't you, then who was it?"

There was silence. My jaw dropped.

"Me?"

"Maybe," he said.

"No, no, you're the Kami." I panicked.

"But you're the one making the ink do weird things. Well… extra weird."

"Look, I've had enough, okay?" I said, feeling sick to my stomach. "I don't want ink following me around. I don't want Yakuza following me around. You need to get this thing under control or I need to switch schools." It was one thing to watch him draw things here, but the idea of the ink permeating my own life, never knowing when it was going to show up…

He smiled.

"Luckily I have a plan," he said. "The wagtail that attacked the others—I couldn't stop it. I've been thinking about the way Takahashi Jun was in control in the kendo match. You know, like he wouldn't let me see what attack was coming next, not a shift of body weight or a glance or anything, and yet he had his moves planned out, everything calculated. If I could learn to keep my thoughts so focused and hidden, maybe I could take control of what I draw. Here, look what I brought."

He lifted a velvet drawstring pouch out of his book bag and slipped its contents into the palm of his hand. His eyes shone as he held them out.

"A bottle of ink," I said. "And a paintbrush. For calligraphy?"

"It's too dangerous for me to paint," he said. "But maybe over time I can use them again."

He rested them gently on the grass and shook his head, tossing his bangs out of his eyes. A useless gesture, because the minute he leaned forward to the notebook, they slid back again.

"This isn't much of a plan," I said. "Focusing your thoughts? Super Zen, but I need the ink to leave *me* alone."

"The ink isn't always bad," he said. "I mean, it's dangerous, but sometimes it's beautiful. At first, I never wanted you to know. I thought I could never tell you. But now I can show you."

He moved his pen in a broad stroke, and then another. And as he drew the lines more quickly, the firefly specks of ink appeared again, shimmering like oil as they rippled in the air.

He drew a butterfly, but its movements blurred on the page. The closer I looked at it, the more my head ached.

"It's because we think it's impossible," he said. "So our brain tells us it isn't moving. Like an optical illusion or something. It used to give me migraines all the time." And the more I watched it, the queasier I got. I had to turn away. Tomohiro smiled, but his eyes never moved from the paper.

And suddenly, as he moved his pen to sketch the wings of another butterfly, the first spiraled upward from the page. It was colorless, with jagged sketched outlines. A stream of ink trailed behind it like a firework, shimmering in shades of black and dark plum. I watched as the butterfly lifted on the breeze, the membranes of its wings thin and transparent. I glanced down at the page, and it was there, too, like the flying one was only a copy.

Three smaller butterflies rose amid a shower of black sparks, beating their wings as they fluttered through the air.

And the whole time Tomohiro grinned and sketched more and more, until a cloud of them hovered in the sky above us.

I watched with my hand to my mouth. Almost fifty of them, swirling around each other as their trails crossed and intertwined in slow, gleaming pinwheels. Such terrifying beauty.

And then Tomohiro scratched through the drawings and they dropped one by one, like black cherry petals crumpling to the ground. It was so horrible that tears welled up in my eyes.

"Don't kill them," I whispered. Tomohiro's eyes widened and he stared at me for a moment.

"I didn't kill them," he said. "They're not alive. They're just drawings."

"But it's horrible to see them fall like that."

"Katie," he said gently, and I felt his warm palm curl around my shoulder. His smooth voice was calm, and he gazed into my eyes through the wisps of his bangs. I felt like the butterflies had tumbled into my rib cage. "It's dangerous not to call them back. If they left Toro and someone else saw them…" He sighed. "I can't let anyone know. It would be the end of me."

"Then stop drawing, Yuu," I said. "Don't bring them to life."

"They aren't alive."

"How do you know?"

"I just know. When I look at them, I can feel them somehow, like they're fluttering around in my head. So I know they're a thought of mine, not real. They're part of me."

It was too awful. Tears rolled down my cheeks and I stood to leave. Tomohiro stumbled to his feet, the notebook slapping closed as it fell off his lap.

"Katie," he said, and I hesitated. "I never asked for this…

ability, you know. It's not something I can walk away from." I looked into his eyes, which seemed deeper and darker than before. "I even have nightmares," he said. "It sounds dumb, but I can't get away from this. I wake up and there's ink dripping on my floor. And I've lost so much because I'm a Kami. I can't lose any more. I can't lose—"

He didn't have to say it.

We stood there for a minute and I really, truly pitied him. He couldn't walk away from it. It was true. And right now he didn't look at all like the jerk Myu had slapped.

He blinked and shook his head. "It was wrong of me to say that," he said. "You have a choice. You can walk away from this, but please just promise you won't tell anyone."

Something about the two sides of Tomo clicked in my head. It was like the sketch in his notebook and the butterfly that lifted; there was some sort of difference there, something between his pleading eyes and his arrogant slouching.

My eyes snapped to his. "This is why you broke up with Myu."

He paused.

"Did she find out about you?"

Another hesitation. "No."

"But she was going to, wasn't she?"

"—yes."

"Did you make it all up? Did you pretend to cheat? Did you pretend to be a jerk, like you do at school?"

"I wasn't a jerk, Katie."

"You were an ass," I said.

"Oi." He sounded annoyed.

"And you let her believe you cheated on her, didn't you?"

He shrugged, leaned back and slouched into the wooden house.

"Things with Myu were breaking down anyway. Too

many questions. I drew a few sketches of Shiori in case anyone went snooping and then just happened to forget my notebook in the *genkan*. I didn't say anything either way and it worked in my favor."

"You're doing it right now," I said.

"Huh?"

"You're being a jerk."

"Am I?"

"Yes."

He blinked at me, his lips curving into a sly smile.

"Tomo, I'm serious. Stop it." It slipped out, just like that. I'd switched to his first name, a shortened one even, and made whatever it was we had closer. He heard it the minute I did, and his face started to turn beet-red. "Anyway," I babbled, "why would you do that to Myu? That's cold."

"Because," he said in a gentle voice, "I had to do it, to protect her."

"You could've been less of a jerk about it."

"If I'd been less of a jerk, she wouldn't hate me like she does now. And I needed her to hate me." And I heard the guilt in his voice, the carefully thought out sacrifice. I saw the way his eyes softened when he talked about her. And despite all the denial I could muster, something flipped over in my stomach when I heard him talk about her like that.

"So why not push me away like you did Myu?" I asked. The heat rushed to my cheeks. I wasn't jealous. I wasn't. I just thought he was being stupid.

He didn't answer at first, and he stared at the ground, the corners of his mouth curved up like he was laughing at me. I wanted to smack him and walk away, but first I wanted an answer.

"You already know, don't you?" he said eventually. "It's

not an easy burden, is it? I didn't want to involve you, but the ink is tied to you. I've known that since— I know. Anyway, how was I supposed to know you would come to Toro Iseki when I was supposed to be at a funeral?"

"Well, don't you think it was going to happen sooner or later? I'm here every week, watching you draw stuff and cross it out."

"Maa." His eyes flashed up and caught mine. "I guess deep down I wanted you to know," he said.

My heart pounded in my ears. "Why me?"

"First, because the ink is hunting you down. I can't keep you in the dark and protect you at the same time. You're part of it somehow. And second, because..."

He walked toward me slowly, his leather shoes pressing down the long grasses. I could feel his breath on my cheek as he leaned forward. My eyes fluttered shut, but I forced them open again. His breath was hot against my lips, and his face blotted out the sky, so I could see nothing but his eyes and the pores of his skin.

"Because," he said in tones of honey and velvet, "I've always had to push away people I cared about. You're the only one who ever pushed back."

The words brushed against my lips and sent the butterflies tumbling again. *He's going to kiss me, he's going to—*

He leaned back and patted me on the head. My cheeks turned tomato-red as I glared at him.

He blinked and stared back, looking completely innocent.

"What?" he said. He took another look at me and burst out laughing. "Did you think I was going to...?" He folded his arms, pressing his fingertips against the insides of his elbows as he laughed.

"I'm glad you think it's so funny," I fumed. Why the hell could he always pull one over on me?

He bit his lip, trying to stop laughing, and bobbed his head at me. "You're right," he said. "I'm sorry. Let me draw something to make it up to you."

"Draw yourself getting smacked in the face."

"Katie," he protested, in the smooth voice he used when he said my name. I said nothing.

A wagtail chirped, and I turned to watch it fly across the clearing, into the ring of trees. And then I felt warmth as Tomohiro stepped forward and wrapped his arms around my shoulders, pressing his head against mine, his chest solid against my back. Tufts of his copper hair tickled against my neck, and his skin was warm, the sound of his breathing calm.

"Warui," he whispered in apology, and I knew then that I couldn't live without him, even when he was infuriating. Which was pretty much all the time.

My only chance was to stop the ink from reacting to me. There had to be a way. I couldn't just bail on him—I had to save us both.

I couldn't walk away, and I knew it. Not until we both could.

Three weeks until summer vacation, and each time we visited Toro Iseki, Tomohiro's ambitions grew. He drew birds and trees, turtles and rabbits. I pleaded with him to try to scratch the drawings out slowly, to see if it could be less traumatic to watch, but nothing seemed to help. Everything keeled over like its soul had been sucked from its body. And the turtle had time to take a chunk out of my finger before it collapsed, the ingrate, so I gave up on my humane-sketching plans. Tomohiro still insisted the creatures were just thoughts, so that made me feel a little better. So did searching recipes for turtle soup.

"They're just extensions of me, I think."

"So which part of you wanted to bite me?" I sneered.

Wrong thing to say. His eyes took on this fiery look and he gave me a wicked grin.

"Okay, grow up. I did not mean *that*."

"Oh, please. It's obvious how you feel about me." He ran a hand through his hair. "Can't say I blame you."

"Ugh," I said. "And so modest, too. That's super attractive."

"Well, it must be working," he said, "because you're the one coming on to me."

"I am not coming on to you! Your stupid pen pal bit me."

"And I took him out for it."

"Well, thanks."

His eyes shone as he curled his hand around mine, and my heart almost stopped. "Anytime."

Yuki invited me to go with her family to Miyajima Island for a couple weeks of summer break. Her older brother was working there, and she pleaded with me to go, too, so she wouldn't be bored out of her mind.

The humidity of the Japanese summer wiped out any energy I'd had for kendo, and I could barely make it through practice drills. But Tomohiro and Ishikawa did the hundred push-ups without complaint, completing round after round of *kiri-kaeshi* as we looked on, dabbing our faces with the handkerchiefs everyone carried around because it was so ridiculously humid. The sweat dripped down their backs as they fought without their *men* on, their headbands damp and their hair slicked down to their necks.

"How come you and Ishikawa dye your hair?" I asked as

Tomohiro chugged back a water bottle. He wiped his mouth with the back of his arm.

"It's Ishikawa's strategy," he said, loud enough for him to hear. "He figures he might blind the opponent with his ugly mop."

"Shut up," Ishikawa said, but the corners of his mouth tugged in a grin.

"So why is yours red?"

"White and red, right?" said Ishikawa. "Because we're rivals." He grabbed Tomohiro in a headlock and they both grinned as they fought. I wondered what Tomohiro had said to Ishikawa, because he seemed like a different person, too. Outside of kendo, they both slouched, looked badass and, in Ishikawa's case, got into a lot of serious trouble. But somehow wearing the *bogu* armor and covering their faces with the *men* actually unmasked them and put them at ease. They were really themselves here, and Ishikawa and I somehow came to a truce. He stopped acting like a jerk, and I pretended his threats had never happened. Every now and then I still caught him glaring at me, though, so I avoided him when I could.

You're keeping him from his destiny. The words haunted me. But he didn't know for sure Tomohiro was a Kami. He only suspected it, and we had to keep it that way.

Watanabe-sensei announced a special kendo retreat, mandatory for those proceeding to the prefecture competition. From our school, only Ishikawa, Tomohiro, two senior girls and one junior boy would attend. Takahashi Jun from Katakou would be there, too. I still couldn't believe he was the same Jun I'd met on the train. He already knew there was a strange boy at my school who drew weird sketches. In my thoughts I pleaded that he wouldn't make the connection to the ink, that he wouldn't question the puddle at the tournament. But then I reminded myself that no one knew about the Kami anymore anyway. There was nothing to put together at all.

That week the school set up a big *sasa* tree by the office. The bamboo leaves splayed out like a Christmas tree, and students crowded a nearby table lined with neatly stacked papers.

"Tanabata," Yuki told me as she chose a soft yellow piece.

"Tanabata?"

"The lovers' festival. Two stars in the sky meet only at this time of year, and the rest of the year they're forced to be apart. When the lovers are reunited, our wishes can come true."

I thought about Tomohiro and his kendo retreat, how he would slave away in the heat while Yuki and I splashed around on the beach. But even when we were together, we had to keep a distance, at least until I figured out how to stop whatever was going on with the ink.

"So what are you wishing for?" I said.

"A boyfriend." Yuki grinned.

"You're going to write that?"

"No, no," she said. "I'm writing good grades and health, like everyone else." She took her slip of yellow paper and wrapped it around one of the branches. "What about you?" she said, offering me the pen. "You already have a boyfriend, so..."

I'd stopped denying it. It wasn't worth the effort. After Tomohiro had held me like he had the other day, there was something in his eyes when he looked at me. And even if I wasn't sure about the label, I knew we were connected now, that we shared a special bond.

"You going to wish for good grades?" Yuki said. I stared thoughtfully at the tree. Then I chose a blue paper, dark enough that students would have to strain to read my words. I wrote in English to try to keep the wish to myself.

I hope Mom has found peace.

Yuki went silent when she saw it, unsure of what to say. I didn't blame her; I didn't know what to say, either.

I took a piece of the yarn and tied my wish to the tree, on a lower branch where it would go unnoticed.

The tree ballooned with wishes as the week went past. Tanaka wrote his wish at the end of the week. *I wish my sister could cook.* Yuki and I raised our eyebrows.

"Did you see my lunches this week?" he said, tapping his finger on the paper for emphasis.

"If you flunk out of high school and have to eat ramen for the rest of your life, it'll be your own fault," I said. "You wasted your wish."

"Obviously you haven't tried my sister's *onigiri,*" Tanaka said. He threaded the yarn through the end of the paper and looked for a spot.

"You waited too long," said Yuki. "The tree's full."

"Here," I said. "Put it beside mine."

I stooped down and found mine quickly enough, the English writing standing out amid the blocky kanji.

"Here it is," I said, reaching my hand out for the twirling paper. But there was a new scribble on it, not in my handwriting. I pulled the tag forward, squinting to read the faint reply to my wish.

Mine, too.

Tears brimmed in my eyes and I tried to blink them back. I dropped my paper before the other two could read it and did my best to smile with Yuki as Tanaka tied his wish next to mine.

10

I grabbed my ticket and hopped on the Roman bus down to Toro Iseki. I'd stayed behind to clean the classroom and had to make up time. It was way too humid to bike anyway. I wiped my face with my handkerchief.

Since Monday, Tomohiro had been grinning at me. His tall figure had loomed in the doorway of our classroom at lunch. He'd waited patiently as the class went from chatting, to noticing, to mumbling and whispering, and finally to tapping me on the shoulder. I'd walked over to the door slowly, the eyes of my classmates burning into my back. Tomohiro seemed to enjoy my embarrassment, which didn't surprise me.

"Are you coming on Wednesday?" he said when I reached the doorway. I could hear the whispers mounting, so I slipped into the hallway and out of sight. Okay, except for the row of windows along our classroom that was suddenly crowded with faces.

"Tomo, we always go on Wednesdays," I said in a hushed voice.

"I know," he said. "I just want to make sure you're going."

"Of course."

"It's the last time before summer break," he said.

"I know."

"I promise I won't draw a turtle."

"Good," I said, looking over my shoulder at my classmates. Their heads dipped below the windows.

He lifted my fingers in his, and the sudden touch made me turn. He flipped my hands over in his, looking for the bite mark where the turtle had snapped me.

"I'm okay now," I said, staring at the top of his head as he scanned my hands gently.

"Good," he said and lifted my fingers to his mouth. His smooth lips brushed over them softly, and the students at the windows whooped like idiots. Then he let go and turned down the hallway, his leather bag slung over his shoulder.

It wasn't just the last time we'd go to Toro Iseki before summer vacation. They'd finished the renovations, and the site was opening to the public at the beginning of August. Tomohiro would have to find a new safe haven to practice his art. So far, we'd come up with Mount Fuji and Antarctica.

I ducked under the chain-link fence and into the mini forest. The breeze pushed the humidity against my body in waves.

Then I heard the chimes.

There were at least forty of them hanging in the tree above me, little Japanese wind chimes tinkling in the hot gasp of wind, their papers floating and rippling as they twisted back and forth. Most *furin* chimes in Japan were bright summer colors, but these were black-and-white with jagged edges, so I knew Tomohiro had drawn them into existence. Some of the chimes sounded mournful, likely the drawings that had gone wrong, but the sound of them all jingling together was one of the most beautiful things I'd ever heard.

He was sitting in the grass, his notebook balanced on his

lap. I watched him for a moment before he realized I'd arrived. He looked up at the sky, the clouds drifting lazily above. He'd loosened the tie around his neck and rolled his sleeves up to his elbows. The top buttons of his shirt were unbuttoned, exposing the defined edges of his collarbone. He seemed lost in the sound of the chimes, and I hesitated, listening to them, too.

Then the pollen of the flowers caught in my nose and I sneezed. He whirled around, his eyes wide until he realized it was me.

"Okaeri," he said, and as much as I'd felt awkward when Diane said it to me, when Tomohiro said it I got goose bumps.

"I'm a bit late," I apologized.

"I'll say," he said with a laugh. "Come see what I'm drawing for you today."

I walked forward and sat beside him in the grass. He opened his notebook, and a half-finished sketch draped across the page. I stared with wide eyes.

"You're serious."

He just grinned and pulled the cap from his pen. I rested my hand on his arm.

"Don't you think people will notice that?"

"In Toro Iseki?" he said. I just stared at him. "Katie, this is our last chance to try this. We won't have another opportunity like this for who knows how long. I want to try."

"You're totally crazy," I said. "It could trample us."

But he placed the nib of his pen on the paper and started filling in the sketch. He drew in the eye, a dark pool of ink on the page. He filled out the ear and the mane, the muzzle and the long, strong flanks that whizzed across the page as he drew them. The sketch tossed its head and turned to bite a fly off its withers.

There was a gentle thud in the grass, and another, and then the horse stepped out from behind a Yayoi hut. There was a ghostly, vacant look in its eyes, and its mane was as jagged as Tomohiro's hurried pen strokes.

Tomohiro drew faster and faster, his own eyes growing vacant and strange like the horse's. He was scribbling in details, fetlocks above the hooves and muscles trailing down the horse's legs.

"I think that's enough," I said.

"Huh?" He broke away like I'd snapped him out of a dream. I pointed to the horse sniffling at the grass with his scribbled black muzzle.

He whispered, "I did it."

He rose to his feet, placing the notebook gently on the grass.

"Stay here," he warned. I knelt, ready to tear the drawing to shreds if I had to. The horse lifted its head high as Tomohiro approached, and then it swallowed back a distressed whinny. Tomohiro whispered as he stepped closer. The horse pawed the ground, then lowered its head.

I watched him reach his gentle hands to the horse's muzzle, and I waited for it to take a big chunk out of him. My fingers bent the corner of the drawing as I waited for the jaw to open.

But the horse merely nuzzled his hands, drank in the spiced smell of him and turned back to the grass. Tomohiro turned to face me, his face brighter than when he won a kendo match.

"Come on!" he shouted. I ripped the page out of the notebook and folded it into my pocket. Just in case.

He lifted me onto the horse's back, then climbed a railing in front of the Yayoi hut and leaped on behind me. Swirls of ink spilled into the grass from the horse's hooves and twisted into the air from his mane. The horse's skin felt like crinkled paper, but he was warm and alive beneath that thin hide. His hair flopped in slow motion, pulled by the wisps of ink that radiated from it. I pressed a tentative hand into the wiry mane and twisted my fingers through the warm, oily ink. The swirls dissipated as my fingers slid through, curving away into new clouds.

"Ready?" Tomohiro said, but he didn't wait for my answer. He kicked in his heels and the horse lurched forward. I almost fell into its neck. I tangled my hands into the mane and gripped its stomach hard with my legs.

The Yayoi huts blurred around us as we galloped forward. Tomohiro's shoulders pressed against mine as his bare arms reached for the mane to steady himself. The humid air pressed against my skin as we raced through Toro Iseki, Tomohiro's laugh ringing in my ears.

We galloped to the southern edge of forest, where the horse slowed to a trot. He wound through the trees and broke through the other side, where the newer excavations were taking place. I held my breath as the horse narrowly missed the pits in the dirt, the tools sprawled around the site. When we reached the end of the clearing, the back of the Toro Iseki Museum, Tomohiro dug his heels in and the horse turned, galloping north again. We went around so many times that everything blurred, everything but the whizzing of the air as it went past and Tomohiro's breath against my cheek.

He hadn't thought to draw any reins or saddle on the horse, but somehow the horse went exactly where Tomohiro wanted him to. Maybe he was right that the horse wasn't entirely alive but an extension of him. Tomohiro tensed and the horse reacted; he turned his head left and the horse followed. It suddenly hit me how much control he had and how little I did. I had no choice but to trust him, and the feeling left me unsettled.

The horse began to cough and shake with the effort, ink trickling down his white neck like black sweat. Tomohiro halted him by the notebook with no effort. A giant grin plastered on his face, he leaped down and I followed, glad to be on the ground and in control again.

"What did you think?" He laughed, stroking the horse's nose.

"Amazing," I said, but anxiety began to spread through my thoughts.

"I should have tried this earlier!"

"Yeah, but you practiced a lot to get to this point."

"And this is only the beginning of what I can draw," he said, and I saw in his eyes how giddy he was, how intoxicated by his own ability.

"We should take it slowly," I said. "Don't forget what happened to Koji." He held out his hand and I passed him the folded paper from my pocket. He collapsed on the grass and drew through the picture of the horse with his pen. The scraping sound almost made me sick.

The horse stretched his leg out to the front and lowered his head, resting his muzzle against his hoof. He sighed, a long shudder that rattled through his rib cage, and then his eyes lost the depth of their light. He collapsed on his side and dissolved into swirls of ink, nothing left on the grass but a sheen of oily black.

"Yeah, but I was too young then. Did you see it?" he said. "It didn't try to hurt anything. It was entirely under my control."

"Yeah," I said, but his tone was making me nervous. "Let's go have some melon ice to celebrate." But he didn't hear me.

He reached into his book bag and pulled out the velvet pouch, shaking the brush and inkwell into his hand.

Shivers ran up the back of my neck. "Tomo."

He pulled the lid from the ink and dipped in the brush.

"Tomo, stop." I stared, my skin pulsing with fear, my ears buzzing.

He flipped to a clean page in his notebook, and the bristles of the brush bent backward as he stroked the stark black across the paper. The ink sank in and spread in little tendrils of black, the pigment too thick for the notebook paper. He was like some kind of addict, completely lost to the thrill of it. He wasn't thinking straight. Whatever control he'd talked about, it was slipping—he'd never acted like this before, at least not with me.

"What are you drawing?" I said, my throat dry.

"You think the horse was amazing," he said, "but anyone can have that experience. I want to give you something that only Kami can feel. Something others can't do."

I watched him draw the expert curves, as if he'd only left calligraphy yesterday. The long strokes snaked across the paper as I desperately tried to guess what he was drawing. What could Kami have that other people couldn't? My mind raced.

I looked at his face, and his eyes startled me. They looked like the horse's, thick and ghostly, vacant of anything familiar. The eyes that had stared me down in the courtyard, that had lit up with his bright laugh in the café—they were gone, replaced by these alien pools of black that stared down at the paper with intensity.

His hand moved faster and faster, the strokes more and more desperate.

My voice was shaky, and I realized my hands were shaking, too. "Tomo, you're scaring me."

"The pen was too weak," he said, but the voice wasn't his. It was raspy, and he panted for breath as he painted faster and faster. "I see that now. It was just the reflection in the water."

"Stop it," I said and grabbed the end of the brush. My wrist hit the inkwell and it tipped over, pouring ink down the side of the notebook and onto the grass. But Tomohiro was stronger than me, and he kept drawing as I tried to pull the brush tip off the paper.

"You know what Kami can do?" he said in the raspy and desperate voice that wasn't his. "What Kami can do but others can't?"

He dropped his voice to a whisper.

"Fly."

He was drawing a dragon, long and angular, and it wriggled on the page like a snake, like the scrap I had picked up that day. The sun glinted on its mouth full of shiny teeth and my whole body went cold.

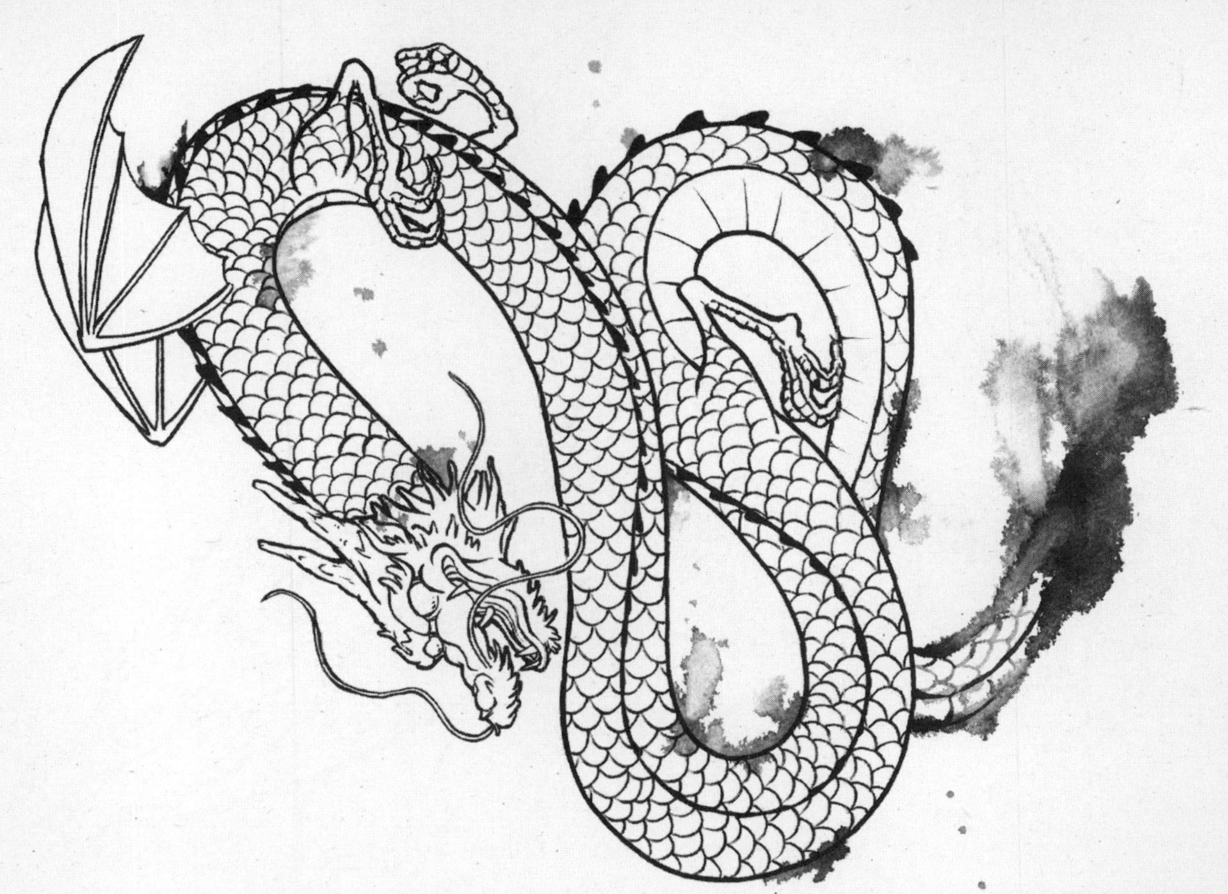

I struggled to snatch the brush from him, but it was like it didn't take any effort to fight me off. No way was I that weak, but it was like Tomohiro suddenly got stronger. A *lot* stronger. He stared down at the paper with his big, vacant eyes, a horrible grin twisting his lips.

And suddenly the dragon's jaws turned on the page, and with a blur they pushed through the paper and clenched down on Tomohiro's wrist.

Tomohiro shrieked as he wrenched his arm out of the dragon's razor teeth. The brush tumbled into the grass, forgotten as he grasped at his wrist. The dragon snapped his paper jaws over and over, just out of reach, while the jagged gash vanished under a torrent of blood, overflowing onto the paper and the ground, onto Tomohiro's clean white shirt. I screamed and reached for my handkerchief, ramming it against the slash and pressing until my fingertips turned white. Tomohiro kept shouting and shouting, but I couldn't hear the words over my own panic. It was like I'd gone deaf or forgotten all my Japanese. I couldn't make sense of anything he said. His eyes weren't vacant anymore but wide and filled with terror.

"The *kami!*" he shouted. "The *kami!*"

I stared as my handkerchief soaked up the blood, the pretty pattern on it staining a deep crimson.

"The *kami!*" he shouted again, and it finally registered.

The paper.

Dark clouds unfurled above, and rain pelted the clearing. Thunder rumbled and flashes of lightning shot through the sky.

"Destroy the drawing!" he shrieked. The blood leaked through the edges of my handkerchief.

I fumbled through the grass for the brush, the rain drenching through my shirt and my hair falling in tangles into my eyes. I screamed as my fingers ran through something wet. I lifted them up—ink.

With my fingers I drew thick lines through the dragon.

"Don't go near his mouth!" Tomohiro shouted. The drawing snapped at me as I sliced its tail from its body with a thick line of ink. The sketch moved so quickly that my head throbbed to watch. I wasn't used to it like Tomohiro, and I thought I might throw up. I hesitated, terrified, then drew a line through its rear legs.

Desperate, I ripped the whole page out and crumpled it, tearing it to shreds. But as the scraps fluttered from my hands, I could see the ink moving and twisting on them.

"It's not working!" I shouted through the thick rain. Tomohiro's copper hair was flattened to his head in awkward spikes. He'd mounded his handkerchief on top of mine, but the dark blood bloomed and spread across it.

"Give me the brush!" he shouted. I dropped to my hands and knees and searched for it in the grass.

A movement blurred where the horse had been, and I looked up. A thick coil of giant snake, wider than the belly of the stallion, wrapped around itself over and over, so that the mound was taller than Tomohiro. The jagged outlines of the snake soaked into long tendrils of ink toward the center of its crackly skin, and as it wound around, it looked like it slithered in two directions at once. It raised its huge head, antlers rising from the top of its silver snout.

The dragon Tomohiro had drawn.

At first I couldn't hear anything but my own scream. The beast stared at me with vacant eyes, its whiskers drooping low below its lips and hanging limp in the drenching rain. Swirls of ink lifted from its whole body, like steam off a horse in a morning mist.

"Katie, the brush!" Tomohiro shouted, but I stood paralyzed as the dragon stared at me.

Tomohiro moved his left hand desperately through the wet

grasses. The handkerchiefs he'd let go of dropped to the ground without the pressure of his hand to hold them there, and the blood streaked down his wrist and along his slender fingers.

The dragon lifted up like a boa ready to strike. Huge claws appeared from the mass of its coiled body, and it pressed them into the earth, bending its long legs. Ink-colored bristles spiked down its spine and twisted into sinewy wings, which it flapped back and forth as it got ready to pounce.

"Tomo!" I shrieked as his fingers closed around the paintbrush.

The dragon leaped up, uncoiling into the air. Tomohiro dove toward the scraps of the page and drew ugly lines through any he could find. High above, the dragon screeched and its leg fell off, dropping in the clearing with an ugly thud and a cloud of ink dust. Tomohiro found another soaked scrap and sliced through it; one of the bristled wings crumbled and the dragon veered sideways in the sky.

Tomohiro flipped over two more pieces before he found the neck. He carved through it in one quick stroke.

The dragon plummeted from the sky. The coils shook the ground as they hit, the tongue lolling out of its mouth before it turned to shimmering dust.

Tomohiro reached into his bag and grabbed his kendo headband, pressing it into the gash as he raced over to me. I fell to my knees in the mud and sobbed while he flung his arms around me.

"I'm sorry, I'm sorry," he cried over and over into the soaked tangle of my hair. *"Gomen, gomen, gomen!"*

The rain poured down from the sky, washing over the shimmering dust, soaking the paper and the notebook until the ink blurred beyond recognition. We clung to each other as our drenched clothes clung to our own skin, and as terrified as I was to let go, I was just as scared to hold on.

11

The blood finally stopped, Tomohiro's kendo headband stained so dark I could barely read the black kanji painted on it. *The Twofold Path of the Pen and Sword,* it said. Only, to Tomohiro the pen and sword might as well be the same thing.

It was a deep gash in his wrist and probably needed stitches, but that would mean explaining to his dad and the doctors, so I knew he wouldn't go to the hospital.

We didn't speak for a while, sitting under the trees for shelter as the rain poured. There wasn't a question I could think of that encompassed everything I wanted to ask. Tomohiro sat beside me, rubbing the headband into his wrist and slicking his dripping bangs behind his ears. I was exhausted and just wanted to go home, but I didn't know what to tell Diane, and so I stayed, trapped in the hell that had once been our paradise.

"What now?" I said, when the silence became too much to bear.

"Let's hope the storm gave us cover," he said. "That and not too many people live around here. They'll say the dragon was a trick of the light. A flash of lightning against the clouds, that kind of thing."

"Really?"

"I hope so. It didn't lift too high up in the clouds."

"Tomo."

"Hmm?"

"I told you to stop drawing, but you didn't listen."

Tomohiro's head slumped forward. "It was strange," he said. "You were right beside me, but your voice sounded a mile away. I couldn't hear what you were saying. It all sounded…fuzzy to me."

"You have to stop drawing."

He said nothing.

"Don't you get it? This was almost Koji all over again. Is this really worth your life?"

He lifted his head slowly, staring at the trampled grass where the dragon's corpse was disintegrating.

"It's worth my life," he said. "But it isn't worth yours."

"How can you say that? It's not worth yours, either."

He shook his head. "Even if I stopped drawing, this…power, curse, whatever the hell it is. It won't go away. I'm a Kami, Katie. This is what I am. My nightmares are so real I could die in my sleep. The kanji I write on my entrance exams could cut open someone's wrist. A lot of the characters have the radical for sword in them, you know. The ink is everywhere I go, and sometimes I…sometimes I lose myself, like when I couldn't hear you. I'm marked for this darkness. This is who I am." He lowered his head. "My only hope is to learn to control it."

"Then maybe I—maybe I need to go."

"What?"

"Because I'm making things worse. I'm some sort of catalyst. And I don't know why."

"It—it might be more dangerous if you leave."

"I'm sorry, what?"

"The way I feel about you, Katie," he said, his brown eyes

searching mine. "What if it's reacting to my emotions or something? If you left, I might— I mean, the Kami power might overtake me. What if I completely lose it, if the nightmares finally get me? But as long as you're safe. It's for the best if the ink destroys me anyway. If I don't wake up, then I can't hurt you."

I stared at him. Did I mean that much to him?

"Too dramatic?" he said with a laugh, shaking his head.

"That's not funny."

"It's not supposed to be. It's lonely being a monster."

"You're not a monster."

He held up his blood-soaked wrist like it was proof. "I am. But it's not damn fair." The rain clung to spikes of his hair, dripping off the tips of it into the grass. "It's not just the ink hunting you, Katie. I'm hunting you. I want you like I've never wanted anything."

Every part of me caught fire. Every nerve pulsed.

"I was trying to push you away, messing with you in the courtyard. I almost couldn't go through with it. You'll think I'm such an asshole, but when I saw you—god. I couldn't get you out of my head. And then you climbed that tree and shouted my name. You weren't afraid of me. You didn't back down. I felt like you could see me, the real me. Myu was a reminder that I was too dangerous to be anything but alone and half-dead. You made me alive again, Katie. If I have to burn for that, then I'll light the damn match myself."

"Tomo," I said. My mind whirled with everything he'd said.

"I know. I'm sorry. I should keep my mouth shut."

"No, I—"

My *keitai* chimed then, its happy metal tune so out of place in the soaked clearing. Tomohiro pressed his back into the rough trunk of a tree while I reached for my phone.

The ID flashed *Diane.* There was no way I could answer it. I sat there frozen, unable to answer, unable to put the phone away.

"What will you do?" Tomohiro asked softly.

"I can't go home like this," I said. The phone stopped ringing. A few seconds later, it started again. "What am I supposed to say?" I was soaked, covered in dirt and ink and blood. My uniform was probably ruined, and I had no clue how to explain this. Even Diane, who didn't believe in curfews, was definitely going to ground me. And I was pretty sure I wouldn't be going to Miyajima with Yuki.

Yuki.

"Wait," I said. "What if I stayed at Yuki's?" But Tomohiro's expression was a few seconds ahead of mine.

"Can you explain the ink and blood to her?" he asked. He bit his lip, then leaned his head back against the tree trunk. "Come to my house," he said.

"What?"

"My father's in Tokyo for work. You can wash your uniform."

"And Diane?"

"Tell her you were caught in the rain. It's the truth after all."

"And tell her I'm staying over at a senior boy's house."

He blinked. "She doesn't know who I am?"

My cheeks turned red.

"She thinks I'm with Tanaka," I said.

He grinned as I felt my face flood with heat. "With Ichirou?" he mused. "I had no idea you thought he was hot."

"Shut up," I said, but I couldn't bring myself to smack him. "I don't."

"Well, you can't go home, that's for certain. So there really is no choice but to let me help you." He grinned slyly. "Unless you want to stay over at Ichirou's."

That time I did smack him in the shoulder. He was right,

of course, even if he was being a smart-ass. It would be hard enough to make my way to his house without anyone staring at us. Hopefully the drenching rains would keep everyone indoors.

He stood up, grabbed his soaked book bag and wiped the raindrops off it with his palm.

"Let's go," he said, reaching out his left hand. I stared at it for a moment, the smoothness of his open palm. Then I nodded and put my hand in his. He pulled me up and led me to the outskirts of the forest, where his bike rested against a plum tree. He tried to wipe the seat off with his hand, but everything was so soaked it made no difference. He laughed then, and I heard my own voice echo it. I wasn't sure how anything could be so funny when we'd almost been mauled by a dragon, but there we were, muddy, bloody and grinning.

We ducked under the fence, slamming it closed. Thunder still rumbled in the clouds above, and the streets were practically bare. Tomohiro got on the bike first and then patted the metal carrier above the rear wheel.

"Isn't that dangerous?"

"You don't want to walk, do you? Anyway," he added, "I wouldn't let you fall."

I sat down on the carrier and lifted my feet. I pressed my hands into the back of the seat, but Tomohiro snorted at me and wrapped my palms around his hips.

"Okay," he said and pressed against the pedal. The bike wobbled and lurched forward, and I squeezed my hands into his stained blazer. He curved around for a bit until he got the hang of steering two people with only one good wrist, and soon we were speeding north, Shizuoka spreading before us. The rain was thick on the streets, but we didn't mind the spray—we really couldn't get much more soaked anyway.

Tomohiro cycled for what seemed like forever, the world around us a blur of gray skies and white umbrellas. The taller buildings shrank away, and we cycled down narrow alleyways behind houses, where cement retaining walls pulled away from us at sheer angles. At last he slowed down, in front of a two-story house with an arched gate in front.

Mounted on the gate above the bell and intercom was a silver nameplate that read *The Yuu Family.*

"You live here?" I gaped. It wasn't a big house, not by American standards, but a detached home like this in over-crowded Shizuoka was a pretty big deal. Tomohiro shrugged and slouched against the gated entrance.

"My dad's head of accounting at ShizuCha," he said casually.

"ShizuCha?" I repeated. "The tea company?" But Tomohiro looked pretty embarrassed about the whole thing, so I dropped it. He pushed the gate open and motioned me through, following behind with his bike.

"We should probably leave our shoes outside," he joked as we reached the front door. I peered down at our muddy, ink-coated shoes as he reached into his pocket and pulled out a key, turning the lock with a loud click.

"Tadaima," he sang as he stepped in, out of habit since no one was home. The entrance tunneled into darkness. The humid, stale air trapped in the house smelled like a snuffed-out candle, thick against our faces but warm compared to the rain outside.

Tomo clunked his shoes against the raised floor to the veranda as I slipped mine off. I peeled off my soaked kneesocks, laying them on top of my shoes like strips of bandage.

He led me toward the bathroom, a sink with the bath and

shower behind a separate door and a laundry machine across the hall.

"Here," he said, opening the lid of the all-in-one washer-dryer. "You can put your *seifuku* in here."

"Don't these kinds of stains need to be scrubbed out?" I asked, but neither of us was really sure.

"Put the skirt in the wash, then," he said. "Leave the shirt in the sink and we can try scrubbing or bleaching it. And go ahead and have a hot bath. I'll find some clothes you can borrow and leave them outside the door."

Embarrassment crept up my neck, but he looked as cool and collected as always. I hated him for it.

"Thanks."

"Don't get ill from the cold," he said, and he reached his hand up to brush wet strands of hair off my face. He tucked them behind my ear, and I hoped he would leave before my knees buckled under me.

Once I heard his footsteps thumping up the stairs, I unbuttoned my shirt. I stared at it critically before leaning it over the sink. I ran some water and scrubbed the sides of the blouse together. There was no way I was going to get the ink out, even if I could get rid of the blood streaks. I sighed and let the shirt crumple into the sink. I threw my skirt into the machine, but left it for Tomohiro to turn on; I couldn't quite make out all the kanji on the buttons. I wasn't sure what to do with my underwear—it was soaked, but there was no way I was leaving it in the laundry room. In the end I brought it with me into the bathroom and laid it flat on the counter, hoping by some miracle it would dry.

The shower spray was hot against my skin and I greedily breathed in the steam. My skin turned pink as I shook off the cold chill from the rainstorm. Blood and ink had crusted under my fingernails and I scrubbed until they came clean. I rinsed off and lifted the bamboo cover off the tub of water on the other side of the tile floor.

I soaked, staring up at the azure ceiling in silence. It hit me then that I hadn't called Diane back yet. I sat up, water sloshing over the side of the tub. I lifted myself out and opened the bath door, where I found a stack of fluffy towels beside the sink.

"Tomo?" I called tentatively by the hallway door. When there was no answer, I creaked it open a bit. Tomohiro had left a neat pile of gray sweatpants and a shirt on the floor. My underwear hadn't dried, obviously, so I shoved it into the pants pocket and gave a grateful sigh the pants were a little bulky. I scrambled into the clothes and called through the house until Tomohiro came downstairs, clean clothes folded in his arms, which he held far away from his chest.

He stopped walking halfway, his eyes wide. My skin felt itchy.

"Cute," he said, and I wanted to hit him. Pins and needles scratched up my arms. "My turn," he added. "My room's upstairs. You'll find it okay."

I nodded, reached for my bag by the entrance and headed up the stairs. I heard the door of the laundry room slide shut.

There were only a couple of doors upstairs and only one was ajar, so I slipped inside. A simple bookshelf and desk sat on one side of his room, his bed across from them with a blue plaid duvet strewn across it at an angle. I felt guilty somehow, like I was trespassing in his room; the feeling thrilled me at the same time it filled me with embarrassment.

I sat on his bed, looking around the room. There were some cute trinkets—a miniature Eiffel Tower, a few plush animals that I wondered with sudden urgency if other girls had given to him. But what really caught my eye were the posters, almost twenty of them plastered on the walls. Rembrandt, Rubens, Monet, Michelangelo—all of them represented. Most of the paintings featured angels trampling demons, judgment dealt out at the end of time. The rain pelted against the roof, and the raindrops running down the windows spread creepy gray blotches of light on the paintings.

I heard the spray of the shower downstairs.

There were other paintings, too, white and black and gray like Tomohiro's sketches. Ghostly images of forests and landscapes, tossing oceans and cherry blossoms floating through the air. Ink-wash paintings, the traditional kind you saw in shrines or tatami rooms. The shadows that fell on them in the silence of his room made the landscapes seem so far away, distant worlds that almost came alive when I stared at them long enough. I wondered if they'd been drawn by Kami, too, but I realized I must be wrong. It would be too dangerous to display works like that. Still, maybe all the creepy posters were the reason Tomohiro had nightmares. I'm not sure I could sleep with all these angels and demons ripping each other to pieces around me.

I took a deep breath and reached into my bag for my phone. The ring echoed in my ear as I waited, still wondering what exactly I was going to say.

The phone clicked on the other end.

"*Moshi moshi,* Greene residence."

"Diane—"

"Katie!" she burst out. "Thank god. Where are you? I called so many times."

"I'm so sorry. I got caught in the rain. I didn't hear the ring."

"It's a mess out there. It's like typhoon season early or something. Where are you?"

"I'm at Yuki's," I lied. "We got totally soaked, so she let me come in and have a bath and put some clean clothes on."

A sigh of relief. "Good thing you girls had common sense. What about Tanaka?"

"Tanaka?"

"Don't you spend every Wednesday together?"

"Oh. Today it was just Yuki and me. After Sewing Club, I mean."

"I'll borrow Morimoto's car and pick you up."

"No!" I shouted. "I mean, um, I was hoping I could stay over. My clothes are going through her laundry anyway, and she has pajamas I can borrow."

A pause. "But you and Yuki aren't the same size."

"It's just for sleeping, Diane. I'll make do."

"I still think you should come home." Her voice sounded off, somehow. Was she onto me? Was I that obvious? I needed to change tactics, and fast.

"Diane," I said. "Look. Moving to Japan has been hard for me, and I'm really starting to make good friends, you know?" I could hear her breathing on the line. "Please let me stay over," I said. I squeezed my eyes shut and hoped the sympathy card would pull through.

It did. I heard a sigh of defeat.

"Okay," Diane said. "As long as you're safe and dry, and as long as Yuki's mom doesn't mind."

"It's fine with her," I said and quickly said my goodbyes before she could change her mind. As much as Diane had protested, I was more interested in what she hadn't said. For example, that there were giant inky dragons floating through the sky.

I dialed Yuki's *keitai* and waited for the tinny ring.

"Katie?" she said when she answered.

"Yuki-chan, I need a favor," I said, wincing as the words

came out of my mouth. God, I sounded thirteen or something. "If Diane calls, can you cover for me?"

"What?"

"I got caught in the rain and my *seifuku* is a mess. If I go home like this, Diane is going to seriously question where I was."

"And where *were* you?"

"On a bike ride with Tomohiro," I said. "But we fell off the bike into the mud."

She squealed. "And now you're staying at his house?" I gritted my teeth, but there was no way around it. I needed her help.

"It's not like that. His dad's here, too. Look, please cover for me, okay? Please?"

"Katie, try to be careful, okay? You don't know for sure that those were all rumors."

"They were," I said. "Promise." I mean, except the attack on Koji, which, when you thought about it, was very much Tomohiro's fault. And had almost happened to me.

"Okay, got it. No problem," Yuki said, like she was in on the secret. I could almost imagine her winking, throwing her fingers up in the peace sign. It's what she would do at school, but at the same time she had no idea what the secret really was, how deep and dark it ran. I closed my *keitai* and shoved it back into my bag.

Safe, for now.

The water shut off downstairs, and a minute later Tomohiro padded up the stairs, toweling his copper hair.

"Ah." He sighed as he came in wearing a gray T-shirt and red plaid pajama bottoms. "Feels good to be dry and out of the rain." He sat down beside me without thinking, and suddenly we were there, sitting on the side of his bed. His cheeks turned a deep red and he stood up.

"C'mon," he said and led me downstairs to the living room.

He flipped on the TV and started switching channels. A fresh bandage was knotted around his wrist, and the tails of it hung down his arm. I clued in suddenly about what he was looking for. He was studying every news report before switching to the next.

"You're looking for the dragon."

"There's no way nobody saw it," he said, and the fear started to sink back into me, colder than the damp rain outside. But he clicked and clicked, and it was nowhere on the news. He sank back into his white couch and sighed.

"Looks like we were lucky," I said.

I jumped when a cheerful chime rang through the room. Tomohiro narrowed his eyes and sat up, padding across the room to his book bag. He pulled out his *keitai,* his tiny *kendouka* charm dangling across the back of his hand.

He stared at the ID on the phone as it rang, rainbow colors spreading across the metal edge where he'd flipped it open. "Shit," he said. "Can't he leave me alone?"

"Ishikawa?" I said.

"Probably needs backup again." He sighed. "I'm tired of saving his ass every time things go wrong, but he doesn't have anyone else to help him. I'm it. I don't wanna see him get thrashed."

"You better go, then," I said.

"I'm not leaving you," he said, his eyes searching my face. "Anyway, I'm pretty sure he'd notice that my wrist is sliced open."

He clicked the cell phone shut, and the phone stopped ringing, the colors fading away. Then it rang again. When that died down, a text chimed in.

"What's his problem?" Tomohiro said, opening the phone

again. "He usually gets the message if I don't answer." He opened the text and his eyes widened, his face turning pale.

"What is it?" I asked. My throat felt thick and dry.

Tomohiro didn't answer, just stood there and stared, his face frozen in horror.

"What? Is the text from someone else? Who's it from, Tomo?"

With a dry voice, he whispered the name.

"Satoshi."

Relief surged through me momentarily. "Ishikawa again?" I said. "Jeez, you scared the crap out of me."

"He saw it."

My blood ran cold. "What?"

"He saw it. I know it."

"Ishikawa—"

"He saw the dragon."

He turned the *keitai* to show me the text scrawled across the screen.

見えた。*I saw it.* So simple, and so terrifying.

Suddenly the phone was alive again, swirling with color, chiming cheerfully in Tomohiro's hand. His palm opened slowly and the *keitai* dropped to the floor, slamming against the hardwood and skidding a little ways, still chiming.

"How do you know that's what he means?" I said. "There's no way—he doesn't even know about Toro Iseki."

"He knows I go there to draw," Tomohiro said.

Panic coursed through me, turning my limbs to jelly. "You told him?"

He shook his head. "You're not the first to think of following me," he said. "He came once, watched me draw, got bored."

The phone stopped ringing. "But how could he have seen?"

"I don't know," he snapped. "I don't know how. But he's

kept a close eye on me since that ink puddle in the kendo match. He knows what Kami are because the Yakuza know about them, and he's tried to get me to admit it before. He thinks I have some stupid destiny as a Yakuza weapon or something." *You're keeping him from his destiny.* Oh. "I convinced him the last couple times he was wrong, that I don't even know what Kami are, but lately I've been losing control."

Because of me. Cue the stifling guilt. "But he's your friend. He'd keep your secret, right?"

"There are more powerful things than friendship that would sway him." His eyes had gone dark, and he sat down on the floor, tucking his knees up to his chin. "Koji defended me until the end. He almost lost his eye and still protected my secret. Sato won't do that. He's in too much trouble to think of anything but protecting himself." It was true. I knew it. Ishikawa was drowning and he'd pull Tomohiro down with him.

"What are we going to do?" Tears welled up in my eyes. I didn't want to run from the Yakuza.

"We're going to deny it," Tomohiro said, pressing his head into his hands. The tails of the bandage splayed across his knees. "You can't let anyone know we were together today."

My stomach flopped as I thought of Yuki. She wouldn't tell anyone, right? She'd keep my secret.

Who was I kidding? She couldn't keep it to herself for five minutes. She was probably on the phone to Tanaka right now.

But it was too late, and his eyes were so sincere. I didn't want to let him down.

"I won't," I said. He nodded. His phone rang again and his eyes glazed over.

"I've lied to him before," he said, but he sounded like he was convincing himself. "I'll do it again. Shit. He must have been doing deals in Ishida again. That's how he saw it."

Ishida. Where they'd cornered the guy in the knit hat, where Jun had rescued me from the hairy, tattooed creep. It was close to Toro Iseki. He could easily have had a view of it from there.

"Tomo," I squeaked out. He looked up, and I must have looked like crap because he snapped out of his mood and strode over, sitting down on the couch with me.

"Don't worry," he said, taking my hands in his. "We'll be okay."

I nodded, but my stomach ached. I blinked back tears and one rolled down my cheek. He reached for it, the tiny drop catching the light on his slender fingers, and then all I could see was the gleaming hazel of his eyes as they searched mine. I tensed, and he leaned in. I could smell the shampoo in his still-damp hair.

I felt his breath against my mouth, and then he pressed his lips against mine, his hand still on my cheek. The heat sent a shock through me, melted away any other thoughts but this, that Yuu Tomohiro was kissing me.

He pulled back then, suddenly. His cheeks flushed red, his eyes round and surprised. He bobbed his head in apology.

"Sorry," he said. "You must be thirsty. I'll get you a drink." He excused himself and practically ran to the kitchen, where I heard way more clatter than necessary to get a glass.

I touched my lips with my fingers, pressed them against each other, feeling the way they'd swelled when he kissed me. I didn't think my face could get any redder; thank god he was taking so long in the kitchen.

Then his *keitai* rang again, spewing rainbow colors across the floor.

"Iced tea okay?" he shouted over it, his voice way too energetic. "I've only got oolong and lemon."

"Sure," I said, staring at the phone.

He returned, putting the cold glass into my hands. He clicked the phone off and threw it onto a side table before sitting beside me. I took a sip of the bitter tea, resting the cup on the coffee table. His eyes never left me.

"Are you okay?" he said. I couldn't help it—a laugh came out.

"Are you kidding?" I said. "We were nearly ripped to shreds by a dragon, and now Ishikawa's going to blurt your secret to his little Yakuza friends. I'm just peachy." But all I could do was stare at his soft lips, wanting to press mine against them. *Stupid, stupid.*

"They don't know what they're dealing with," Tomohiro said, his eyes dark. "You think they're scary?"

"Um, they're gangsters."

"And I'm the shadow lurking around the corner. I'm the *youkai* demon dragging them screaming into the night."

"One, that's creepy. Two, stop with the monster business. You're not evil, Tomo. You were there when I needed you. You saved me from the dragon, but you also saved me when I couldn't be myself, when everyone else told me to heal and get over it. You're risking everything to be with me, everything to help me. You're…you're—" I could barely speak with him staring at me like that. He put his oolong tea down gently on the coffee table, his eyes never moving from my face.

"O-re sa," he whispered, leaning closer. *I, you know…* I remembered the first time he'd started to confess those words to me, in the lush green of Toro Iseki.

His fingers slid along my jaw, each like a spark on my skin.

"Kimi no koto ga…" About you, I… And he rested his lips on my jaw, where his fingers had been. The warmth of it pulsed through me.

His lips were so close to mine, grazing along my skin to my mouth. *"Suki,"* he breathed, *I love you,* and then the softness of his lips pressed against mine and the world caught fire, everything light and flame and burning.

His fingers wound in my hair, the cloth wrapped around his wrist sliding along my collarbone as he moved. I reached for him, letting my hands trail along his jaw and around his neck, twisting the spikes of his hair flat between my fingers. His feathery bangs tickled against my skin as his kisses brushed against my lips, my cheek, the corner of my jaw. He trailed down to my neck. He was fireworks and radiance, glare and tingling frostbite.

My voice was quiet, a crackle in the fire. *"Suki,"* I whispered, and the ocean of him churned against me, his kisses deepening like he was drowning. His arms closed around me, the heat of his fingertips splayed against the skin of my waist. He pressed his fingers under the hem of the shirt he'd lent me, scorching lines of warmth up my back. I slid my hands down his back to the edge of his T-shirt, then looped them under. My fingers felt like ice against the heat of his skin, as if they were melting, and he moaned softly into my neck, the vibration of it pulsing on my skin.

Everything was floating. Everything was burning. Everything was drowning.

"Shit!" he groaned and pulled away, his hands slipping from my back, my fingers left holding emptiness.

Red bloomed across the bandage on his wrist, trails of blood and ink streaking down his arm in zigzags like rain on a window.

"Are you okay?" I said between breaths. Stupid question, but it was hard enough to think straight, like I'd been pulled from a dream, lost in that moment when you couldn't move and you weren't sure which world was real.

His eyes squeezed shut as he cradled his arm. "It stings

like hell," he said. He walked down the hall to the bathroom, where I heard the spray of the tap. A minute later he came back, a new cloth bandage wrapped around the wound. I guess if you cut yourself drawing as often as he did, you'd have supplies lying around.

"I'm sorry," I said, mostly because I felt awkward. But he sat beside me, tracing my ear with the fingers on his left hand.

"Well *that* got the blood going," he grinned.

"God, you're so stupid sometimes."

"That's part of my charm," he said. Then he winced again.

"You need to go to the hospital," I said, but he shook his head.

"Can't. It'll be fine. I just need to rest it and, you know, keep the blood flow calm. And you're not helping with that last part, by the way." His head hunched toward his chest, his bangs covering his eyes from view. I couldn't tell if they were closed, but I knew he was in more pain than he was admitting.

"Do you have any painkillers?" I asked.

"In the kitchen," he rasped. "In the cupboard by the fridge." I went into the kitchen and pulled out the bottle, shaking two into my hand.

"Here," I said, and he knocked them back with the oolong tea.

"Thanks," he said, wiping the back of his mouth with his good wrist. "But I should warn you, those are the kind that knock me out like nobody's business." Of course I'd grabbed the wrong ones—I could barely read the kanji on the bottles. He leaned back into the couch, curled on his side.

"Do you want me to help you upstairs?"

"I'll sleep down here," he said. "You can have my room. We have futons in the tatami room, but my dad will wonder why I pulled them out, so I better just take the couch."

"Are you sure?" I said. His eyes already looked droopy, but maybe I was overthinking it.

"Sorry," he said. "It's for the best since I clearly can't control myself." He breathed in suddenly at the pain. "Could you pass me that blanket?" I looked behind and found it, then tucked it around him. He grabbed my fingers with his left hand, resting them on his lips. His eyes looked watery and distant, but they gleamed as he stared at me. Through the tips of my fingers he said, "I'll protect you. I promise."

I stroked his hair, running my fingers through the copper silk of it, until he lifted my hand urgently from his head.

"The blood flow," he gasped.

"You're an idiot," I said, and he grinned.

In the darkness of his room, I crawled into bed. The rain made shadows on the ink-wash paintings, as if the drops ran down the painted trees themselves.

"What do you want?" I whispered to the darkness. "Why am I the catalyst?" I hated myself for thinking it, but how much of his feelings for me were really him, and how much were…the other part of him, the part hunting me? Was it his feelings for me that were making the ink do weird things?

It couldn't be. He hadn't even really known me when my pen exploded.

Tomohiro had an alarm clock beside his bed that went *tick, tick,* annoyingly loud, as I squeezed my eyes shut.

I listened to the rain pattering on the roof. I pulled the blue duvet tighter around my shoulders, surrounded by the smell of him, my skin still pulsing where his touch had scored itself into my memory.

And once I drifted to sleep, the dragon rose in my dreams, Ishikawa standing fearlessly beside it.

12

I awoke to Tomohiro knocking on the door and racing back down the stairs. I rubbed my eyes at first, then jolted up when I saw the alarm. I dashed downstairs and found him in the kitchen, grinning at me. I paused and thought about my hair, my face and my unbrushed teeth. My cheeks went red.

"Ohayo," he said, waving his hand up in the air, a fresh skin-colored bandage wound tightly around his wrist. He was already dressed for school and frying up sausages in a pan.

"You're going to school with your wrist like that?" I said.

"I don't really have a choice. It's kind of suspicious if I don't show up," he said. "My school blazer will cover it. Don't worry."

I was nothing *but* worried. "It's kind of warm to wear your blazer all day."

He smiled. "I'll manage. I left your *seifuku* outside the door."

"Ah, thanks!" I shouted, running up the stairs. I saw him roll his eyes and turn back to cooking. I grabbed my *seifuku* and flipped the skirt back and forth. It was not only clean, but pressed, too—embarrassment spread through me as I realized how early he must have gotten up to iron the pleats, especially with his wrist chewed open. There was a bloodstain running along the hem, but it didn't show up well unless you were looking for it. Thank god our school used dark navy skirts.

The blouse wasn't in quite as good shape. The bleach had helped, but it looked pretty battered. The stains weren't noticeably blood, though—mostly ink or mud. It's not like I had a choice anyway, so I buttoned it up and tied the satin handkerchief around my neck. At least the long ends of the ribbon covered some of the shirt. I combed my hands through my hair and pulled on my kneesocks, practically brown with stains. Then I hurried back downstairs, where Tomohiro rolled two sausages out of the pan and onto my plate.

"Thanks," I said, pressing my palms together. *"Itadakimasu."* He nodded and put the pan back in the kitchen. There were two bowls of miso soup, two sausages each, a piece of lettuce, and a cut-up tomato.

We ate in silence, but between bites I peeked at him, dressed sharply in a clean uniform. His bangs fell into his eyes as he leaned down to scoop tofu out of the soup, the motion a little sloppy with his left hand.

"Um, so you cook," I said, after the silence became awkward. He looked at me, a smile curving onto his lips. I hated him for being so cool and collected again when I was still a mess. I couldn't even look him in the eye without feeling his lips against mine.

"My dad's cooking is pretty bad," he said. "So I thought I'd better learn before we starved to death." I hesitated, not sure how to react to that. But then Tomohiro laughed so hard the tofu fell off his spoon back into the bowl. "You always look ready to pick a fight," he grinned.

"Sorry," I said. "I was just thinking about your mom, that's all."

"She was a great cook. She used to make sweet egg for

my *bentou* every day. Not exactly a gourmet dish, but comfort food, you know? I'm pretty good now, but my sweet egg never tastes like hers did."

"I miss my mom's cooking, too," I said. "She used to make this awesome pasta. Mushrooms and some kind of white sauce. It tasted like heaven. God, I'm glad I can talk to you about it."

"Of course," he said. "I hope you took my very good advice and let yourself be changed."

"I did."

"The first time the ink attacked me was about a year after I lost her. It's like the Kami bloodline realized she was gone, so it moved on to me."

"Does it work like that?"

"Nah, coincidence, I think. Hits when you're not a kid anymore. Otherwise there'd be some big ink-related disasters."

"Makes sense," I said.

"Hell of a genetic parting gift she left me."

He tipped the bowl of miso soup into his mouth, clawing with a spare chopstick at the seaweed stuck on the bottom.

"You told me I could be angry, Tomo. That she's gone."

"You can feel any way you want to," he said, clanking the bowl down on the table. "Any way you need to."

"Are you angry?"

"Angry as hell."

It shouldn't have, but it made me smile. Tomo smiled, too, and stood up suddenly, pushing his dishes to either side. He reached across the table and pressed his lips to mine. He smelled of tofu and seaweed and miso paste, his hair gel like sweet vanilla.

When he pulled away, I said quietly, "What happened to her, Tomo?"

He frowned, tracing circles on my jaws with his thumbs.

"The nightmares," he said. "They can be so bad. It's not like I have them all the time, but when I do—god. Things made of shadow calling for you, chasing you, forcing you into corners and revealing the darkness inside you. Telling you horrible things they say they know you want, the things you don't want, so when you wake up you don't know what's real anymore. And you— Never mind. I don't really want to talk about it, but they're sick." He looked jittery, his eyes staring at something far away. I couldn't believe anything could shake him up like this. "I know. They can't really hurt you, right? They're just dreams. But even dreams can kill you if they're scary enough. Heart attack in your sleep, and that's it."

"They killed her?" I whispered. Was it just like what had happened to Mom? But he shook his head.

"She couldn't sleep at night," he said. "She couldn't face them. She'd wake up screaming all the time but wouldn't tell me why. She'd stay up as late as she could, terrified to close her eyes. Sometimes she'd be awake for days at a time. She was a wreck. And then—"

He slumped down into his chair.

"I forgot my lunch. She was bringing it to me. When she heard the crosswalk chime, she didn't even check which direction it was. She didn't even look before she stepped out."

My hand went to my mouth. "Oh god."

"I remember running to the window of my classroom, the sound of all the sirens. The rice and sweet egg all over the road."

My eyes filled with tears. "I'm so sorry."

"So you bet I'm angry. And that's why I won't lose anything else to the ink. Not my life, not my mind—not you."

The table was a barrier, Tomohiro so far away. I skirted it

desperately and wrapped my arms around him, sinking into his warmth.

"I'm okay," he said. "It was almost eight years ago."

"It's horrible."

"Sorry," he said. "I didn't want to make you sad. I'm fine, just changed. And mad." He brushed the hair out of my face and tucked it behind my ears with his good wrist. "And now we need to get to school before we're both late."

I dabbed my eyes, nodding, and I felt a small thrill then, that I knew Tomohiro better than anyone at school, that he trusted me more than Myu or Ishikawa or anyone. It was a stupid thrill in the face of such a story, but I couldn't help feeling it.

I left the house first, walking south a few blocks before turning west. That way I would still come from the south side of Shizuoka Station and wouldn't stand out. Tomohiro would ride his bike north and come along the stone wall, the one he often jumped over to look badass, to cover that he was really sneaking off to draw.

The rain had cleared some of the humidity, and the crisp morning air felt refreshing against my bare arms. I passed OLs—office ladies—in suits on their way to work, salarymen and schoolteachers, students wearing other uniforms. One of them, a guy from another school, walked the same way I did for a while; I got a little paranoid. If he hadn't been in front of me, I would've sworn he was following me. I wasn't sure about which school uniform he wore—from behind I couldn't see the tie, and the white shirt and dark pants were pretty basic—but then he turned his head to look across the street, and I saw the shock of blond hair tucked behind his ears, the silver earring glinting in the sunlight.

Jun.

He saw me, too, and stared at my Suntaba uniform. He smiled broadly, lifting his hand and bobbing his head.

"Good morning!" he said.

"Morning," I stammered. He stopped and waited for me.

"You get caught in the storm last night?" he said.

"What?" Oh god, how did everyone know? Did I radiate guilt or something?

"The mud," he said, pointing at the stains that pretty much covered me head to toe.

"Oh. Yeah." *Jeez, Katie. Can we bring the tension down a notch?*

He stared at me another minute. "So you're on Suntaba's kendo team, huh? I was surprised to see you at the tournament."

Of course he'd noticed. I was the only blond-haired girl in the school, for god's sake.

"Yeah," I said politely, stifling my inner monologue. "So you're the famous Takahashi."

"I guess I am." He grinned. "Just a sport I'm into, right?" His hair slipped from behind his ear and he tucked it back again. "This weekend is the kendo retreat with some *kendouka* from your school. Are you going, too?" We were walking together now, but I wasn't sure how it had happened.

"I'm not going," I said, waving my hand in front of me. "I'm not good enough. Mostly the seniors are going."

"Ah," he said, tilting his head backward and looking up at the bright blue sky. "Too bad."

He was just being polite, I knew. But somehow his subtle compliment made the hairs stand up on the back of my neck.

"That ink thing was weird, huh?" he said.

"What?"

"At the tournament."

"Oh," I said. "Yeah, that was super weird."

"Made me think of that story you told me at the station.

You know, with that boy at your school who was drawing things."

Not good. Not. Good. *Get out, get out now!*

"Oh, yeah, he transferred," I said. "Haven't seen him since."

Jun paused. "Oh. Guess it wasn't him, then."

Thank you, Brain. For once.

"We always run into each other, but did you know we've never been properly introduced?" he said, swinging his book bag back and forth. The green-and-navy tie on his neck bounced against his shirt as he walked. "You know I'm Jun, but after all this time I still don't know your name. After a while it was kind of embarrassing to ask."

"Really?" I said. But when I thought about it, it was true. I'd never told him. He looked at me with genuine, friendly interest, and I don't know why it made me blush. Okay, I did know. He was gorgeous. And he'd saved me in Ishida and plucked that cherry petal from my hair. But Tomohiro was right about Jun keeping his thoughts hidden; he smiled, but his piercing eyes didn't give away any emotion at all. They felt like they could reach deep inside you.

Why was I staring into his eyes? I looked away, self-conscious. "I'm Katie Greene."

"Greene-san," he said. "Ah, like the color of spring, *ne?*"

Yeah, or puke. Now he was just overdoing it. I wondered if I should hint around that Tomohiro and I were…well, whatever we were.

"So are you looking forward to the prefecture tournament?" I said, feeling stupid for asking. What would he say, *no?*

"I am, but there's a lot to do. I'm looking forward to training with Suntaba's best."

"I think they have more to learn from you." I laughed.

But then I felt like I'd betrayed Tomohiro somehow and bit my lip. Jun smiled.

"My school is just east of yours," he said. "I thought it would probably be too wet to take my bike today. I'm glad we can walk together, and I can get to know the competition."

"Ha," I said. But really I was trying to come up with some reason not to walk together. The sidewalk narrowed and we ended up squished together, like we were some kind of couple. Already some students and salarymen had passed by and looked us over, and I wondered if they would get the wrong idea. I didn't want a rumor going around Suntaba in case it got back to Tomohiro.

It's not like I'm doing anything wrong, I thought, but Jun still made me uneasy.

"Ano sa," he said as we descended the stairs into the underground walkway below Shizuoka Station. "Who's your favorite composer?"

"What?" I couldn't have heard him right.

He laughed. "You know. Do you like classical music?"

"Yeah, but…that's a strange question."

"Sorry. I guess I'm a strange guy." He grinned, and his bangs tumbled from behind his ear. He tucked them back again. "I'd still like to know."

I thought for a minute. "I guess Tchaikovsky," I said. "I used to dance ballet back in New York. Not seriously or anything, just for fun. But as a kid I was pretty obsessed with *Swan Lake* and *Sleeping Beauty.*"

"Ah," he said. "Good choice."

"You?"

He smiled. "I like Beethoven," he said. "His songs are often mournful, but there's always a glimmer of hope in them. I like that, the belief that there's hope for this world."

"Of course there is," I said, but he was silent. "So…you must play, then, to ask me a question like that."

He nodded. "Music and kendo," he said. "My two passions."

"They're fairly opposite," I said.

"Not really. They're both composed of intricate patterns, both movements of great artistry, *ne?*"

"I guess they are, if you think of it like that."

We walked in silence for a minute, then resurfaced from the tunnels near the entrance to Sunpu Park. "Do you miss dance?" Jun said.

I shook my head. "I wasn't that good."

"I think you're lying." He grinned. "I saw how you moved in the kendo match. I'm not surprised you've danced before."

My cheeks blazed red. I hadn't thought about him watching my kendo match. I'd done all right, but I was nowhere near his level of grace.

We rounded the corner, and I was suddenly very glad not to be alone.

Ishikawa stood in the middle of the bridge leaning against the cement railing, two guys standing with him. They weren't dressed in school uniforms—they were definitely older, with jagged haircuts and bulging arms. One of them smoked a cigarette, which he stepped on as we approached. My heart almost stopped. Were they…could they be Yakuza?

Ishikawa stared at me and narrowed his eyes. The night came back to me, his frightening text to Tomohiro. Did I look suspicious? But he didn't know I'd been with Tomohiro when it happened. My heart pounded in my ears and I thought my legs would give way underneath me. I'd never seen Ishikawa with actual Yakuza members, if that's who they were. I slowed down, almost stopped, but remembering the plan to deny everything, I knew stopping would give away more than walking ahead.

Jun noticed my hesitation, and his face crumpled with concern.

"Is that… Are they waiting for you?" he asked quietly.

"I don't know."

As we got closer, a snide smirk crossed Ishikawa's face.

"*Oi,* Greene!"

"Ishikawa," I said, my throat dry and thick. I hoped he wouldn't notice my hands shaking.

"Where's Yuuto?" he said gruffly, stepping toward me with his hands in his pockets. His bleached hair bounced a little as he walked.

"Why would I know?" He walked too close, the way Tomohiro always did, but he smelled different. He smelled of tobacco and soba.

"You can't fool me," he whispered. "I saw it."

"Saw what?" I said through gritted teeth.

He sighed. "I've known Yuuto longer than you have, and I know what he's capable of. And I bet you were there. You think he'd do something like that just for fun? No, he was trying to impress someone. Don't hang out with him. He'll get you in big trouble." Ishikawa placed his hand on my shoulder and I shrugged it away.

"Hey, hey," Jun said, stepping in front of me. "Ishikawa, isn't it? From the kendo tournament?" Ishikawa's eyes skipped from me to him, sizing him up.

"You," he said. "From Katakou School."

Jun nodded, his cold eyes searching Ishikawa's face. "Yeah, Takahashi Jun. I'm looking forward to competing with you and Yuu again." Ishikawa's eyes shifted from Jun to me, then to the two ghastly companions who waited on the bridge.

Panic shuddered through me as I watched him struggle with the intrusion.

"Look, Takahashi, I'd just like to have a talk with Greene for a minute. I'm sure you understand."

"Of course," Jun said. "I'll wait for her."

Ishikawa blinked. "Are you two friends?"

I opened my mouth to speak, but before I could, Jun said, "Yes, of course. *Ne,* Greene?"

"Yeah," I managed, staring at the men on the bridge. One of them spat into the moat below. *Well, that's attractive.*

Ishikawa stood, stunned into silence. He looked like he was going to explode.

"Let's go," he said to the men suddenly, and they skulked toward him. As they passed us, the one who'd spat into the moat spat again, this time at the ground just beside Jun's shoe.

"Lucky he was here," he drawled at me. "Watch your back." My blood turned to ice, and as he walked past, the guy bumped his shoulder harshly into Jun.

Jun blinked his cold eyes and suddenly grabbed the guy by his shirt collar. The guy let out a cry of surprise.

"Don't threaten her," Jun said.

"Jun," I said, and Ishikawa stopped walking, his mouth dropping open and his hand reaching for his pocket.

"What the hell do you think you're doing?" the guy said, pulling Jun's hand off him. "You want a fight, is that it, pretty boy?" He swaggered toward Jun.

"Hey, break it up," Ishikawa said, looking rattled. "What the hell, Sugi? It's broad daylight. Forget it."

"Shut up, Satoshi," Sugi growled.

"Jun," I said, tugging on his arm. "Let's go." His eyes were frost. Ishikawa looked around, his eyes wild. So much for controlling his own goons.

"Sugi, we're going. Right now." Sugi raised a fist and lunged at Jun, but Jun sidestepped and pulled on the goon's arm, spinning him around in a circle so he nearly lost his balance.

"Call your friend off, Ishikawa," Jun warned.

And then Ishikawa pulled his closed knife out, tracing his fingers over it like he was reassuring himself he was in control. Except we all knew he wasn't. His hands were shaking. "Sugi! Leave them alone, damn it!" Sugi's whole face was red, and he lunged toward Ishikawa, grabbing the knife out of his hands and snicking it open. *Oh god.* A scream died in my throat as he thrust the weapon toward Jun.

Jun stepped away, grabbing hold of Sugi's shirt with one hand. In a fluid movement, he detangled the knife from the thug's hand and pressed it against his throat. Sugi took a sharp breath, his skin touching the blade.

"Don't ever threaten us again, got it?" Jun said coolly.

"Damn it, Sugi! I'm sorry," Ishikawa said, his eyes flicking between Jun and me. "I just wanted to talk to her. I swear."

"I don't care," Jun said. "If you can't control your thugs, then leave them at home." His eyes flicked to Ishikawa. "Now, get out of here." He closed the knife, dropping it into Ishikawa's hand.

Ishikawa stared at me, a cross between horror and embarrassment. Then he and the two guys took off running.

I realized I was holding my breath and I let it out in a gasp.

"Close one, yes?" said Jun, bending forward and pressing his hands against his knees. "Are you okay?"

I didn't know what to say.

He looked at me, smiling kindly.

"Jun, what the hell was that?"

"Ah," he said. "I don't like gangsters. And he threatened you."

"Yeah, but—"

"You have to mean business with them," he said, "or they won't leave you alone." His piercing eyes stared back as he smoothed a blond highlight behind his ear. "I'm sorry if I scared you," he said. "You can't take them lightly, Katie. Those guys are dangerous."

"If you hadn't been here—"

"Don't worry," Jun said. "You're Yuu's friend, right? And Ishikawa and Yuu are friends. So he wouldn't hurt you. And now that I've shown him his goons don't listen, hopefully he'll distance himself from them."

"Maybe."

"I didn't mean to frighten you. Listen, could I give you my *keitai* number?" I opened my mouth, but he held up a hand. "I know. I'm not going to ask you for coffee again." He smiled. "But I'd just feel a lot better if I knew you could get ahold of me."

He was himself again, gentle and calm and gorgeous. I wished he hadn't let Sugi get to him with the whole bumping-into-his-shoulder thing. But it did feel nice that he'd defended me and that I could count on him.

"Okay," I said, pulling out my *keitai*. He smiled, pushing a button on his phone to send through his number. My *keitai* beeped with his info.

And suddenly his warm fingers wrapped around my hand, which sent a shock through me.

"I think you have someone you like," he said. "But if things change, would you consider me? I'd really like to get to know you better."

My heart felt like it stopped.

Then he scratched the back of his head, laughing. "I'm

sorry. *Hazui,* I'm so awkward sometimes. Forget I said it. I go this way now, so…"

"Oh. Oh, okay. Thanks."

"Bai bai," he said, the same as the English *goodbye,* and he actually winked, shaking a thumbs-up at me. Yes, really. He turned and I watched his tall frame walk around the outskirts of Sunpu Park. He walked gracefully, not the swagger Ishikawa and Tomohiro sometimes tried when others were watching, and he swung his book bag back and forth alongside him. I watched him for another minute, then raced through Sunpu Park to class.

My mind fell apart as I listened to the gravel crunch beneath my feet. I just wanted a day where no one pulled a knife or released an ancient dragon into the sky. Too much to ask, apparently.

Ishikawa had seen the dragon after all. It was harder to deny than I'd thought. I was a bad actor. Good thing school was ending for summer break soon. I wouldn't be able to make it much longer.

Ishikawa was waiting in the courtyard after school, but it wasn't for me. I saw him standing among the clutter of bikes, his arms folded across his chest and the sun shining off his shock of white hair. He leaned against the metal bar, eyes narrowed, watching the door of the *genkan* as students filed past him.

I backed up to the cubby where I'd placed my slippers and waited. I had to get to cram school, but there was no way I could go out there now.

The door to the school hallway slid open and the scraping noise made me jump. I looked over my shoulder and saw Tomohiro there. He gave me a small nod, eyes scanning over the students in the *genkan*. When he saw Ishikawa outside, he grimaced. He shook the slippers off his feet and shoved them into his cubby on the other side of the room. Then, without looking back, he left the school. *Deny everything.*

Ishikawa spotted him and walked halfway over. I watched, holding my breath. Tomohiro was acting casual, slouching over and running his hand through his hair. Ishikawa looked a little calmer than the morning, too, but he wasn't smiling.

"Hey!" Someone clapped me on the back and I jumped a mile. Tanaka stood there grinning at me.

"Don't do that," I hissed.

"Sorry."

"It's okay. I'm just… Never mind."

"Hey, should we go for ramen together?"

"I have cram school."

"So skip," he said. "It's almost summer break. Let's go for ice cream at least, okay? Make memories to carry us through the lonely summer, stuff like that."

"What?"

"Come on, come on," Tanaka said, pushing me out the door. "Yuki's waiting outside." The wave of afternoon humidity pressed against my face, like walking into an oven. Tomohiro would definitely be sweltering in his blazer, just to cover up his wrist. Ishikawa looked over as I stepped out, his face pale. He put his hand on Tomohiro's arm, pushing him away gently as he approached me.

"Greene," he said, and I didn't want to stop walking, but Tanaka had no idea and stopped, looking around the courtyard for Yuki. He saw her by the tennis court with her friends and waved her over. Ishikawa was in front of me now, Tomohiro a step or two behind.

"Leave me alone," I said quietly, but Ishikawa's head bobbed down in front of me. A half bow, an apology.

"I'm sorry," he said. "I'm sorry about what happened. I didn't mean for it to happen, I swear."

"What happened?" Tomohiro said, walking over.

"Nothing," I said. "Ishikawa's mobsters just decided they'd have a go at me."

Tomohiro looked at Ishikawa, his face darkening.

"You pulled that shit in front of Katie?" he said.

I watched the plan disintegrating in front of my face.

"Katie-chan!" Yuki cried as she joined our group. She saw Tanaka's confused face and added, "What's wrong?"

"I didn't know your friend would be provoked by that," Ishikawa said. "Sugi shouldn't have done it, but your friend could've turned away."

"What friend?" Tomohiro said.

"Takahashi," Ishikawa said, and Tomohiro looked at me funny.

"I ran into him on the way to school," I said. The sun felt too warm, and I wanted to leave.

"He said you're friends," Ishikawa said.

Crap. I couldn't deny it or Ishikawa would know I'd been lying, and that would put me in more trouble. I looked at Tomohiro and bit my lip. But so what if I had other guy friends? He wouldn't take it that way, would he?

"Yeah," I said quietly, "we're friends."

"Katie, everything okay?" said Tanaka.

"Everything's fine," I said. "Let's go." Tanaka nodded, and we started to leave.

That wasn't so awful, I thought. It could've been worse.

"I hope you took care of Katie last night, Yuu-san," Yuki blurted out with a wicked smile, and my heart stopped.

Tomohiro opened his mouth to speak, but no words came out. His face started to pale.

"So you *were* together last night?" said Ishikawa.

"Yuki!" I hissed.

"We weren't," Tomohiro said.

Yuki looked confused. "But…"

"We weren't," I echoed. "I was helping my aunt with papers all night. Really boring. Listen, I'm going to be late for cram school. I'm—I'm sorry."

I did the only thing I could do in that situation. I ran. Yuki and Tanaka followed as I tried to lose myself in Sunpu Park, but I couldn't. I knew the park too well now. The bells by the central fountain chimed beside me as I slowed to catch my breath.

"Katie, wait up!" Yuki called. She and Tanaka were at my side a minute later.

"What happened to not telling anyone?" I said.

"I'm so sorry! I thought you just didn't want your aunt to know!"

"Wait, why is this a secret?" said Tanaka.

"It isn't," I said, running my fingers through the tangles in my hair. "It's just…" How much did I want to involve them? The less they knew, the better. "I just don't want Ishikawa to know anything about us. He's creepy."

"I'm sorry," Yuki said again. "I'll buy the ice cream. My treat."

What could I do? It was done.

Tanaka chatted about cakes and drinks as we walked, and I forced myself to look down, to not look back. I squeezed my hands into fists as we walked. I tried to focus on the beauty of Sunpu Park, but the greenery had faded to the brown of a too-hot summer. I hoped Tomohiro was a smooth liar. I guess he'd had a lot of practice.

We bought extravagant ice creams from the stall at Shizuoka Station, warm waffle cones dripping with green-tea ice cream and sweet-bean topping, vanilla-and-strawberry swirl with melon and mango sauce drizzled on top. I tried to forget everything at that moment, to just enjoy the normalcy of it.

How much had changed that eating sweet beans in a waffle cone at a bullet-train station had become normal?

At the last kendo practice, Ishikawa tried again. I was drinking from my water bottle, and when I tilted my head down and pulled the bottle from my lips, he was there, standing too close. I almost spat the water out into his face.

"Greene," he said quietly. "Yuuto is my friend. I don't understand why he's keeping this from me."

"What do you mean?" I said as casually as I could. Ishikawa stared at me. I hadn't noticed before how deep his eyes were, how they drew you in like prey.

"Listen," he said, wrapping his wrist around my arm gently. "Has Yuuto told you about the Kami?"

"You mean Shinto gods?" I said. Ishikawa swore under his breath. Behind us, the clack of *shinai* hitting against each other and the *kiai* shouts of opponents filled the gym.

"Look, pretend all you want. The Kami were scattered at the end of the war. But they're uniting now, in secrecy. They have been for the last ten, twenty years. And not all the Kami are gentle or good-hearted, or naïve, like Yuuto." He leaned in closer, his voice a hot whisper crawling on my skin. "Yakuza aren't the most dangerous people in Japan. Do you have any idea what these Kami will do to claim Yuuto as their own?"

I was silent. Was he making it all up? Tomohiro hadn't mentioned some secret society of others like him. It's not like I saw strange creatures made of ink floating through the sky every day. People would pick up on that sort of thing.

I'd hesitated, and Ishikawa's eyes gleamed. A smile hovered on his lips, like he'd convinced me to admit the truth. I didn't know if he was lying about the other Kami, but I knew I had to protect Tomohiro. "Ishikawa, I have no clue what you're talking about. Maybe it's my poor Japanese."

The light blinked out of his eyes and he screamed right in my face, shaking his head from side to side. "Don't talk shit!"

"Hey, hey!" called out Watanabe-sensei. "Ishikawa, Greene, back to your *kiri-kaeshi* now!" Ishikawa sighed, his shoulders hunching as he tried to calm down. His grip tightened around my wrist.

"Do you think I'm the only one who saw the dragon?" he whispered roughly. "You're sorely mistaken. Yuuto won't admit it, but you can save him, Greene. Let me help him. Let us protect him from *them*." He let go of my wrist then, slamming his *men* over his head, and fell back into line before I could respond.

My whole body shook and I felt like I was going to throw up. I pushed in the door of the girls' change room and shrank to the floor, tears trailing down my cheeks. What was the truth? What was going on? It was probably all lies, spun by Ishikawa to get me to spill what had happened. I rocked on my heels, crying and crying, and then slipped out of the gym before the girls came in from Kendo Club, before Ishikawa could confront me again. I hurried along the edge of the gym, and I could feel Tomohiro's eyes on me as I slipped out of sight.

13

Yuki's mother picked me up at seven the next morning and drove us to Shizuoka Station. Diane was busy packing for a teacher's conference in Osaka, so it was a quick hug and goodbyes, and off we went. The Shinkansen train sped across Honshu, the mainland of Japan. I stared out the window at rice fields and hundreds of low buildings, built with earthquakes in mind. Yuki chattered excitedly about how we were going almost two hundred miles per hour, but it just made my ears pop and ache the whole way.

Yuki and I got off the bullet train in Hiroshima and switched to the local trains for the big red-and-white ferry to Miyajima. We saw the giant o-Torii gate in the distance, an archway of bright orange reflected in the deep blue water. Itsukushima Shrine splayed out on its stilt legs above the tide, which swelled around the barnacle-encrusted base of the snaking orange hallways. Against the blue of the sky and the dark green forested mountains, the sight took my breath away.

Yuki squeezed my arm. "It's beautiful, right? It's the one thing I like about visiting my brother."

I grinned. "Is he that awful?"

"Worse," she said, and we laughed. I breathed in the smell

of the sea, the motor of the ferry whirring in my ears. And in the back of my mind, I felt the happy thrill of a summer vacation with friends.

But whenever I closed my eyes, the imprint of the ink dragon leaped at me, Ishikawa's words filling me with doubt and dread. What sort of world was Tomohiro walking into at his kendo training retreat? Could he hold out against Ishikawa?

And if there really was a secret society of Kami—a dangerous one at that—why the hell didn't he tell me? Did he really not know? So how come Ishikawa did? As if the Yakuza were really the good guys, and I was supposed to fall for that.

But no matter how I played the scene out in my head, I was never fully convinced that I'd figured it out. It didn't add up.

The ferry docked and Yuki's brother was there, waving wildly at us.

"Niichan!" Yuki shouted.

"Yuki!" he shouted back.

Niichan was short and slender, and looked an awful lot like Yuki. They had the same round, warm face, and the same willowy fingers.

"So good to see you," he said, when we'd finally docked at the Miyajima Terminal. "And this is your friend Katie?"

"Nice to meet you," I said, and we bowed to each other.

"I'm Watabe Sousuke," Niichan said. "But you can call me Niichan, too, if you like."

"Thanks." I smiled. I'd never had any siblings, and it was nice to have a brother, even if he was a surrogate.

He took our suitcases, one in each hand, and loaded them into his white three-wheeled truck. We puttered up a few side streets and then scaled the side of the mountain.

He pulled into a narrow driveway and there it was, a little two-room house halfway up the mountainside and out of the way of the tourists. The view was amazing, the ocean stretching out to tiny islands that rose from its depths. From the inside of the house, the roar of the waves was a gentle lapping, a pleasant sound that filled the house.

Niichan put our suitcases in the corner of the main room and then walked over to the little stove to boil some water. He made us each a cup of tea, and we sat down together on the tatami floor.

"Yuki's glad you could come this year," he said, passing a plate of cookies. I sat up straight on my knees, ready to put into practice what I'd learned at Tea Ceremony Club. But Yuki sat with her legs sprawled to the side, so I collapsed, too, relieved but a little deflated. So much for tea-ceremony studies. "She always complains about how bored she is."

"How could you be bored here? It's beautiful!"

Yuki groaned. "It's beautiful," she said, "and tiny. Once you've been here every summer for the last four years, it starts to wear on you."

"Well, at least you can show Katie around this time, *ne?*" Niichan said, and I blushed at the familiarity of hearing my first name from a stranger. I guess I'd been in Japan long enough for it to affect me like that. "Listen, Katie, if you're interested, I can show you around Itsukushima Shrine."

"Isn't that the one we saw from the ferry?"

Yuki nodded. "Niichan works there."

My eyes almost popped out of my head. "You're a monk?"

He laughed. "No, no," he said. "Just a caretaker. I maintain the website for the priests, clean the grounds, lead tours, that sort of thing."

"Oh." But my heart was still pounding. If he worked at a Shinto shrine, wouldn't he know a lot about Kami?

After the tea, we took a walk along the shoreline of Miyajima, the giant orange arch of Itsukushima in the distance. We had dinner at a café, and on the way home, Niichan bought us each a maple leaf–shaped custard cake, the pastry warm in our hands. He laid out futons for us in the living room, which was also the kitchen, and was now a bedroom. He slept in the other room, which was his bedroom and had a Western-style bed in it. Diane's mansion had Western beds, too, and I wasn't used to the tatami pressing against my spine through the thin futon as I tried to sleep. Yuki and I whispered for a while, but when she fell asleep I stared into the darkness, listening to the lapping of the ocean outside the window.

Suntaba School and my life there felt so far away, the happiness and the danger Tomohiro brought into my world. I wasn't sure how I'd managed to get mixed in with gangsters and secret societies. I wished I'd fallen for Tanaka, that I'd called Tomohiro on the jerk he was and just stayed away from him. But I'd seen the real him, that he was deeper and different and changed. Now I couldn't imagine a world without him in it. My heart was glass—easy to see through, simple to break.

I wondered if this was how Mom had felt after Dad. It was enough to make me swear off boys forever.

The ocean breeze blew in through the window, the rich, salty smell of the sea pressing against my face. I thought of riding the horse through Toro Iseki, galloping freely through the clearing and laughing until tears swelled at the corners of our eyes and our stomachs ached.

A buzzing noise sounded in my purse. My *keitai.* I pulled back the futon duvet and crawled over the scratchy tatami, fumbling around in the bag until my fingers touched the cool metal. The darkness flooded with rainbow colors as I flipped open the top.

A text from Tomohiro. Of course.

How is Miyajima? Training started today. Katakou's sensei is tough. Sato thinks you and I are spending too much time together. He's joking that you're seeing Takahashi on the side. —Tomo

I read the message again, scouring it for the messages hidden underneath. If Ishikawa thought we were spending too much time together, it must mean he was pestering Tomohiro about the Kami thing. My cheeks flushed when I read about Jun. Was he actually worried about it? I didn't want to explain myself and come off looking dumb. Or worse, defensive.

I thought carefully, then typed a response.

Miyajima is beautiful, more fun than a sweaty old kendo summer. I only saw Takahashi at Sunpu when Ishikawa was being a—I deleted what I'd originally put, and tried again—jerk.

I stared at it for a while, then clicked Send. I couldn't risk any hidden messages of my own, anything that might give him away. I hoped my concern went with the message, because I was out of my mind over here on this tranquil island, unable to do anything to help.

In the morning, we took the ropeway up the mountain and searched for monkeys with Niichan's binoculars. When the afternoon got too hot, we had plenty of summer homework to keep us occupied in the little house while we blasted the air-con.

Niichan and I went for a walk while Yuki perfected her chicken curry for dinner. We talked about the weather, the sights in Miyajima, about New York and Canada, and my life straddled between the two. When we reached Itsukushima Shrine, we wandered straight in, walking along the boardwalk planks above the water, through the long tunnels of orange and white that snaked along the building.

"Niichan," I said, looking down at the big koi circling the stilts of the shrine.

"Hmm?"

"Could you tell me about the *kami?*"

"There are so many." He laughed. "Here at Itsukushima the principal *kami* are the three daughters of Susanou."

"Susanou," I said. The name sounded familiar.

Niichan nodded. "The god of storms," he said. "Amaterasu's brother."

My blood froze, but I forced my feet on so Niichan wouldn't notice. Amaterasu was the source of power, Tomohiro had said. All the Kami's abilities came from her.

"Do you—do you think," I stuttered, hoping I wouldn't sound ridiculous. I squeezed my eyes shut. "Do you think the *kami* were real?"

Niichan's footsteps stopped. I opened my eyes and saw his face creased in all sorts of worry lines. I'd gone too far now, I thought, but then he smiled. "All I know is that there is a lot of power in the shrines," he said. "If you pray, you get your wish, you know? I've seen it happen many times."

"But what about… I mean, what about the ink-wash drawings some of the priests do? Do you think there's power in those?"

I'd overdone it; he was looking at me funny. We reached the other end of the boardwalk and turned toward the main shrine in the center.

"I think," he said slowly, "that there are those who have

great talents in this world. And surely these talents are given for a purpose."

I wondered what purpose Tomohiro's ability had, what this dark curse on him could be for.

"Listen, there's something I think you'd be interested to see," he said as we neared the main shrine. Past the slotted wooden box for tithes was an old wooden door, and Niichan stopped outside it. He reached into his pocket and pulled out a small ring of keys, then unlocked the door and slid it to the side, revealing a dark, dusty room. He flicked on the light switch as we stepped inside.

"These are some of the national treasures we keep here at the shrine," he said. "Some of them are very old, so we rotate the collection and keep them in this fireproof room."

The room smelled of antiques, ancient wood and lacquer, dust and straw tatami on the floor. In the middle of the ceiling hung a square lamp, which cast shadows on the statues and paintings covering the walls. Fierce dogs of stone, teeth bared; bronze statues of bald-headed, chubby priests or princes or who knew what. Colorful woodblock paintings and several ink-wash landscapes.

"They're beautiful," I said. It was strange to think of all the history silently locked away in this room, half-forgotten.

"I thought you'd be interested because of the paintings you mentioned." He smiled. "Many of these pieces are hundreds of years old, saved from the various fires Itsukushima Shrine went through. Some are more recent, of course."

I approached one of the woodblocks, a painting in three panels shadowed by the square lamp above. A man stretched backward in agony, women and what might be diplomats in bright kimonos in desperate prayer beside him. Around him swirled horrible green-skinned demons and red-faced monsters, hands reaching for him and flames spiraling into inky darkness. The chaos in it unnerved me.

"That's one of the most priceless in our collection," Niichan said behind me. "One of the last woodblocks by Yoshitoshi."

"Who's the man?" I said, pointing to the arch of his back as he recoiled from the apparitions. The room felt stuffy, too warm for my liking.

"Taira no Kiyomori," Niichan said. "A powerful leader in older times. He funded the restoration of this shrine in the twelfth century, which is why we have so many pieces relating to him. He was vicious at times, merciful at others, but very ambitious. He controlled Japanese politics by force for many years, creating ranks of samurai in the government. He even forced the emperor to abdicate so he could place his own son on the throne."

"Is that why all the demons?" I said, staring at the painting. I felt ill just looking at it, and yet I couldn't look away. A bead of sweat rolled down my face.

"Ah." Niichan nodded. "When Taira was older, he fell into a horrible fever. Vivid nightmares every night, demons approaching him, shadow monsters whispering horrible things. His fever burned everyone who touched him, they say. Eventually it killed him."

My heart pounded in my ears. A powerful man with ties to the imperial family, hunted by nightmares until they killed him. Could he be a Kami, too?

And suddenly I saw that the flames in the picture were moving, flickering back and forth in the inky darkness. I jumped back.

"Daijoubu?" Niichan asked.

"I'm not okay," I whispered. "I thought I saw… There! Did you see it?"

"What?"

Of course he'd think I was crazy. But I knew I'd seen it. "Never mind," I said, backing away from the woodblock. "It must be the heat. Do you guys keep this room so warm to preserve the treasures or something?"

"Katie," Niichan said, and I looked at him. Suddenly the room was freezing.

"What's going on?" I said, and Niichan's face twisted with confusion.

"You saw the flames move, didn't you?"

"What do you mean? That's impossible," I lied. Niichan shook his head.

"You felt the fire. Taira was a Kami, Katie, and so was Yoshitoshi, who painted this piece. But if you saw it move—I don't understand." He leaned against the wall, crossing his arms over his chest. "I don't know how, Katie, but I think you're a Kami."

Reality shattered, everything around me slowing. "Me?"

"If you weren't, the flames wouldn't have danced for you. Yoshitoshi's Kami bloodline was faint. His ink only reacts to those whose Kami blood has been awakened."

"I'm…I'm not…"

"You know what a Kami is," Niichan said, and shocked by his words, I nodded. There was no sense denying it. "You'd have to know, to ask me the questions you did. Your drawings move, don't they?"

"They don't." Except one time, but Tomohiro had been there. "And I couldn't be a Kami." I lifted a tangle of blond hair in my hand.

"That's true," Niichan said. "It shouldn't be reacting to you, but it is. You must be tied to the Kami somehow. Why?"

I don't know. But that's the problem, isn't it? That's why Tomohiro's drawings are going haywire, "Niichan," I said, nervous to spill the secret. "I know someone who—whose drawings move. But it's worse when I'm around. The ink jumps off the page."

Niichan's eyebrows shot up. "You know such a powerful Kami? Be careful, Katie. Most aren't capable of such things. And if you're influencing the ink, then it might be best if you don't go near this Kami. Who knows what could happen?"

Like a dragon lifting into the sky? Too late.

"How do you know about Kami anyway?" I said. "You're… you're not one, are you?"

He shook his head. "You just hear things when you work at a shrine, especially one with ancient connections like Itsukushima. Most people have forgotten about Kami. I shouldn't even let on that I know, but you're Yuki's friend. I was worried when you started asking about drawings having power."

"Thank you," I said. "It's hard to find anything out about the Kami. I guess it's a big secret to keep."

Niichan moved forward, resting his hands on my shoulders. "Don't tell anyone, Katie. Not even Yuki. She's a good friend, but she has a big mouth." I nodded and he dropped his hands, stepping out of the room as I followed behind. I felt nothing but ice and numbness as he slid the door shut and locked up the room of treasures, the room of the flickering fire. It occurred to me the room was fireproof to keep the painting from burning down the rest of the shrine, not to protect the treasures inside.

I walked in silence as we scaled the mountain, toward the wafting smell of Yuki's curry bubbling.

I wasn't a Kami, but I was tied to the ink somehow. And if I stayed with Tomohiro, we could lose everything.

I wondered what hope there was for him, what hope there was for me.

As I stood on the ferry waving goodbye to Niichan, Miyajima and the giant o-Torii gate dropped from sight. We sped through Hiroshima on the bullet train, through Osaka and Kyoto, moving closer and closer to Shizuoka. My mind was buzzing, despite the earache the train gave me. Could I really be connected to the Kami? I didn't like the thought that whatever haunted Tomohiro was in my veins, too. The text from Tomohiro had been the only one I'd received, and after sending two or three unanswered, I'd stopped. I didn't want to look desperate, and anyway, he must have a good reason for not replying. Or at least he better. Maybe Ishikawa had been looming over his shoulder all the time. And maybe he was actually getting some kendo training done.

Diane was still away for another week, and I was supposed to stay with Yuki's family until she came back, so naturally I didn't breathe a word of it to Yuki and came home to an empty mansion, mine alone for a whole week.

I dropped onto the couch and surfed through TV channels, mindlessly watching variety shows for a while. I tried to ignore the possibility that Niichan was right, but how could he be wrong? Though he'd admitted he didn't have all the answers. Maybe I wasn't tied to the Kami. Maybe the painting reacted to me because of my time with Tomohiro or something like that.

I sighed. I didn't want to deal with this, especially on an empty stomach. I searched the kitchen cupboards but only came up with shrimp chips and bitter oolong tea.

I sat down with a bowl of the shrimp chips and flipped open my *keitai.* Still no messages. I phoned Tomohiro's *keitai,* but it was off. I dialed his home phone, but it rang and rang. When I got the answering machine, I hung up.

The panic was creeping through me, but I hadn't wanted to admit it, not in Miyajima. But now, alone in my thoughts and alone in Shizuoka, I couldn't put it off any longer.

What if the Yakuza got to him while I was away? What if something had happened to him?

No, it was ridiculous. He was probably just busy. And what were they going to do with him anyway? Just how dangerous could a paintbrush be?

The image of Tomohiro's slashed wrist jumped to the front of my mind, all the cuts up and down his arm.

I phoned again, but still no answer. I watched the variety shows a little longer.

When I couldn't stand the thoughts flashing through my head, I pulled on a light sweater and headed out to the *conbini* store to get some dinner.

I walked farther than I needed to, the cool night air calming me down. In the mansion, the thoughts seemed to bounce off the walls and come back at me again, but out here they lifted into the air like clouds of glittering ink.

The doors of the *conbini* slid open as I approached, and I dropped my eyes from the teen clerk, heading straight to the refrigerated aisle. My eyes fell on the desserts, then the *bentous.* I picked out *unagi* with rice and *gyoza* on the side, and then chose a *purin* pudding for dessert. Then I stared at the drinks for a while, trying with effort to read all the different choices.

"Katie?" My body froze, but my thoughts took off at top speed, rattling around in my head until I didn't know whether to run or face the voice. I turned, slowly, and saw a familiar face tilting at me, eyes filled with curiosity. The lick of blond at his ears. The glint of his silver earring.

"Jun," I said, the panic reining itself in. He smiled at me, and I realized I'd probably looked like a nervous idiot the way I'd jumped.

"What a coincidence," he said. Then, deciding it wasn't too rude to comment on my jitters, he added, "Are you okay?"

"Oh, I'm fine," I mumbled. "Just getting some dinner." I motioned at him with the eel dinner box.

"Ah," he said, smiling broadly again. He looked different out of his school uniform, all casual flare with a white T-shirt, jeans and a short-sleeved black jacket draped over his broad shoulders. He wore one of those thick black bracelets around his wrist, the kind with silver spikes on it. It looked ridiculous.

"Um," I said, because he was still smiling and waiting for me to say something. "How was the kendo retreat?"

"Tough, but we learned a lot. It was great to get to know Yuu and Ishikawa better."

"Oh," I said, and relief flooded through me. So nothing weird had happened.

"I thought you'd have heard from Yuu by now," he said, and I felt the heat rise up my neck.

"What do you mean?" I said. He looked down at the floor with a grin and bobbed his head, like he was apologizing for bringing it up.

"Because you and Yuu are friends," he said. Which was all he needed to say, really. I hoped Tomohiro wasn't going around bragging like a jerk. It would definitely line up with the idiot who looked up my skirt. But then I dismissed it. I knew he wasn't really like that at all.

"Anyway," Jun continued, "I learned a lot training with them. It turns out we have some things in common."

"Oh," I said, wondering why Yuu hadn't called me if things were all fine. It didn't even sound like Ishikawa had pestered him much about the dragon. "That's nice."

"You know, I knew from the way Yuu held his *shinai* the first time that he'd done calligraphy."

My blood ran cold. "Calligraphy?" I choked out, but Jun looked unfazed. Of course he did. There wasn't anything weird about calligraphy. Usually.

He nodded. "There's something artistic about the way he moves. I've been in the Calligraphy Club since junior high, and I can see it in his swordsmanship. You know, they have a lot in common."

"Who does?"

"I mean calligraphy and kendo." He smiled patiently.

I felt stupid suddenly, hot and itchy and wishing I could just go up to the bored clerk and pay for my *bentou* so I could get out of there. Instead I asked, "They do?"

"They're both Zen traditions," Jun said. "Calming your mind, looking within yourself for beauty and inspiration."

"Uh-huh."

Jun smiled yet again. "I guess I'm talking too much. Anyway, I tried to get Yuu to draw with me, but he wouldn't do it. You'll have to convince him to show me his work sometime."

I paled. "Sure thing."

"Well..." he said, bobbing his head and lifting up a bottle of cold tea. He went to the front to pay and I stared down at my *bentou,* waiting for him to vanish. But just as he was ready to walk through the open doors, he turned and walked back to me.

"I forgot to ask you," he said, his face twisting with concern. "How is Yuu's wrist doing?"

The shelves in the *conbini* seemed to blur out of focus. I opened my mouth, but only an awful squeaking sound came out.

"Didn't…didn't he tell you?" Jun said, his face full of surprise. "On the first day of training, he brought his *shinai* down hard on Ishikawa's *men* and his wrist split open. Must have been an earlier injury he didn't take care of. He had to go to the hospital for stitches."

I just stared at him with my mouth open. Ishikawa would've seen it, then. The truth, on display in front of the one person it shouldn't be. Ishikawa would put it together, the strange jagged wound on Tomohiro's wrist appearing on the same day a dragon lifted into the sky.

"Oh," he said, rubbing the back of his head. "I'm sorry you heard from me. He probably didn't want to worry you. Training was okay after that, don't worry, but it just seemed like an awfully deep wound. It's a shame, with the tournament coming up. And Ishikawa said Yuu is so good at calligraphy, so he'll have to take a break from that, too. I hope it heals up."

"Oh," I finally squeaked out.

"Give him my regards, okay? Hope he is all healed up for the prefecture finals." He gave a friendly wave and curved out the door.

As soon as I paid for my *unagi* and *purin,* I bolted out the door and down the dark streets. I turned down the alleyways, not even thinking of my own safety. I almost crashed into a boy on a bike as I twisted through the streets, until the houses got bigger and the crowds got smaller.

I didn't stop until the iron gate was in sight. My lungs

burned as I hunched over, panting, the crinkle of my *conbini* bag the only other sound in the thick night air. I pressed my hand against the cold metal nameplate above the intercom button. Once I'd caught my breath, I pushed the button in. The metal gate was closed.

"Yes?" came a tinny voice across the intercom, and a thought fired through my brain.

Tomohiro.

But a moment later I realized it wasn't Tomohiro but an older, rougher version of his voice. His dad.

"I'm looking for Yuu Tomohiro," I said.

"He's out" came the reply.

"I really need to talk to him," I said, because really, what else could I say?

"Sorry." The voice vibrated through the speaker. "I don't know where he is. You could try his *keitai.*"

Because that had worked so well over the past week.

"Thank you," I said and turned down the street, wondering where to go next.

Toro Iseki, obviously, but as soon as I started sprinting down the street, I slowed down. There's no way he'd be there, not this late. Would he?

I imagined his drawings fluttering through the darkness, as white as ghosts.

I flipped open my *keitai,* staring at his phone number on the bright screen. My finger circled the send button, but I couldn't bring myself to do it again. It started to dawn on me, the only things I knew for sure:

Yuu Tomohiro was not kidnapped by the Yakuza (yes, I had been worried about this).

Yuu Tomohiro's wrist was seriously injured, more than he'd let on. And Ishikawa had seen it.

Yuu Tomohiro was avoiding me.

My heart felt like it had collapsed in on itself. Was that last one really true? Was it all in my head? There was this nagging unsettled feeling, like the balance of the world was tipping.

I twisted through the streets, not sure where to go. Toro Iseki was a long way to go if I was wrong, and I felt like I was. With his wrist that damaged, could he really draw anything? And would he want to draw anymore, after what had happened?

It's worth my life, but it isn't worth yours.

Was my life for sure at risk?

I had to find him. I stared down the street, the lights of Shizuoka blurring as I spun my head around. He was somewhere. I just had to figure it out.

I walked back to Shizuoka Station; it wasn't like I had a better idea, and the station was the central nerve of the city. On a board in the station, tourist flyers splayed out of little cubbyholes. Most of them had majestic views of Fuji or Shizuoka tea fields sprawled across them, but one was for Toro Iseki. I flipped the brochure open and saw the open hours. Definitely closed by now, but that wouldn't stop Tomohiro anyway. I debated about the twenty-minute bus ride, the long walk back if I was wrong. And if I was wrong, I sure didn't want to break into Toro Iseki at dark. I shuddered, imagining my hand touching the wet snakeskin of the dragon, though of course his body was long gone by now.

Some places in the city didn't close when the sun set. Ramen-noodle-house signs gleamed in the darkness. *Conbini* stores glowed with their shiny mopped floors. I snuck a peek at the café where we'd had dinner together, but no luck. What else might be open?

And what was Tomohiro thinking anyway, running off

to places at night where I couldn't find him? Didn't he have entrance exams to worry about? And didn't he need every spare moment of study time in between all those practices for the kendo tournament?

I stopped dead in the whirlwind of travelers that pulsed around the station.

Kendo.

I ran through Sunpu Park under the dim lamplight and the bare *sakura* branches, past lovers and friends strolling through, salarymen stumbling home from nights of drinking with coworkers. I ran until my lungs burned, until the roof of Sunpu Castle gleamed in the distant moonlight, and then I crossed the northern bridge toward Suntaba School.

I had to make sure Tomohiro was okay. Had Ishikawa backed off? No more swarming with creepy Yakuza members? After talking to Jun, I had to know. I had to know if everything was all right.

Most of the lights in the school had blinked out and it looked deserted, empty, like the shell of a distant memory.

Deserted except for the bright fluorescent lights that gleamed from the gym doorway.

I ran toward the door, my lungs about to burst and my legs about to give way. The warm light from the gym spread across the shadows of the rear courtyard, lighting up the tennis-court lines in a ghostly shade of yellow.

I stopped as I reached the open door, pressing myself against the frame as I peered in.

Tomohiro was inside, alone and decked out in kendo armor, swinging his *shinai* through the air. He turned, moving through the katas and *kiri-kaeshis* like a dancer in slow motion, silently at first, then with shouts of determination.

Even from here I could see how unsatisfied he was with the

movements. He'd swipe through the air, curse as he walked back into place, then strike again. The *shinai* shook in his hands; he lost his grip and the sword fell an inch—not at lot, but enough to distinguish a point from a miss.

It wasn't like him to struggle with the easier movements. It took me five seconds to realize it was his wrist, because although the strength in a *shinai* swing comes from the left hand, it's the right that guides the hit. And Tomohiro's was going all over the place.

He swore and got back into place, shaking his head, clearing his thoughts. He thrust again, swung for a hit. He got it, but then the *shinai* fell again; better than I could do, but not like him at all.

I watched him struggle. I wasn't sure what to do, whether I should let him know I was there. But why did I go all the way to Suntaba if I wasn't even going to talk to him?

I stepped into the splash of artificial lights and walked toward him. He noticed me after a moment, lowering the *shinai* and pulling the *men* off his shoulders. I tried not to notice the way he stared at me, surprised and silent. I tried to stay focused on the fact that he was possibly avoiding me, and not to let on that I knew. Or to come off all mad at him. Something like that.

"You're back," he said, advancing toward me across the gym floor.

I squeezed the grain of annoyance in my mind as it struggled to get away.

"We got back this morning," I said.

"Okaeri." His voice was too gentle, passive almost. The whole thing felt off.

"Thanks. How about you? You're hard at work, I see."

"Yeah, well…" And he looked away. Was he avoiding me because he was embarrassed about his wrist? Or maybe the kissing in his living room? Now that I thought about it, it was kind of awkward.

"Um…so how was the training retreat?" I said. *I'm connected to the Kami,* I wanted to blurt out, but everything about him felt weird. He started to unbuckle the armor and reached for his water bottle on the bench nearby.

"Fine," he said. "I might have learned enough of Takahashi's moves to beat him next time."

"Great," I said. "And Ishikawa?"

"Ishikawa's fast," he said, chugging down the water. He wiped his mouth with the back of his arm and screwed the lid back onto the bottle. "But there's a good chance we won't be paired in the tournament. Usually they don't pit team members against each other."

"Oh." Pause. "So, um, how is your wrist doing?"

He hesitated and stopped pulling off his glove so it sat there half on, half off, the laces dangling down.

"I mean because of before," I said. His eyes were glaring, like I'd hit a sore spot. But he didn't know Jun had told me about it, right? I could just be innocently asking.

"It's fine," he said, grabbing the fingers of the glove and yanking it off, dropping his arm down before I could see.

Jeez, touchy much?

"That's great," I said. "So Ishikawa…?"

Another pause. "We're getting along fine."

I felt like I was standing in the middle of a quiet street, just waiting to get run over. Why was his voice so cold?

Then, as he looked into my eyes, his voice softened. He untied the *tare* around his waist and placed it with the rest of the armor. I noticed the new headband in his hair, not a bloodstain on it. He pulled it backward off his head, and his copper hair flopped down around his ears.

"Did you have fun in Miyajima?"

"Yeah, it was okay." *I might be a Kami.* I couldn't say it. It felt wrong, like I was intruding on the pain he suffered. But Niichan's alternative, keeping my distance from Tomohiro—it scared me more. "I…I went to a Shinto shrine. I think maybe I learned why the ink moves."

"What?"

I swallowed. "What if I'm a Kami, Tomo?"

He stared at me for a moment.

"You can't be," he said.

"What if there's some other way, though? What if I'm connected somehow?"

"Do you have nightmares?" he said. "Like the ones I told you about?"

"What? No."

"Then you're not. All Kami have nightmares." I thought of the painting of Taira no Kiyomori, the demons and shadows encircling him. "Not all Kami's drawings move, right? But all Kami have the nightmares."

"Oh." Niichan hadn't said that.

"There's some other reason you're moving the ink. I'm not sure why. But don't worry about it, okay? You're not a monster, not like me. *Ii ka?*"

"O-okay."

"Good." He stooped down and packed his *shinai,* gloves and *hakama* into his navy sports bag, carrying the rest to the storage room at the back of the gym. "So…want to go for some ramen?"

Not really. Why was it so awkward?

"Sure."

When I got home, the phone was ringing. I hurried over to pick it up, but when I heard the voice on the other end, my mistake occurred to me.

"How'd you know I'd be here?" I said, scrambling for an excuse. Diane did half a laugh on the phone.

"I'd be more surprised if you weren't," she said. "C'mon, what teenager doesn't want the house to herself for a week?"

"Diane, I promise, I'll be really careful and take good care of myself."

"I know," she said. "If I thought you'd throw a house party, I'd have confiscated your key."

"Does that mean—?"

"Yes, yes." She sighed. "You can stay. But if anything happens, you call Yuki's mom, okay?"

"I will," I promised.

"So how was Miyajima?"

"Really nice."

"Uh-huh."

"I brought some *manju* home. You know, those cakes with custard in them."

"Oh, that's even better. Try and save some until I get home."

"I will."

"What did you have for dinner tonight?"

I stared at the *unagi bentou,* still in the bag. I wondered if it was ruined by now.

"Unagi," I said. She didn't say anything for a minute. "Diane?"

"I'm here," she said. "It's just, you're sounding...well, not so much like a *gaijin* anymore." Diane laughed, and even though

I felt like I should be annoyed, I felt kind of proud. "Just like Nan," she said. "You could be planted anywhere and bloom."

"Comes with the genes," I said. "Well, I mean, for you and me." Mom had only wanted to bloom in familiar territory. I don't think she would have gone for shrimp chips and seaweed.

"I'm in Osaka for a few more days and then I'll be back, okay? Call me if you need anything."

"I will."

"Love you," Diane said, and before I could answer, she hung up.

"Love you, too," I said to the dial tone.

I put the *unagi* in the fridge and went into my room to pull on my pajamas. I sprawled out on my bed, staring at the ceiling.

I thought about how dim Tomohiro's eyes had been, not lit up the way they were when he was happy or even when he was delighting in being a jerk. Was he really so upset about his wrist?

I rolled onto my side and curled up. It made sense when I thought about it. He'd had to quit calligraphy, the one thing he loved, because of this dark ability. And now the other passion in his life, kendo, was tainted, too. He couldn't get away from this power, a dark inkblot on his life that controlled him unless he could find a way to control it.

So far, the ink was winning.

14

The sound of my *keitai* beeping woke me the next morning. I rubbed my eyes until they turned red.

"What time is it?" I mumbled, fingers splayed out as they searched the table beside me for the phone. I flipped the *keitai* open and looked at the text message from Tomohiro.

Meet me at 1pm, Shizuoka Station. —Yuu

I stared at the name he'd written. Yuu felt distant and strange, but maybe he'd just made a mistake. He did seem a little off since the kendo retreat.

I stayed too long in the shower, until my skin turned pink and taut under all the steam. I put on my pretty pink shirt and a cream skirt, and even tried to do my hair up, which didn't really work that well, but hey, points for effort, right?

I waited outside the bus loop until I saw him stride over, his eyes cold and distant. He had the same look from school, the way he'd look staring at me from across the courtyard.

"Come on," he said, looping his fingers around my wrist.

"Hey," I said, following behind him. I pulled my hand out of his grip as I followed him. "What's up with you today?"

"Sorry," he said, looking down at the ground. "It's my wrist. It's really bugging me." He pulled up the black wristband he wore to cover it and I gasped. The stitches were still visible, and the gash looked way bigger than I remembered.

"Will it…will it leave a scar?"

He hesitated for a second, then smirked and slipped the soft wristband back over the cut.

"I've got quite the collection," he said, but the joke just made my stomach twist.

He led me through the winding, narrow streets of the Oguro neighborhood, until I'd completely lost track of where we were. He reached again for my arm and pulled incessantly, checking his watch again and again. So much for a nice date. My pink-and-cream outfit looked completely out of place against the monotonous gray of the streets.

At last he led me toward a tall building. I couldn't read the kanji, which wasn't new. When he stopped abruptly, I almost crashed into his back.

"Close your eyes," he said, turning his head to the side and not meeting my eyes.

"Tomo."

"It's okay," he said. "Trust me."

I raised an eyebrow. "*Trust you,* Mr. Cheesy?"

He gave me an agitated sigh. *"Ii kara!"*

"Fine, fine."

"Okay." His voice was heavy, but I closed my eyes and let him lead me up the stairs and through some glass door.

The building inside smelled of dried flowers and musty carpet. We went up some more stairs and down a hallway, and I opened my eyes to peek. The hallway was lit with yellow lights glaring from above, an ugly carpet on the floor. Doors flanked both sides of the wall, like an apartment building.

Only, I was wrong.

Tomohiro stopped at one door and fiddled with a key in his pocket. He slid the lock open and led me in. The door clicked behind us, his hands on my shoulders. I stepped forward slowly, panic rising up my shoulders, buzzing in my ears.

I could barely get the words out. "What is this?" My throat felt like it had seized up.

"It's a love hotel." And there it was.

"What?" I couldn't have heard him right.

"It's popular in Japan," he said, isolating me as he said it. "It's a place where we can be alone." He turned around then, a sly smile on his face.

The room was huge, with a big soaker tub on the other side with marble steps leading up to it. And behind him, a neatly made bed. The whole thing looked like a very fancy hotel room, and I felt the lump in my throat growing.

He kissed me then, but it wasn't at all like the kisses in his living room. His arms wrapped around me, but they weren't gentle.

My world no longer felt like it was slipping out of balance. It had tilted right over and I was falling, tumbling into space, into the flames below.

Yeah, he was gorgeous, and it wasn't like I hadn't thought about him a lot since that night at his house. But it was too fast, way too fast. There was no way I was ready for this.

His kisses trailed to my shoulder, and the panic burned through me. My ears hummed like I'd been surrounded by screaming tweens at an Arashi concert.

"Tomo," I said. "I don't— I think— I'm not really ready for this." I tried to lift his hands off me, but they snaked away and landed on my arms, my back, my hips. I stepped away from his lips as he leaned in, but his hands pressed me into the wall and he kissed me so hard I swore my lips would bruise.

I grabbed his shoulders with my hands and shoved him away. "I said quit it!"

The look on his face was horrible, an ugly sneer that made me look ungrateful. It made me feel like garbage, like he thought I was utter garbage.

"Typical Western girl," he snapped, and time stopped. Hot tears sprang to my eyes and my stomach churned. He leaned in to kiss me again, but I turned away. I darted for the door and stumbled into the hallway.

"Katie!" I heard him call after me, but I ran faster, throttled down the stairs as my heart pounded in my chest. The tears wouldn't stop, tracing down my cheeks and blurring my vision as I ran. I didn't know where to go, but when I stared down the first-floor hallway, I saw that one end led to an array of doors and the other a glass door to the street.

I burst onto the sidewalk, clacking down the stairs in the shoes I'd so carefully chosen to go with my outfit. It seemed ridiculous now; all the warning signs, and yet I'd never admitted to myself what kind of guy he really was.

I raced down the street, choking back sobs. I stumbled as a shape rose in front of me, a person I hadn't seen through my blurry vision. I tried to stop before we crashed, but my shoe twisted underneath me and I collapsed. He caught me before I hit the cement.

I looked up with horror.

Ishikawa.

"Greene?" he said, looking puzzled. His forehead creased as he looked at me with concern. "Are you okay?"

"Leave me alone," I said, struggling out of his arms. I ran forward, but I could feel his eyes burning into my back as I sprinted away.

Oguro was a messy labyrinth of streets. I hurried onward,

getting more and more lost, feeling like a dragon coiling in on its own tail, until my legs gave out. I fell to my knees, my lungs burning, and I cried there, cried and cried until the sobs ran dry.

I spent the night watching variety shows on TV, eating melon ice with a miniature wooden spoon they gave me at the *conbini* store. My head was spinning, even though I'd already downed two headache tablets with a slug of bitter oolong tea.

All the signs had been there. Didn't I know better than to go for that kind of guy, thinking I had seen a different side of him and just excusing the way he acted the rest of the time? I watched the variety-show panel as they jumped on little trampolines and shot hoops, and then talked about the history of *onigiri* rice balls.

I flinched when the phone rang. I didn't want to answer it in case it was Tomohiro, although he hadn't tried my *keitai* yet, so I figured he was pretty pissed.

Well, good. I was way more pissed.

The phone kept ringing. If it was Diane and I didn't answer, then she'd worry and I'd never be allowed to be by myself again. Although that wasn't really the worst punishment; apparently I wasn't capable of making good judgments anymore.

The phone rang again. Maybe it was Yuki or Tanaka. They could pull me out of this spiral of misery. I swallowed hard, lifted the receiver and put it to my ear.

"Hello?"

"Um, hello?" It was a girl's voice, gentle but unfamiliar. I wondered if it was a wrong number.

"Yes?"

"Is this, um, Katie Greene?"

"Unfortunately, it is."

A confused hesitation. "What?"

"Sorry," I said. "Yes, it's me."

"Oh." Pause. She sounded so nervous. Why the heck was she calling me? "I'm sorry to bother you. My name is Yamada Shiori."

My head buzzed with a migraine, but the name hit some sort of recognition. How did I know that name?

"I go to a girls' school near Sunpu Park. I'm a friend of Yuu Tomohiro…?"

It struck me like a hit between the eyes, like a *shinai* cracking down on my head.

Shiori. The pregnant "girlfriend."

"Oh, hi," I said weakly. She gave an embarrassed laugh on the phone, like she was relieved I knew who she was.

"I wanted to ask you about Tomo-kun," she said, and I felt like I would throw up. That was the last thing I wanted to talk about. I bet she really *was* his girlfriend after all. Nothing would surprise me at this point.

I dug the wooden spoon into the melon ice while I held the phone with my shoulder. "Yeah?"

"Well, have you noticed anything strange lately?"

The world that had been spinning stopped suddenly. I fell back into the couch and cupped the receiver with both hands. "What do you mean?"

"Well, he's been coming to visit me and help me with my… situation. Our mothers were best friends before, um, before the accident. But he hasn't been coming around lately, and he's been sort of…cold, somehow. Tough."

I couldn't speak.

"The thing is, Yuu has some friends who are no good. I'm a little scared that he's in trouble. You know, with his last girlfriend, when she was in trouble with them, he actually—I know it sounds cruel but—he asked if he could sketch me so she would think he was cheating. He said he had to do something severe to protect her."

Her words blurred in my ears. Yuu's last girlfriend. Saeda Myu. The name cracked into my head.

Point. Two wins the match.

It hit me then, in a horrible way. The argument between Myu and Tomohiro in the *genkan* at school, the way he'd been a total ass to her. The betrayal in her eyes, that she'd thought he was different, and his confession to me later in Toro Iseki.

I had to hurt her to protect her, to keep her safe from what I am.

My thoughts spun. I could hear Shiori calling my name, but I couldn't respond.

I was a moron. An absolute, total moron.

It wasn't like Tomohiro to take me to a love hotel, to say the things he'd said. He was messing with me to get me to hate him.

To save me.

"Katie?" Shiori's gentle voice reached through the chaos swirling in my head.

"Shiori," I said. "I think he's in trouble. I'm going to find him." I copied down her number, promising to call her back, and slammed the phone down.

I grabbed my purse and pushed open the sliding door to the deck, where Diane's bike gleamed in the setting sun. I lifted the handlebars over my shoulder and dragged the bike to the door, shoving it into the elevator and cramming it through the lobby doors.

The wheels hit the pavement and I was off, snaking away from the sunset over Shizuoka, into the end-of-day humidity. I wove through cars, motorbikes and taxis. The clouds above gathered and the rain started to drizzle down, not much more than a fog around me.

How could I have been so stupid? How could I fall for it so easily?

The more I thought about it, the sicker I felt. What were the chances in a city of seven hundred thousand people that I would run into Ishikawa *right outside the hotel?* That's why Tomohiro kept checking his watch—he'd asked Ishikawa to wait outside so he could see us break up. It was a setup to throw off the Yakuza. I could see that now. And I'd fallen for it.

He really pissed me off.

I wound past Shizuoka Station and up into the streets of Oguro, where I was a bit lost. It had been hours since it had happened, so why would he still be here? I followed the way as well as I could remember, which really wasn't that well.

The streets were deserted in the rain, and the darkness fell quickly. Before I knew it, I was biking through Oguro alone, the roads lit by the humming fluorescent lights of the *conbini* stores every few blocks.

I stopped in front of one and flipped open my *keitai.* I dialed Tomohiro, but his phone was off and it went straight to his voice mail. I pedaled forward again, hunting through the maze of Oguro, searching for…something.

An hour later, the backs of my legs ached and I hadn't found anything. I decided on a new plan and set out for Shizuoka Station. And then came a loud crash.

There was an overturned garbage can near the mouth of Sunpu Park, and beside it on the bridge I saw a familiar shock of white hair.

I slowed down, lifting my leg over the bike. I coasted on

one pedal the way Tomohiro always did. I jumped off as I neared the bridge, slipping behind a white truck parked there.

Ishikawa pulled himself up onto the cement railing of the bridge, kicking his legs against the stone. Two of his unshaven cronies stood with him, one wearing sunglasses, the other smoking a cigarette. I wondered if they were the same ones who'd confronted me when I was with Jun, but they didn't look familiar. How many Yakuza were in Shizuoka anyway? It wasn't like it was Tokyo or Kobe, the center of their headquarters. What the hell were they here for? The fields of tea?

Oh. Probably.

And then I saw Tomohiro standing across from them, his navy gym bag at his feet, surrounded, with no hope of escaping.

He didn't look stressed, though. He leaned against a *sakura* trunk, hands in his pockets, slouching. He wore a short-sleeved cream jacket over his black T-shirt and jeans, the soft color catching the dim lights around the bridge. He looked down at the ground, his bangs fanning into his eyes.

"How long are you going to deny it?" Ishikawa said. I pressed my fingers into the cold metal edge of the truck and slid down to squat on my heels. Alarm bells blared in my head. Should I call the police? Or would that be even more exposure Tomohiro didn't want?

Tomohiro didn't answer, and Ishikawa laughed, smacking his fist against the railing.

"It doesn't really matter if you admit it or not," he said. "We know you drew the dragon, Yuuto. I'm just trying to give you a chance. We've been best friends a long time. I want to help you, man. I know you're scared."

It sounded like the speech he gave me. And Tomohiro smirked at it, too, staring Ishikawa straight in the eye.

"Scared of what?" he said. "You're talking shit."

"Scared of your power," Ishikawa said. "Scared of the possibilities. You think you're the only Kami in Shizuoka? I heard about the nightmares you 'gifted ones' have. And shit are you gifted, Yuuto. You think all Kami can make dragons?"

Tomohiro smirked and looked away. "Like I said, you're crazy, Sato."

"Oh? How'd you get that scar on your wrist, Yuuto?"

Tomohiro wrapped his slender fingers around his wristband and twisted it back and forth.

"Fuck you," he spat. The two guys beside Ishikawa lurched forward and Tomohiro uncoiled, balling his hands into fists. My breath caught in my throat.

"Yuuto," Ishikawa said, his eyes gleaming in the darkness. There was something tender in his voice. "I don't want it to go this way." He leaped to his feet and strode forward, in front of the brawly guys. "Please don't make me do this."

"Walk away from this, Sato," Tomohiro said. "You think you're in control of this situation? You think you're important to them?"

Ishikawa stared at him for a minute, his face turning red.

"They're using you, Sato. And you're letting them."

"Shut up!" Ishikawa shouted, his voice cracking as the words buzzed in my ears. "You want to see me in control, Yuuto? Fine!"

"Sato—"

"Screw you!" He turned to the thugs, tears in his eyes, his voice broken. "Bring him! If you break his wrist, I'll break yours."

The men were on him suddenly, and Tomohiro was pushing, shoving them away. I heard a horrible crack and saw Tomohiro's fist outstretched, one of the men ricocheting away.

The guy in the sunglasses dove for Tomohiro's knees and they buckled, the two men tumbling to the ground. He punched Tomohiro in the face and pulled at his hair, his hand coming away with a wad of copper strands. Tomohiro kicked and squirmed, slamming the man against the tree trunk. He was up again and the guy with the cigarette was on him, blood dripping from his bottom lip. Ishikawa stayed out of it, backed against the bridge. He was shaking, like he wanted to call the goons off. His face was full of regret and his mouth opened, but he closed it again, looking down.

He didn't have the guts to stop them. Some best friend.

Or maybe he couldn't. Maybe they wouldn't listen anyway, like Sugi hadn't with Jun.

Cigarette punched Tomohiro in the stomach and he doubled over. I let out a silent scream, but when Ishikawa's eyes shot toward me, I realized it hadn't been silent at all.

Crap.

"Katie," Ishikawa said, renewed resolve in his voice. "Grab her!" I rose to my feet, but they felt like blocks of lead. I turned and ran, trying to get my leg over the bike as I scooted forward on one pedal. When that didn't work, I threw the bike down, fumbling in my purse for my phone as I ran.

"Katie!" shouted Tomohiro, and he was up like a shot. The men reached me first, linking their fat arms around mine and dragging me backward. My phone clattered to the ground. I cried out and struggled in their grip, and as I pulled from side to side, Tomohiro's image shook in front of me, his eyes filled with terror.

"Greene, you're just not having a good day, are you?" Ishikawa shouted, but all I could see was Tomohiro scrambling forward, blood trickling down his face.

Cigarette yanked my arms behind my back while Sunglasses stood there with his hand on my neck. They both reeked of sweat and tobacco.

"Fuck you, Satoshi!" Tomohiro screamed, and the smile faded from Ishikawa's face. He looked embarrassed, even. "Leave her out of this!"

"I thought you two broke up," Ishikawa said. "But it doesn't look that way, does it?"

I heard my own voice, trembling, vibrating under the meaty fingers of Sunglasses. "We broke up," I said.

"Really?" Ishikawa said. "Why's that, then? Did you find out about him? Who he really is?"

"I don't know what you're talking about," I lied. He smirked.

"Is that true? You don't know the monster lurking inside him? He's a danger to all of Japan, Greene, all of the world. You don't know what he's capable of."

"I didn't know what *you* were capable of," I spat. The goons jerked me backward.

Ishikawa shouted, "Yuuto! Work with us, and we'll let her go."

No. He was going to use me as bait. Tomohiro's eyes met mine, and in them there was none of the darkness that I had seen in the hotel, no ugliness or hatred. I saw only our link, the axis that kept our worlds spinning, that kept us in balance. And I knew that neither of us could leave the other.

Tomohiro started to shake. He turned to Ishikawa and his back was toward me, his navy kendo bag trampled on the ground. Fresh blood leaked between the stitches across his wrist and curled up his fingers, dripping to the ground. His body heaved with every breath, and I knew he would give himself up. I could almost hear the words rounding on his lips, giving them up to save me. Destroying himself for me.

But the words didn't come. He shook, more and more

violently, and then something glinted in the darkness, sparkling like a jewel. Ink shimmered on the ground where it had oozed out of his duffel bag, out of the corner of velvet that lay torn at the mouth of the zipper. And then something reflected off Tomohiro's hip. The glint grew darker, more encompassing and thicker. Ink dripped from under his cream jacket, spreading in two swirling clouds around him like the glittering dust that had trailed the wagtail.

When the ink clouds touched the ground they curled upward, like waves encircling him in slow motion. The ink from the kendo bag sprawled upward and joined them, trailing up his spine in slow motion and spreading out at his shoulders.

His fists shook violently. The men holding me swore and released their grip as they watched.

"What the hell?" Sunglasses shrieked.

Ishikawa's face was pale, as papery as anything Tomohiro had drawn. He fell to the ground, scrambling backward until his back pressed against the scratchy stone of the bridge.

Tomohiro moaned as the inky clouds swirled around him. There was a vague shout gathering on the air, but it wasn't coming from him. I could hear it rattling around in my head, but there was no sound in my ears. The traces of the voice grew louder and louder until it was yelling in my head. I put my hands over my ears, but the sound seemed to come from inside. An icy breeze blew along my neck, racing toward Tomohiro as the clouds glinted and spread.

The ink feathered into monstrous black wings on his back. Two streams of ink spread upward, taller than Tomohiro—seven feet, then twelve, taller and taller like great spiraling horns. The goons had backed up now, and I should have run to Tomohiro—or run away—but we were all frozen by the horrible apparition.

The ink carved itself into a jawbone, cheekbones, deep-set eyes. Four sharp horns grew from the top of the smoky ink as it towered over us.

Ishikawa screamed as the ink assembled a horrible, demonic face that laughed gleefully the harder Ishikawa shrieked. I was glad I couldn't see its features from behind Tomohiro; I'd never seen Ishikawa act like that, so paralyzed with horror. He stared, his own face whiter than his hair, and my blood ran cold watching him.

Suddenly the ink fell like a waterfall. It splashed downward, Tomohiro collapsing with it, the ink splattering everywhere like blood. It sprayed against my face, warm and tingling on my skin.

I stumbled forward, snatching my *keitai* off the ground and shoving it into my pocket as I ran.

I knelt over Tomohiro; he was unconscious.

"Tomo!" I cried. The ink that pooled around him began to trace paths along the cement, reaching toward me like grasping fingers.

"It's you," Ishikawa said, and I barely heard him.

"Tomo! Can you hear me?"

"You're the key to all this, aren't you?"

"Can you shut it?" I shouted. "He needs an ambulance or something!"

"The ink. It reacted to you. There wasn't a drop until you got here."

Shut up, I thought, but I was shaking.

Because he was right.

15

I grabbed Tomohiro's shoulders and shook them.

"Tomo!" I shrieked, but his head rolled from side to side as I shook. He coughed, and ink spilled out of his mouth.

A meaty pair of hands grabbed me and yanked me backward.

"Forget it!" I heard Ishikawa say. "Let's just get out of here!"

"Screw you!" yelled Sunglasses. His thick fingers cut into my arms as I struggled. "You gonna let a freak that powerful just walk around? He's gonna hunt us down. Let's deal with this now."

"No Kami, no pay," said Cigarette. He reached over and pulled Tomohiro off the ground.

"Let go!" I screamed. Cigarette hoisted Tomohiro over his shoulder, bracing himself under the weight. He headed toward the unmarked truck I'd hidden behind, and threw the doors open with a sour metal clang.

Ishikawa got to his feet, his hands squeezed into fists. His face was pale and he stumbled as he moved forward.

"What makes you think we can control him, huh?" Ishikawa said. His eyes were wild and full of fear. I'd seen him scared before, but not like this. I could see his fists shaking as he struggled to keep them balled. "I know Yuuto. He'll leave us alone if we leave now." Cigarette slumped Tomohiro across the floor of the truck, then hopped in behind and dragged him by his shoulders into the darkness.

"Tomo!" I yelled. I kicked my shoes into Sunglasses's legs over and over, but it was like he couldn't even feel it.

"Having second thoughts, Satoshi?" Sunglasses said. "You know what we think of cowards like you."

"It's not like that," he said. And then Sunglasses yanked me over to the truck. "Shit, man," Ishikawa said. "Leave Katie here."

"So she can report us, you mean?" said Cigarette. "She's the missing piece, if you didn't notice. She's the freaking ink magnet. The inkwell." He emerged from the shadows, lighting a new cigarette and holding it between two fingers.

Fear rattled down my spine and spread its icy grip to every limb. I knew I was kicking, but I couldn't feel my legs moving anymore. The darkness of the truck loomed closer and closer, until Sunglasses threw me into it. I skidded across the metal floor, cold and studded with metal bolts that caught and sliced across my finger. My shoulder ached, but I sat up as quickly as I could, lunging toward the doors Cigarette was closing.

"Greene!" yelled Ishikawa.

I saw Sunglasses turn around and slug Ishikawa in the jaw, and then the doors slammed in my face.

"Let me out!" I banged my fists on the doors over and over. The sound of a metal bolt sliding into place echoed in the emptiness of the truck. I hit the door again.

Footsteps, the driver's door opening and banging shut, the engine roaring to life.

"Shit!" I shrieked, hot tears blurring in my eyes. My cut finger burned as I slammed my fists into the metal over and over.

The truck lurched and I tumbled backward, half on top of Tomohiro.

I cried out in panic for a minute, Tomohiro's limp legs pressed against mine. I screamed at my brain to think.

My *keitai.*

I grabbed it out of my pocket and flipped it open, the LCD screen illuminating the darkness of the truck. I dialed 911, pressed the send button and squeezed the phone against my ear.

Come on, come on…

A strange beeping noise and a recorded woman's voice babbling in Japanese.

What the crap? I dialed again.

How can the number not be in service?

And then it dawned on me. The emergency number in Japan is not 911.

But what the hell is it?

I stared at my phone, willing myself to know the number to call.

But I didn't.

I stared down at Tomohiro, putting my hand on the small of his back and shaking him gently.

"Tomo?" I said, my voice trembling.

The wings were still there, feathers of ink sprawled over him and draped onto the floor. There was a gaping hole in the wings where my hand touched his back. I lifted my fingers; the ink felt greasy and warm as it dripped down my hand and over the blood from my cut.

"Tomo." I shook him gently. But he was out cold, and the truck was driving us farther and farther into trouble.

My *keitai* screen blinked out suddenly, the truck dark except for a faint candlelike glimmer around the ink melting off Tomohiro's back.

I scrolled through the names in my address book, thinking who else I could call. Diane was in Osaka and I didn't have a contact number with me. I stared at each name as it illuminated on the screen.

There weren't many of them to choose from.

Then *Tanaka* flashed up on the display.

I mashed the buttons and pressed the phone to my ear.

It rang and rang. The truck lurched to the left and picked up speed. The ink and blood dripped off my wrist and onto my *keitai.* I switched hands and rubbed the gunk off on my jeans, making a big, ugly splotch.

"Moshi moshi?" said the voice on the phone, and I was too shaken up to realize it didn't sound familiar.

"Tanaka," I blurted out, "call the police. These Yakuza attacked us and we're in a truck and I don't know where they're taking us." I choked up and started to cry.

And then I realized from the confusion on the other end that something was wrong.

"Katie?"

It wasn't Tanaka. It was Takahashi.

I'd hit the wrong button and got the wrong name. But it didn't matter, because anyone could help us.

"Jun," I said. "Please help me."

"Oh god, Katie. Are you okay? Where are you?"

"I don't know!" I said through tears. My throat felt thick and I could barely get the words out. "We were at Sunpu Park. I think maybe we're on a highway. We're moving really fast."

"Don't panic," Jun said, and I felt like smacking him. *Don't panic? That's your best advice?* "I'll call the police. Katie, did they say why they took you? Was it that Ishikawa guy again?"

"Tomohiro's here, too," I sobbed.

"Yuu's there?" Silence. "Katie, do you know what they want?"

I opened my mouth but clamped it shut again. I cursed silently. I'd almost given away everything. Did it even matter anymore? They might be able to use Tomohiro, but not me. They'd— Oh my god. They'd kill me.

"Jun, please help me."

"Katie, I'm going to hang up so I can call the police. Try to keep your phone with you, okay? Put it in manner mode so they won't find it. I'm coming for you. Hold tight."

I didn't want to hang up, to sever the only link I had to help. But I didn't have to. Jun hung up first and my LCD dimmed, leaving me in darkness again.

"Tomo," I said, flipping my *keitai* closed and open again, and resting it beside us. The wings had melted, little pools of black trailing away from him, turning to dust and lifting slowly like dull fireflies.

His eyes were closed, his copper hair lined with sweat and clinging to the sides of his face. There was a dark pool near his mouth and I panicked. I grabbed the *keitai* and put it beside his face, then breathed out in relief.

It was ink dripping out of the corner of his mouth. Creepy, but it wasn't blood, so I figured he was okay.

I looked at my finger again to see how bad the cut was. It had stopped bleeding, but the truck was rusty. I hoped it wouldn't get infected. I reached into my pocket and pulled out a tissue, wrapped it around the cut and pressed my fingers together to hold it there.

I checked Tomohiro again and made sure he was breathing. Then I sat back and stared at the truck, looking for any means of escape.

The *keitai* screen blacked out again, and this time I folded it up, shoving it into my pocket. As chilling as it was to sit here in the dark, I needed to save the battery.

The truck pulled us forward, and I rocked back and forth in the darkness, nothing to do but wait.

"Katie?"

The voice startled me in the darkness, and I shot forward onto my hands and knees. "Tomo?"

He groaned, and I heard the slide of fabric as he pushed himself up. I lifted the *keitai* out of my pocket and saw him hunched over in the dim light.

"What happened?" he said, rubbing his jaw.

"You passed out," I said. "They took us somewhere. I don't know where. They killed the engine an hour ago, but no one's come for us yet."

He moaned, running his fingers through his hair. Even sweaty, bloody and shoved in the back of a gangster truck, he still made my stomach jittery when he did that. He made a face, lolling his tongue out. "Ugh, my mouth tastes like a pen exploded."

Okay, a little less attractive.

And then he snapped out of it and looked at me.

"Are you okay?" he said, and my *keitai* blinked out. "Did they hurt you?"

"I'm fine," I said, folding the phone and shoving it into my pocket. I felt the warmth of his breath as he moved closer, his palms sliding up my arms to my shoulders. The rough calluses from kendo practice scraped against my skin followed by the towellike wristband covering his scar.

"What happened?" he said again, his voice raw. "I remember shouting your name, and then this intense…pain, like I was burning alive."

"I don't know what happened," I said. Even trying to think back to it made me shudder. "There was ink everywhere. It made these…wings, on your back. And some kind of ugly, horned face above your head."

"Wings? A face?"

I smirked. "It scared the crap out of Ishikawa."

Tomohiro's voice was stone. "Good."

"He told them to leave us alone after that. But they didn't listen."

"Katie. You have to get out of here." His cool fingertips traced down my arms, sending shivers up my spine. They rested on my fingers, hesitated on my makeshift tissue bandage.

"Yeah, because I've just been sitting around in this truck for fun," I said. "Like there's a way out."

There was silence, and I felt a little guilty for being snarky. Just a little.

There was a distant sound, a crash not too far away. My heart jumped and I felt like I was going to puke.

"They're coming," I said.

"I'll protect you," Tomohiro said, squeezing my hands in his. "Go to the back of the truck." He dropped my hands and stood. A light flipped on outside the truck, a little stream of light filtering between the truck doors. I could see Tomohiro's hands balled into fists.

"You're kidding, right?" I said. "They'll kill you."

"Go to the back of the truck."

"Not a chance." My legs felt like they were made of stone, but I numbly dragged myself toward him.

The doors flung open to blinding light. I'd been sitting in the truck for so long that pins and needles started to spark in my legs. I stumbled backward.

My eyes adjusted and I saw three men, two of them covered in rainbows of sprawling tattoos. They held guns pointed straight at Tomohiro, and the chill spread through me.

Guns are illegal in Japan. Most police don't even carry them.

Which meant the police would be no match for these guys, even if they knew where to find us.

"Get out," said the third man, his hands folded behind his back. He wore a black business suit and looked fairly normal—almost pleasant. "And don't try anything."

At first Tomohiro didn't move. My brain practically screamed at him.

Then his feet dragged forward.

One of the guns followed his movement. The other one pointed at me.

Tomohiro's eyes went wide. "Let her go," he said.

I blinked back hot tears.

"It's okay," the suit guy said, staring at me. He lifted his hand, and the gun pointing at me lowered. "We're just businessmen here. We're hoping to come to an arrangement." He smiled, reaching his hand out to help me out of the truck. "We don't want to do anything drastic, either."

I stared at his chubby fingers until he pulled them back again.

"The thing is," he said to me, as I sat on the edge of the truck and slid myself down, "we don't know what he's capable of. Even he doesn't know. So we're just being cautious."

"Leave us alone," I said.

The man didn't say anything, but the tattooed, gun-toting guys motioned at us to get moving.

The room was a big parking garage, and our steps sounded hollow against the concrete floor. They marched us through a side door, into a maze of a house that felt way too big to be in Japan. Golden light filtered through the rice-paper walls as we approached a large tatami room. The *shouji* paper door stood before us, and as the businessman slid it aside, the full glare of the meeting room shone through the dark hallway.

We stumbled through the *shouji,* pushed by the men with guns.

There were about twenty men in the room and some tough-looking women. Some of them had ragged haircuts, tattoos racing down their arms and vanishing under their too-tight vests. Others looked friendlier, wearing suits like the businessman and smiling as we entered. Four rows of low-set tables were spread across the floor, some of the men kneeling at them and shoving sushi into their mouths with silver chopsticks. A Mohawked guy stood in the corner chugging a bottle of green tea as he spoke what sounded like rapid Korean with one of the businessmen.

And kneeling alone at one of the tables, looking dejected, was Ishikawa, a big, ugly bruise circling his right eye and three wide scratches across his jaw. His nose had swelled up so much he looked like the cartoon Anpanman.

"Satoshi," Tomohiro said under his breath, but Ishikawa stared intensely at the tabletop, grimacing.

"Have a seat," said the businessman, and a few of the others scattered to clear a table for us. Tomohiro and I just stared at him. One of the men cocked a gun and started to raise it. The businessman smiled and gestured at the table with his arm.

I wished I could punch him in the gut. But Tomohiro's

slender fingers curled around my wrist and he pulled me with him toward the table. We knelt down, two tough-looking guys closing in the sides of the table. At least Sunglasses and Cigarette were nowhere to be seen.

"We haven't been properly introduced," the businessman said. "You can call me Hanchi." Tomohiro looked down at the tabletop, his hands still in fists.

Hanchi waited for a minute, looking at us thoughtfully. Then he drew in a quick breath.

"Well," he said, "I guess we should get down to it. We're not here to threaten you, Yuu. We think you are a boy of incredible talent. Ishikawa speaks highly of you, you know."

Tomohiro said nothing. The Korean guy came over and slammed a bottle of green tea in front of me. I looked up at his face, but he was already turning away.

"I think we could do a lot for each other," said Hanchi.

"Not interested." Tomohiro's voice sounded so dark it almost made me shiver. It was like his don't-give-a-crap attitude but more intimidating, like he could actually hold his own against these guys.

"Ah," said Hanchi. "But I don't think you've considered what a spectacle you made of yourself when you sketched that dragon."

Tomohiro's eyes went wide for a moment before he forced the expression off his face. I wondered if anyone else noticed.

"We can protect you, Yuu. We can take care of those close to you. We can protect your girlfriend."

In a sharp voice, he said, "Ex-girlfriend. She's not part of this." The word ripped through me; it was probably a trick to throw them off, but I remembered then that we hadn't made up. Maybe we were broken up. Or maybe he was protecting me the only way he could. So how come it still hurt so much to hear it?

And reality check, why do I even care in a room with gangsters and loaded guns? Still working on the priorities, I see, Greene.

"Ah," said Hanchi. "Well. But I've heard you still draw inspiration from her, so the specifics don't matter." He muttered something and one of the men tossed a pad of paper in front of Tomohiro. Hanchi reached into his shirt pocket and pulled out a pen, clicking the end and placing it down on the pad.

"What's this for?" Tomohiro said.

Hanchi smiled. "You don't have to pretend with us. You're not the first Kami we've come across. But it's been a while. Most of them can't get the drawing off the page, Yuu. I know you can do better."

"What's a Kami?" Tomohiro said in a bored tone. He looked up at Hanchi, and I could see the dark challenge that radiated from Tomohiro's narrowed eyes. A slick smile curved its way onto his lips.

What the hell? *It better be an act,* I thought. *These guys could kill us, and he's enjoying it?*

Hanchi frowned, squeezing his hand into a fist.

"Don't play around, Yuu," he said. The friendliness was starting to drop from his voice.

Tomohiro reached for the tea bottle and twisted the cap, chugging down a mouthful and wiping his mouth with the back of his arm.

"So what's that for?" Hanchi smirked, pointing at the wristband.

Shit.

"I play kendo," Tomohiro said. "I have a weak wrist."

Hanchi motioned at the Korean guy, who stalked toward Tomohiro and yanked the wristband off his arm, revealing the stitched-up gash along his wrist for all of them to gape at. It was pink around the edges, crisscrossed by the dozens of other cuts and scars that trailed up his arm.

"Those kendo injuries?" the Korean guy sneered.

"I'm a cutter," Tomohiro said through gritted teeth. "I have entrance exams coming up. It's stressful. You do the math."

Hanchi laughed. "Sorry, Yuu," he said. "We're not buying it. I heard from Ishikawa you used to be quite the artist in the day. Let's start with something simple." He reached into his back pocket and pulled out a wallet. He spread the leather and flipped through, the bills slicking against each other as he pulled one out. He bent over the table and spread the ten thousand yen at the top of the pad. "Draw this," he said. "If you can do it, you can keep it. My gift to you."

"I can't draw," said Tomohiro.

The Korean guy pulled a gun from his back and slowly lifted it to me. My heart drummed in my ears.

"Can you draw now?" Hanchi said.

Tomohiro stared for a minute, his fists shaking.

"If you're not a Kami, then why is it a problem?" asked Hanchi.

The Korean guy cocked the gun.

"Shit, Yuuto, draw the damn bill!" Ishikawa shouted. I looked over at his swollen face, riddled with blue-and-yellow bruises. He looked so defeated, so small among these punks.

Tomohiro's fingers slid along the paper until they reached the pen. He closed them gently around it, lifting it upright to draw.

It's worth my life, but it isn't worth yours.

"Tomo, don't draw," I whispered.

He didn't answer. And then his hand slid across the page,

the patchwork of scars gliding along the table edge as we watched, his secret exposed to everyone.

He sketched slowly, looking from the bill to the page. Beads of sweat trailed down his forehead and clung to his bangs. I knew he was trying to control the ink, to disguise what he was. But with me beside him, he didn't have a chance.

He shaded in the details, sketching in the two pheasants on the back of the note. I saw the edges of the bill flicker, almost move. He hesitated for a minute, his head falling forward and his bangs fanning into his eyes. Then he shook them out and kept shading.

The corner of the sketch was curling up, the way the real bill did. The pheasants starting flicking their heads around, pecking at the ground.

"Tomo, stop," I whispered. I looked at his eyes. They were flooding with black, his pupils growing too large. "You have to stop."

I reached over and pinched the back of his leg as hard as I could.

He dropped the pen and it rolled in a slow circle across the page.

"Let's see," said Hanchi, reaching over to pick the paper up.

As he lifted the pad, the sketch fell right off the page and fluttered to the table.

Hanchi reached over and picked up the bill.

"Su-ge," he said in a low voice. Everyone watched in stunned silence.

The sketch looked just like the bill. There was still a drawing on the paper, but it looked blurry and made my head ache when I stared at it.

"One problem, though," Hanchi said as he flipped it back

and forth in his hands. He held the note right in front of Tomohiro's eyes. "It's black-and-white."

"It's a pen sketch," I said. "What did you expect?"

"I can't use this," Hanchi said. "Are you messing around with me?"

Tomohiro shook his head, breathing heavily. A trail of ink trickled from his shirtsleeve down to his wrist, where it dripped onto the paper.

Splotch, splotch.

"All my drawings are black-and-white," Tomohiro said. "I only do calligraphy and ink wash."

"This is no good," Hanchi said. "Draw something else. Get him a *sumi* and an inkstone."

"No!" I said, then clamped my hand over my mouth. Hanchi raised an eyebrow.

"Ah, I think we've hit on something here," he said with a smile. "Your…abilities only work with raw ink."

"Look," Tomohiro snapped. "I'm not interested in working for the Yakuza, and I don't know what Satoshi told you, but I can't make dragons appear in the sky. Do you know how crazy that sounds?"

"You just sketched counterfeit money, Yuu."

"And you saw how pathetic it was. I'm no good at this, okay? Let us go."

Hanchi sighed, pinching the bridge of his nose with two fingers. "Let's try again, hmm?"

Sunglasses came in, and the sight of him sent prickles up my spine. He put down an inkstone, a *sumi* ink stick and a *sumi* brush for Tomohiro, while the Korean guy brought a small dish of water. They backed into the group of Yakuza watching curiously.

"So you can't draw money. There are other things we need.

Drugs, guns, your basic underworld stereotypes. In fact, as long as the other gangs know we have a member who can create monsters—that alone is all the power we need to run things properly.

"So," said Hanchi, reaching behind his back and pulling out a gun, "let's try again." He pulled out the clip and reset it with a loud click. Then he tossed the gun onto the table. I watched as it spun around on the glossy surface, slowing until the end pointed at Tomohiro. "And there's no point in trying anything," Hanchi added. "Gun's empty. So draw."

Tomohiro picked up the *sumi* brush, gliding his fingers over the length of it, plying the bristles back and forth.

"Horsehair," he said without looking up.

"Ganbare," said Hanchi. *Do your best.*

Tomohiro placed the brush back on the table. He gripped the *sumi* ink stick tightly and moved it to the *suzuri* inkstone. His hands shook just a little, but no one seemed to notice but me. He took a little water and poured it on the *suzuri,* then started grinding the *sumi.* The ink bled into the water, making it thick and dark. His hand twisted and twisted around the inkstone, the scraping filling the silent room. His bangs slipped from behind his ear and fanned downward, hiding his eyes from me.

I felt so powerless it was driving me crazy.

As Tomohiro ground the ink, the Yakuza began to crowd the table, curiosity overtaking them. Even Ishikawa rose, creeping forward on socked feet to peer over our shoulders. I wished I could sock *him* one, but I guessed it wouldn't be the best move. I'd have to punch him later.

If there was a later.

The ink thickened and pooled in the *suzuri* stone. A faint sheen swirled through the ink, the edges of the liquid floating in ways they shouldn't. At first my brain tried to ignore it, and no one else seemed to notice except Ishikawa, whose face crumpled in confusion. But I'd watched Tomohiro draw before, and I knew when the ink stopped being ink and started being…well, something else.

Tomohiro stopped, pouring a little of the ink into a bowl and adding some water for a lighter gray shade. I pinched the back of his leg. *This isn't art class, idiot.* Why put in the effort? But as the Yakuza leaned in, I did, too, and when I saw his eyes, the pupils were huge. And growing.

Shit. Those alien eyes. I'd lost him now.

"Tomo, stop," I said, pinching him harder.

He said nothing, staring down at the paper with those vast, vacant eyes. He blotted the brush and dipped it into the black ink. He lifted it in a slow arc to the *hanshi* paper.

He drew a stroke downward, then one sideways.

Each stroke was delicate, determined. The whole room watched in silence.

He blotted the brush, shaded the handle of the gun with the gray ink. The gun was more artistic and less realistic than the ten-thousand-yen note. I hoped the design was part of some plan he had, but the look in his eyes terrified me. The Kami blood in him had taken over.

Now his eyes were gleaming, his hand moving faster and faster.

I'd lost him, just like I'd lost him when he sketched the dragon. If bottled ink had been too much for him then, how the hell could he handle hand-ground *sumi* ink?

The answer rang out in my head.

He couldn't.

Damn it.

The gun started spinning on the page slowly, his hand following it around, painting it as it moved.

"Tomo," I said louder. "Stop." I grabbed his arm with my hands, and his whole body shuddered. He jolted his arm back with so much force that I fell backward; he barely missed a stroke.

Ink spread from my fingertips down my arms, coating my skin with a black sheen.

"Katie!" Ishikawa's bleached hair loomed over me, his face twisted with concern. His hands reached out to pull me up.

"Don't touch me!" I yelled. When I looked at my arms again, the ink was gone.

The Yakuza didn't notice. They were staring at Tomohiro and getting nervous. The gun was spinning slowly again, pointing at each Yakuza as it went past and stopping for a brief moment. They leaned back, eyes wide.

"Yuuto, what happened to your eyes?" said Ishikawa.

"Hanchi!" said the Korean guy, but Hanchi waved it away. "Wait," he said.

Tomohiro kept drawing, filling in the sketch, adding depth. Ishikawa looked at my arms with their lack of ink. He stared at Tomohiro's alien eyes and at the drawing.

The ink was dripping sideways off the paper. It was reaching slowly, drop by drop, toward me.

"Yuuto," Ishikawa whispered, like he finally got it. Like he finally realized how much danger we were in. "Yuuto, listen to Katie and stop."

I wanted to tell him to piss off, but even more I wanted Tomohiro to listen.

"Yuuto," Ishikawa said, putting a hand on his shoulder.

Tomohiro thrust his arm back and Ishikawa tumbled into a

group of Yakuza. They collapsed into the table behind them, and two of its legs shattered under the weight.

"Hanchi!" the Korean said again. This time Hanchi looked worried.

"Yuu, that's enough," he said, but Tomohiro's hand whirred between the ink bowls and the *hanshi* paper. *"Mou ii!"* he said again. Nothing.

Hanchi's eyes narrowed. He reached forward, grabbed the Korean's gun and pointed it at Tomohiro.

"Yamero!" he shouted. *Stop!*

And suddenly the gun stopped spinning. The sketch rotated upright, so that the gun barrel pointed directly at Tomohiro. And I screamed as I saw the trigger pulling back.

"Yuuto!" shouted Ishikawa and leaped forward.

Bang.

I screamed.

Tomohiro and Ishikawa collapsed to the floor.

Blood streamed up Ishikawa's shoulder, trickling through his bleached-white hair and pooling in his ear.

Another loud bang shook the building.

"What the hell was that?" shouted Hanchi.

"Hanchi!" yelled Sunglasses, pointing at the doorway.

At least twenty snakes made of ink wriggled under the rice-paper door.

Only, Tomohiro hadn't drawn them.

"Sato," Tomohiro groaned, and I slumped Ishikawa off him.

"Tomo," I said as I clawed at his chest and arms searching for wounds. But we could both see Ishikawa sprawled unconscious on the floor, the blood soaking through his shirt.

More and more snakes streamed in, and something was crashing through the hallway toward us. The Yakuza scattered, firing at the snakes, screaming as the papery serpents wrapped around their ankles and sank in their inky teeth.

"We have to go!" I said. I grabbed Tomohiro's arm and pulled him up with me, but he crouched back down again.

"We can't leave him!" We stared at Ishikawa and how pathetic he looked, how the blood was retracing the lines back down to his shoulder now that Tomohiro was pulling him upright, the stark red threading through his white hair.

Tomohiro ducked under Ishikawa's injured arm and I pulled on the other. Together we adjusted him over Tomohiro's shoulders.

Ishikawa groaned.

"Sato," said Tomohiro. "Come on, man, help me here."

Ishikawa wrapped one arm tighter around Tomohiro. He tried to wrap the other and yelled out when he couldn't.

"It's burning," he rasped. *"I-te, i-te!"*

"It's okay," Tomohiro said. "Let's go."

The crashing sound got louder, and suddenly the whole *shouji* door collapsed into the room, a serpent as tall as me hissing at the shrieking Yakuza.

Ink dripped off his fangs and pooled on the floor.

And behind him, a man dressed in black, blond highlights tucked behind his pierced ear.

What the hell?

Takahashi Jun.

16

"Katie!" Jun yelled. He ran toward me, grabbing me by the shoulders; and even though ink-sketched snakes were swarming the room, even though a giant serpent slithered toward the shrieking Sunglasses, all I could feel was the heat of his palms through the cotton of my shirt.

"Daijoubu ka?"

"I'm fine," I said, "but what—? How—?"

"Yuu," he said, and at first I thought he meant *you,* but then he let go of my shoulders and walked toward Tomohiro, taking Ishikawa's other arm and draping it over his back.

"Takahashi," Tomohiro said, staring at the giant snake cornering Sunglasses on the other side of the room. "You… made these?"

"We need to go. Now," said Jun, and just like that he and Tomohiro started dragging Ishikawa to the collapsed rice-paper door.

I hurried after them, leaving behind the shrieks of the Yakuza and hisses of snakes that buzzed in my ears.

We wound through the building, moving as quickly as we could. Ishikawa groaned as the other two shouldered him through the narrow hallways.

My mind buzzed with the same thoughts over and over.

Because I knew Tomohiro didn't draw any snakes.

We came out in the same garage; there was the truck. But the garage door was in pieces on the ground, puddles of thick ink oozing across the floor.

"Come on," Jun said, leading us through the gaping hole of the garage. The humid summer air hit as I stepped out into the smell of night flowers and the hum of vending machines. In the dark, three motorbike engines revved to life and I blinked as the beams of light splayed onto the walls. Three people dressed in dark clothes straddled the bikes, hands on the handles and helmets shining my reflection back at me. One of the riders carried a beat-up-looking navy duffel bag—I knew it instantly. Tomohiro's kendo bag, which meant they'd started searching for us at Sunpu Park.

Tomohiro jumped back, but Jun slipped out from under Ishikawa's arm and raised his hands.

"It's okay," he said. "They're with me. *Oi!*" he called to one of them. "We need to get Ishikawa to Kenritsu fast."

"No," Ishikawa gasped.

"Are you totally mental?" I snapped. "You've got a gunshot wound, for god's sake!"

"That's the point," Ishikawa said between breaths. "They'll… ask questions."

"So, what, you'd rather die?"

"Satoshi, go to the hospital," Tomohiro said.

"Yuuto—"

"Please, Sato."

"I'll take him," said one of the riders. She lifted the helmet off her head and held it under her arm. "I'll cover the questions."

How is she going to do that? I wondered. But the girl reached out her arm and helped Tomohiro hoist Ishikawa onto the back of the bike.

"Can you hang on?" she asked.

Ishikawa didn't answer, but the weight of his body pressed against her back. She revved the engine and zoomed into the darkness, Ishikawa slumped over as they went.

"Katie," Jun said, gesturing to another of his companions, "go with Ikeda. She'll take you back to your aunt's place."

"You're kidding, right?"

"I don't think they'll come after you. Ikeda will stay with you if you're worried."

I stared at Jun. I definitely appreciated the fact that he'd followed up on my call, busted us out of Yakuza hell and was now giving us an escape, but I had questions burning in my mind that wouldn't go away.

Why didn't he call the police?

How did he know where to find us?

Where the hell did those snakes come from?

"I'm not sending Katie home alone," Tomohiro said.

Jun grabbed a fourth motorbike, shiny black and parked in the shadows of the Yakuza building. He swung his leg over and revved the engine to life.

"Yuu, you may still be in danger. If you stay near Katie, she is, too. Get it?"

Tomohiro balled his hands into fists and looked down at the pavement.

"You don't get it," I said. "I'm in danger whether he's near me or not."

"What do you mean?" Jun said.

"Nothing," Tomohiro said.

"Look," said Ikeda, "we can't stick around here."

"Yuu, come with me," said Jun. "I know somewhere safe you can go for now."

The anger and fear boiled inside me. I couldn't take it anymore, all of them talking like I wasn't there, like I wasn't part of this. Wasn't it me that snuck into Toro Iseki with Tomohiro, watched him sketch the dragon and the wagtail and the horse? I'd been through just as much as him. I'd seen the way he struggled between his passion and his curse.

What had Cigarette said? I was an ink magnet. I was making the ink do things. Niichan said I was connected to the Kami. I was definitely part of this, and there was no way I could just go home.

I walked up to Jun and sat behind him on the bike.

"Wherever you're taking Tomohiro, I'm damn well going, too."

Jun stiffened, the bike idling underneath us, kicking up smelly fumes that flooded my nose.

"Jun," Ikeda urged. "We've gotta go."

"Okay," Jun said at last. "Hold on."

I nodded and wrapped my arms around his waist. His skin was warm and hard through his shirt, and I knew Tomohiro was staring at me as he sat on the bike behind Ikeda. I kept looking forward, not letting him know I saw him watching.

What was I supposed to do, let go of Jun and fall off the bike?

Jun only had one helmet, and he plunked it down on my head before we took off. We lurched forward into Shizuoka traffic, zipping in and out of the lanes. I'd never ridden on a motorbike, and before I knew it, I was pressing myself against Jun, my knuckles white as I clutched at his shirt rippling in the humid breeze.

"Where are we?" I shouted over the roar of the engine.

"Yakuza meet-up place in Aoi Ward," Jun said. The red light turned blue-green and we raced forward. "About an hour from Shizuoka Station."

Only an hour north of Sunpu Park, then, an hour from home.

"How did you know where to find me?" I yelled. My hands felt like they were slipping, and for the hundredth time I readjusted them around his broad frame.

He tilted his head back, the blond highlights whipping around in the wind and the traffic lights sparkling in his silver earring.

"I've had a few run-ins with them before," he said.

What was that supposed to mean? Like the knife incident with Sugi? I remembered what he'd said then. *I don't like gangsters.* I looked back at the other two motorbikes and watched them zip after us. Ikeda and Tomohiro passed us, his arms wrapped tightly around her.

Well.

"Jun." The wind whipped my words back at me. "Did you make those snakes appear?"

"What?" He sped up.

"The snakes!" I said.

He didn't say anything, which was answer enough.

Which meant he was one of them, too. He was a Kami.

My mind reeled. The ink at the kendo match—he must have realized what it was. I thought back to how he'd pressed me in the convenience store, in the stations, on the way to school. *How's Tomohiro's wrist? I always knew he'd done calligraphy. Would you get him to show me his drawings sometime?*

Damn. It was all a trick, and I'd let it all pass over my head. How long ago did he figure it out?

I tried to think of anything that gave Jun away. Was there ink on his hands? Did he have a notebook with him?

I craned my neck to look over his shoulder, but the bike wobbled underneath us. He wasn't carrying anything with him, but that didn't mean anything anymore, not after I'd seen what Tomohiro could do without drawing anything.

Or more like what the power could do to Tomohiro.

But that was with my influence. So what were the chances Jun could do that? Pretty slim. No, there had to be some paper involved somewhere.

Jun was tall and I didn't want the bike to flip as I shifted around, so I gave up and slouched behind him, resting my head against his shoulder to avoid the strong winds battering my face.

Then I noticed the way his arms bent to grab the handlebars of the motorbike. At this angle I could see the muscular curve of his kendo-champion arms.

And I saw it on the inside flesh of his left arm, near his wrist.

A kanji carved into his own skin, fresh welts rising on the pink surface of the strokes.

蛇.

Snakes.

The blood drained from my face as I stared at the carved kanji. It moved in and out of view, Jun oblivious to the fact that I'd noticed it.

It made me sick to think he'd carved it into his own skin, even if the wound wasn't much deeper than a paper cut.

But he'd saved us. He'd told me to come to him if I ever needed help, and now I understood why. He'd figured us out a long time ago. Had we been so transparent?

We made our way south, the roads starting to look more and more familiar. The streets were almost deserted and I pulled my *keitai* out of my pocket to check the time. Just past 2:00 a.m., but adrenaline pumped through my veins as the lights of *conbini* and vending machines whirred past us.

I saw it in the distance when we stopped at a red light, the walls and tiled roof in shadow, away from the glare of the city lights. There was no mistaking what it was. The traffic light flicked to blue-green and we sped toward it.

Sunpu-jou. The castle at the heart of Sunpu Park.

Jun slowed down, the bikers killing their headlights and coasting forward as the castle rose before us.

A sign hung on the end of the bridge to keep cyclists out. The castle always closed at night; if you stayed late at Suntaba for clubs, you had to cut through the southern or western bridges.

Jun stopped in front of the bridge to Sunpu Castle and shut off the engine.

"Here?" I asked. The others had already climbed off their motorbikes, twisting them around the wooden barrier placed to deter after-hours cyclists. Jun didn't answer at first, lifting himself off the motorbike and waiting for me to do the same. I tugged at the straps of the helmet, shoving the heavy black plastic into his waiting hands. He hooked it around the handlebars. "You think we'll be safe in the middle of the night in the deserted park where they first nabbed me? Are you kidding?"

Jun looked at me with curiosity, then pointed at the tall glass tower at the southern end of the park, its glossy windows dwarfing Sunpu Castle. "Under the nose of the police headquarters?" he said. "I think we're safe from them here, yes. And who said anything about deserted?"

He turned to cross the bridge, and that's when I saw them,

the others dressed in dark shirts and jeans, clustered at the door of the castle and peering out at us. There were seven of them in all, parting to let the motorbikes through and into the courtyard. I stood there in the cool air, listening to the crunch of the gravel under the tires.

Tomohiro stepped toward me as I folded my arms across my chest.

"What the hell is this?" I said.

"That's what I want to know," he said. He rested a hand on my shoulder and it sent a jolt through my body to feel his fingers closing around me, to feel the warmth of the pads of his fingertips.

Ikeda and the other rider waited behind us.

"You need to get moving," she said to us. "The Yakuza might not be far behind. We'll be safe in the park for now. Safer than out here, anyway."

I peeked at Tomohiro, but he looked more unsure than I was.

Jun turned around, waiting.

We stepped forward and clambered across the stone bridge. Fish bobbed up and down in the dark waters below, sending ripples spinning through the murky water.

Our sneakers crunched on the gravel as we passed through the giant doorway of the castle.

Ikeda and the other rider followed, pulling their bikes up to the others and dropping Tomohiro's kendo bag beside the mini makeshift parking lot. Then a few of Jun's friends pulled at the giant castle doors. The slabs of wood groaned as the doors ground shut.

"Are you allowed to do that?" I said, but no one answered me.

I looked at them, huddling around Jun like a timid goth

following. They ranged in age, the youngest maybe twelve and the oldest in his twenties. They all wore the same dark clothes, the same grim look on their faces. Jun stood in front, his lean arms folded across his chest.

"What's going on?" said Tomohiro.

"Yuu, I want you to know you and Katie are safe here."

"What are you talking about?" I said. His voice was strange, his eyes gleaming. My heart pulsed in my ears. Something was off here. Way off.

"I want to help," Jun said. "I've always wanted to help."

"I don't need help," Tomohiro said.

"You need to trust me," Jun said, "so I'm going to tell you everything about what happened."

"You don't need to tell us," I said. "I saw the mark on your arm."

Jun's eyes widened for a moment, and he loosened his grip around his elbows, rubbing his fingers over his wrist.

"This?" he said, opening his arms to reveal the pale skin on the inside, the welts raised in the kanji for *snake.* "Yeah," he said. "I'm a Kami. Like you, Yuu."

"You made those snakes," Tomohiro said.

"Yes."

"How did you know where to find us?"

"Like I told Katie, we've had run-ins with the Yakuza before."

"We?"

Jun motioned to the group around him.

I looked at Ikeda, lifting the motorbike helmet off her head. She saw me looking and put the helmet on the ground, pulling back the sleeve of her jacket.

A ribbon of cuts ran up the inside of her arm.

Shit.

"You're *all* Kami?"

"Try to understand," said Jun. "It's not something to be afraid of, Yuu."

Tomohiro didn't answer, but I swore I saw his hands shaking.

"The power you wield—it's not something to turn away from. We're descendants of Amaterasu, kin of the imperial family. I know you're afraid of it, Yuu. But we've all had the nightmares. We've all seen what you have seen."

I looked at Tomohiro, but he looked away, his eyes cast down to the gravel. I wondered what kind of horrible visions haunted him at night. I shuddered, remembering the demons and shadows in the Taira painting.

"Some can bear it better than others. Some are more gifted than others. And you are gifted, Yuu. Incredibly gifted. Not many Kami can call on their power without sketching a single line."

"I don't know what you're talking about."

"You don't have to pretend with us," Jun said. "We've all seen our drawings move on the page. We can help you."

Tomohiro's eyes filled with suspicion. I touched his arm to reassure him. Jun had always been kind to me, and now he'd rescued me again. I knew he could help Tomohiro control the power.

"It's okay," I said quietly. "We can trust him."

"Because he's your friend," Tomohiro said, and the way he said it made my cheeks blaze.

"Yeah," I said. I didn't feel like explaining myself to him. It was 2:00 a.m. and we'd been kidnapped by Yakuza and freed by Kami. If he was jealous, he could deal with it.

Tomohiro looked at Jun for a moment. "What do I need to do?" he said at last.

Jun smiled. "We can help you, Tomohiro. Or rather, you can help us. We've been looking for someone with your ability for some time. So first, we'll offer you a gift." He reached his hand out to Ikeda, who shuffled in the pocket of her jacket for a small notebook and pen. Jun took them and walked toward us, placing them in Tomohiro's hands.

"You want me to draw?" Tomohiro said. "Draw what?"

"Hanchi," Jun said. "The Yakuza boss. Dead."

The pen dropped from Tomohiro's hand and hit the gravel below.

"Kill him?" I breathed.

Jun blinked, tilting his head to the side. "You need to send a message to the Yakuza. You don't want them coming after you again."

"Yeah, but—" I started, but Jun held up a hand.

"I've never killed anyone before," Tomohiro said quietly. "I didn't even think it was… Can we do that?"

"Go ahead, Yuu," Jun said. "The honor is yours."

"Honor?" Tomohiro's voice was shaking. "What honor is there in killing a man on paper?"

"You show a lot of mercy to the man who kidnapped you and Katie," Jun snapped, and I saw Tomohiro flinch as Jun used my first name. Jun tucked his blond highlights behind his ears with force; he was getting frustrated. His eyes were dark pools of ice. "You think he would've shown you the same kindness? He's been responsible for lots of deaths. As a Kami, you can exact judgment."

Tomohiro dropped the notebook on the ground, disgusted.

"I'm not killing someone," he said.

"Jun, that's excessive," I said. "What's the point of killing someone?"

"I think you'll see, in time," Jun said. "The world is crying out for the judgment of the Kami."

"What does that even mean?" I said.

"Japan was ruled by Kami a long time ago," Jun said. "The major samurai families of Heian Japan? Almost all Kami. Some were stronger than others, like me and Yuu." I glanced at the kanji engraved on Jun's arm. He didn't even use paper or a pen to control the ink—what was he capable of? "The world's falling apart, decaying before our eyes. The Yakuza are spreading across the country, spilling into other parts of the world—is that a world you want to live in? We're destined to take it back, Yuu. We can rule Japan like gods, like the *kami* once did."

"Are you crazy?" Tomohiro said. "Rule Japan? What the hell are you on, Takahashi?"

Jun laughed, but there was no humor in his voice. "I'm declaring war on the Yakuza," he said. "But war requires weapons. I'll make them all pay for what they've done. They'll beg forgiveness at my feet or I'll wipe out every last one of them, whatever it takes until Japan is safe. The Kami will reclaim our place as rulers, the way it used to be. The ink wants blood. It always wants blood. Yours, or someone else's. Let us help you."

"I told you," Tomohiro snapped. "I don't need h—"

"Stop acting like you're human!" Jun spat. The comment stung me, and Tomohiro stumbled backward like he'd been slapped. "You think you're so much stronger than your Kami blood? You think you can go around life with a blowtorch and it's okay because you have a little candle snuffer? Wake up, Yuu! Before you hurt someone." Jun looked directly at me. "Before someone gets burned. You're a weapon, and you have to decide which side will wield you."

I wanted to punch him. What the hell did he know about us? I'd seen the control Tomohiro had, the way he scratched out his drawings in time. But the image of the wagtail dropping midflight flashed in my mind, the horrible way it had attacked the other birds. I thought about the way Tomohiro's eyes grew vacant when he sketched, how I'd pinched him and he couldn't stop. How I lost him, how he couldn't hear me. The scars climbing his arm, the dragon spiraling into the sky.

"Stop acting like you're normal," Jun said, his voice softening. "The blood of Amaterasu runs in your veins." He stepped forward, extending his hand. "You can be a prince in the new world we'll create. Once we take control of Japan, with the emperor as our puppet, we'll rule like we did before. We're marked for this. You're more than human, Yuu. You're superior."

"Superior?" Tomohiro whispered. He hunched over, clutching his hand to his heart. I heard a splotch and looked down. Ink carved down his arms and dripped onto his sneakers. "Superior?" he said again, his voice trembling. "How can this be superior? My own sketches try to kill me. My dreams hunt me down. Being a Kami took my mother's life from her, and it took my mother from me! How the hell is that superior?"

"We've all lost something. But it's time to stop running from who you really are."

"That's it, then," Tomohiro said. *Splotch, splotch.* "Destined to take over Japan, no matter the price, no matter the blood? So this normal life I've tried to create—it's all an act. I've always known. Always known what I really was."

"Gifted," said Jun, stepping forward again.

Tomohiro shook his head, his whole body heaving with every breath.

"Evil." He looked up, a darkness in his eyes.

"Tomo," I said, but icy fear tingled in every part of my body.

"I'm a monster," he said, raising his hand to point at Jun, "and so are all of you."

"The human in you fears the Kami that flows in your veins. Once you stop struggling, things will be easier."

"I'll fight this as long as I live," Tomohiro hissed.

"And if you hurt others in the process?"

Silence.

"What's a guilty man's death compared with many innocents'?"

"Because!" Tomohiro shouted. "It's not my choice to make!"

"You're still talking like you're not a Kami," Jun snapped back. "It *is* our choice. It's our responsibility to protect them. When others get hurt because of your inaction—what then?"

My body tensed, looking for some way out, some way to end this. But doubt pressed against me. The kanji for *sword,* the dragon, the gun—they'd all tried to kill Tomohiro. What if he really was so dangerous he was unconsciously trying to stop himself?

What if he—the ink— What if it killed me, too? It was already seeping into my life in every way possible. What if—

I swallowed, my throat so thick I could barely breathe.

"What then, Yuu?"

"Then it's better if I'm not alive."

It's worth my life, but it isn't worth yours.

"You can do so much more with your life," Jun said. "Don't settle for this. Don't let it haunt you."

In the breeze I could hear a whisper of that voice again, that gathering noise like a million voices talking at once. It was the same voice that had taken him over when we'd faced Ishikawa and his thugs. The sound was overwhelming, moans of pain and cries for help, animalistic screeches and overlapping voices. *Monster,* they said. *Demon. Murderer.*

"No!" Tomohiro cried out and fell to his knees, hands clutched over his ears. He could hear it, too, like high-pitched feedback that bounced around inside your head. Only, the way he writhed, I knew that whatever I was hearing, his was tenfold.

My mind reeled. I had to stop this torture for him.

I stared at the motorbikes, useless with the castle doors closed. And then I spotted Tomohiro's kendo bag, its white zipper gleaming in the moonlight.

I stooped over, grabbing the pull with shaking hands. I rummaged through the bag, the smell of worn leather filling every breath, the armor slipping across my palms as I searched.

The smooth touch of bamboo as my hands closed around the *shinai.*

I wheeled around, the others watching me with confusion. I stepped in front of Tomohiro, swung the *shinai* forward and pointed it at Jun's throat.

"Leave us the hell alone," I said.

"Katie," he said, lifting his arms in front of him. "What are you doing?"

The *shinai* shook in my hands as I tried to hold it steady.

Jun stepped toward me. "We're trying to help."

"The hell you are."

"Tell me you've never felt afraid of him. Tell me he's never endangered you."

My cheeks flushed red. "You don't understand anything!" I shouted. I swung the *shinai* at him and he leaped back.

"And you think you do? How long have you known him,

a few months? Do you have any idea what Yuu is capable of? Does he?"

Splotch, splotch. Only, now the ink was dripping onto the gravel from Jun, spreading across his back into feathered black wings. The ink dribbled down Jun's arm and pooled in the palm of his hand. It stretched out on itself, building like an icicle of ink until it was as long as the *shinai* in my hand.

"I didn't want to involve you in this. I wanted to protect you. Can you expect the same from him?"

"Shut up!" I snapped. "You're the same as the Yakuza. You just want to use him, too!" I pushed off the back of my foot and swung the *shinai* at him. "Do you hear how crazy you sound? You're just thugs trying to take over Japan!" My *kiai* shout rang in my ears. It was so loud I could barely believe it was my own voice.

He lifted his ink *shinai* to block my attack, and the force of the block pushed me backward. Ink splattered onto both of us, sprayed across the ground like dark blood.

Jun's eyes flashed. "I'm not the same as the Yakuza. They can all rot and die."

"Jun," called out Ikeda, but he threw his hand back to them.

"No one touches her," he said. Then to me, "Katie, please. Don't fight this. We're on the same side."

I circled him, but the other Kami backed up. He held his *shinai* ready, moving faster through the stances than I could.

Like I had a chance of beating the sixth-place national kendo champion.

But I had to try.

He was on the defensive, not lunging at me, which only pissed me off even more. It was like he knew I didn't have a chance, like he wanted to humor me.

I shouted again, going for a right *kote* shot. If I could take out his wrists, wasn't that the source of the Kami's power? But he turned at the last moment and I stumbled forward, leaving my *dou* wide open for a hit.

He didn't take it.

"We're not like them," Jun said as he circled me, his leather shoes crunching the gravel slippery with ink. "All they think about is money and drugs, useless street power. I'm talking about real power, carving out a new future for Japan. Yuu belongs with us. He *is* one of us!"

"He'll never be like you!"

Jun pointed the *shinai* down at the ground, his hands spread apart. He thought I wouldn't fight him.

He was wrong. I swung and the tip grazed his wrist. He stumbled backward, letting go of the *shinai* with his left hand and shaking his fingers back and forth.

He inhaled a sharp breath. *"I-te!"*

Point.

I swung again, but he twisted out of the way. Now he was advancing toward me, a fire lit in his eyes. Ink feathers spread across his back, splaying out as they formed wings.

He yelled his *kiai* and lunged at me, his sword clacking under mine and pulling up with such force that I tumbled into the gravel.

"Katie," he said, his voice full of concern. The sharp edges of the stones sliced across my knees as I fell, but I grabbed on to the *shinai* with everything left in me.

I was not going to lose, not like this. I couldn't win, but I wouldn't give up.

I rolled across the stones and onto my feet. My scraped knees burned, but I ran toward Jun anyway. I lifted the *shinai* over my head and screamed as I brought it down on his *shinai*.

Ink splattered everywhere as his *shinai* shattered. It showered the ground as he stared at me, and then the ink slowly dripped upward, re-forming into the slats of the sword again.

"It's you," he whispered.

"Damn right it is."

"You manipulated the ink."

I felt exposed, frightened. I didn't want them to use me.

"The ink's reacting to you, isn't it?" Jun said. "Even my *shinai*. It was you at the tournament. You're why I lost control in the match." So the pool of ink hadn't been Tomohiro; it had been Jun. "Katie, you're in serious danger."

I paled, my *shinai* still thrust out at his. "Why?"

"His power," he said, pointing at Tomohiro, who hunched over in agony as a pair of ink wings spread on his back. He opened his mouth to scream, but only trickles of ink came out. "It's reacting to you. The longer you're near him, the stronger and more deadly he's going to grow."

"You're lying." But it was an echo of what Niichan had said to me in the temple.

"Why would I? I'm your friend."

"Huh, suddenly I feel all warm and fuzzy."

"Katie," he said, and I hated myself for the goose bumps that prickled along my skin.

"I'm not a Kami," I said. "I don't have the nightmares."

"I never said you were a Kami. I said you're in danger."

Tomohiro writhed beside me, still unable to hear anything but the voices shouting. It was horrifying to watch. I bent down and rested a hand on his arm, stroking his back and wishing it would stop. Jun watched with his piercing eyes. I hated him for knowing more about it than me. I hated all of this. I couldn't take it.

"So what am I, if you're such a genius?" I shouted. "Yeah,

okay? The ink's bitten me. It's trailed me, whispered to me, blown my pen up in class. It likes me, okay? I get it! But can you tell me why, Jun? Can you tell me why the hell the ink finds me so interesting? What does it want?"

"I don't know how, but you have ink in your blood," he said. "I've heard of it happening before. The ink inside you calls to the Kami blood. It's trying to awaken in you any way it can."

"Why?" I whispered. "What does the ink want?"

"Power," Jun said. "The ink senses something of its own in Yuu and is drawn to it, like a stream to a lake. It augments our ability. It knows how he—how he feels about you." His voice sounded bitter, and he looked away from my hand on Tomohiro's back. "It'll use those feelings to get the most out of him until—"

"Until what?" I breathed.

Jun looked at me with sad eyes. "Until the power overtakes him. Until his emotions for you make him lose control and he becomes only Kami."

I rose to my feet, my hands clenched in fists. "So to save myself I just have to stay away from him? No going for coffee? That's lame, Jun. Got anything else?"

"You don't get it!" he shouted, and I took a step back. He was looking at me like he was going to break. He'd never looked so fragile. His eyes were melted ice, warmth spilling everywhere. "It's going to kill you, Katie! If the ink kills you, Tomohiro will never regain control, and that's what it wants!"

My ears stopped hearing. My eyes stopped seeing. All I could feel was my heart pounding, pulsing through my whole body.

"You're lying," I whispered.

"I hope so. I hope to hell I'm wrong."

"You *are* wrong," I said. "That can't be it." Tomohiro's love for me, was it all just the ink attracted to something within me? Just power seeking its own like magnets, not caring if it crushed me to death?

Impossible.

Tomohiro moaned on his side, clawing away demons that weren't there. His pupils were huge and alien, like he was living in some other world. And then the whispers dissipated and he stopped struggling, his breathing shallow. He blinked as his pupils shrank to their normal size, concentrating as he tried to focus them on me. He'd made it through whatever hell he'd trod, from being more Kami than human. But what about the next time? What if he didn't come back?

"The ink doesn't care about right or wrong," Jun said quietly. "If you read the myths, the ancient *kami* are terrifying because they don't share human judgments of right and wrong. We can wield the power, or the power can destroy us. Tomohiro needs our help or he'll…he'll destroy you. You need to stay away from him. Please."

A world alone, without him. The flowers around the void in my heart wilted, crumpled beneath the weight of the truth. Going back to being alone.

I screamed and thrust the *shinai* at Jun. "Don't you dare tell Tomohiro that crap."

"And what, wait for you to die? I can't do that."

"Don't you understand? If he thinks the power will kill me—" I fell to my knees, the tears spilling over my cheeks. "If he knows it, that might be enough to send him over the edge."

He hesitated, because we both knew I was right. We were holding a ticking time bomb. Wait and it explodes. Try to defuse it and *boom*. We all die.

Unless one of us was wrong.

"What will you do?" Jun said.

And then I felt the warmth of Tomohiro's fingers as they wrapped around mine on the *shinai.* He pulled us upright, the *shinai* pointed at Jun's throat. Something slick squished against my shoulder and I turned to see Tomohiro's inky wings spread out to match Jun's, warm ink oozing down my skin where the feathers touched me. He squinted a little, his eyes still having trouble focusing, and his shoulder leaned into me as he legs wobbled underneath him.

"We're done here," he said faintly, and Jun smirked.

"Get it through your head. We're not the enemy."

"Could've fooled me."

Jun looked at me hard, lowering his *shinai* and dropping it to the ground. It splashed into a puddle of ink as it hit the stones.

"The power is hunting you both, Yuu. What if it gets to you first?"

"Then at least it'll keep me out of your hands," Tomohiro spat.

Jun squeezed his hands into fists so tight the veins popped along the strokes of the snake kanji on his skin.

He said, "You don't know how to handle your gift."

Translation: you may accidentally kill your girlfriend, which I can't tell you in case you blow up and kill us all right here and now.

Tomohiro smacked the *shinai* into Jun's right wrist so hard the bamboo slats rattled. I heard the snap of bone as Jun fell to the ground with a cry.

"Jun!" said Ikeda, running to his side.

"It's my life!" Tomohiro shouted. "I'll live it how I want. I don't owe you anything!" He threw the *shinai* to the ground and grabbed me by the wrist, pulling us toward the closed castle doors. He yanked on the heavy handles, but they wouldn't budge.

I looked back at Jun, the way he was sprawled on the gravel with Ikeda's arms wrapped around him. He lifted his head, his face covered with sweat and dirt, his fingers scratched raw by the sharp stones he'd fallen into. He looked so pathetic cradling his broken wrist that I almost felt sorry for him. Almost.

"You have no idea," Jun rasped. "You've barely seen the surface of what you're capable of."

Tomohiro wrapped his arms around me tightly, the warmth of his body pressed against mine so hard I could barely breathe.

"Then we'll find out together," he said and flapped his dark wings, lifting us upward. The walls of Sunpu Castle slicked past, my sneaker tapping against the clay roof tiles as we lifted. The Kami scattered as we hovered an inch above the shingles, slamming into the drain spout on the other side of the castle wall. Tomohiro's wings gave out and we collapsed onto the rail of the bridge, the ink feathers melting and splashing into the dark water below. Tomohiro tipped forward toward the water, but I pulled him back as hard as I could and we tumbled onto the bridge.

We could hear the groan of the wooden doors as the Kami pulled on them, the rumble of the motorbikes revving to life.

But as the gate opened to the scene of Jun crumpled on the ground, we heard his voice, hollow and defeated.

"Mou ii," he said. *That's enough.*

"But—" Ikeda said.

"It's enough!" he yelled. "He'll come back when he sees his mistake."

I stared at him, but Tomohiro grabbed my wrist and started running, and my eyes fell off the shape of Jun, off the wings that were pooling into puddles of ink below him like thick black tears. We ran until the tunnels of the underground walkway swallowed us up, until we stumbled through the glaring lights of the empty train station, where our footsteps echoed in the silence.

We ran until tears streamed down my face, blurring the streetlights as we walked toward Diane's mansion.

17

We rode up the elevator in silence, and my hands shook as I fumbled to turn the key in the door. Tomohiro locked it behind us, the slide of the bolt flooding me with relief. We stood there in the *genkan* staring at each other, streaked in ink, dirt and dried blood.

I wanted to reach out for him, but I was scared I would burst into tears if he touched me. I wondered if he was thinking the same thing, so we just stood there like idiots for a while.

Then he pulled out his *keitai,* the little kendo warrior swinging back and forth on his phone strap.

"I'm going to call Kenritsu," he said, flipping the phone open.

"Okay," I said. His cell phone beeped as he typed in the hiragana, searching online for the hospital number. I wondered if he wanted to be alone when he called, so I slowly backed toward the bathroom. I left the door ajar and heard his smooth voice after a pause.

"Moshi mosh? Yuu Tomohiro desu ga," he said. I wondered how he could sound so calm, like nothing had happened.

I turned on the tap and let the water splash onto my hands

while I stared into the sink and listened to Tomohiro. *I'm connected to the Kami. The ink is somehow trapped inside me.* I looked in the mirror, studying the lines of dirt caked on my skin. I looked like crap. I had to wash my face twice to get all the dirt off.

I heard Tomohiro's phone slam shut, heard him curse under his breath. As I dabbed my face on the towel, he pushed the bathroom door open a little.

"They won't give me any info because I'm not family," he said. "They probably think I'm one of the Yakuza trying to find him."

"I'm sure he's okay," I said.

Tomohiro stared at me as I hung the towel back on the ring.

"Um," I said. "Do you want to go to the hospital?"

He shook his head. "Tomorrow."

"Okay," I said, but his stare was so intense that the back of my neck felt prickly.

He reached his hand up to my cheek but stopped short of touching me when he saw the ink caked on his hands.

"I—" he said.

"It's okay."

"It's not. I almost got us—"

"You didn't," I said. "*They* did." He stood there staring into space, so I turned on the water for him and stepped out of the way.

He washed his hands, the dark ink spiraling down into the drain.

"I'm going to get some tea," I said.

"Okay."

I padded into the kitchen and pulled open the fridge, grabbing the bottle of black-bean tea and pouring it into two glasses. Tomohiro turned off the water and met me in the kitchen, his face and hands scrubbed pink. He took the glass with both hands but didn't drink. Just kept staring.

So I said quietly, "Don't draw anymore, Tomo."

His voice was barely a whisper. "I can't."

"I know, but—"

"I mean I can't," he said. "What Takahashi said about the dreams, the whispers…it's all true. I don't even need to draw anymore. The ink just uses me as its canvas." He held out his arms, striped with pale ink stains.

"But…"

"It's going to keep hunting me, until I give in or it destroys me."

I felt hollow, like all my Japanese had spilled onto the floor and I couldn't understand anything anymore.

"Tomo."

He walked slowly to Diane's ugly couch and pressed his back into the purple leather. He lowered his head and his bangs fanned over his eyes. The chill of the tea glass pressed against my fingers.

"I don't know how to fight it," he said. "How do you win when you're up against yourself?"

I thought for a minute. "I don't know," I said. "But if there are so many Kami, there must be a way. It's not like you see people's chemistry notes exploding all the time."

I hoped he'd smirk, but at this angle I couldn't see his face. His fingers gripped the glass tightly as it rested on his lap. I sat down beside him, placing my glass on the coffee table. I wrapped my fingers around his glass, pried it out of his fingers and placed it on the table beside mine. His hands free, Tomohiro buried his head in them.

"I'm a monster," he said. "I have to go somewhere."

"What? Where?"

"Somewhere I won't hurt you. Somewhere I won't hurt anyone."

"Look, don't listen to those idiots. If they're all Kami and living in Shizuoka, and we didn't know… I mean, he's probably just trying to scare you into joining them. There's no way Jun has enough power to take on the Yakuza or restore the Kami as rulers of Japan, or whatever crap he was spouting."

"How do I know?" Tomohiro said. "How do I know you'll be safe?"

And then I suddenly realized how his leg was pressed against mine, the heat of it through his jeans. The shame came flooding back to me, the anger with it.

"Tomo," I said. "It was an act, right?"

He didn't answer.

"I mean the—" I could feel the blood rushing to my face. "The love hotel."

Silence.

"Damn it. Say something!"

He lifted his head slowly, exhaustion in his eyes. It wasn't much longer until the sun would rise.

"I *told* you to stay away from me," he said, but his eyes gleamed as he stared at me.

There was no smirk, like there had been for Myu. There was no slouching, no look of disgust. No lies.

He reached his hand up and tucked my hair behind my ear with tenderness. *"Gomen,"* he apologized, his soft voice almost beyond hearing. I bit my lip as hot tears rushed to my eyes. I blinked them back; no way in hell was I going to cry now. He started to lean in, and I pushed him back, my palms smacking his chest.

"You're such a jerk!"

"I know," he said and wrapped his arms tightly around me. The warmth of him pressed in around me and I breathed in the smell of dirt, sweat and ink. He held on tightly, like he was going to break if he let go. We lay there clinging to each other, knowing the world would tilt if we let go, that without each other everything would fall out of balance.

The muffled sound of the phone woke me, and I opened my eyes to the sunlight muted by the thick curtains draped over the balcony windows. It took me a minute to figure out where I was. Tomohiro's face rested next to mine, his hot breath ticklish on my neck. We'd fallen asleep on the couch, and somehow by tangling our limbs into the cushions we'd managed not to fall onto the floor.

The phone stopped ringing as I tried to inch off the couch without waking Tomohiro. Not a problem—he slept like a stone. My neck and back throbbed from sleeping like a yoga pretzel.

I slid off the end of the couch and arched my back, stretching out all my sore muscles. It felt like I'd been kicked around the block, which wasn't that far from the truth.

I jumped when the phone rang again. I walked over and stared at the lit-up ID.

From Osaka.

I lifted the headset out of the cradle and to my ear.

"Moshi mosh?"

"Katie!" Diane said, but the crackling on the line was awful. "I know you kids can really sleep in, but honestly? I've called five times."

"Huh?" I glanced around the room, looking for some clock to figure out what time it was. "Sorry."

"Is—okay?" Her voice cut out.

"Yeah, everything's fine," I said, rubbing the back of my neck. *Just been kidnapped by the Yakuza, freed by some freaky mob with superpowers that may kill me, learned I'm connected to the Kami and slept on the couch with a senior boy. And I think I know which one of those will bother you the most.* "I'm fine."

"Okay, listen. I'm—*crackle*—coming back tonight, but—*hiss*—need you to turn on the fax machine, okay?"

"What?"

"The fax machine. It's—*ksshhh*—the bookshelf by the dinner table."

I stared across the table at it.

"Are you listening?"

"Yeah, but it's a bad connection."

"I know. Turn on the machine, hon, and we'll talk—*kssshh*—get back, okay?"

"Okay," I said, and Diane hung up. Had she ever called me "hon" before?

I stumbled toward the fax machine and pushed the button. It beeped a few times and hummed to life. Behind me I heard Tomohiro flip over on the couch. I was half-surprised he didn't tumble right off onto the floor.

I turned to look at him, his eyes closed and his breathing slow. He looked so peaceful lying there. It was hard to imagine the nightmares haunting him. Was it true that someday he might not wake up from the horrible dreams? Or that one day he'd lose himself and come after me? I couldn't picture it as he lay there.

Lies. They had to be. But they scared the crap out of me.

The phone rang again. The fax machine picked up the call with a high-pitched slew of beeps, and then the machine shook as it fed the blank paper through.

I stepped forward, covering a yawn with the back of my

hand. My back throbbed as I leaned over to peek at the message. Probably some kind of school forms or something for Diane.

But I hesitated. The fax being spit out was in English.

For once, I stumbled over my fluency. As weird as it seemed, I wasn't used to reading without concentrating to try, and the fax paper was printing upside down, so it took me a minute to read the page.

The machine spat it out and started on the next page. I picked the paper up and turned it around.

It was for me.

All the beeping and printing woke Tomohiro, and I heard the couch creak as he stretched. I spun around, the paper pressed between the pads of my fingers.

He looked around slowly, but when he saw me, he bolted upright like he'd just remembered where he was. He face flushed a deep red and his eyes were big and round.

"Ah," he stammered. *"O-ohayo."*

"Um, morning," I said, but as awkward as I felt—*did it count as sleeping together? Oh god*—I couldn't tear my eyes away from the paper.

To the attention of Diane Greene, RE: Katie

"What's that?" Tomohiro said.

Katie, sweetie, hope you've received our emails and phone messages. Here are the forms.

What messages? What forms?

Please fill them out with Diane ASAP so we can book the ticket. Love you, sweetie! Can't wait for you to come home.
Nan & Gramps

What ticket?

Tomohiro padded over. He stood so close behind me I could feel his hot breath on my neck. It sent shivers up my skin.

My fingers started to tremble.

I grabbed for the forms as they fed through the fax machine, thumbing through them, freaking out.

"Are you okay?" Tomohiro said.

Hot tears formed in my eyes and I blinked them back.

They were custody papers. Gramps was in remission.

My head buzzed, and when Tomohiro wrapped his slender fingers around my shoulders, it took all the strength I had left not to collapse to the floor.

"They want me to go home," I said.

"Home?"

"My grandparents. They're booking me a ticket to Canada."

Tomohiro was silent, his grip loose. "When?" he whispered.

"As soon as they can," I said.

He didn't say anything, and I just stared at the papers, my hands shaking.

I didn't get it. This was what I'd waited for.

Wasn't it?

So why the hell did I feel like someone had stabbed me?

"That's great," Tomohiro said eventually, and he lifted his hands off my shoulders. I turned around to face him and he looked so sincere, except his eyes didn't match the rest of his face.

"But—" I said.

"It's your home," he said, but his words sounded so hollow. "It's not the same as New York with your mom, but it's where you wanted to be, right? With your grandparents."

"Well, yeah, I thought so," I said. "But I'm not sure anymore."

"Katie," Tomohiro said, and the low voice he used just about knocked me over. How did he look so stunning when his hair was standing at funny angles from sleeping on an ugly couch sized for Lilliputians?

"Tomo, I'm not sure I want to go back."

"I think it might be a good idea."

"Traitor."

"If the Yakuza and the Kami come after you again… And I don't think they're going to stop…"

"And what about you? It's okay if they come after you?"

Tomohiro gave me a hard look, his eyes like gleaming stones. "It doesn't matter what they do to me," he said. "It might even be better if they—stop me. But I need to know you're safe."

"Oh, and so what you need is so important?" I spat, but really I was shaking at what he'd said. More like what he hadn't quite said. "How can I know you're safe if I'm not here to save your pretty ass?"

"Katie—"

"Don't 'Katie' me!" I shouted. "You all think you know what's best for me. It's my life! I get to choose!" He stepped back, stunned, and the tears spilled down my face. "You want to be in control of your life. Well, I do too!"

I let the tears curve down my cheeks, not caring if I looked awful. And suddenly Tomohiro blurred toward me, and his arms wrapped around me. He held me so tightly I thought I might break, and then he let go a little and my lips found his.

He gently reached up and smoothed my hair over my shoulders, cupping my neck with his warm hands. He kissed the tears off my cheeks, until my head buzzed with the warmth of him, until I forgot about the black hole about to swallow me up.

He leaned back, shaking the bangs out of his eyes. A second later they fell in again.

"Do you really think my ass is pretty?"

"Shut up," I said, and he grinned.

The doorbell rang, and we stood there stunned. The grin dropped from his lips, and the warmth in me turned icy cold.

"Is it—" I whispered.

Tomohiro curled his hands into fists.

The doorbell rang again.

"Stay here," he said and padded toward the door.

"Don't answer it!" I hissed as I followed him around the corner. The papers dropped from my hand as I grabbed the phone off the table to call 911. No, wait—crap! Why did I still not know who to call?

Tomohiro pulled the door open and peered out.

Tanaka and Yuki stared into the *genkan,* and their faces flooded with red as quickly as ours did. I panicked. We must have looked like crap, still in our dirt- and ink-stained clothes from yesterday, our hair totally messy, and—*oh god.* And our lips swollen from kissing. We stood there, all four of us looking like tomatoes.

"Tomo-kun!" Tanaka stammered.

"I-Ichirou."

Yuki put her hand to her mouth and stared at me, the edges of a huge grin visible between her fingers. I knew exactly what she was thinking. And I had no clue how to convince her it wasn't what it looked like.

"Um," I said. *Wow, real articulate.*

"Ohayo," Yuki said, bowing to Tomohiro. He folded his hands across his chest, trying his tough-jerk look from school, but I'd never seen his face so red.

And knowing he was thinking about *that* made me go lobster-red. I swear my ears felt like they were burning.

"It's great weather today! Um, can we come in?" Yuki said, looking at me funny. She was trying to save me.

"Of course," I said.

They shuffled into the *genkan* and slipped out of their shoes, while Tomohiro and I moved back to give them room.

"We tried to call, but you didn't pick up," Tanaka said, tugging at his shoelaces. "Yuki-chan got worried, so we came to check on you."

"Because you're supposed to be staying at my house while your aunt is away," she said. "But of course, I see you're fine."

"Um, I wasn't— I, um, we were practicing kendo at school yesterday and he came over afterward. We were so tired we just—"

Yuki started waving her hands madly. "Oh, I know, I know," she said, which meant she totally didn't believe a word I was saying. "Don't worry about it."

"Maybe we should go," said Tanaka.

"It's fine," said Tomohiro. "Come in. Did you have breakfast yet?"

They exchanged glances.

"What?"

"It's almost noon," Tanaka said. Yuki looked like she was going to burst. She kept stifling her nervous giggles.

"Well, lunch, then." Tomohiro grinned. Somehow the color had returned to his face and he looked filled with confidence.

I really hated him.

Tomohiro pawed through the fridge and pried out various bowls and bottles. He lifted a pot onto the stove top and started mixing dashi powder into a stock.

Yuki grabbed my elbow and yanked me into the hallway.

"I can't believe it!" she squealed in a whispered voice. "You and Yuu last night!"

"It's not like that."

"What's he like?" she said. "I bet his tough thing is a facade. He's got a gentle touch, right?"

"Yuki!"

"Okay, okay." She giggled. "But he cooks? I never expected our kendo champ to cook. Next thing you'll be telling me Ishikawa does creative dance."

I listened to her babble while Tanaka chatted with Tomohiro in the kitchen. The smell of bonito fish and miso wafted from the kitchen, Yuki's excited Japanese curling off her tongue.

Why were all these things so familiar to me now?

Did I really want to leave all this behind?

18

After lunch, Yuki squeezed my hand and told me she and Tanaka were going for karaoke. For a minute I swore Tanaka was blushing, but the next minute he looked normal.

"I can't," Tomohiro said. "I have to visit a friend in the hospital."

"I'm going, too," I said.

"You don't have to."

"I know."

We waved to Tanaka and Yuki in the lobby of the mansion and walked to Shizuoka Station, where we hopped on a yellow-and-green bus bound for Kenritsu Hospital.

Ishikawa was on the second floor, in a room with white walls, a white floor and white sheets. Everything was white, which made his bleached hair fit right in. The only splash of color was the purple ring around his eye, the bruises all over his face and arms.

His shoulder was plastered with wrapped bandages and his arm hung in a funny way around the bulky cloth.

He'd been staring out the window when we came in, but at the sound of our footsteps, he turned his head.

"Oi," he said quietly. He looked so defeated, like all the strength and fight had been punched out of him.

Tomohiro held out the flowers he'd bought in the lobby; white, like the room.

"Oh. *Sankyu,*" said Ishikawa, an English *thank you* that had been absorbed into Japanese culture. Kind of like I had.

Tomohiro set them down on a tray near Ishikawa's bed and unwrapped them from the crinkly cellophane.

"How are you feeling?" he asked.

"Like shit," Ishikawa said.

"Just as well," Tomohiro said, reaching for an empty vase behind the hospital bed. "I would've beaten the crap out of you anyway."

"Ha," Ishikawa said, but the laugh spluttered out and turned into a rattling cough.

Tomohiro passed me the vase and I looked for a sink in the room where I could fill it up. I found one and walked over, while Tomohiro put his hand on Ishikawa's shoulder as he coughed.

I felt oddly betrayed and jealous. Shouldn't he be pissed off for the danger Ishikawa had put us in? Why were we even here?

I watched the water rise up the stalks.

But Ishikawa had taken the hit when it mattered. He'd changed his mind and tried to save us. And if he hadn't jumped in front of that bullet— The water overflowed the vase and I twisted the tap shut.

Ishikawa had stopped coughing, and as I put the vase down by the window, he didn't meet my eyes.

"Guess you'll win the prefecture tournament, Yuuto," he said after a minute.

I'm sorry, was I the only one who'd experienced the past two days?

But Tomohiro acted like this whole conversation was perfectly normal.

"I would've won anyway," he smirked.

"Just look out for Takahashi," said Ishikawa.

Tomohiro shrugged. "I don't think he's a problem, either."

"Huh?"

"Broken wrist."

Ishikawa grinned. "Busy night, huh?"

"Guess so."

Silence, then. The hospital room was stuffy and the air was stale. I could feel the sweat filming on my skin. I wished I could run out of the room.

Just when I couldn't stand it anymore, Tomohiro said, "Well, I guess…"

"Yuuto," Ishikawa said. He took a heavy, rattling breath and I thought he might start coughing again. "I didn't— I mean, I—"

Tomohiro looked down. "Power is an ugly thing," he said. "Run from it while you can." He strode toward the door and I followed behind him. I watched him reach for the door handle to slide it closed, stared at the wristband slipped over the crisscrossing of old scars, and then I knew what he meant.

They were different types of power, but Ishikawa and Tomohiro were both trapped. And despite how much I wanted to punch Ishikawa in the gut, I started to understand why the two could be best friends, even after all this.

They were both afraid and alone, in over their heads with no way out.

And now I was going to abandon Tomohiro, too.

When Diane arrived home with her roller suitcase in tow, I was slouched on the couch flipping through Japanese game shows. I stumbled to my feet and met her in the *genkan,* while she bent her leg to pull off her blue pumps.

"Tadaima," she said, surprise in her eyes. I probably looked like a raving lunatic, and it was time for the raving part.

"We need to talk," I said.

She hesitated. "Did you read the fax?"

I nodded. Then the tears I'd been holding back started to sneak down my cheeks. I brushed them away, but Diane lunged forward and wrapped her arms around me.

And somehow her embrace felt a lot like Mom's.

"Oh, hon," she said, squeezing me into her navy blouse and the smells of fresh makeup. She let go then, her hands on my arms as she studied me. "But it's good news, right? Gramps in remission."

"Yeah," I said. Every inch of my body felt numb, like I was hearing her through a tunnel.

"Nan told me they cleaned out the attic for you. They're fixing it up really nicely. They want to know when you want to book the ticket."

"The thing is," I said, feeling ready to explode, "I'm not sure I want to go."

Diane hesitated, her eyes growing big and wide. Then she shook her head.

"Let me get some tea," she said, "and we'll talk."

"Okay."

She went into the bathroom first, so I poured what was left of the black-bean tea into two glasses. When she came out, I was already sitting on the couch, so she grabbed her cup and sat down on the *zabuton* cushion across from me.

"What's changed?" she said, and the directness of the question hit me. I felt like guilt was oozing out of every pore in my body. I should say that I liked living with her, that I liked her curry rice and her nutty game shows. And partially it was true. I liked my life here, even if reading signs was still a bit like deciphering hieroglyphs. I liked my friends—hell, even the kendo I enjoyed. But above all that, the events of the past few days throbbed through my mind.

What's changed?

Tomohiro. Period. That's it.

And how stupid would that be, to throw away my life for a guy? Even if he was a gorgeous kendo star, even if his drawings were so beautiful they sent butterflies knocking around my stomach. Even if he loved me.

My whole life was ahead of me: university, career, everything. And if I stayed here, I might be choosing death. And how the hell was I supposed to tell Diane that?

And that wasn't the only thing that had changed. I had ink inside me somehow. I was connected to the Kami. If I left now, I would never really know who I was or what I was capable of. I'd never know how far my own power might reach or why there was ink lost in my veins.

"Katie?" Diane said, and I looked at her, how her shoulders hunched over the way Mom's always did when she worried about me. She was waiting for an answer, but I didn't know how to give one.

What's changed?

"I have," I said. My mouth felt dry, but I tried to swallow anyway. "I've changed."

"You don't want to move back?"

"I don't know," I said. "It's so complicated."

"Well, let's work it out."

"I can't."

"What do you mean, you can't?"

"I mean, I can't just make a pros-and-cons list of my life," I said. "How am I supposed to know what's the right thing to do, where I should go? Sure, Nan and Gramps will be happy if I move back, but what about my life here? We're halfway through the Japanese semester. They don't start the school year in September like they do in Canada. If I move back, how is that going to work? And—" *And I like living with you.* But I wasn't about to admit it after all the whining I'd done about moving back. How could I have known how well Diane and I would fit together as a family?

"I'm sure the schedule can be worked out, so that's not an issue," said Diane. "Knowing where we're headed in life isn't easy for anyone. No one really knows what's going to happen. We just sort of keep moving forward because we have to."

"I think it's deeper than that," I said.

"Deeper?"

I looked at Diane, wondering if she understood what I was saying. *Give it four or five months,* she'd said. "It's been four or five months." *I belong here.*

It took her a minute to get it, but when she did, the smile curled along her lips.

"Katie," she said. "Don't be afraid to go. It won't make Japan any less important in your life. You can give living with Nan and Gramps four or five months, too."

"I know," I said. I slouched back on the couch, deep in thought.

"Katie?"

"Yeah?"

"Does this have to do with Tanaka?"

"Tanaka?" *Oh.* "Ew, no."

"Are you sure this isn't about a guy? Because staying for a guy is—"

"I know," I said quickly. "It isn't about a guy."

"Take the night to think about it," she said. "Nan is waiting to book the ticket, but give it a day, okay?"

I nodded and trudged to my room. Had she heard a word I'd said?

I wasn't staying for a guy. But who was going to look out for him if I wasn't here? And what about the life that had taken root here? I'd given it the time, and the plant was only starting to bud. Why should I hack it out of the ground before it had time to bloom?

And as dumb as it seemed, like a moth to a flame, I needed to know. Was the ink really trying to kill me? What if it was something else? What if I was part of something important, something that could stop the other Kami for good?

What would Mom do? God, I missed her. I could do anything, she'd told me over and over. But I needed to hear her say it again, that she believed in me.

I stared into the void in my heart, searching for her. I hugged my pillow to my chest and stared at the ceiling, but I couldn't stop wondering if Tomohiro was safe, if the Kami would come back to get us.

I need to know you're safe, he'd said.

Shit. I *was* staying for a guy. And he wanted me to leave, because if I didn't, terrible things were lurking around every corner.

My *keitai* went off in the middle of the night. I jolted awake, fear twisting up and down my spine.

"Moshi mosh?" I said, shocked to find myself speaking Japanese even half-asleep.

"Katie," said Tomohiro's smooth voice. I fell back onto my pillow with relief.

"God, I thought you were Jun calling to threaten me or something."

"Sorry," he said. He sounded pretty sheepish. "I know it's late. I just wanted to make sure you were okay."

"Fine," I said. "Except I can't sleep."

"Really?"

"Yeah," I said. "This jerk called my *keitai* in the middle of the night."

I heard him snort.

"I'll go beat him up," he said.

"Good."

"Wait, why does Jun have your *keitai* number?"

"Never mind," I said. "It was when he was trying to protect me from Ishikawa. It's nothing."

"You sure?"

"Well, maybe I'm not sure, 'cause evil Kami are so hot."

"Hidoi na," Tomohiro whined. "Don't break my heart now."

"Let me sketch him. He might be pregnant."

"*Oi,*" he said, but I could just about hear the grin on his face. "Did you talk to Diane yet?"

"Yeah."

"And?"

"I told her I want to stay in Japan."

"Shit, Katie." He sounded all irritated, the way he talked at school.

"Look, it's my life, okay? I get to make the decisions."

"I know," he said. "But being with me is a bad one. Look, my dad found out about the Kami contacting me. He's talking about moving."

"What?" I sat upright, turning up my air conditioner so Diane wouldn't hear us. "How did that happen?"

"They came to my door tonight."

"Shit," I said.

"Katie," he said, and his voice turned all soft. "I lost my mom. I can't lose you, too."

The same reason I wanted to stay in Japan, thrown back at me. And suddenly my choice felt selfish.

"Where are you going to go?"

"He's trying to pull strings and get transferred to Takatsuki, but I'm trying to convince him to stay. It's not like there won't be Kami in Osaka, too. And I can't switch schools in the middle of studying for entrance exams. I'd fail for sure."

"What if you came with me?"

"To Canada?"

"Yeah."

"And what about my dad? I know I'm endangering him by existing, but if I'm not here, how do I know they won't go after him? I'm all he has left."

The tears streamed down my face and I grabbed a tissue off my night table, trying not to sound like I was crying.

"I'll be fine," he said, but we both knew he was lying.

"I want to stay with you," I said. "Even if it means…even if…"

He was silent for a minute, because we both knew what I was going to say. When he spoke again, his voice was so small I could barely hear him.

"Katie, I know it's your life. But please…live it. Please live."

I listened to the sound of our breath whispering against the receivers, and then we both hung up, and the silence of the night pushed in around me.

If I left Japan, we'd both be safe. His drawings would be under control, and the ink in me would probably go back to being dormant.

I loved him. And I knew what I had to do.

"Okay," I whispered into the darkness. "Okay."

19

Nan sent the ticket express mail, and by Friday it was poking out of our mailbox in the lobby, the printed address of the travel agency in glaring black English letters. There was a little picture of a plane circling a globe in the corner.

Tomohiro left for a second kendo training camp the Saturday morning, and even though I begged him not to attend, freaked out that the Kami would surround him, Jun never showed up at the retreat. Guess he couldn't do much with a broken wrist.

I spent the weekend sorting through my things, while Diane made phone calls to both schools to make sure my enrollment and withdrawal were under control. Tricky, considering neither school was well staffed in early August.

The sweat of the Japanese summer clung to my skin as I packed up my *purikura* album with photos of Yuki and Tanaka, and my headband from my kendo uniform. *The Twofold Path of the Pen and Sword,* it read, the motto of our club. I folded it neatly, the kanji collapsing in on themselves, smaller and smaller.

Mostly I left my room the way it was, because neither Diane nor I could bear to see it pared down to the spare room it had been before I arrived. Not that we were going to admit it to each other.

Not that it needed to be said anyway. It was obvious.

Tomohiro sent me a couple of texts from the training camp, mostly passing on messages he got from Ishikawa that the Yakuza were going to rethink their plan of dealing with Tomohiro. I guess an artist who draws a gun that fires on him isn't the most useful to have around. The Kami were too quiet, though, and I found myself peering out my window at night, wondering if they were watching us, waiting to make a move.

Yuki and Tanaka came over in the afternoon with little parting gifts. Yuki dabbed her eyes and said over and over again how she couldn't believe I was leaving. I tried to comfort her, but how could I? I couldn't believe it, either.

She gave me a cartoon teacup, to remember our time in Tea Ceremony Club, and Tanaka gave me a DVD set of *Lost,* his favorite American series, one we'd watched over and over again in English Club. His cheeks turned a deep red when I hugged him at the door, yet another casual mistake that showed I didn't belong in Japan. I probably should've bowed or something.

I mailed off a parcel to Nan and Gramps, mostly *omiyage* souvenirs for them and for friends when I got there. I stuck in a few curry-rice mixes, not sure if I could buy them in Deep River, not sure if I could survive life without the comforting smell of Japanese curry wafting from the steel pot in the kitchen. I studied Diane's *nikujaga* and meat spaghetti, willing myself to remember all thc dctails, eating thick toast for breakfast every morning slathered in honey. Buying *purin* puddings and green *matcha* cream horns from the *conbini* stores until my stomach felt satisfyingly ill. If I had to leave Japan, I'd go out with a five-pound bang.

While I was folding clothes for the suitcase, my *keitai* rang with an unknown number. I picked up, hands trembling.

"Hello?"

Nothing but the sound of breathing.

I started to panic, wondering how they got my number.

"Greene," Ishikawa said quietly. *"Ki wo tsukete na,"* he managed before a rattling cough started up. Halfway through the coughing fit, he hung up. *Take care.* A peace offering, I guess.

Well. He wasn't my best friend, so I could still be pissed at him. Even if he'd saved Tomohiro's life.

The day before my flight, I was supposed to meet Tomo in front of Shizuoka Station, so I was completely shocked when he knocked on our front door. Diane answered it, a bizarre look on her face. I peeked around the corner from the bathroom, my heart drumming in my ears. Now I'd have to explain everything. As the door swung open, I imagined the worst: Tomohiro slouching in the doorway, hand pressed to the back of his head and his scars fully visible. Maybe a split lip from some fight he got into on the way over here. What if Diane somehow knew the rumors about his pregnant girlfriend? Oh god, my life would be over.

But he was standing normally when she opened the door, and he gave her a crisp, overeager bow, flooding the *genkan* with superpolite Japanese. I didn't think I'd ever heard his sentences end in all those *masus* before. But Diane raised her eyebrows at his copper hair, the thick silver chain around his neck and the rips in his jeans. She probably thought he was a bit of a cleaned-up punk, which I guess he was.

She turned around and I ducked back into the bathroom, my face totally red and the heat rushing up the back of my neck.

"Katie," she called out. "Um, Yuu Tomohiro is here to see you."

"Thanks," I said. She filled the frame of the doorway.

"He's not Tanaka," she said slowly.

"Um," I said. "For the record, I always told you Tanaka and I are just friends."

"You also never mentioned Tomohiro."

"It slipped my mind?"

Diane gave me a stern look.

"Sorry," I said. "I just didn't want you to be worried."

"Why would I be worried?"

"Because of his reputation?"

"Okay, now I'm worried."

"He's not really like that," I said. "Trust me, Diane." She frowned.

"Trust you because you've been lying all this time?"

"Touché."

"If you were staying, we'd have a talk about this."

"I know. I'm sorry. But I swear, he's nice. And our planned activities are PG, I promise."

"That doesn't fill me with confidence."

From the hallway, Tomohiro cleared his throat.

"Diane!" I whined.

"Home by nine," she said. "Or I get a shotgun." And then she couldn't help herself and grinned.

Small victories, I guess. It wasn't like she was going to pull the staying-for-a-boy line on me, because I wasn't staying.

"We're going for *kakigori,*" I said. "Um. I have my *keitai* with me."

"Okay," Diane said, but she kept staring at me. "Have a good time. I'll call you." She emphasized that part.

"Um, okay," I said and closed the door behind us. I tried

to punch Tomohiro in the arm, but he sidestepped it, a bright grin breaking onto his face.

"What's that for?" he said.

"Like you don't know! Couldn't you have dressed like a normal person?" I swung again. He jumped back, his arms up in the air and the smirk plastered on his face.

We walked to the food floor of the department store off Miyuki Road, debating which café had the most impressive spread of wax desserts in their floor-to-ceiling windows. We ducked under the cloth *noren* hanging from the doorway and sat down at a table. We ordered *kakigori,* shaved ice, mine melon and his strawberry with extra condensed milk.

"That's disgusting," I said, watching him drown the syrupy ice with runny cream.

He shrugged. "I'm not sharing."

"I wouldn't want any. One bite and I'll give my *grandkids* cavities."

The nightmare of the Kami and the Yakuza hovered on the edge of our memories, and I found myself wondering if it had really happened or if it had all just been a bad dream.

"Ishikawa's getting out of the hospital this week," he said.

"Oh." Back to reality.

"I'll be careful," he said.

I mashed the melting ice with my spoon. "I didn't say anything."

"You didn't have to."

He finished the last bite of his *kakigori* and then reached across the table for mine.

"Hey!" I said, but all I could think about was the softness of his wristband against my skin as he pulled the dessert toward him.

"Don't complain," he said, scooping a huge bite into his

mouth. "I'm saving your grandkids hundreds in dental bills. And do you know how many calories are in this?" He squirted more condensed milk on top.

"About a hundred more now?"

"I need to bulk up for the kendo tournament."

"With *kakigori*."

"Never say I don't sacrifice for my sport."

We walked around Sunpu Park, avoiding the castle. The cherry blossoms were long gone, but a few cicadas still whirred in the hot summer air. He reached for my hand, his wristband pressed against the inside of my wrist, the scars up his arm scraping against my skin as we walked.

It was almost dinnertime and the sky started to streak with colors; our last day was ending. Tomohiro pulled me into a *conbini* store and bought *bentous* for us, which the clerk heated up in a silver microwave. We boarded the puttering Roman bus, the smell of teriyaki and *katsu* curry flooding our noses.

I didn't have to ask where we were going. I knew.

They'd finished the renovations at Toro Iseki, and most of the chain-link fence lay stacked in piles ready to take away. A couple of university students walked around the site, the girl with her arms wrapped tightly around the guy. Near the Toro Museum at the other side of the forest edge, a group of elementary school students laughed and joked.

I stared, feeling like something was slipping away from me.

"Guess I'll have to find a new studio," Tomohiro said, but his voice sounded as hollow as I felt.

We stepped through the trees in silence. The wagtails called to each other, ready to roost in the *ume* trees for the night. The ancient Yayoi huts stood against the orange sky, the once long grasses around them trimmed neatly for the tourist season.

An ugly patch of brown grass was shorter still where it had

burned under the dragon's looped corpse, but that was the only mark left of what had happened to us.

Tomohiro squeezed my hand and pulled me forward. We ducked into one of the huts before we could get caught. Above us, the sun gleamed through the gaps in the thatched roof.

"We'll get in trouble," I hissed.

"What's new?" He grinned and then leaned over to kiss me.

We sat pressed against the walls a long time, staring up at the sky as the colors twisted and darkened. We watched as our last day together faded, as life grew over the shape of what had once been.

I turned the wrong way when we walked back to the bus stop. That's how much my world was shifting under my feet.

Tomohiro couldn't make it to the airport in Tokyo, but at my front door—Diane's front door—he'd stuffed an envelope into my hand and made me promise to read it on the plane. Then he'd pressed a kiss onto my lips, deep and hungry and sweet, and pulled away before I could say goodbye, his hand raised to his face as he turned the corner for the elevator. I'd leaned against the wall, listening until the elevator doors slid shut. And then ink had dripped back down the hallway toward me, leaving inky trails that looked like fingers grasping, stretching.

Never quite reaching me.

"Want a sandwich for the flight?" Diane asked at the airport. I shook my head. My stomach felt like it was pressing in on me. There was no way I could eat. "Tea? Anything?"

It was like we were strangers again, like she was shoving hors d'oeuvres at me at Mom's funeral, keeping a silver plate between us. And yet I'd really started to think that looking for ourselves on the other side of the world, we'd found each other. She wasn't the piece that didn't fit—she was the piece that completed everything.

We stood at the security gate, as far as she could take me.

"Well," she said.

Well.

"Say hi to Nan and Gramps for me," she said. She reached up and stroked my hair. She had that same wavering smile Mom always had when she was pretending not to be sad. "They're going to be so happy to see you."

"Thanks," I said.

"No problem," Diane answered.

"No," I said, looking her right in the eye. "I mean, thanks. For everything."

She looked at me, her eyes filming over with tears. Then she hugged me tightly.

"Oh, hon," she said, her eyes squeezed shut. "If you need anything, you call me, okay? Don't worry about the time difference."

"Okay," I said. She stepped back and looked at me, her eyes shining.

"Your mom would be so proud of you," she said, and my eyes filled with tears. "It was always so hard for her to put down roots outside her comfort zone. And you managed it in a different language, even."

"It's no big deal," I said, which meant *don't say any more or I'll start bawling in the middle of Narita Airport.*

I guess she got the message, because she closed her mouth and stepped back.

"Bye," I choked.

"You've always got a home here," she said. "Okay?"

"Yeah."

I turned and went through the security check. Once I

stepped through the metal detector, I turned to look back at Diane, but she was lost in the crowd.

I adjusted my backpack and rolled my carry-on toward the empty benches near my gate. I wished the floor would open and swallow me up so I wouldn't have to feel anything anymore.

I sat down on one of the hard leather benches by the door. Clusters of *gaijin* and Japanese tourists sat in the rows around me, while two flight attendants talked in hushed tones. I stared out the giant windows at the planes moving slowly around the concrete plaza.

The whole thing felt surreal. To think that five months ago this was what I had wanted. To go home.

But home wasn't there anymore, and it wasn't even Japan, really.

I think it was inside myself.

And it was in him.

And that's why I had to leave. Because I couldn't stand to break him.

I pulled out the envelope and tapped it against my top lip, staring at the luggage trains and the clumsy maneuvers of the planes. They looked so awkward on the ground, big, flailing machines that tipped from side to side as they stumbled forward.

I looked down at the envelope in my hands.

I was practically on the plane. It was close enough.

I pulled the edge of the envelope up and slid my finger along the top, the paper ripping into little puckered edges. I pulled out the note, a plain piece of white paper, and unfolded it carefully.

I'd wondered what he would say to me, agonized over what he would write and what it would mean. And here in red pen was a single word at the top of the page.

いってらしゃい。

いってらっしゃい。

Itterasshai.

Go and come back safely.

Like I was leaving on a vacation and returning to him.

A sketch spanned the rest of the paper, a haunting black-and-white rose chained to the page by five thick X marks, the lines scribbled and rescribbled to bind the drawing. Even then it was risky, but it was only pen, and he'd always managed to keep tabs on his school notes and doodles.

The rose barely moved as I looked at it, its petals fluttering softly in the drafty airport. It almost looked normal. In fact it was beautiful, the same beauty I saw in Tomohiro's eyes when he gazed at the wagtails or the *sakura* trees, when he gave them life in his notebook. The look in his eyes when he gazed at me.

The tears rolled down my cheeks, curving under my chin and dripping onto the paper. The ink ran where they fell, smearing into blots on the leaves and the petals.

But it was done now. He wanted me to go, to be safe. I wanted to be safe, too. The Yakuza and the Kami scared me. Tomohiro scared me. And by leaving, I was keeping Tomohiro's power under control and out of Jun's hands.

I traced the rose with my fingers, trying to imitate the movements of his pen. I'd never been much of an artist, and I pretended that each stroke was mine, that I could capture the soul of a rose the way he had.

My hand ran down the stem, and a hot pain seared through my fingertip.

I yanked my hand backward, flipping it over to inspect the paper cut. A dark bead of blood pooled on the pad of my index finger. It stung like crazy.

I looked down at the sketch.

A thorn. It wasn't a paper cut—I'd cut myself on the thorn.

"*Okyaku-sama,* we apologize for the wait. This is your boarding call for Flight 1093 to Ottawa…."

The blood trickled down the side of my finger and fell onto the page with a sound like someone flicking the paper.

Tak, tak, tak.

The other guests rose around me, businessmen with leather bags on wheels, mothers with sprawling infants wrapped to their fronts, carry-ons of every color whirling by the glass wall where our bulky, awkward plane waited on the concrete.

Tak.

I couldn't do anything now. Nan had bought the ticket. Diane had left for the bullet train back to Shizuoka.

Tak.

I'd promised Tomohiro I would leave.

If I stay, I might die.

I stared at the blood, stark red on the paper—the only color on the page, except for the single word Tomohiro had left me with.

Itterasshai.

Come back safely.

Come back.

But it was last call for the airplane. I couldn't just run out of the airport. That wasn't the way real life worked. Maybe in Japanese dramas, or the bad Hollywood flicks we watched in English Club. But I had a ticket in my jeans pocket, a suitcase on the seat beside me. You can't just pick up and leave in real life.

Tak.

Can you?

I rose to my feet slowly, my whole body shaking. My pulse thumped in my ears, drummed through every vein in my body.

It wasn't running away. If the decision to leave was wrong… changing it wouldn't be running away. Would it?

Please…live.

Come back safely.

I balled my hands into fists, the stickiness of the blood against my palm.

It wasn't about what Tomohiro said or wanted. It wasn't ever about him, not really.

It was my life and my choice.

Because running away, giving up the life that mattered to me, wasn't living.

There's only one chance. I only get one life. If the ink reacts to me, then maybe I can stop it. And if I don't, then we're not the only ones who are going to suffer.

I stepped forward, my legs like stone. I walked away from the row of seats, away from the gate where a few stragglers fumbled with their passports and carry-ons.

I stumbled and then began to run through the monochrome pathways of the airport, Tomohiro's note crumpled around my fingers. I felt alive, the power surging through me stronger than any fear that had pulsed there.

It was my destiny.

I was going to face it.

It was my life.

I was going to live it.

★ ★ ★ ★ ★

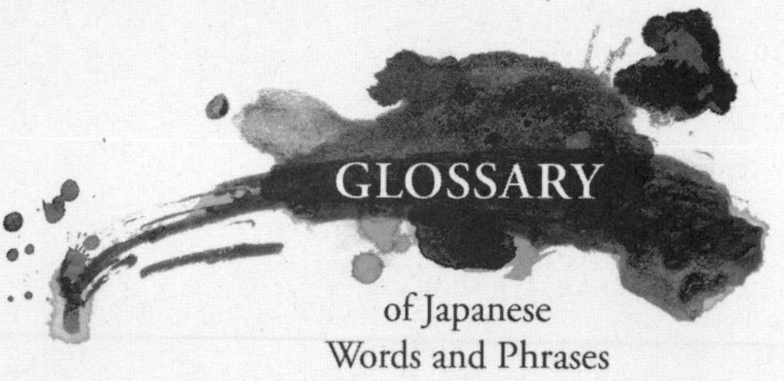

GLOSSARY

of Japanese
Words and Phrases

Amerika-jin:
An American

Ano:
"Um," a filler word telling the speaker you have something to say

A-re:
A word expressing surprise

Bai bai:
"Bye-bye" pronounced just like the English

Baka ja nai no?:
"Are you stupid or something?"

Betsu ni:
"Nothing special" or "nothing in particular"

Bogu:
The set of kendo armor

Chan:
Suffix used for girl friends or those younger than the speaker

Chawan:
The special tea bowl used in a Tea Ceremony

Che:
“Damn it!”

Conbini:
A convenience store

Daiji na hito:
An important person, big shot, etc.

Daijoubu:
“Are you all right?” or “I’m/it’s all right”

Dango:
Dumplings made of rice flour, often sweet and eaten during flower viewing

Domo:
As used in *Ink,* “Hi” or “Hey”

Dou:
The breastplate of kendo armor

Faito:
An encouraging phrase meaning to fight with one’s might or do one’s best

Furikake:
A seasoning to sprinkle over white rice

Furin:
A traditional Japanese wind chime

Gaijin:
A person from a foreign country

Ganbare:
“Do your best,” said to encourage one in academics, sports or life

Genkan:
The foyer or entrance of a Japanese building. Usually the floor of the genkan is lower than the rest of the building, to keep shoes and outside things separate from the clean raised floor inside

Gomen:
"I'm sorry"

Guzen da:
"What a coincidence!"

Gyoza:
Dumplings

Gyudon:
Sauced beef on rice

Hai?:
"Yes?" but used as it is in *Ink,* it expresses surprise, such as "I'm sorry?"

Hakama:
The skirtlike clothing worn by *kendouka*

Hana yori dango:
"Dumplings over flowers," meaning substance over appearance

Hanami:
Flower viewing, in particular cherry blossoms

Hanshi:
Special paper used for calligraphy

Hazui:
"Embarrassing," slang form of *hazukashii*

Hebi:
Snakes

Hidoi na:
"You're cruel!" or "That's mean/harsh!"

Ii ka:
"Okay?"

Ii kara:
"It's okay (so just do it)"

Ikemen:
A good-looking guy

Ikuzo:
"Let's go," said in a tough slang

Itadakimasu:
"I'm going to receive," said before a meal like "bon appétit"

I-te/Itai:
"Ouch" or "It hurts"

Ittekimasu:
"I'm leaving (and coming back)," said when leaving the home

Itterasshai:
"Go (and come back) safely," said to the one leaving home

Jaa ne:
"See you later"

Kado:
The tradion of flower arranging, also known as ikebana

Kakigori:
Shaved ice with syrup, much like a snow cone

Kankenai darou:
"It's none of your business" or "It doesn't concern you"

Karaage:
Bite-size fried chicken

Kata:
A series of memorized movements in kendo or other martial arts

Keigoki:
The soft top worn under the kendo armor

Keiji-san:
Detective

Keitai:
Cell phone

Kendouka:
A kendo participant

Ki wo tsukete na:
"Take care"

Kiai:
A shout made by *kendouka* to intimidate opponents and tighten stomach muscles for self-defense

Kiri-kaeshi:
A kendo exercise drill

Koibito:
"Lovers," dating couple

Kote:
Gloves worn during kendo

Kun:
Suffix generally used for guy friends

Maa:

"Well," but it can be used as a subtle way of affirming something ("Well, yes")

Maji de:

"No way"

Manju:

Small Japanese cakes, usually with some sort of filling inside

Matte:

"Wait"

Men:

The helmet warn during kendo

Migi-kote:

The right glove

Mieta:

"I saw it"

Momiji:

Maple tree

Moshi mosh(i):

Said when answering the phone

Mou ii:

"That's enough"

Naaa:

"Hey" or "You know," a filler word that indicates the speaker is going to say something

Nasubi:

Eggplant

Ne:

"Isn't it?" It can also be used as "Hey!" to get someone's attention (like "*Ne*, Tanaka")

Nerikiri:

A sweet white-bean-paste cake eaten during a tea ceremony

Nikujaga:

A Japanese dish of meat and potatoes

Noren:

An awning hung over the doorway of a shop

Ohayo:

"Good morning"

Oi:

"Hey"

Okaeri:

"Welcome home," said when one arrives home

Okonomiyaki:

A Japanese pancake or pizza-type dish where diners choose the ingredients that go into the dish, such as cabbage or other veggies, noodles, meat or fish

Okyaku-sama:

Guests/customers

Omiyage:

Souvenirs

Onigiri:

Rice balls

Ore sa, kimi no koto ga...(suki):

"I like you" or more literally "About you, I, you know... (like you)." This is a common way for a boy to confess he likes someone

O-Torii:

The giant orange Shinto gate at Itsukushima Shrine

Peko peko:

"I'm starving," usually said by younger children or girls to be cute

Purikura:

Print Club, little sticker pictures taken and printed by machines at arcades or department stores

Purin:

A popular Japanese pudding

Sado:

The tradition of tea ceremony

Saitei:

"You're the worst," something despicable

Sakura:

The cherry blossoms

Sankyu:

"Thank you"

Sasa:

A bamboo tree used for Tanabata festivities

Seifuku:

Japanese school uniform based on the look of old sailor uniforms

Seiza:

A kneeling stance used in kendo

Senpai:

A student older than the speaker

Shinai:

A sword made of bamboo slats tied together, used for kendo

Shinkansen:

The bullet train

Shoudo:

The tradition of calligraphy

Shouji:

A traditional rice-paper door

Sonna wake nai jan:

"It's not like that!"

Sou da na:

"I guess that's right."

Sou ka:

"Is that right?"

Sou mitai:

"Looks that way"

Sou ne:

"You're right, aren't you?" or "That's right, isn't it?"

Su-ge:

"Wow," slang form of *sugoi*

Suki:

"I like you"

Sumi:

An ink stick, ground against the *suzuri* to make ink

Sunpu-jou:

Sunpu Castle

Suzuri:

An inkstone, used in making liquid ink

Tadaima:

"I'm home," said by one arriving home

Taihen da ne:

"That's tough" or "That's a difficult situation."

Tanabata:

A holiday celebrating the stars Altair and Vega reuniting in the sky

Tatami:

Traditional mat flooring made of woven straw

Teme:

A really foul way to call someone "you." Usage is not advised!

Tenugui:

A headband tied under the *men* helmet

Tomodachi:

"Friends"

(Ton)katsu:

A breaded, deep-fried (pork) cutlet

Tsuki:

A kendo hit to the throat

Ume:
Plum tree

Unagi:
Eel

Warui:
"Bad," sometimes used as an apology

Yamero:
"Stop"

Yatta:
"I did it!" or as a general "Yay!"

Yosh(i):
"Good" or "Okay"

Youkai:
A demon

Yuu Tomohiro desu ga...:
"My name is Yuu Tomohiro..."

Zabuton:
A cushion used for sitting on the floor

Zenzen:
"Not at all"

ACKNOWLEDGMENTS

I am so grateful to everyone who put their heart, soul and energy into making *Ink* a reality. Without all of you, this book would never have become everything I had hoped it to be.

Mary Sheldon, this book would not exist without you. The passion and conviction with which you live your life and advocate for reading are an inspiration to me. You are a spark of color in this life, a vibrant example of what the world should and can be. I continue to aspire to the faith you place in me, for the world is changed because of you.

Thank you to my family at Harlequin TEEN, to Natashya Wilson for believing in Katie and Tomo from the start, to Adam Wilson for my first fan mail, to Giselle Regus for your hard work behind the scenes, to the digital and sales teams and copy editors, and to those who inspire me—Debbie Soares, Amy Jones, Erin Craig and Lisa Wray. Thank you to Gigi Lau for the gorgeous cover, and for taking so much care in breathing life into the book of my heart.

To my fantastic editor, T.S. Ferguson. TiduS, you have loved my world and characters as your own, and your thoughtful and brilliant advice allowed me to take the story to a level I didn't know was possible. Your wit and kindness continue to inspire me, and I'm so fortunate to have you as my editor and friend. I look forward to the great things we will accomplish together.

Thank you to my agent, Melissa Jeglinski, for your advice, confidence and support. I am so grateful to you for your hard work and passion, and for saying what I need to hear when I need to hear it. Thank you for believing in me, and in *Ink*.

Without my family's support, I could never have reached this point. Thank you, Mum and Dad, for always believing in my writing and in me. Kevin and Emily, thank you for those trips to the park so I could meet my deadlines, and for the long plot discussions you were always willing to have with me. Thank you, Nathan Conquergood, for reading my early novels and doing book reports on them in school, and Bridget Ball, for passing around a petition at school to publish my book. I so appreciate your enthusiasm and faith in my work.

Thank you, Mio Matsui, for making sure Tomohiro speaks like a real Japanese teen. Thank you, Harumi Sugino and the Hasegawa family, Nobuko, Yoko and all my friends in Japan. Because you opened your arms to me, I can now share that love through *Ink*. ありがとうございました。

Thank you to Caroline Schmeing and Diana Jardine, who read every piece of fan fiction, every full notebook passed under the table in class. To Terry Lim, Clélie Rich and Walter Davies for cheerleading every step of the way. To Alex Neary for my beautiful author photo, and my fellow Lucky

13s for their support. To Nerdfighteria for being a haven where I am understood.

And finally to my readers. Thank you for sharing this journey with me. Wherever you may go in life—*itterasshai.*

Q&A

with Amanda Sun

Q. What inspired you to write *Ink* and why did you choose to set the story in Japan?

A. I lived on exchange in Osaka during my time in high school. Even after I returned from the exchange, the culture and mythology stayed an integral part of my interests. I wanted to make the experience of living in Japan accessible to anyone. At the same time, I was devouring piles of YA books. While watching Japanese dramas for language practice, the two interests merged in my head.

Ink is also inspired by my study of the history of writing. Ancient Chinese characters were originally written down to communicate with the gods. And in ancient Egypt, the snake hieroglyphs on tomb walls were often sliced through the middle by paint or a chisel to prevent them from becoming real snakes in the afterworld. I started wondering what would happen if what we wrote and drew came to life in such a dangerous way, and then I realized that the Tomohiro I'd envisioned would do just that.

Q. How did you come up with the Kami and their abilities to control ink and make drawings come to life?

A. Something I really enjoy about multicultural YAs are the new and sometimes unfamiliar mythologies the authors draw on for their books. I've always found the myths of the *kami* fascinating because the spirits' reactions and sense of justice are so different from our modern-day thinking. The *kami* were unpredictable and dangerous, perfect for a darker paranormal. I thought about how the emperors claimed lineage to Amaterasu and how they were forced to deny this divinity during World War Two. And combining that with kanji characters' original use as a way to interact with the spiritual world, I started wondering what would have happened if Amaterasu was real. What if the emperors really were descended from her? And what if kanji still held some sort of power? And, like Jun, I wanted to blur the lines between whether that power was being used for right or wrong, just like in the old myths.

Q. What artistic abilities, if any, do you have, and what would you create if you could make your creations come to life?

A. I've always wanted to be able to draw, but my sketching skills are lacking! I find other ways to express myself through art—I make costumes. Other than writing, my main hobby is cosplay, which is a Japanese term that combines *costume* with *play.* I make elaborate costumes from scratch, learning a little of everything along the way, including sewing, props, armor, wig-styling—you name it! When the costume is complete, I usually enter competitions and perform onstage. I've won a few awards so far, but what I like best is the community and all the wonderful people I meet through cosplay.

If I could make my sketches come to life, though, I'd want to make impossible things, things that aren't and should be. I'd be tempted to sketch a dragon of my own that I could ride around on—a friendly one, of course!

Q. What do you think are the best qualities of your main characters?

A. I think Katie's best quality is her bravery. Here she is without her mom, in a country she doesn't fully understand, and she's doing her best to keep moving forward. Even when Yuki gives her the option to speak English, Katie keeps trying to speak Japanese, to push herself and rise to the challenge. She knows there's more to Tomohiro, too, and won't let anything stop her from reaching the truth. I also admire that she's a kindhearted person and a loyal friend who does the right thing simply because it's right.

For Tomohiro, I think it's his perseverance. Despite the struggle with his Kami power, he keeps fighting. He doesn't want to be a monster. He's living under a dark shadow and yet he wants to do good with his life. He wants his life to matter and to belong to him, and he won't let anything or anyone stop him. I know how hard it can be to keep going when life looks bleak, and Tomo's courage inspires me—and I hope it inspires you, too!

Q. Was it hard to write about a culture you didn't grow up in? How did your stay in Japan inform what you wrote, and how did you fill in the knowledge gaps as the story started taking shape?

A. I wanted to be as accurate as possible in *Ink,* so I did as much research as I could. While living in Osaka, I kept a daily journal of all my experiences there, from the temples and shrines I visited to daily life and meals with my host family. I've kept in close contact with my friends there, and also hosted students from Shizuoka. While writing *Ink,* I visited Shizuoka again and took numerous photos, wandering through Sunpu Park, touring one of my host students' schools and sitting in the grasses at Toro Iseki.

Katie was an ideal protagonist for me because she is an outsider looking in, and so it was a POV I could identify with and write with confidence. For school life and Japanese culture, I made sure to check with my friends in Japan as much as possible. I also watched every Japanese school-based drama I could get my hands on to see school life in action.

Q. What was the hardest scene for you to write? What was the most fun scene to write?

A. I think the hardest scene for me to write was the love hotel. Beneath the facade he constructs, I know Tomohiro is a kind, gentle person, and I didn't like to see him acting that way toward Katie. I wanted to shove him in a corner and tell him to think about how he acted! So while it was hurting Tomohiro to act that way to Katie to save her, it was hurting me, too. Poor guy.

The scenes that are the most fun for me to write are when Tomo and Katie interact. From one snarky comment to the next, they have that attitude where they want to one-up each other, but never in a belittling way. Sometimes their replies to each other are so snappy that I have to rush to type them down and I have to separate them in my mind to catch up! I love that they're competitive in a friendly way.

And of course I love writing the ink scenes. It's fun to see what sinister way the ink will twist in next.

Q. What are some of your favorite books and/or authors, and did any of them in particular inspire you to become a writer?

A. I always wanted to be a writer. Growing up, my biggest influences were Jane Yolen, Bruce Coville, Lloyd Alexander and C.S. Lewis. I loved traditional fantasy, but then TV shows like *Gargoyles* and *Beauty and the Beast,* where an impossible thing was happening in our world, became so appealing to me. I loved Narnia because it made the fantasy world accessible to me, and I started to search out similar stories that were possible in our world.

I took a turn into slightly darker-edged YAs after reading books like the Chaos Walking trilogy by Patrick Ness, *Half World* by Hiromi Goto and *The Graveyard Book* by Neil Gaiman. I love those books because they aren't afraid to take you into the darker places, to let the worst possible things happen before they lead you out again. Also, reading lighter fantasy by Terry Pratchett reminded me to keep my books both realistic and human. I didn't want flat characters. I wanted bad guys who were likable and had good traits, good guys who had flaws and reasons why they were shaped that way. I love complex characters because we learn so much about ourselves from reading about them.

Q. Without giving away spoilers, can you tell us a bit about what's going to happen to Katie and Tomo in Book Two?

A. Katie and Tomo are going to have to face some serious consequences to their decisions in *Ink.* With Katie returning to understand her connection to the Kami, her closeness is going to cause Tomo further loss of control unless he figures out how to contain his power. The Yakuza aren't going to take their embarrassment lightly, and Jun isn't going to give up on recruiting Tomo to his idea of the future. It's going to take everything Katie and Tomo have to save each other. I hope you'll look forward to it!

QUESTIONS FOR DISCUSSION

1. At the beginning of *Ink,* Katie has to leave everything familiar and move in with her aunt in Shizuoka. Have you ever been in an unfamiliar situation out of your comfort zone? How did it make you feel? Did you learn something from the experience?

2. Imagine you have the Kami power to draw anything and it will become real. What would you draw? What if there was the possibility that your drawing could turn against you? Would you still take the chance?

3. Shiori, Tomohiro's sisterlike friend, finds herself the target of bullying because of her pregnancy. Did it surprise you that she'd be bullied for keeping the baby? How did you deal with an instance in which you were bullied? Is there any effective way to stop bullying?

4. Ishikawa is always calling Tomohiro to bail him out of bad situations with the Yakuza. Do you think Tomohiro is really helping Ishikawa by rushing to his aid? How else could Tomohiro help him? What would you do to help a friend like this?

5. Tomohiro struggles against his powers, determined to shape his own fate. Is there something you wanted to achieve that you had to struggle for? What sort of obstacles did you face, and how did you motivate yourself to keep going? What is something you would fight for until the end?

6. What did you think of Tomohiro's decision to push Katie away to protect her? Have you ever had to step away from someone or something you cared about? If you were a Kami, how would you protect your loved ones?

7. At the end of the story, Katie says, "It was my life. I was going to live it." Have you ever gone against expectation for something important to you or acted in an unexpected way? What was the reaction of others around you?

8. What do you think of Jun's goal to rid the world of the Yakuza, criminals and corrupt governments, no matter the cost? If you were a Kami, how would you feel about being used as a weapon of war for a peaceful goal? Does peace require war? Is force justified to reach an important goal?

Katie has decided
to stay in Japan,
and Tomohiro is more
determined than ever
to fight the darkness
inside him…
…but destiny isn’t an
easy thing to change.
Turn the page for a
sneak peek at the next novel
in THE PAPER GODS series

Chapter One

"Hold still," Yuki said, threading the thick obi ribbon through the back of the bow. She pulled the loops tight. "Okay, now breathe in."

I stared down at my *keitai,* flipping through the call history.

"Katie?"

"Hmm?"

"Breathe in."

I took a deep breath and she shifted the bow to the center of my back. "How's that?"

"Looks great," I mumbled, flipping through my messages. Empty.

"You didn't even look up," Yuki said.

"Mmm-hmm. Hey!" Yuki snatched the phone out of my hands.

"Ano ne," she said. "Listen. Yuu will call you—I'm sure of it. You don't want to be the panicky girlfriend, right?"

I didn't say anything. How could I? Yuki didn't know that not being able to get ahold of Tomohiro could mean the Yakuza had him, or the Kami had kidnapped him, or that he'd drowned in an ocean of his own sketching.

Yuki grinned and sidestepped, tugging the creases out of the sleeves of my *yukata,* the summer kimono she was lending me. "Now look," she commanded, pointing at the mirror.

I looked.

The *yukata* made me look elegant, the soft yellow fabric draped and folded around me like an origami dress. Pink *sakura* blossoms floated down the woven material, which Yuki had complemented by lending me her pink obi to tie around my waist.

"*Dou?* How is it?"

"It's beautiful," I said. "Thank you."

She grinned, smoothing her own soft blue *yukata* with her hands.

"Yuu is a jerk for not calling," she said. "But let's forget about it for now. It's Shizuoka Matsuri, and you're still here with us. So let's go celebrate!"

Was he being a jerk? I hadn't been able to get ahold of him since deciding to stay in Japan. It didn't make sense, unless he was in trouble. Or avoiding me, in which case he'd clearly learned nothing from the first attempt and I would pound the lesson into him tomorrow when school started again.

It didn't matter if he was avoiding me. Sooner or later, I'd have to get in touch with him. Because as much as I'd wanted to stay in Japan to be with him, I'd also had no choice. If Jun was right, Tomohiro was a ticking time bomb, and I was the only one who could defuse him.

Diane entered my room carrying a tray of glasses filled with cold black-bean tea. The ice clinked against the sides of the cups as she set them down. A pink spray of flowers unfurled in a corner of the tray.

"Don't you girls look beautiful," she said. "Katie, I picked this up for you on my way home." She lifted the spray of pink flowers off the tray, the little plastic buds swaying back and forth on pink strings. She tucked it into the twist Yuki had pulled my hair into.

"Kawaii." Yuki grinned. "You look so cute!" I turned a little red as Yuki stood next to Diane, both of them with their hands on their hips as they looked me up and down. They were starting to fuss a little too much.

"Thanks," I said. "Um. We should get going."

"Yes, I think Tanaka's starting to sweat a little out there," Diane said.

Yuki took a gulp of tea and slid the door to my room open, where Tanaka was waiting in jeans and a T-shirt.

"You guys are taking forever," he said. "Can we go now?"

"Let's go," I said, the long yellow *yukata* sleeves tangling around my wrists as I slipped on my flip-flops and shoved my *keitai* into a pink drawstring bag I'd bought at the *depato* store.

"You look cute," Tanaka said to us with a smile.

"So do you," Yuki said. She stuck her tongue out at him as he turned red. She grabbed my hand and we headed out the door.

"Itterasshai!" Diane called after us.

Go and come back safely.

The only word Tomohiro had written on his letter, the word that had sent me running from the airport, that had me tripping over my own feet to catch Diane at the Narita Express platform on the way back to Shizuoka.

Tanaka pushed the button for the elevator.

We'll find out together, Tomohiro had said to Jun. Tomohiro and I would find out what the ink wanted and how to control it together, without the help of his society of Kami who wanted to overthrow the government and kill off anyone who stood in their way.

It didn't make sense. Why would Tomohiro push me away again now, when I was so determined to help?

The light was fading outside as we stepped into the heat. It was the last week of summer holidays, before school started for the second semester, and the hot weather wasn't going to give up easily. We clattered down the street in our *zori,* or in my case flip-flops, hopping onto the local train for Abekawa Station.

"We're gonna be late," whined Tanaka.

"It's fine," Yuki said. "We'll still be in good time for the fire-works."

The train lurched around the corner and I tried not to press into Tanaka's side.

"If the *takoyaki*'s all gone by the time we get there, I'll blame you."

"How would that even happen?" I said. "They won't run out."

"Right?" Yuki agreed. "Tan-kun, you and your stomach."

By the time the train pulled into Abekawa the sun had blinked below the horizon. We stumbled through the musty train air toward the music and sounds of crowds.

It felt like all of Shizuoka was here, the sidewalks packed with festivalgoers while dancers in *happi* coats paraded down the street. Lanterns swung from floats and street signs glowed, and above everything, we could hear about three different songs competing for attention above the crowded roads. It was a little claustrophobic, sure, but filled with life.

"What should we do first?" Yuki shouted, but I could barely hear her. She grabbed my hand and we pressed through the thick crowd toward a *takoyaki* stand. Tanaka rubbed his hands together as the vendor squeezed mayonnaise over the bite-size batter stuffed with octopus.

"Anything's fine with me," I said. Translation: no idea.

"I'm good, too, now that I have my *takoyaki,*" Tanaka said. "Want one?" The bonito fish flakes on the hot batter shriveled as if they were alive.

"Um, maybe later."

"We should try to get a good spot for fireworks soon, though," Yuki said. "Near the Abe River bridge would be best."

"What's the big deal about the fireworks?" I said. "You keep bringing it up." I mean, I loved fireworks as much as anyone, but she seemed a little fixated on it.

Yuki pulled me over, whispering in my ear. Her voice was hot and smelled of the fishy batter.

"Because," she hissed, "if you watch the fireworks with someone special, you're destined to be with them forever."

"Oh." Jeez, I could be so stupid. So this was some big scheme for her and Tanaka. "Do you want space or something?"

"No, no!" She waved her hand frantically. "Not like that. Let's stick together, okay?"

"Sure," I said. As if she'd tell me if that was the plan anyway.

We rounded the corner to two rows of brightly lit tents. All the thick, fatty smells of festival foods filled the air. Fried chicken, fried squid, steaming sweet-potato fries, roasted corn, strawberry and melon *kakigori* ice. My stomach rumbled and I moved forward, heading for the baked sweet potatoes. I handed over the yen and pocketed the change. Then I pulled back the aluminum foil to take a bite, the steam flooding my mouth. Beside me, kids dipped red plastic ladles into a water table while an old motor whirred little plastic toys round and round. The toys bobbed in and out of the ladles while the kids shrieked with excitement.

A flash of color caught my eye, and I turned. I strained to

hear the sound above the music and chatter of the crowd, but it was there—faintly. The tinkle of the colorful *furin,* the delicate glass wind chimes like the ones Tomohiro had sketched into the tree in Toro Iseki.

Across from me, the *furin* booth glowed with electric light, catching on the gleaming chimes as they twirled in the night breeze.

"Hello!" The vendor greeted me in English, but his welcome barely registered as I stepped into the tent. Almost a hundred of the chimes hung suspended around me in a rainbow of glittering colors, spinning above my head in neat rows. Tomo's *furin* had been black-and-white, like all his sketches, but they'd held the same magic, the same chorus together that my ears could never forget.

"You like the *furin?*" The vendor smiled. He had a kind, worn face and the early startings of a gray beard.

"They're beautiful."

"The sound of summer, *ne?* The sound of possibility."

I reached out, cradling a glass *furin* in my hand. Possibility.

"Yuki-chan, look—" I turned.

I'd lost her to the crowd.

Panic started to rise in my throat. She wasn't one to abandon me on purpose. Even if she did want alone time with Tanaka, I knew she wouldn't leave me stranded.

Anyway, it wasn't like I couldn't get home safely. Taking trains around Shizuoka wasn't a big deal anymore. Festivals just weren't as fun by yourself, and the loneliness stung a little. I clutched my fingers more tightly around the *furin.*

"You looking for someone?" the man asked.

"I'm okay," I said, stepping back into the darkness between the bright tents. I pulled out my *keitai,* ready to call Yuki, and then stopped with my finger on the button. She'd wanted time with Tanaka anyway. I should just grow up and do something for her for a change, even something little like this.

I slipped my phone back into my bag and pulled the drawstring tight. I watched the water table a little longer and then strolled down the row of tents.

I stared at the different festival games interspersed with the food. Eel scooping, pet bugs, *yoyo tsuri* balloons on strings floating in the water. I finished my sweet potato, balling up the aluminum with a satisfying scrunch. In the next tent a pool of goldfish darted around, slipping out of the way of the paper paddles dipped into the water to catch them. I watched for a minute as the fish snaked out of the way, their scales shining under the hot, buzzing lamps of the tent. The paper paddles broke and kids shouted in dismay, while the vendor gave a good-natured laugh.

I shuffled closer to the tent as the group of kids left, now just a teen couple left trying to catch a fish. The girl followed a goldfish slowly with the paddle, her movements deliberate and cautious, her giggle sounding when the fish caught on and sped away. She crouched on the ground beside the pool, paddle in one hand and bowl in the other, her red-and-gold *yukata* crinkling around her *zori* sandals.

And then I realized I knew this girl.

The pregnant bump of her stomach under the light cotton of the *yukata*.

And the boy beside her. Tomohiro.

Not kidnapped. Not falling apart. Not dead.

Scooping goldfish with Shiori.

I stepped back. He hadn't noticed me yet, the two of them laughing as Shiori tried to maneuver a different fish into her bowl.

I knew right away he wasn't cheating. It had only been two

weeks since I'd returned, and he wasn't like that. Maybe that was the attitude he portrayed at school, but I knew better. I knew he was with Shiori as a friend, supporting her.

But it still bothered me. I felt stupid then, tall and ugly and awkward in my borrowed *yukata*. Flip-flops on my feet because I couldn't find *zori* sandals large enough to fit me.

Maybe Tomohiro wasn't as dangerous as Jun had led me to believe. He seemed normal enough squatting beside Shiori, eyes following the goldfish, a smile on his face. He wore jeans and a dark T-shirt, the usual thick wristband around his right wrist. I could still see faint ink stains streaking up his arms, the scars hidden on the other side, but it was the only trace of what had happened. He looked so…normal.

Maybe staying in Japan had been the wrong choice. Maybe I wasn't useful to the Kami after all. Maybe they didn't need me—maybe *he* didn't need me.

"Yatta!" Shiori shouted. The fish had slipped from her paddle into the bowl. The vendor smiled and filled a plastic bag with water, ready for the new pet.

"Yatta ne." Tomohiro grinned, reaching his fingers into the bowl to chase the fish. It swam between his fingertips, the ones that had trailed along my skin, the ones that had tucked my hair behind my ear.

I stepped back and my flip-flop scraped against the street. Tomohiro and Shiori looked up.

I stared into Tomohiro's dark eyes. I couldn't look away, like prey. I felt ridiculous.

Shiori stood up, a hand on her belly. "Oh! It couldn't be… Katie-chan? Is that right?" Tomohiro stayed crouched on the ground, unable to move.

I opened my mouth, but no sound came out.

"I thought you returned to America," Shiori said.

"Canada," I said. My throat felt sticky and dry.

"Hai," the vendor said, thrusting the newly bagged goldfish at Shiori.

"Thank you." She smiled, reaching for the bag. And all this time, Tomohiro and I couldn't move.

"Katie," Tomohiro said finally, his voice deep and beautiful and just how I'd waited to hear it. My mind broke.

"Sorry," I whispered and turned to walk away. I pressed my way through the thick crowd, desperate to get away. I knew I was being stupid. I knew it was nothing between him and Shiori. But it stung, and I had to get away from it.

Behind me, even in the midst of all the festival noise, I was sure I heard Tomohiro call my name, but I kept walking. I wanted to see him, but not like this. I thought he'd been losing his mind, that he'd been in danger of the ink taking over—what had happened that now he seemed just fine, as though I'd never even existed in his life?

I pushed past the *takoyaki* stand and the rows of roasted corn, turning down a darker street where shrine-goers rang a bell and carried lanterns. I wove in between them toward the big Abe River bridge. It was late, probably almost time for the fireworks. If I could just find Yuki and Tanaka, maybe I could forget all this had happened.

"Katie!" Tomohiro called out. I kept walking, but I could hear his footsteps in the quiet alleyway, the soles of his shoes clicking as he ran toward me. His fingers wrapped around my wrist and pulled. *"Matte!"* he said. *Wait,* like Myu had said to him in the *genkan*.

I stood for a moment, staring at the swaying lanterns as the small group of shrine pilgrims walked past. He held my wrist gingerly, and I knew I could shrug him away if I wanted to.

"Why?" he panted. "Why are you here? In Japan?"

"Good to see you, too," I said.

"Hey, that's not—"

"Hey nothing!" I turned to face him. "You've had your *keitai* off for two weeks! I thought you were taken by the Yakuza or the Kami or something, and you're just scooping goldfish with Shiori?"

"Shiori showed up at my house crying. I'm just trying to be a friend. It's nothing!"

"I know." This time I did pull my wrist out from under his fingers. "I know that already." I walked toward a nearby bench and sat down. Tomohiro followed and crouched in front of me.

"I didn't know you were here," he said. He ran a hand through his hair, the wristband snagging on the strands. "How the hell didn't I know? The ink didn't—it didn't react at all."

"I chose to stay," I said. "I couldn't do it—I couldn't get on the plane."

Tomo's eyes turned dark. He sat still for a minute, then buried his head in his hands.

"Shit, Katie!"

"It's not your choice!" I said. "I need to stay. You're not okay by yourself. You're going to need help—my help. I'm linked to the Kami, remember?"

"What are you going to do if the Yakuza get involved again?"

"Look, I thought about it, okay? But there are people I care about here, Tomo. Diane, Yuki… Do you even think I'll be safe on the other side of the world if things blow up here?"

Tomohiro stood and paced back and forth in front of the bench. Then he swung out a fist and slammed it against the garbage can. The hollow echo made me jump.

"Shit!" he said again.

"Would you cut it out?" I snapped. "You're right, okay? Maybe it was better for me to leave. But it was my choice! It's got nothing to do with you. I'm not leaving, so just get it through your head."

He looked at me, eyes blazing. "And what if what you choose is selfish?" he said. "What then, Katie? If it hurts others, if it puts others at risk?" I felt sick. How had this happened? All I'd wanted was to come back to his open arms.

He collapsed in a slump on the ground. In a quiet voice, he added, "What choice do I have? I'm a Kami. Anything I choose will hurt others. I have no choices."

This was not going at all how I'd envisioned. "I didn't stay to hurt you," I said, my voice wavering. I was not going to cry in front of him, but already my eyes were starting to blur. I held on with everything I could.

And then he snapped out of it. He heard the tremble in my voice. He rose slowly to his feet, his eyes deep and lovely and melting everything else away.

"Katie-chan," he whispered. I stood with my arms folded, biting my lip to keep the tears from welling over. I grasped for the last of my anger.

"I didn't stay to ruin things for you," I managed.

And then his arms were around me, my face buried in the warmth of his shoulder. His heart beat rapidly under my cheek, his breath labored as he clung to me as if in a storm.

"Hontou ka?" he said. "You're really here?"

"I'm here," I whispered.

He stepped back, tilting my face up to his, and he kissed me gently, as though he thought I might break or disappear completely. Like I was a ghost, a dream. I closed my eyes, drifting on the moment. His warmth, his touch, the smell of his hair gel. Everything the same as I'd remembered.

"Tomo-kun!" shouted Shiori, and the moment ended. We stepped back as she walked toward us, her new goldfish swimming round and round the plastic bag as it swayed in her hand. I didn't like to hear her call him Tomo-kun, especially knowing that Myu had never been allowed to call him such a close name. He'd held her at a distance and made her call him by his last name, Yuu. Was Shiori really only a friend?

But that's stupid of me, right?

"Shiori," Tomohiro said. "Katie's staying in Japan."

"Ah, really? You're not going back?" She smiled. "I'm glad! I was so sad to not even meet you after we talked on the phone that time." She squeezed my hand, and I thought, *She really means it. She is really clueless about the awkwardness of this.*

"On the phone?" Tomohiro asked.

Shiori pointed her finger at him, poking him in the chest. "The time you decided to be an idiot," she said.

"Oi," he stuttered, annoyed.

Shiori smiled. "Katie, are you hungry? We could get some yakitori before the fireworks start."

"Oh, um…"

"Shiori," Tomohiro said, his voice flat. The seriousness of it made me shiver a little.

"Nani?" she said. "What is it, Tomo-kun?"

"I've just discovered my girlfriend is staying in Shizuoka. Permanently. Do you think maybe we could…you know, meet up in a bit?" The words hit me like a wall. Did he actually just ask that?

"Oh…oh, no problem. I'll get something to eat and meet you after, okay?"

"Shiori," I said, reaching my hand out.

She waved it away and shook her head. "No, no, it's okay!" she said. Her voice was far too cheerful. "I'll catch up in a bit. This baby is always hungry." She circled her stomach with her fingers, smiling too widely. Then she turned, and she was gone.

Tomo reached for my shoulders, wrapping his arms around them from behind, but I sidestepped his embrace.

"Don't you think that was kind of rude?"

"Yeah, it was," he said. "But I just want to be with you right now." And he leaned in to kiss me again, and this time was not fragile at all, but filled with hunger. "You look beautiful in that *yukata*."

I felt my cheeks go hot. "It's Yuki's."

"Come on," he said, squeezing my hand. "Fireworks start soon, and I know a great spot." He took off running and dragged me along for a couple paces until my feet started working. I let him pull me around the side streets, Tomo laughing when we almost crashed into some serious-looking lantern carriers on their way to the shrine. It was a nice change, running but not for our lives. Maybe things weren't really as serious as I'd thought.

We rounded another corner, and there was a cast-iron bridge looming over the Abe River. A few small boats blinked with lanterns as they bobbed in the darkness. Tomohiro pushed his way along the crowds near the metal stairs down to the beach and grabbed a spot against the railing.

"Well?"

"Beautiful," I said, looking out at the lights on the water. Lanterns in a rainbow of colors hung from the railings, and the opposite shore gleamed with matching strands of lights. The humidity of the air and the close-pressing crowds weren't so bad here by the freshness of the river.

"Too muddy on the beach, but you'll get a great view up here. Do you want a drink?"

"I'm okay."

"You sure? I'm thirsty. There's a vending machine over there. Iced coffee? Milk tea? Melon soda?" With each suggestion, he pressed his lips closer and closer to my neck until I laughed nervously.

"Okay, okay," I relented. "Milk tea."

"Got it." And then he was gone, and the humid air felt colder.

I looked out at the lights on the boats, still bobbing. Everyone was chatting and laughing, waiting for the fireworks. I hoped Yuki and Tanaka had managed a good spot, too, and Shiori—god, she'd made me feel awkward but I hadn't wished that on her. Watching the fireworks alone, snubbed by one of the only friends she had. Maybe it wasn't too late. Tomo could call her and—

"Katie?"

My name, deep and velvet on a familiar voice.

Except it wasn't Tomo's.

I clasped my hands tightly around the railing, clinging to the cool metal as I turned slowly. Black T-shirt, black jeans—he almost faded into the darkness. Blue lantern light glinted on his silver earring as he moved forward.

"Katie," he said again.

My whole body seized up with fear. I stepped backward, pressing my back against the railing. "Jun," I whispered.

"It's okay," he said, lifting a hand to calm me. "I'm not going to hurt you, remember?" And then I saw his other hand, wrapped in a ghostly pale cast at his side. His broken wrist, the one Tomohiro had shattered with his *shinai*. I stared at it, trying to figure out if I should run. "I'm on your side," he said.

"Look, I don't want to be friends with you," I said. "I don't want anything to do with your little society."

"You're right," he said. "I didn't mean for it to happen like that. I wasn't sure what kind of showdown we'd have with the Yakuza, so I called a few friends. I just wanted to be prepared."

That gave me pause. I'd been so wrapped up in his weird Kami cult that I'd forgotten how he'd saved me and Tomo. That without his help, we might have been—

One of the blond streaks in his hair fell forward into his face, and he lifted his hand to tuck it behind his ear. The motion brought back the memory of him plucking the cherry blossom from my hair. And then the way he'd protected me from Ishikawa on the Sunpu bridge. I felt so confused. Jun was the enemy—right?

"I'm your friend," he said, as though he'd plucked the thought from my mind. I shivered—he could read me too well.

"Then don't stalk me," I said. "Stay away and give me space."

"Katie," he said. "I just want to help. You know as well as I do that Yuu is dangerous. But I'm not here looking for you, if that's what you mean. You make that choice—if you want help, I'm there."

"So why are you here?" I said. "Out of all the places in Shizuoka, why are you right here?"

Silence, and then he smiled.

"Because this is the best place to see the fireworks," he said.

"Oh."

"Katie?" Tomo arrived from the other side of the road, a

can of milk tea in each hand. When he saw Jun, his eyes narrowed. "Takahashi."

"Yuu." Jun grinned, his eyes gleaming. He lifted his arm so we could see his bandaged wrist clearly. "Want to sign my cast?"

Tomohiro pressed the milk tea into my hands, his eyes never leaving Jun. "If you don't get out of here, I'll give you another to match."

"I'm just here to watch the fireworks, Yuu. I can go somewhere else if you want."

"Yeah. You can go to hell."

Things were escalating, and I felt powerless to stop it. So much for being linked to the Kami. I couldn't even handle two idiot guys tripped out on testosterone.

"Tomo—"

"No, it's okay," Jun said. "I'll leave."

And then *boom!*

I jumped a mile, terrified. Did he shoot him?

Another boom, and the sky flooded with light.

The fireworks. I breathed out shakily.

We all stared into the sky, the fight momentarily dropped, as bursts of color spread across the city. The crowd around us swelled, pressing the three of us closer together against the railings. I became the barrier between Tomo and Jun, and it was not comfortable. Not at all.

And then I remembered Yuki's words, that whoever I watched the fireworks with would be there for me forever.

Could I really trust Jun? Even Tomohiro was unpredictable. He'd treated Shiori like a jerk tonight. What if he did that to me—again? Who was really telling the truth here? I needed a better hand of cards to compete. I had to learn what it really meant to have ink trapped inside me, to be linked to the Kami.

Another burst of sound in the sky, but no color, just a brief oily shimmer as it splayed across the sky. And then suddenly everyone was screaming and scattering across the road.

Ink descended on us like a black rain, warm as the drops splattered down my face and stained the sleeves of my *yukata*.

Another firework burst, all ink instead of color, raining down on the crowd with a faint sheen. A woman ran past, covering her head with her hands. She bumped me into the railing and I fell forward. I dropped the milk tea, trying to grab at the railing before I fell headfirst onto the beach. And then two sets of strong hands grabbed me by my shoulders and pulled me back.

Tomo. And Jun. Saving me together.

"Let's get out of here!" Tomohiro shouted. I nodded and he grabbed my wrist, pushing his way through the crowd. I turned to look at Jun. He stood there silently watching me leave, the ink dripping down his cast, running down his skin in trails of black. When I looked back again, he was gone in the frantic swarm of people.

"Was it you?" I shouted, but Tomo didn't answer. I couldn't have heard him over the screams anyway. The black ink pounded down as we ran for the train station, as we were soaked by the very truth of it.

Nothing was normal, and I'd known it, deep down. It wasn't something I could run from. The ink hadn't forgotten me.

My fate was raining down from the sky.

About the Artists

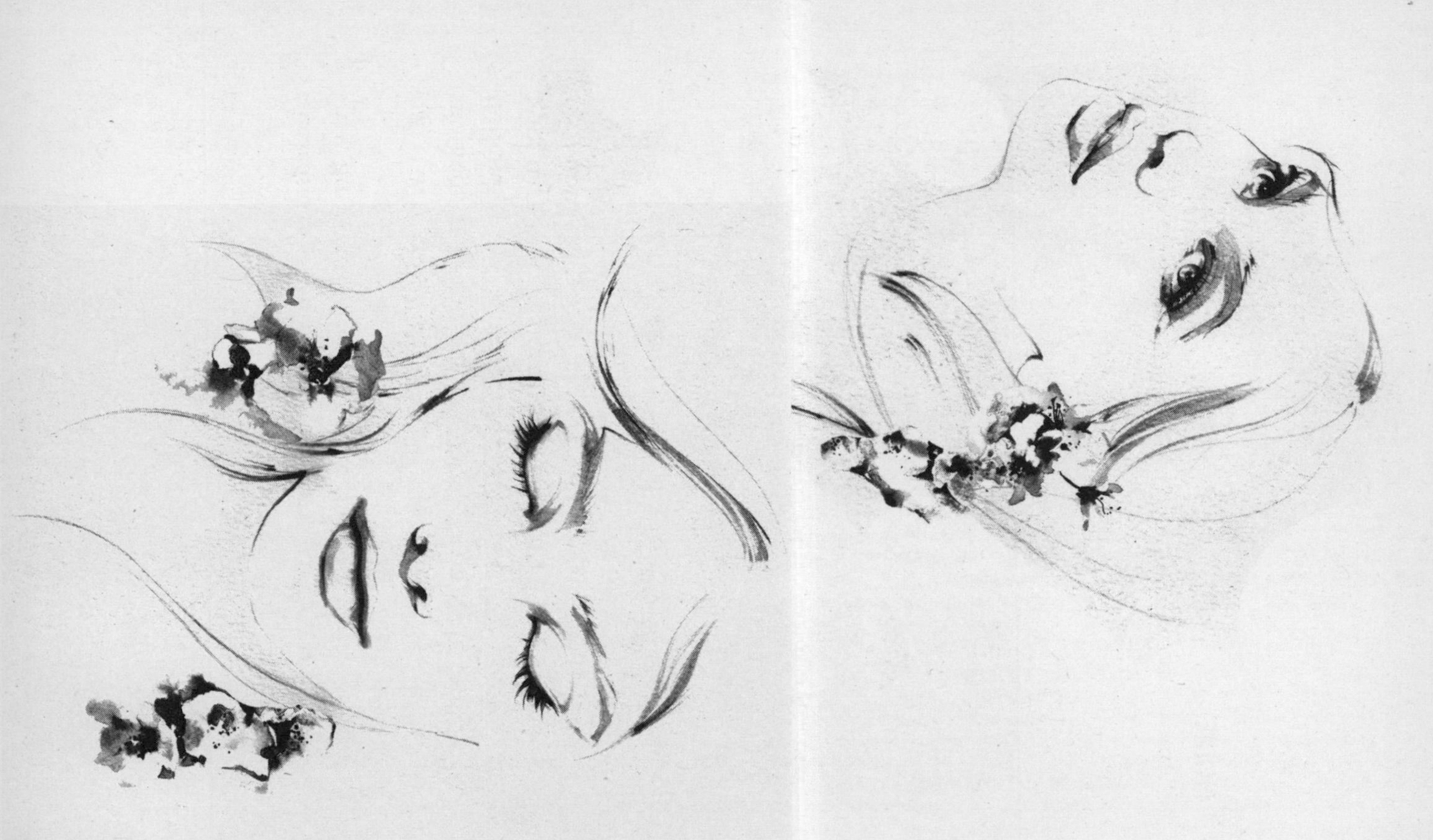

MEET THE COVER ARTIST, PETRA DUFKOVA

HOME:

Petra was born in Uherské Hradiště, Czech Republic, and currently lives in Munich, Germany, where she is busy with her new son, Maximilian.

EDUCATION:

Petra studied art at a technical school for applied arts. She earned her modelist/stylist degree from the international fashion school ESMOD in Munich, with a prêt-à-porter collection.

AWARDS:

2008 Best Illustration Award for her collection at the China Fashion Week, in addition to numerous design awards.

MORE ABOUT THE ARTIST:

Today Petra works as a freelance illustrator, stylist and as a fashion designer for Marcel Ostertag. Her illustration style is a combination of traditional method and modern look with a focus on fashion, beauty and lifestyle. Her inspiration comes from many areas—books, magazines, art exhibitions and fashion shows, and just walking around her city with her eyes open.

Petra developed her art style after experimenting with aquarelle, a traditional technique of painting in transparent, rather than opaque, watercolors. From there, she developed her own art style, which often combines watercolors with ink. The cover art for *Ink* is an example of this style.

A Q&A WITH ROSS SIU, INTERIOR SKETCH ARTIST

WHERE WERE YOU BORN AND RAISED?

I was born in Hong Kong and lived there until age seven. I was then raised in the very rainy but beautiful city of Vancouver. Right now I reside in Osaka, Japan.

WHAT IS YOUR EDUCATIONAL BACKGROUND?

I am a graduate of the IDEA Program of Capilano University in North Vancouver.

WHAT MADE YOU WANT TO BE AN ARTIST?

I don't think I ever actually *decided* to be an artist. Creating art was always a part of my being. It has been that way probably since I was first exposed to drawing, which, as far as I can recall, began when a family friend taught me how to draw robots when I was around four years old.

WHAT MATERIALS DID YOU USE TO MAKE THE DRAWINGS FOR *INK*?

I used pencil crayons to sketch; a bit of tracing paper; then finished with fine-liner, oil-based markers and Chinese calligraphy ink.

TELL US A BIT ABOUT THE PROCESS OF CREATING THE DRAWINGS.

The creative process was very pleasant. We had good communication; the author and creative team knew what they wanted and were very encouraging to me. I am pleased that they are happy with the results.

WHAT ELEMENTS OF JAPANESE CULTURE HAVE INFLUENCED YOU AS AN ARTIST?

Their modesty and humbleness, respect for tradition, attention to detail, obsession with perfection, and their loyalty to those things have always influenced me as an artist.

YOU CURRENTLY LIVE IN OSAKA—ARE THE CITY OR PEOPLE AN INSPIRATION FOR YOU?

The people here do inspire me, because their attitude is more laid-back and casual. They laugh and joke around a lot more than people do in other parts of Japan, which is important to me.

DO YOU IDENTIFY WITH BEING A FOREIGNER IN OSAKA? IS IT A PLACE YOU COULD STAY AND MAKE YOUR HOME?

I enjoy many things about Osaka. The convenience of transportation; the abundance of great restaurants; the truly convenient convenience stores; the great routes for bike rides; the beautiful, unique scenery—all these things have made the city really easy to get comfortable with. That said, the space feels too confined here for me to want to make it a permanent home. But who knows what the future will bring!

WHERE HAS YOUR WORK BEEN ON EXHIBIT?

My exhibitions include:
Vorld (2008)—Chickennot Gallery (Kyoto, Japan)
Personal Circles (2009)—iTohen Gallery (Osaka, Japan)
Can I Have an Easy Life (2012)—Galaxy Gallery (Osaka, Japan)

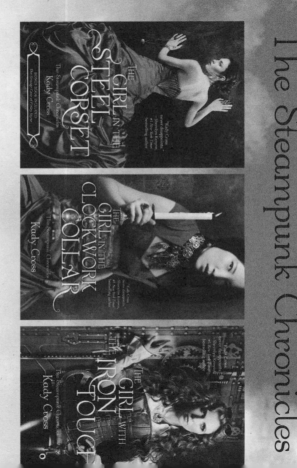

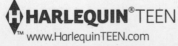

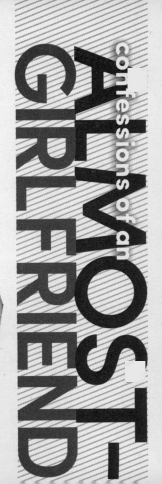

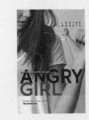

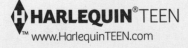

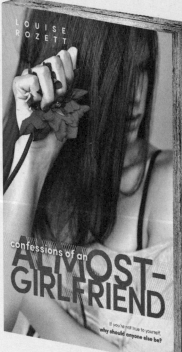

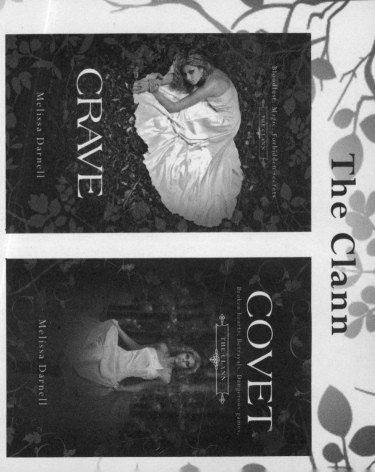

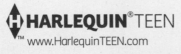